A BROTHERS IN LAW NOVEL

MY WAY TO YOU

LYNDELL WILLIAMS

DEEN LOVE BOOKS
NEW YORK

My Way to You by Lyndell Williams

Printed in 2018
All Rights Reserved

Published by:
Deen Love Books
New York, NY

Cover design by Taria Reed
Content Edited by Tiffani Burnett Velez
Copy Edited and Proofread by Nakia Jackson

ISBN 10: 1-68411-647-3
ISBN 13: 978-1-68411-647-8
www.laylawriteslove.com

For all the interracial couples struggling against bigotry and intolerance to be in each other's arms.

And in this gauntlet of Love
that life has put us through
Beyond the hurdles of your heart
Is how I'll find my way, to you.

ALKEBULAUN

1-Back in New York 7

2-A Working Dinner 17

3-Can You Go Somewhere? 27

4-Dinner and a Cab 33

5-You Forgot Me 41

6-Vince Deckland 51

7-Enjoying the Ride 59

8-Let's Keep This Between Us 67

9-Basketball with Marcus 73

10-Jamaica Station 83

11-Samantha 93

12 - Am I Forgiven? 101

13 – Strap on a Helmet 109

14 -Regina Makes Breakfast 117

15 - Cocktail Party from Hell 125

16 - Simon's Place 137

17 – Kimchi 143

18 - Regina Meets Alice 149

19 – Subway 154

20 – Instagram 165

21 - Be a Man About Yours 175

22 - Marcus Confronts Simon 185

23 - Heart to Heart 193

24 - You Can Go Now 201

25 - I Need to Find Her 207

26 – D.C. 215

27 - Condom Break 225

28 – Boardroom 233

29 - Red Line 241

30 - Skinny Girls' Pill 253

31 - I Need Space 259

32 - Regina and Jeremy 267

33 – Emergency 275

34 - Shower 283

35 - Eggs with Alice 293

36 - Courthouse 301

37 - Give it to Vince 309

38 - Doin' It Well 319

39 - Justine Young 329

1-BACK IN NEW YORK

SIMON'S CHEST SWELLED as he let the box of books hit the wood floor with a loud thud. He surveyed his new digs. Although the Brooklyn Heights apartment was not the same as his mother's sprawling house in Jamaica Estates, it was good to be officially a New Yorker again. He achieved his goals in Boston, but his longing for home nagged him the entire four years he'd lived there. He also couldn't wait to get away from the pain and bad memories.

There wasn't much left to do in the apartment. Save for a few boxes and pictures leaning on the walls where they were to be hung, he was pretty much set. All the furniture was in place, the handiwork of his mother, who oversaw the deliveries like a drill sergeant. Alice Young had gotten straight to business. She made certain that her son's new abode was as comfortable and organized as his childhood home. Getting his bearings at the new law firm that recruited him after his first summer internship was challenging, and the last thing he had time for was to supervise painters and handymen. *I have to do something nice for her as soon as things settle down at work.*

He reached for the buzzing phone on the counter. "Hi, Ma." Simon pressed the phone against his ear and began stocking small jars from a bag on the floor into the empty refrigerator.

"Hello, Simon. Are you all settled?"

"Yes."

"*Did you put the kimchi in the refrigerator?*"

"I did." The last jar rattled against the rest. "Thanks for making them for me." He closed the refrigerator and rubbed his growling stomach. As good as his mother's *kimchi* was, he had a hankering for something else.

"*Of course. Let me know when you want more.*"

"Will do."

"I packed the rest of your things here. I can have them mailed to you."

"No, Ma. That's okay." Simon grabbed the keys off the counter and shoved his wallet into his jacket pocket. "I'll get them the next time I come out there."

"*I'll leave them in your old room then. Have you eaten?*"

"That sounds good." Simon stood in front of the entryway mirror, combing his fingers through the top of his hair, still amazed at how intuitive his mother was. "I'm going to get somethin' now." The soft click of the apartment door's lock echoed down the hall as he headed for the elevators.

"*Eating out? You know you can't live like that, Simon. It's not healthy.*"

"I know, Ma. Don't worry. I'll go grocery shopping tomorrow. Lots of fruits and vegetables. I promise." He endured his mother's subsequent lecture about proper nutrition all the way to the subway platform, injecting the requisite yeses, confirming that he was dutifully listening. "Ma, I gotta go. I'll call you tomorrow?"

"*I'm sure you will.*" Alice's tone conveyed the perfect combination of sarcasm and warning. "*But I'll be busy getting ready for my trip, so we can talk when I get back. Love you.*"

"Okay, ma. Love you too," Simon shouted into the phone, unsure if she heard him over the screeching sound of the train.

᭥᭥᭥᭥

Simon weaved through the rows of tables, then sat and inhaled the glorious mixture of aromas wafting around him. He typed *I'm here, man* before setting down his phone. The tapestry of people testified to the popularity of Sylvia's Tiny Kitchen and proved that it was worth the subway ride from Brooklyn to dine. Sitting in the middle of the soul food restaurant reminded him of days spent travelling on the train across the city with his dad, who was a hard-core fan of the cuisine and passed it onto his son.

He raised his hand to catch the attention of a waiter. After weeks of newness, it was finally time to enjoy something that solidified that he was truly home. Just like the traditional Korean and Irish dishes served at the Young residence, the steaming plates at the Harlem landmark represented a staple of his life. He scanned the menu. *I want some catfish.*

"Welcome to Sylvia's. What would you like today?"

He opened his mouth to order, but was interrupted by a voice from across the crowded restaurant. "Simon!" He turned, and his gaze fell upon two men weaving towards him. The tall, muscular man led the pair. His eyes flashed recognition; the corners of his mouth pulled back exposing shining white teeth. Simon bolted out of his seat and gripped the broad forearm.

"Hey, man." Familiarity fueled Simon's excitement at the sight of his best friend Marcus Kent's warm, brown face. He wrapped his free arm around the brawny man, giving as firm a squeeze as he got. Marcus stepped back, keeping one hand on Simon's shoulder.

"You look good, man. Did you have an easy time findin' the place?" Marcus's hand came down on Simon's shoulder in a few hearty pats.

"Please," Simon gave Marcus's bicep a playful jab, "I've been coming to Sylvia's since I was a kid. You're the Long Islander."

Marcus belted out a baritone laugh. "True. I hope you don't mind, I brought my intern." Marcus slapped the back of the young man next to him, whose head towered over even a man of his stature. "Simon, meet Jeremy Stacks. He's pursuing a future in law as well."

"Absolutely. Nice to meet you, Jeremy."

The waitress cleared her throat. Simon looked over to the woman standing, tapping her order pad. "So, that'll be three?" Her tapping moved from her pad to the floor with her foot.

"Yes, thank you," said Simon with a sheepish smile. The men sat and quickly ordered before returning to their conversation. Simon read his phone.

Missy: *How about we chill tonight?*
Simon: *Sure, I can't come until later tonight though.*
Missy: *I'll wait up.*
He smiled at the sexy picture that appeared on his phone.

"So," Marcus leaned back in his chair and smirked, "you still have the women fallin' all over you and that sexy Asian game of yours?"

Simon let out a soft chuckle. "I do aight. How's Toni?"

"She's good. Her practice is thriving. Now, let me guess, you're at that big law firm that was sniffing after you?"

"Pretty much. As I recall, the headhunters were chasing you big time too. Did you choose a firm?"

Marcus shook his head. "Nah, man. I decided against churning in the legal machine. I launched a small, multi-service not-for-profit. I want to make a direct difference for folks catching hell around here."

The waitress returned with drinks and bread. Simon bit pensively into a roll. "You always said you wanted to get involved in community organizing. I just thought it would be after you established a legal career."

Marcus took a long drink from his glass before setting it down. "Well, there are more than enough lawyers ready to work for rich folks. It's the poor who struggle for justice. Now I'm helping them with that struggle." The playfulness vanished from his eyes. "I remember when that was important to you as well."

Simon shifted in his chair. Marcus always shot straight from the hip and made no apologies. His former college roommate was particularly careful at making sure he didn't stray too far from his humanitarian commitments while he pursued success. "Yeah, it still is." The waitress placed the hot plates on the table. Simon reached for the pepper and sprinkled his catfish. "I haven't forgotten how important it is to give back. Didn't I always volunteer with you?"

Marcus grinned while he cut into the chicken in front of him. "Indeed, you did." He lifted the forkful of food and pointed it at Simon. "You stayed committed to whatever needed to be done. So, what are you doing to give back now?" The fork disappeared into his mouth.

A pang of guilt grew in Simon's stomach. "I haven't found an endeavor of interest," he said before putting his glass to his mouth.

Marcus's brows shot up. "Really? I find that surprising that no organization wants to avail themselves of someone as shrewd as you."

"Yeah, go figure." Simon chomped down on his fish. He shifted his gaze to Marcus's young companion, who he'd forgotten was even there. *Does he even talk? What am I gonna do? With this busy schedule of mine, I never considered volunteering anywhere, but Marc is right.* "Maybe," Simon raised his eyebrows at Marcus, "there's something I can do for you?"

Marcus lifted the napkin from his lap and wiped his fingers. "We do offer free legal services. Would you be interested in volunteering?"

"Definitely. Where are you located?"

A card appeared from Marcus's shirt pocket. "Harlem." He dropped it on the table next to Simon's plate. "We've a committee that meets once a month to strategize about initiatives and funding. I think it would be a good idea for you to come and sit."

"Sounds good." Pulling the wallet from his jacket, Simon shoved Marcus's card in before retrieving his. "But I'll need two or three weeks before committing to anything. I'm still gettin' my bearings at work."

Marcus flipped Simon's card front and back before placing it into his shirt pocket. "Uh-huh." He jabbed at his plate until his fork was refilled. "You were always organized and quick on the uptake. Unless things have changed, I'm sure you already have your bearings." The last mound of food disappeared and Marcus signaled for the check.

Simon rubbed the back of his neck. Marcus made it obvious that he would not be put off and expected a shorter time frame for his friend to join him in the cause. "One week?"

Marcus slammed his hand on the table as he rose, rattling the plates and glasses. "Great. I knew you still had it in you. We're meeting this Thursday at 7:30."

"That's not one week."

"The address is on the card." Marcus thanked the waitress and grabbed the check.

"No, Marcus. I got it." Simon attempted to take the small slip from his friend, but it was moved out of his reach.

Marcus surveyed the check, then pulled a bunch of bills from his wallet. "Too late," he smiled at the waitress, "Keep the change."

The waitress's eyes lit at Marcus's generosity. "Thank you, sir. Enjoy your evening."

Stuffing his wallet into his back pocket, He looked down at Simon with a smug grin. "I plan to."

Jeremy reminded the men of his existence by rising and standing behind Marcus. "It was nice meeting you," the young man said pushing his glasses up his nose. Was this the future of law? His face was so smooth, it indicated that shaving wasn't even necessary.

"So, Simon. I'll see you on Thursday?"

Simon raised his hands in defeat. "I'll put it on my schedule."

Marcus clamped down onto the back of his neck like when they were in college. "I knew you would. Great seein' you, bro." The two men weaved their way out of the restaurant and disappeared into the street.

Simon asked the waitress to put the rest of his meal in a to-go container, and headed for the subway. A series of notifications—each containing an image of his *friend* in fewer clothes—reminded him that he wasn't going straight home to Brooklyn and needed to take different train.

ง♦ง♦ง♦ง♦

The following morning, Simon strode through the maze of cubicles. His black leather backpack flung behind his back, he navigated the twists and turns while balancing not one but two coffee cups. It only took a couple of weeks for him to devise a system to efficiently navigate through the entire building, which involved walking past the right offices while avoiding others.

"Good morning, Agnes," Simon smiled at the executive assistant for one of the senior partners, tilting his coffee in celebration of the day.

"'Morning, Simon."

The matronly-dressed woman's smile revealed a set of highly-polished dentures. Simon was always generally cordial to people, but he made it a special point to charm the firm's staff. It never hurt to have them on your side.

He turned a corner. His assistant, Corella was working at her desk.

"Good morning, Corella." His face beaming like a school boy with an apple for the teacher, Simon presented a coffee cup to her. "Two creams, no sugar."

Corella pulled off her reading glasses. "Thanks, Simon."

He dipped his head. "You're welcome." He stood in front of the desk, immobile, while his assistant checked out the caffeinated morning libations.

Corella's nose crinkled a little. She sniffed, carefully took one sip and smiled "You didn't have to."

Simon turned on his heel. "But I did." He strutted into his office.

She was the best assistant the firm had to offer. Years working with attorneys from associates to senior partners not only meant she had tons of experience but knowledge of the firm's inner workings. She knew where the bodies were buried. As a result, many feared her, but more so, they respected her.

She was valued enough at the firm that she could choose her own assignment. Simon was fortunate. Corella had tired of working with the last attorney and was looking to team up with another when he started. She selected him after a 10-minute conversation in his office. She was smart, organized, and efficient, and he did his best to make sure that she knew he appreciated her hard work.

Simon sat at his office desk. It was a small but respectable workspace. One wall hosted built in shelves and a closet, where he kept extra clothes. His L-shaped desk held his computer and a few drawers. On one side of the desk was his chair and opposite it was another for clients. It was a lot better than being stuck in the maze of cubicles, and there was a huge window that let in plenty of light.

Simon hung his jacket on the back of the door, sat at his desk and rolled his sleeves.

"Simon?" Corella called from the doorway, concentrating on her tablet screen.

"Yes, Corella?"

Without looking, she glided to the front of his desk. "I have an email you sent me yesterday. You need to clear part of your afternoon schedule one Thursday a month?"

Oh boy, Marcus. Simon scratched his head and swung his chair back and forth. "Yes, I'm going to be doing some pro-bono work for an organization in Harlem."

Corella's groomed brows drew close together as she looked up from her tablet.

"It's important. I just need to switch my schedule around to accommodate leaving an hour early on some Thursdays."

"Okay." Corella returned her attention to the screen. "That can be arranged. What's the name of the organization?"

Simon stood. He pulled out and searched his wallet. Retrieving Marcus's card, he held it in front of himself and tilted his head.

"May I see the card?" Corella held out her hand. "I'd like to enter the information in your contacts."

"Sure." Simon smiled and took a deep breath. "Thanks."

"You're welcome." Corella slowly disappeared behind the closing office door.

Simon reclined in his chair and stared at the ceiling. *Good thing Corella reminded me about Thursday. There's no way I would ever flake on Marcus—not after everything he's done for me. Besides, it's high-time I started giving back again.*

He punched the numbers on the desk phone to cease the red light flashing on it. He stiffened at the high-pitched saccharine voice in the first voicemail.

Hi, Simon. He peered at the wall hanging of a black figure brandishing a swivel chair like a sword. *I'm in New York, and I was hoping we could catch up.*

A knot twisted at the base of his neck and his heart raced out of control. Shutting his eyes, he hit the erase key and inhaled until the beating settled.

2-A WORKING DINNER

Is TONI AWARE OF THIS LITTLE MAN-CRUSH you got goin' on?" Regina couldn't hold her tongue any longer. She'd watched her brother patter around for the last 20 minutes talking about the mythical Simon Young. "I mean, really, should we sacrifice a virgin or somethin' to commemorate his arrival?"

"Ha, you really think you're a riot?"

Reclining in big brother's office chair, Regina fluffed her coils and smirked. "Yup."

"Look, Gina, Simon and I weren't only college roommates, we had each other's backs when it came to dealing with some of those white, privileged assholes around campus." He pulled freshly-printed paper out of the machine. "*And* he and I did some pretty significant things together in the surrounding area." Marcus motioned to the wall behind him, where a multitude of award plaques he'd earned while in law school hung. Regina briefly skimmed the wall before inspecting her nails for any manicure flaws. "He's smart and dedicated. He may have forgotten for a minute, but now he's here, and we're damn lucky to have him."

Regina snickered and continued needling her brother, a skill she'd honed over the years. "Yeah, yeah. I'm sure he walks on water and all that." She glanced at the clock next to the Afrocentric poster of Martin Luther King, Barack Obama, Malcolm X, Nelson Mandela and Bob Marley on the wall. She was irked at the reminder of how sexist pro-black culture can be but decided to continue to test Marcus's patience than go into a debate about the cross-cultural erasure of black women. "So, where's your wunderkind? I thought he was on time all the time?"

Marcus caught his bottom lip between his teeth and looked down at his watch. "He'll be here. Let's just go wait in the conference room. Trust me. You're gonna be impressed."

♟♟♟♟

Simon hiked the strap of his black backpack further up his shoulder and raced up the subway steps. He zigged-zagged between pedestrians at a hurried pace, stopping only to scan the bustling street, searching for the "large red brick building" Marcus described. He glanced down at the GPS on his phone and let out a sigh. The center wasn't far, but even at break-neck speed, he was going to be at least 3-5 minutes late. *I'm gonna have to leave work even earlier and make up the time.*

He saw the same numbers on the business card Marcus gave him brandished on the brick building across the street. He switched his gaze between it and the little red man on the traffic light. The speed of the cars made jaywalking a hazardous endeavor. Simon's constructed apologies in his mind with each flash of the red figure until its white counterpart appeared. He raced across the lanes. Entering the glass door, he was greeted by a young woman with a bright smile.

"Hello. How can I help you?"

"Hi, I'm here to meet with Marcus Kent. My name is Simon Young."

The receptionist gave him the once over, wheeled her chair closer to the desk and took the phone receiver in her hand. "Sign in please." She flipped her long curly hair and pointed to a clipboard with a flirty smile. "I'll let him know that you're here."

"Thank you." His backpack made a quiet thump on the floor. Instead of exploring the woman's obvious interest like he normally would, Simon paced the small welcome area lined with resin chairs along the windowed walls and focused on calming his panting. It was nothing like the large complex maze of floors at the massive law firm, but it was someplace that offered him a chance to do more than acquisitions.

It's going to be great working with Marcus again. They'd managed to get their degrees and pass the bar while helping the high-needs communities surrounding their law school. They founded two after-school programs in Boston that were still operating. Marcus and he also assisted legal teams that helped liberate at least five unjustly imprisoned people. It was all fulfilling.

"You can go in, sir." The receptionist twirled a curl around her finger. "Just go down the corridor to the conference room. It's the last door."

"Thanks." The conference room was already full of people standing and chatting in clusters as well as a few who sat sipping from paper coffee cups. Simon searched for Marcus's familiar face. He noticed the young man from the restaurant, whose head loomed over everyone else's. *There's—what's his name—Jeremy. The way he stuck to Marcus at the restaurant, he has to be in here somewhere.* Marcus's wave caught Simon's attention.

"Okay everyone," Marcus called out over the chatter, "please sit. We're going to get started."

People began to circle the long conference table to sit in what appeared to be predetermined seating. The air rushed out of Simon from another firm handshake and hug from Marcus, who then turned his friend to face the seated crowd.

"Everyone, this is Simon Young. He's agreed to do some pro bono work for us. He is a brilliant attorney. I thought he would be a good addition to the advisory board."

A chorus of welcomes filled the room. Simon adjusted the strap of his backpack and stood in a confident stance. "Hello, everyone. It's great to be here, and I'm excited at the prospect of engaging in some substantial work with all of you." He noticed that Jeremy was not yet seated. The young man strolled around the table, landing his lanky frame next to an extremely stunning woman. Her heart-shaped face framed full lips, a Nubian nose and sparkling upturned russet eyes.

An explosion of black coils crowned her head, and her flawless brown skin glowed.

"Just grab a seat anywhere, man. You can introduce yourself to everyone after the meeting." Marcus took his place at the head of the conference table, right next to the woman, who cast a radiant smile at him.

To his chagrin, Simon realized that the only seat available was at the far end of the conference table, probably the furthest from the beauty. He walked around the room, unable to keep from staring at her, making it necessary to issue multiple apologies as he hit the backs of chairs along the way. His awkwardness caught her attention along with everyone else's. Her eyes sparkled with amusement, and she pursed her full lips as she and the rest of the room watched him make his way to his seat. *Great. I've managed to look like a complete idiot.* He glanced at Marcus, who looked at him with a cocked eyebrow.

Marcus squinted at the sheepish grin Simon offered. "Okay, I was recently made aware of a new grant opportunity." He flipped through a stack of papers in front of him as he spoke. Simon struggled to keep track of what was being said. His attention remained doggedly stuck on the woman. She sat regally poised in the chair, taking notes as Marcus spoke.

"It's highly competitive, but I think we have a shot at getting it if the proposal is really tight with a dynamic narrative. Regina, your flair for prose will be a great asset."

So, that's her name? How appropriate. I heard it before somewhere but where? Get a grip. She's not the first pretty face you've seen.

"Maybe you can lead the proposal writing team?" Marcus passed the papers to Regina.

She scanned them. The pensive expression on her face made her even more striking, if that was possible. Simon chided himself inwardly. *Why was she having such a strange effect on me?*

"I can contribute some content, but there are a ton of specifics that require a level of technical writing that is beyond the scope of my abilities. I'll need someone with the right skill sets to execute this proposal."

"I think I can help with that, Regina." Confidence burgeoned in Simon's chest. He was quite proficient at grant writing, giving him a chance to redeem himself from his earlier buffoonery.

Regina shot him a wary gaze across the table. "Are you sure you want to jump into a project like this on your first day volunteering? It can be overwhelming and requires a lot of commitment."

Simon sat straight and smoothed his tie. *She may be gorgeous, but I'm not gonna sit here and let anyone impugn my abilities.* He opened his mouth.

"This is definitely in Simon's wheelhouse, Gina," Marcus interjected. She fixed her doubtful stare on him; her tapping resumed and quickened in cadence. "It's similar to proposals we completed to fund projects in Boston, so his expertise on the team will raise the potential of us getting it." The beating sound dominated the room. It was obvious that no one would dare impose their opinion on the duo staring each other down as if they were about to draw guns at high noon.

"Fine." The papers glided across the shiny wood. Simon stopped them before they flew off the table. Her accuracy at aiming the papers so they reached him without breaking her stare-off with Marcus was admirable.

"But you know how important this funding is," said Regina with undertones of warning.

"I do, and I've every confidence that you two will produce exactly what we need."

Simon raised an eyebrow. The strain in Marcus's voice was unusual. He was not one to tolerate being challenged, especially when he was in charge. It was surprising how he handled Regina questioning his judgement with so much reserve. She was indeed an intriguing woman.

Simon scanned the room. Some people continued to watch the showdown while others shot him a sympathetic glance.

Jeremy's long fingers settled on Regina's arm; she turned her head as he leaned in to whisper quietly in her ear. An irrational pang of jealousy poked at Simon.

"I can help with the content edits and proofing, Marcus." Jeremy's crackling voice grated Simon's nerves even more than before.

"Looks like you've got your team, Gina." Marcus lunged from his chair, ratcheting the tense atmosphere. "Email me your timeline, and let me know when you want to organize a review panel."

While the board members were clearly on pins and needles, Regina seemed unfazed by Marcus's imposing physique towering over her. "Of course. Will there be a dining budget, or do you just want us to pick a few leaves from the trees out front?"

Marcus's lips formed a thin line. "Submit the receipts to Graciella," he quipped before heading towards the door. It wasn't until it closed behind him that anyone dared move. The room quickly filled with voices that faded as people began emptying into the hall.

Simon set his backpack on the table and began to stuff the papers into it when a voice came from behind him. "Hello, Simon." He turned. A short, balding man stood with an outstretched hand. "Harold Reynolds, it's nice to have you on board." Simon peered over the man's head and spotted Regina hooking her handbag in the crook of her arm and walking behind the row of chairs. She stopped briefly to respond to someone while eyeing her phone and the doorway. She passed the two men, not even acknowledging their existence.

Simon grasped Harold Whoever's forearm and shook. "Thanks. Will you excuse me?" He turned and made a beeline to Regina without waiting for a reply. "Regina?" She stopped and waited for him to reach her.

"So, you're Simon?" She crossed her arms and sized him up. "I have to say you're not at all like I pictured," she jibed while resuming her progress out the door.

"You know me?" He followed her, struggling to respectfully refrain from ogling her plump, round bottom as she walked in front of him; it was tough. *Eyes up! The last thing you want is to come off as a lecherous creep on top of being a dork.* He quickened his pace and walked beside her as soon as they were out of the corridor.

"My brother has mentioned you quite a bit over the years, more so in the past week. He's been excited about you joining the advisory committee."

Simon held his forehead. *That's where I've heard the name.* "You're Marc's little sister."

"Younger sister. I guess he hasn't mentioned me nearly as much." Simon gently caught her arm. They stood in the middle of the waiting room, eye to eye, with people buzzing around them.

"No, he has. You're a writer. You work at a newspaper." Simon stared at the ceiling as if the name he was searching for was there. "The—"

"Not any more. I've my own blog now."

His gaze returned to her face. "That sounds great."

"It is." Regina tilted her head as she smiled. She put a hand on her hip. "Marc tells me you work for a large firm."

Simon stuffed his hands into his coat pocket and rocked on his heels. "Yeah. I just started."

"So, this," Regina said waving her arm, "must be a stark difference."

"It is, but this," Simon mimicked her motion, "is nothing new to me. I've done a lot of work in underprivileged communities."

Regina's eyebrow shot towards the ceiling. "Slumming?"

"Not as far as I'm concerned. I like to help people." Simon grinned. "Are you slumming? I've been to your parents' home. You were definitely not brought up in the hood."

Regina opened her mouth and then clamped it shut "That's a fair enough observation, Young." She pulled her phone from her handbag and slid one manicured finger across the screen as she moved closer to him. "Why don't you drop call my number so we can arrange for our first meeting?"

A flowery smell from her springy coils wafted into his nose and fogged his mind. He shook his head and retrieved his phone from his suit pocket. No way he wanted to be caught off guard around this woman again. "Sure." Simon took a step towards Regina, accidentally bumping his arm against hers. He felt the warmth rushing up his neck. "When would you like to start?"

"Well, we still need to coordinate with J."

"J?"

"Jeremy."

"Oh, yes. Jeremy." Simon plugged the numbers on Regina's screen into his phone. Their hands brushed, sending an electric charge through his arm and body. The goosebumps he spied bursting on Regina's arm made him want to see where they ended.

He called the new number. Regina stared at him. "What?" He flashed a self-assured smile.

"You're all red."

"Am I?"

"Yeah." Regina leaned to one side of his head. "Especially around your ears."

Simon rubbed an earlobe and grunted. "I guess the heat here is a little too high."

"Yeah, I bet that's it. You know," Regina said with a mischievous glint in her eyes, "we won't really need Jeremy's help until we're at the editing stage, and having to arrange schedules with one less person will make things easier."

As if on cue, Simon noticed Jeremy emerging from Marcus's office down the hall. *Oh, not now, man.* "I agree. Why take him away from Marcus until it's absolutely necessary?" He pressed his palm against Regina's upper back and guided her towards the door. "I'm sure the two of us can get things done."

Not wanting to take a chance that Jeremy would find them, he guided her a little down the block before waving for a cab. "How about dinner?"

"We could stay here and order in. Marcus gave us a food budget."

He saw Jeremy peering over the heads of the passersby, searching up and down the street. *Come on. What, did he put a GPS implant in her or somethin'?* To his relief, a cab stopped in front of them just as they were spotted by Stretch. "I would prefer a nice restaurant." Simon opened the door. "We can make it a workin' dinner. I know a great place."

"That sounds good."

"Regina!" The sound of Jeremy's bellow drifted into the cab just as Simon slammed it shut.

"Is someone calling me?"

"I didn't hear anything." Simon threw an arm over the back of cab seat. "What's up man," he said to the driver while tapping the headrest, "let's hit it." He watched with satisfaction as Jeremy's tall body shrunk in the distance. There was no shaking his attraction to this woman, and he was going to do whatever it took to explore it further—without a third wheel.

His gut flipped when the traffic light switched from red to yellow. *There's no way he'll catch up to us.*

"Regina!" Her name seeped through the windows. The couple gazed out the back in unison. Simon clenched his fist. There Jeremy was, running towards them.

"Look, there's J." Regina sighed. She waved in the back window.

Jeremy reached and banged on the trunk of the cab after only a few strides of his long legs.

You've gotta be kidding me. Simon's blank stare hid the irritation stirring inside him.

Jeremy approached the passenger door. Simon rolled down the window just a crack.

"Hey guys. Where're you goin'," Jeremy panted. Beads of sweat dripped down the sides of his head and disappeared into the wetness of his dress shirt.

"Dinner."

"Are you talking about the grant proposal? I can join you." Before Simon could tell him just where he could go, Jeremy jumped into the cab's front passenger seat.

Simon read the text message that chimed on his phone as the cab moved past the greenlight.

Regina: Some other time?

He glanced over to her and was greeted by sympathetic eyes. He then peered at Jeremy's head bobbing in the front seat.

Note to self. Use faster cabs.

3-Can You Go Somewhere?

SIMON LEANED IN THE HIGH-BACK executive chair at the head of the boardroom table, glowering at Jeremy, who stood over a seated Regina. She was so deeply engrossed in proofing the grant proposal draft that she didn't even notice how closely Jeremy was positioned next to her, but it wasn't lost on him.

For the past three weeks, Simon spent every free moment working with her and the ever-present intern. Regina's schedule clashed with his, so finding time to do anything other than research and writing the proposal was impossible. He'd hoped that there would be at least one time that he could meet with just her, but unlike the two of them, Jeremy's calendar was overly-accommodating.

Uptown or downtown, neither was an issue for the young man. His class schedule didn't even present a problem, and no matter how hard Simon tried, Jeremy managed to be the one sitting next to Regina. If he was late, the urchin would already be there. If he was early or on time, the pest arrived with her. *If he wasn't such a thorn in my side, I'd have to respect the boy's game.*

His elbow resting on the arm of the chair, Simon hid his clenched teeth behind his hand, watching the pesky cock blocker gaze at Regina with puppy dog eyes. Of course, she didn't see his game. To her, he was "J," the office innocent with the boyish grin. Everything he did in her eyes was harmless or an accident, but he wasn't fooling Simon. *I'm sick of Lurch's hovering. Enough was enough.*

While he managed to keep his upper body composed, his left leg shook incessantly.

"Everything okay?" Regina caught Simon's attention and then cast her gaze down to his shaking leg.

Simon stilled his leg with his hand. "Dandy." He bolted upright in his seat and folded his outstretched hands on the table. "We've proofread the proposal twice already. I think it's time to call for a review committee."

Regina stiffened her back and returned to examining the proposal. "If you're in a hurry, you can leave. J and I can handle this."

Jeremy gloated behind her, and it was all Simon could do not to jump across the table.

"No, staying isn't a problem. It's just been my experience that overworking a proposal can negatively affect the final presentation." He rested his elbow on the conference table and held out his hand to Regina. "We don't wanna overthink it. How about I ask my assistant to take a look? It's always good to have a fresh pair of eyes." He spread his lips into a heartening smile.

Regina gave Simon the papers and laid her hands on the table. "I guess we're done here." She pulled her shoulders back and pivoted her chair until her long legs emerged from under it.

"Great." Simon stood and put the papers in his backpack. "I'll talk to my assistant in the morning. How about I escort you home?"

"Thank you, but that's not necessary. I'm a big girl." She thinned her lips and shot him a piercing stare.

"Please." Simon mustered a flirtatious smile. "Allow me. It's late, and I'd feel better about it." He picked up her purse with one hand and help his arm to invite her to stand.

Regina's gold hoop earrings swayed as she tilted her head to one side. Simon gleaned the twinkle in her eyes before she lowered them. "Okay." Her mouth curved into a slight smile. She stood and took her purse. "I'll get my coat."

Simon walked over to Jeremy, grabbed his hand and pat him on the arm. "It's been a pleasure working with you, Jeremy. You must be exhausted from all the runnin' around."

Jeremy flinched and looked at Simon like he was speaking gibberish. "It's been fine." He turned his head, following Regina. "I can still help with more."

Simon tugged the young man's arm, regaining his attention. "No, you've gone above and beyond here," he continued despite Jeremy's thin-lipped smile. "I'll have to make sure and tell Marcus how impressed I am with you." After throwing his backpack strap over his shoulder, he reached to put his arm around Jeremy's. "Now why don't you go have some fun?" *I'm gonna get you as far away from Regina as possible tonight. It's past time I had Ms. Kent to myself.*

Regina looked back at Simon talking to Jeremy. *I guess he is a man who knows how to take care of business.* The clumsy first impression dissipated around the erect Simon brandishing a confident grin. She walked towards the coat room but noticed light filtering out of her brother's cracked office door. His voice drifted into the hallway as she approached.

"I'm gonna try and get home soon, sweetness."

Another late night? Is he trying to make things between him and Toni harder? She opened the door and leaned against the door jamb.

The heels of Marcus's shoes clicked against the hardwood floor as he paced the span of the room. "No, I won't be going to the gym." He fixed his gaze towards the ceiling, rubbing his head. "I already promised not to go until the treatments were over. Can't you just trust I'll be there?"

Regina knocked on the door, making sure to smile. They were fighting about the fertility treatments again. Now was not the time to be flippant or contrary.

Marcus motioned her into the room before flopping in his chair. "Toni, Toni." He rested his arm on the desk and rubbed his forehead. "I know that Toni. I'm heading home in about an hour. Damn it, we have enough time. Hello?" Marcus slammed the phone in front of him.

Regina flipped the phone and checked the screen. "Toni upset?"

"That's putting it lightly. These injections make her crazy. I'm trying to be an understanding husband, but she lashes out for no reason sometimes."

"Oh, boo-hoo. She's the one going through all the procedures. Suck it up and stop makin' it about your ego."

"You're biased."

"Damn straight, and I make no apologies about it. I love you and Toni. You're the best couple I know outside of mom and dad. I don't want you guys messing things up because of crazy hormones."

"Oh, you think I do? I've dealt with all this shit during the first round of treatment, and now we're doing the same thing again. We never used to fight before. Now it's a sick cycle of anger and tears."

Regina's phone chimed.

Simon: *Did you leave?*

Regina: *No, I'm in the office with Marcus. I'm going to need a few minutes. You don't have to wait.*

Simon: *But I will.*

"Is that Toni? How mad is she?" Marcus began shifting stacks of folders on his desk.

Regina put her hand on her hip. "You really like taking advantage of the fact that your wife and sister are best friends."

Marcus snorted. "Trust me, it's more of a liability than an asset." He reclined in his large black executive chair.

Regina slipped her phone in her bag. "No, it's not Toni."

"Jeremy?"

Regina scoffed. "No."

Marcus squinted and sat straight. "Who is it then?"

She bent over the desk. "Why are you in my business? You need to go home and handle yours."

She flung the door open.

"See how easy it is to walk out? Try it. The woman you love is somewhere crying. Fix it."

Marcus's booming voice followed her into the hall. "You still didn't tell me who was on the phone."

"And I ain't gonna." She hurried back to the conference room. Disappointment ebbed at her when she walked into the dark emptiness. She sighed and pulled her purse strap further up her shoulder. *Simon must have run out of patience and decided I'm not worth the wait. His loss.* She went to get her coat, shaking off the realization that she was looking forward to spending some time with him alone, even if it was just to take her home.

They'd had some pretty nice conversations between the times they worked on the proposal. Simon was smart and funny. *Tonight could've been a chance for me to get to know him better, but he obviously isn't all that interested if he couldn't wait a few minutes.*

Once inside the dimly-lit waiting room, Regina stopped. Her stomach fluttered at the sight of Simon leaning against the reception desk with his long, crossed legs extending from his full-length black coat.

He glanced from his phone and smiled. "Ready?"

"I thought you left." Simon reached for her coat and held it in the air.

His arms enveloped her as she stepped into it. "I told you I would wait." He slid his hands over her shoulders and down her arms.

Regina trembled at his touch. "Indeed, you did." She turned her head. Their lips almost touched and for a moment, time and her breath stood still. She lifted her lids. A slight redness blushed behind his light freckles. She'd never noticed them before. They invited her to smooth her lips across them. She concentrated on buttoning her coat before she gave into the temptation to do so as well as bite his luscious bottom lip. "Where's Jeremy?"

"We'll not have the honor of Mr. Stack's company tonight." Regina cast her gaze down and smiled. Simon leaned closer. The smell of his cologne drifted into her nose and titillated her already stimulated senses. "It's just us. I hope that's okay." The promised mischievousness twinkling in his gorgeous angular eyes sent a charge of excitement down her spine.

She swallowed the lump in her throat. "I'm fine with that." She quaked at the feel of his hand against the small of her back but managed to appear composed despite the craving burgeoning inside her.

He raised his hand towards the door and tilted his head. "Let's go."

4-Dinner and a Cab

S IMON WOUND THROUGH TABLES AND CHAIRS,
leading Regina through the restaurant. The maître d' led them
past the bar and into the tent-themed dining area. Cloth hung
across the ceiling and down the walls, where electric lanterns
provided a soft glow. Regina glided onto the chair Simon held out
for her. The sight of her radiant face in the flickering candlelight
made his pulse race. He tried his best to make sure he didn't reveal
the raging passion growing at the base of his stomach. This was the
first chance he had to talk to her outside of their volunteer work
without Jeremy. *I'm gonna make the best of this.*

"Would you like to see the wine list?" asked the waiter, handing
them each a menu.

"Oh, I don't drink," announced Regina, shooting Simon a
quizzical glance. "I hope that won't be a problem?"

"That's fine," chuckled Simon. "I hope you don't mind if I
imbibe?

Regina raised her palm and slowly blinked. "Knock yourself out."

"Then I'll have a beer. What would you like, Regina?"

"Do you have Shirley Temples?" She attempted to sound as adult
as possible while ordering a drink typically reserved for little girls.
Simon fought the smile tugging at the corners of his mouth.

"We do, ma'am."

"I'll have one, please, and may I have two cherries?"

"Of course. I can give you three, if you like."

Regina giggled. "No, thank you. Two is fine."

"Anything you want, ma'am." The waiter closed his pad and gave Simon an approving grin before dashing towards the bar.

Regina gazed down at the menu. She had the ability to remain strong and even intimidating to the strongest opponent. He'd read the quick work she made of some of her blog commentators. However, at this moment, she was ordering kiddie drinks. He was interested and excited to learn more about what made her tick.

Regina looked at him and shrugged one shoulder. "What?"

"A Shirley Temple?" He ended the futile effort to keep from smiling.

"Shut up, Young." Her pout, feigning hurt, enhanced her beauty. "I had it once at a wedding when I was ten and got hooked."

After ordering dinner, Simon watched as Regina looked around the restaurant. Throughout the weeks of trying to shake the tall tagalong, He'd thought hard about the perfect place to bring her. The impressed look on her face proved he made the right choice.

"So, shall I start asking you the usual questions one asks a date?" She slid a finger up and down the dewy glass of water.

Simon raised his eyebrows and poured beer into his glass. "You consider this a date, then?"

Regina's eyelashes fluttered and she adjusted the napkin on her lap. "Perhaps, dinner between friends would be more appropriate."

There was a certain sense of accomplishment in watching her squirm in her chair. The impromptu dinner plans were working. "Honestly." He caressed her wrist, temporarily mesmerized by the goose pimples forming under his touch. "I have no intention of being just friends."

Lamp flames flickered in her sparkling eyes. "You're pretty sure of yourself, Young."

"About things I want, yes." He clasped her hand and passed his lips over her knuckles.

Regina grabbed her necklace and slid the small charm on it back and forth across the gold chain. "Interesting." She squeezed his hand and leaned slightly over the table. "I can be the same way."

Simon took a drink with his free hand and cleared the lump in his throat. "So, what's your first question?"

"Sorry?"

"Your first date question. What do you want to know?"

Regina glided her tongue across her lower lip before holding it between her teeth. Everything evaporated around them for Simon. He waited for the first query about his life, not completely sure if he wanted to answer.

The waiter approached the table with a large serving tray. "Your food."

Simon released Regina's hand to accommodate the steaming plates laid in front of them. "Is there anything else I can get for you?"

"Did you want anything, Regina?"

"No, I'm good."

Simon glanced at the waiter. "No, thank you. We have everything we need for now."

Regina wrapped her full lips around a stuffed grape leaf, closed her eyes and made a soft moan. "You have to try these."

"I can't wait." He held her gaze and slowly opened his mouth.

She placed the rest of the grape leaf on his tongue. He circled her wrist and closed his lips over her finger tips. Putting the leaf in the back of his mouth, he softly licked each tapered fingertip before releasing his grip.

Regina bit her bottom lip. Her eyes fixed on his mouth as he chewed.

He wiped his mouth with the napkin and shot her a boyish grin. "I'm dying to answer your question."

"Oh, yes. My question." She poked her fork at the food on her plate. "Why did you become a lawyer?"

"My dad. He was a great lawyer." Simon stared and turned the beer bottle on the table. "I remember him bringing me to his office sometimes. There'd always be a client needing his help. He helped everyone he could until his illness prevented him." He erected and grabbed his fork. "He was a great father too. I want to be everything he was."

"I'm sorry for your loss." Regina's eyes glistened with sympathy.

"Thank you. I was small when he died. He made sure my mom and I were financially secured. It was still hard, but, we had each other and pulled through." He took a deep breath. The conversation was not going in the direction he wanted. He cut a piece of meat and held it in front of Regina. "My turn."

Regina laid her hand over his and pulled the food into her mouth. She swallowed and licked one corner of her mouth with the tip of her tongue. Simon's insides jolted with hunger, and not the type satisfied by food. This was one the best meals he ever experienced. "Very good, but at this rate, we'll never finish dinner."

He let out a low chuckle, and they continued to eat. "What about you?" He asked between forkfuls, "what made you decide to become a social justice blogger of all things?"

"I'm an intelligent Black woman with a lot to say. How else can I get people to listen to me?" Regina popped a kebab in her mouth and laid one hand over the other while looking into the dim restaurant. "I do write for other publications, but I like having my own platform."

Simon studied her as she spoke, admiring the confidence in her voice and demeanor. He was fully absorbed by everything about the woman sitting across from him.

"I watched my mother struggle for years with the nonsense in academia. As a Black female professor, she caught a lot of crap from people who really didn't want to hear what she had to say. With my blog, I'm in control. Even if only one person reads it, it's still mine."

"I agree." Simon presented another forkful of food to Regina. She smiled and returned in kind. "I read some of your articles."

Regina tilted her head and played with an earring. "When?"

"Honestly, as soon as I decided that I wanted to know as much about you as possible." Simon looked at her over his glass as he drank.

She braced her chin in the palm of her hand. "And, let me guess," she pronounced in a dry tone, "I'm too aggressive. I focus on race too much, and I need to do away with all the feminist talk."

"Actually, no. I think a lot of what you write is spot on."

"Really?" Regina lifted her head and smiled. She played with a lock of her hair. "That's refreshing to hear. Normally, someone has a problem with at least one aspect of my approach."

"Not me. I've a lot of respect for smart women who aren't afraid to express their opinions."

"You do?"

"Yes." Simon concentrated on making tiny circles on the back of her hand. "As long as there isn't a problem when I express mine."

He made sure to leave the waiter a generous tip before leading Regina out of the restaurant. Rain poured on the street. People dashed by the doorway suspending umbrellas or anything over their heads that would help keep them as dry as possible. A black car stopped in front of restaurant. "You wait here," Simon directed Regina, "I'll make sure it's ours."

"Okay."

Simon held his coat over his head ducked to talk in the open window. He then turned back to get Regina from under the restaurant awning. He guided her to the car, itching to slide his hand below the small of her back but didn't want to risk a slap. He was bold but not reckless.

They settled into the back seat for the trip back uptown. The rain caused her soft coils to tighten, allowing Simon to gaze at the nape of her slender neck as she looked out the car window. He tried to calm the urge to nibble it. Resting his arm across her shoulders, he shifted his body closer to hers. "Are we almost there?"

"The next block." Regina turned her head. Their lips almost touched. Light from the street filtered through the back window and cascaded on her dreamy eyes and full lips. Simon caressed a round cheek. Regina's lips parted. He slid the side of his thumb down her delicate jaw and leaned his head to one side, closing the distance between their lips.

The car jerked to a stop, breaking the trance. "You're at your destination, sir."

Regina turned to open the door. Simon huffed and shot the driver an irritated glance. "Thanks, man."

Her soft giggle relaxed him. His body shivered at the rush of cold air swirling around him and filling the space left by her as she stepped outside.

She bent over and peeked inside. "You comin', Young?"

He paid the driver and hopped onto the curb. Wind swirled around them, making the hems of their coats flutter against their legs. He put his hands in his coat pockets and leaned into the wind. They walked towards the tall brick building. Once in the elevator, Regina stood at the back. Simon braced his back against a side wall and looked at the floor numbers over the door. She pressed her body against his. Her cold hands on his cheeks didn't extinguish the fire building inside him.

"Now," She slanted her head and moved in closer until their lips barely met, "where were we?"

"Hold." A loud voice shot into the elevator as the doors slowly closed. Regina hastily moved to the side. Simon extended his arm to stop the doors from completely closing.

A man hurried inside. "Thanks." He held his hand to his chest and panted. "You know how long this thing takes to move. Almost as long as it takes for the doors to close."

"No problem." Simon forced a smile. The doors creaked to a close and the elevator proceeded to creep up the shaft at a snail's pace.

The man smiled at Simon and lifted his hat to stare at the numbers over the door. During their slow ascent, Simon edged nearer to Regina. "Does it take this long all the time?"

"All the time, but you get used to it."

Simon lifted her fingers and pressed them to his lips. "I plan to." He leaned towards her smiling lips.

"Ahem." They turned their heads towards the man, who peered at them with his dark brown lips upturned in a scowl. He scanned them from head to toe and back.

Regina pushed at Simon's chest. His quest to finally taste the lips that've been teasing him for weeks was once again thwarted. *What's this dude's deal? He's never seen people kiss before?* The man continued to look back at them during the rest of the ride. Not that he cared, but he noticed Regina rocking back and forth and staring at the floor.

The elevator came to a merciful halt. The man walked out, but not until he gave the couple the once over again. Before the doors creaked completely shut, he yelled "sellout" from the hall. Regina's head popped up. Her lips formed a line, and her eyes flashed with anger.

Simon squinted. "What did he just say?"

"Nothing," she spat between clenched teeth, "He didn't say anything." She jammed her hands in her coat pocket and sniffed while tears welled in her eyes.

5-You Forgot Me

THE GRINDING SOUND OF THE ELEVATOR DOORS churning open cut through the silence. Simon wiped the last tear from under Regina's eyes when she pushed off the wall and bolted. Her handbag jostled at her side as she hurried down the corridor. Simon reached and kept pace with her. "Which one is yours?"

"The last one on the left." She looked straight ahead—her eyes vacant and emotionless.

A familiar aching feeling crept over Simon. *I know that look.* He'd seen it on Marcus plenty of times while they were in college. Although he'd encountered his share of racist bull, some unimaginable stuff happened to his best friend. Professors were especially condescending and offered Marcus far less face time. Cops followed him around, and he was frisked in the street more than once because he "fit the description." The world makes sure that people with darker skin do not have an easy time of it.

Like then, his gut twisted in knots and the back of his neck tightened. He walked by Regina's side in complete silence, waiting for her to say something—she didn't.

Regina's hands shook as she fumbled her keys in front of the apartment door. Simon held out his. She looked at him. Her eyes now showed an intense mixture of pain and anger. He motioned towards his hands with his. Regina's shoulders slumped before she dropped the keys in his palm.

The rattling in the lock crackled through the air. "You know," he said trying to make sure his voice was just the right tone, "I wanna listen if you wanna talk." The line always worked whenever he or Marcus needed to get something off their chest.

"I don't." He paused. Her tone shut him down and out. He searched her face. The angry expression softened and her eyes shifted from side to side. She touched his chest. "I'm sorry. I just can't."

"I get it. I'm not totally clueless, though."

She smiled. "I know. I just don't want to give it any more energy."

Simon opened the door. "Enough said." Light from the hall fell on the tile floor of the apartment entryway. He braced an arm on the wall, looking at the blackness inside and then Regina.

"Thanks for understanding." She turned just at the door and grabbed her keys. "Goodnight." Tight-lipped, she cast her gaze downward and closed it.

Simon flattened his back against the wall and glared at the ceiling. "I don't believe this," he grunted to the air. "The whole evening ruined by one jerk." He strode down the hallway. His thoughts quickened with the vein thumping at the side of his neck. *I understand why she's angry. She should be. The guy was a complete douche, but why shut me out?*

He pushed the elevator button and groaned when he heard the churning sound. He looked around for the stairs, but then slumped his shoulders and paced. Staring down the hall towards Regina's apartment door, his heartbeat steadied. They had such a good time at dinner, and the chemistry between them was potent. If it wasn't for the idiot on the elevator, he would be holding her in his arms, something he waited so long to do. "No. This isn't ending like this." He took a deep breath and hiked his backpack higher on his shoulder. Undeterred by the nervous sensation creeping through his spine, he strode back to Regina's door and knocked. He placed his outstretched hand on the door jamb, closed his eyes and breathed deeply with his head down.

She appeared in her bare feet, skirt and tank top. "Simon?"

He cleared his throat. "Hi." She stepped a little closer and his pulse pounded so hard that he felt it through his entire body.

She looked down the hall. "Is everything okay?"

Simon stepped until his shoes met her painted toes. "Yes. You just forgot something."

Her eyes darted in their sockets as she searched his face. "What?"

Simon held the back of her neck between his hands. He grazed her lips. The light touch sent charges of desire through his body. "Me."

Regina's eyes became alit with passion. He felt the rush of her breath tickle his top lip. She wrapped her arms around his shoulders and smashed her lips against his. They parted, and his tongue explored the sweet warmth of her mouth. Regina backed into the apartment, pulling him with her. The sound of the elevator door churning open drifted into the apartment just before the door closed.

"Let me hang your coat," she ordered breathlessly. Simon complied and followed her to the coat rack hanging on the entryway wall. He kicked off his shoes next to hers and shrugged off his suit jacket, standing behind her to hang it. Every nerve in his body was on fire. He slid his hand up her arms and kissed her neck. Regina gasped and turned to face him. "Would you like something to drink?" she asked loosening his tie and unbuttoning the top of his shirt.

He smiled at her scrambling fingers. She was excited too. He pulled the shirt out of his pants and started to undo the buttons at the bottom. Their hands met at the middle. "No." He pulled the shirt off and hung it, never breaking their passion-filled stare. "I only want you." He tore off his white tank. His chest and ab muscles heaved and skin tingled under her touch as she made a trail down the front of his body. Her hand stopped just above his belt buckle.

"I didn't' know you had all of this hidden under that shirt."

Simon took her hand and kissed the inside of her wrist. "There's more."

Letting out a nervous laugh, she took his hand and walked him to the bedroom. They stopped at the side of the bed. Fluffy pillows flew into the air and disappeared on the other side. She tore back the comforter. He pulled her against his body when she stood. "Let me take off your clothes," he whispered in her ear. It was both a command and supplication. He stroked just beneath her breast. "I've been dying to touch you."

He nibbled her ear before pulling her top over her head. He fulfilled his long-sought desire and explored his new treasure. Slipping his fingertips down her neck and across her shoulders. "You feel like silk." He cupped each breast and circled each nipple until he felt them pebble through the bra. Her shutters and moans drove him to distraction. No one was going to keep him from having her now.

Regina turned her head towards his. He captured her lips while his hand stole up her back. Releasing the bra clasps with ease, he slipped it off and let it drop to the floor. He turned his lover around and gently laid her on the bed. Round breasts floated in the light. "Magnificent," he panted before circling one tight nipple with his tongue and gently tugging the other between his thumb and finger. He wanted to taste all of her but wasn't sure he had the patience to wait. He was already so hard to the point of splendid pain. He couldn't remember wanting a woman so much.

Regina arched her back and ran her fingers through his hair. "Mmm, Simon," she moaned. She robbed him of her delectable breast by rolling over. She then re-embarked on the journey down his body. He shook under the kisses down his neck and across his chest. This time, Regina's hand didn't stop at his belt buckle. She popped it open and undid his pants. His cock jumped out and jerked at the touch of her fingertips sliding up and down its shaft.

"Regina," he groaned. "You don't know what you're doing to me."

She brought her mouth to his ear. "Yes." She squeezed him hard. "I do."

His body ached with hunger. He couldn't keep it at bay. He filled his hand with her lush coils and gently yanked her head back to expose her neck. He bit her soft flesh. "I'm going to lose it."

"What are you waiting for?"

Her body bounced as Simon jumped off the bed. He pulled a small blue packet from his pocket, removed the rest of their clothes and ripped it opened with his teeth. He settled between her thick, warm thighs, rubbing his tip against her hot folds. Assured that she was ready, he plunged inside of her.

His body stiffened at the sound of his lover's gasp and whimper. His heart thumped wildly; every inch of him shuddered, protesting the sudden stillness. He yearned to continue——to take them both to release, but a feeling of dread crept into him and stirred with intense passion her body triggered until his head ached. "I'm hurting you?"

"Just a little. It's okay." She drew his mouth to hers and shot her soft tongue inside. He melted into the kiss. She tasted so sweet. "Don't," she panted, propelling her hips forward. "Don't stop, Simon."

He happily submitted. Soft creaks from the bed permeated the room, becoming more frequent and louder with his increasing thrusts. The headboard joined the erotic symphony of creaks, grunts and ragged breathing. When Regina slid her hand down his sweaty back and dug her nails into his flexing rear muscles, Simon almost gave into the sensations. He tried running case law through his mind to slow down the building urge, but to no avail. The feel and smell of Regina along with her hot moans in his ear overtook his senses. *This—feels—too—good.*

Just before his battle was lost, Regina wrapped her legs around his waist, threw her head back and let out a primal scream. He stopped to enjoy her insides pulsating around him then slammed in and out of her deep, hard and fast until his body locked in an explosion. Regaining control of his muscles, Simon pulled out of his new lover and laid next to her.

"Come here." He brought her against his body and laid a series of light kisses on her mouth. She placed her head on his chest and entwined one leg with his. The room became quieter as their breathing eased. "I'm sorry I hurt you." Simon broke the silence. "Was this your first time?" he asked stroking her arm with one finger, trying to appear causal while his stomach tightened in anticipation of her answer.

"No." Regina wriggled and stretched her arm across his chest. Her hair tickled his chin. "Don't worry, Simon. You didn't deflower me," she giggled. "It's just been a while."

That's a relief. At least I don't have to worry about explaining to Marcus how I took his sister's virginity. Simon stopped his finger. "How long?"

She lifted her head. "How long has it been for you?"

"I refuse to answer that question on the grounds that—"

"Mmm-hmm." She placed her head back on his chest.

He squeezed her closer. "I'm sorry. That was intrusive. It's none of my business."

She pressed her lips to his. "No, it's not, but I forgive you. After your performance tonight, I'm willing to overlook a small sexual *faux pas.*"

His laugh shook their bodies. "I appreciate that." He rose and walked to the bedroom door. "Which way is the bathroom?"

"To your left."

"I'll be right back."

After disposing of the condom, Simon returned to the bedroom to find the light on and Regina braiding her hair in front of the mirror wearing a tank top and pajama shorts with the words *S*L*E*E*P* across the back. He certainly didn't want to. She glanced at him through the reflection. "My hair is trashed, Young." She took a silk scarf out of the top drawer. "Lucky for you, I'm workin' from home tomorrow." He celebrated how everything sprang into a delightful bounce as she tied down her tendrils.

He strode naked across the room and kissed her neck. "I could make it messier, if you'd like.

"That's quite alright."

He watched her backside jiggle as she walked to the bed and put back pillows and blankets. "Are you sure?" He rounded the bed and stood akimbo opposite her, presenting his stiff eagerness. "I would be more than happy to accommodate."

Regina rubbed the side of her neck with her fingers and cast her eyes to one side. She dashed under the covers. "You'll need to get up early to make it downtown. That is if you're staying."

He eyed the empty space in the bed. Normally, he would have had his pants on as soon as the condom hit the bottom of the trash can. Sleepovers were not something he did. They made things too complicated and sent a message that he was into a woman more than he was. By now, he would have formulated a dozen excuses in his mind to head out the door. Instead, train numbers and routes that would get him to work on time in the morning ran through it. He couldn't make his way to the door or form the words for any lame excuses. It petrified him, but he wanted nothing more than to wake up next to Regina.

He flashed a full grin. "Try to stop me." He dove into the bed and pulled Regina into the crook of his body.

"You're going to sleep naked?"

"I've got you to keep me warm."

ᥫᩡᥫᩡᥫᩡᥫᩡ

"Uh." Simon reached over Regina's soft body nestled against his towards the strange nightstand, fruitlessly searching for his cell phone to end the offending screech emanating from it. *Man.* Nothing but cool wood and the realization that the noise was coming from his slacks laying on the floor halfway across the room. He caressed her bare shoulder and gingerly slid his arm from underneath her head. "I'm sorry." He padded across the room in his bare feet. "It's set for me to get up for work." *Which I'll probably be late for.* He held the pants in front of his groin. His stomach tensed. It was going to be a mad dash downtown. Fortunately, he always kept fresh clothes in the small closet at his office.

"It's okay." Regina let out a soft sigh as she arched her back and stretched. One of her long brown legs escaped the confines of the white sheet. "I understand."

Simon ached to climb back into the bed with her but couldn't risk being too late. He hadn't been at the firm that long, and making a good impression was still very important. The partners were watching, and there was plenty of competition that would jump at the chance to make him look bad.

"I'm going have to head out. Do you mind if I use your shower?"

"Be my guest."

"Care to join me?" He couldn't help offering the invitation. His mind raced with excuses for his tardiness if she accepted.

She let out a soft laugh. "Then you would never make it into work." She slid off the bed and walked towards him. A mischievous glint danced in her dark brown eyes. Having her so close unraveled his sensibilities. He drew her closer, cupped the back of her scarfed head and kissed hungrily at her inviting lips. Morning breath be damned. There was no way he was leaving without having her again.

The ring and vibration saved him from losing all abandon and returning to bed to execute the ideas he had about what to do to Regina's sensual body. He let out a groan while reading the name on the screen—*Corella. It's like she can read my mind.* "Hi, Corella." Simon tried to sound as calm as possible despite Regina nuzzling his neck.

"*Hello, Simon.*" Clicking sounds from her keyboard drifted through the phone. "*I just wanted to let you know that Mrs. Blakeside called. She needed to reschedule and push her meeting with you ahead to 11:15.*"

"Shoot. Thanks, Corella. I'll be there. Can you—"

"*The files are already on your desk, and I've rearranged your calendar to accommodate her.*"

"You're the best."

"*I know. I'll see you when you get here. Bye.*" Corella didn't wait for a response. She never did when she wanted to make it clear to Simon that he needed to be front, center and all business.

"I really have to go." Simon's lips barely touched Regina's as he dashed into the bathroom. He had to put as much distance between them to regain some composure. Few things rattled him, and he typically remained in control–especially when it came to women. After what happened in college, he'd learned to keep his passions in check. Unchecked desire for a beautiful woman nearly destroyed him emotionally. He wasn't going risk that amount of heartbreak again. *A cold shower is in order.*

Simon rubbed at the field of goosebumps spread across his arm as he dashed out of the bathroom. *Maybe, the shower was colder than it had to be.* His self-possession returned, the smell of coffee drew him directly to the kitchen, where he found his hostess standing behind her kitchen peninsula pouring fresh brew from a glass coffee pot into a metal thermos.

"Feeling better?" she asked with a knowing smile. The thin straps of her tank top peeked from under a long emerald green robe. More clothes didn't make her any less desirable. "I've some croissants. You can take a couple on the subway." She handed him two pastries from the carton along with the thermos full of coffee. "Milk, no sugar."

Morning sustenance in hand, Simon gently prevented Regina from turning away and wrapped his arms around her waist. "Well, someone has been paying attention." He pulled her closer for a kiss, groaning as her hands slid up his back. He tightened his embrace, kissing harder, crushing her breasts against his chest.

"Simon," gasped Regina as she broke the kiss.

"Mmm?" He pressed his lips against her jaw and then made a trail of kisses down her neck.

"Your train." Her hoarse voice barely sounded the words. She pushed on his chest. "You're going to be late." His kisses continued down the opening of her robe. "Mrs. Whoever is waiting."

"Mmm-hmm." The ringing phone in his pocket interrupted his descent just as he reached the two splendid mounds peeking from the robe. "Man, just when it was getting good." He relaxed his arms, and set the thermos on the counter. "Simon Young." Regina smiled as she wriggled out of his embrace. He fixed his gaze on her jiggling behind as she walked to the door. She held it open, dangling his backpack in one hand.

"Yes, we'll finalize everything this afternoon." He wedged the phone between his head and shoulder and wriggled an arm through the strap hole of his backpack before dashing into the hallway. "No, that is not what was negotiated." He turned; the door closed in his face. He hefted the backpack on his shoulder and dashed towards the elevator. "We're not going to haggle any more about this. The offer stands as is."

6-VINCE DECKLAND

H IS BODY CRUSHED BETWEEN THE SUBWAY DOORS, a grunt escaped Simon's lips. Falling against them once he managed to squeeze inside the train, he gulped air into his lungs. Simon searched down the packed subway car, peering between the throngs of commuters for an empty seat. Nothing. He scanned the notifications on his phone. There were emails, texts and phone calls from colleagues, clients, friends and family—everyone— except the one person he wanted to hear from the most.

He popped the last bit of crescent in his mouth and grabbed a pole, positioning his stance for the endless starts and stops ahead. As with any New York City train, there was a host of interesting-looking people, but it was the popping sound of gum and the feeling that he was being watched that drew his attention to a little girl sitting in the seat directly below him. Her small mouth was going a mile a minute as she stared at him through thick glasses. The little afro puffs on either side of her head were held by pink ribbons, each tied in a neat bow.

"Hi," she chimed, twirling a ribbon around her small finger.

"Hey." He smiled back.

"You know, you're a man, but you smell like my mom's soap."

"Really? Thanks, kid." Simon wrinkled his nose. Not something he would normally choose, but that was the last thing on his mind when he'd grabbed from a bunch of bottles of body washes hoarded in the corner of Regina's shower.

"You smell like flowers. My dad has a special soap for men. It doesn't smell like flowers. He says flowers are for ladies. Why are you wearing ladies' soap?"

He shot a self-assured smile at his little inquisitor. "I like smelling like flowers. It makes me feel pretty."

She wrinkled her nose, her head bobbing with the sway of the train. "You're weird."

"Yeah, I get that a lot." Simon looked around the car and then out the window for the name of the station that the train was approaching. He sighed. The trek from Harlem to downtown was proving to be a chore, especially when the trip came with an over inquisitive kid. The girl stopped gnashing the gum and poised her lips to speak. "It was nice talking to you," Simon blurted before she had a chance to say a word. "Have fun at school or wherever it is you're going." While passengers poured out, he made his way to the other end of the train car, where he struck gold—a seat. He plopped on the hunk of plastic and opened and closed his hand in quick motions. *I'm gonna have to bring a manlier soap with me the next time I stay at Regina's. If there is a next time. She didn't look too pleased shufflin' me out the door. Maybe last night was a one-time thing.* Hearing the phone chime, Simon reached in his pocket and read the message.

Regina: *Did you catch the train?*
Simon: *Barely. I had to dive for the doors.*
Regina: *Aww! Perhaps try setting the alarm earlier?*
Simon: *Good idea.*
Regina: *I tend to have those. Have a safe trip downtown.*
Simon: *Thanks.*

Simon leaned back in his seat and drank down the last of the coffee in his thermos. "Oh yeah, there's gonna be a next time."

ও৶ও৶ও৶ও৶

The firm was in its usual morning commotion. Simon weaved through the halls and cubicles towards his office. Corella looked at him as he approached and then her watch.

"Good morning, Corella." He tried to sound as commanding as possible but couldn't quite pull it off when confronted with Corella's motherly stare over her designer glasses. He dashed by her like a school boy late for class.

"'Morning, Simon." Corella's fingers slid across the screen of her tablet while she trailed him into the office. "Your meeting is in 45 minutes. I'm assuming you'll be changing?"

"Yes." Simon shrugged off his coat, which Corella quickly grabbed and hung on the back of the office door while he took a shirt from his small closet. "Thanks."

"I suggest the red tie. Mrs. Blakeside seems to like you in it."

"Agreed."

"Have you had breakfast?"

"Affirmative." Simon held up the empty thermos.

"Good. Do you want to have lunch ordered in?"

"You don't have to."

Corella held up her hand. "It's going to be a long day. What would you like?"

"Surprise me."

"You got it. By the way, nice fragrance."

"Yeah," He pulled at his shirt cuffs and let out a nervous chuckle. "I decided to try something new." He opened a cabinet holding his travel bag full of toiletries and pulled out a bottle of cologne.

"No, that'll only make it worse." She went back to swiping her tablet. "Just go with smelling like a fresh meadow for today. Is there an address?"

"An address?"

"To send flowers. I know a great florist who can have them delivered by this afternoon."

"Oh, no." Simon moved his gaze to his desk and curved his lips into a smile. "She's not the flowers type."

"I like her already. You have 40 minutes." She grabbed the thermos and turned towards the door. "I'll have this refilled for you."

"You're the best." Simon scrolled through his phone's contact list, stopping at the R's.

"I know." The door barely closed behind her when Vince Deckland strutted in. A knot grew in the pit of Simon's gut as the tall blonde in a perfectly-tailored suit waltzed to his desk.

"Hey, Si. How's it going?" Vince scanned Simon's desk. "Yeah, that's great. I was wondering if you could do me a favor."

Simon sighed, set his phone face down on the desk and braced his fists on his hips. "I'm busy Vince."

Vince lifted his hands and pumped his palms in Simon's direction. "I know, I know. We all are." He teetered the picture of Simon's mother in his hand. His gaudy man's ring twinkled in the light. "I have a couple of clients in my office," Vince sniggered, "and let's just say that English is barely their second language." He jabbed the picture towards Simon before sitting it on the edge of the desk. "I was hoping you could help translate."

"Where're they from?"

"China, I think."

"I'm Korean." Simon grabbed his mother's picture and returned it to its rightful place. "Now if you'll excuse me, I need to prepare for a meeting."

"But, isn't it the same thing?"

Simon scoffed. "No, It's not the same thing. China and Korea are two different countries, and the people in China speak a bunch of different languages." It baffled him how ignorant so many of the college-educated people at his firm were. They lived their lives in myopic bubbles void of any culture or perspectives outside of theirs. He walked across his office and stood right outside of the doorway. "I suggest you try getting one of the firm's translators."

Vince cocked an eyebrow as he walked out the doorway. "We have those?"

"Yes. Get your assistant to request one." Simon noticed Corella holding a yellow sticky note out of the corner of his eye. He strutted to her desk. "Thank you, Corella."

"No problem, Simon," she answered and returned to her tasks.

Simon held the small square of paper under Vince's nose. "Make sure she knows what language she needs to request to be translated. Start by asking your clients. Bye Vince."

"Great. Thanks Si!"

"Simon," he corrected.

"Yeah. Thanks, Simon." Vince walked down the hall, becoming a microaggressive memory.

Simon crossed his arms and pressed his lips together. Corella was peering over her glasses and gently shaking her head as she rolled her eyes. "I told you it was going to be a long day." She glanced at her watch. "You have 35 minutes."

ꙮ ꙮ ꙮ ꙮ

"Okay, Mrs. Blakeside." Simon smiled and straightened his shoulders as he opened his office door. "I think we'll be able to have this matter settled within a week."

"Thank you, Simon." The older woman picked up her designer handbag and rose gracefully from her seat. "I knew you would handle this for me. Some may consider it a minor thing, but I wanted it taken care of before I left." She extended a skinny wrinkled hand and gently rubbed the top of his head. "I told you he was my little legal machine."

Simon slowly blinked as he forced a grin. "That's what I'm here for." They made their way down the corridor.

"Are you sure he knows what he is doing," asked another equally older woman walking behind them. "This is very important." The trio stopped in front of the elevator. Simon pressed the button with a little more force than necessary.

Mrs. Blakeside patted her sister on the shoulder. "I'm sure it's just fine."

"Yes, Ms.?" Simon raised his eyebrows.

"Ripley."

"Ms. Ripley. I've assisted clients with this type of thing before. Your sister is in good hands."

She sized Simon up with a suspicious side glance before turning her attention to her sister. "I just don't know. This place has plenty of lawyers. Perhaps he can get another one to check his work."

Simon clenched his teeth behind his smile. "If you would like another opinion, I can ask a colleague to look at the contracts."

"No," Mrs. Blakeside responded as the elevator opened. "You see, Agnes. You've insulted the boy." The geriatric duo stepped inside.

"I'm sure plenty of people ask. I mean he is," Ms. Ripley tilted her head and squinted, "young."

Simon clasped his hands behind his back and watched as the two women talked as if he wasn't there. "You worry too much. His people are very smart."

Simon's shoulders slid down as the elevator door closed. *Good thing I haven't had lunch yet. It's hard to deal with bigots on a full stomach.* On cue, his belly growled as he made his way back to his office.

He approached his assistant's desk. "Corella." She held a bag with the name of his favorite diner on the front.

"I figured you could use a treat."

"You're the best."

"I know."

Corella handed him the lunch bag and put on her glasses. "Oh." She picked up a pile of sticky notes. "I have 5 messages from a Samantha. She couldn't get in contact with you and asked to speak to your assistant. She seems pretty anxious to talk to you."

"I'm not available to speak to her, ever." He stormed into his office and paced the floor. *Why can't she just leave me alone? I swear, she must've gone mental or something.* He turned, Corella was perched on her chair, looking at him with a concerned expression.

Simon walked back her desk and rubbed his forehead with his fingertips. "I'm sorry." He swallowed and shifted his weight. "It's complicated. Let's just say the best thing is for me not to talk with that person."

"Understood."

"Thanks, Corella."

"You're welcome." The phone rang. "Hello, this is Corella Banks." She made eye contact with him. "May I ask who's calling? Samantha?" Simon filled his lungs through his flaring nostrils. "I'm sorry, Simon's not available at the moment. "Would you like to leave a message?" was the last thing he heard before shutting the door.

7-Enjoying the Ride

REGINA PEERED AT THE COMPUTER SCREEN and began vigorously typing. *And you're obviously clueless about the role racism plays in your life. I suggest opening a book.*

After Simon left, she'd decided to shower and get right to work on her next blog post, but memories of the previous night made it impossible to concentrate. She followed his last trail of kisses down her neck with her fingers. Simon's kisses and touches were emblazoned along every nerve of her body, making it hard to properly serve an indignant slap down to the ignorant and juvenile comments from the bigoted racists trolling her site.

The Blackness of Kent garnered an impressive number of followers and disparagers over the years. Regina created it as a platform to empower people constantly traumatized by racism, so having detractors and sleazy trolls was inevitable. Normally, she was more than ready for a fight, but not today. Today, Simon Young clouded her mind and dulled her wits. She tapped her finger on the mouse, holding her head in her hand, scouring her brain for a dismissive retort. She had nothing.

She straightened her back in the chair. *How about you go fuck yourself?!* flashed across the screen. "There," she pronounced to an empty apartment, "my work is done." Regina closed her laptop and dialed the phone. She needed to talk to somebody about her previous night of passion and purge the hodgepodge of excitement and anxiety jumbling her brain.

"*Toni Kent.*"

"Hey, Toni."

"What's up girl." The professional tone faded from Toni's voice.

"Nothing. I was wondering if you were free for lunch?"

"Ahh. It'll be tight. I've a packed schedule. I was really just plannin' to eat in my office. How about you come over tonight for dinner?"

Regina sucked air through her teeth and scratched through her coils. "Umm. I was kinda hoping to talk to you without Marcus around."

"Really? About what?"

"How about I bring you a sandwich?"

"Okay," said Toni in a tone that made her suspicion clear. She and Regina had been friends for years—much to Marcus's vexation—so she could tell immediately when something was afoot. *"I scheduled to have lunch between 12 and 1."*

"Perfect. Extra pickles?"

"You know it."

꿈 꿈 꿈 꿈

The tip of Regina's tongue protruded from the corner of her lipsticked mouth as she clicked her thumbs vigorously at the cell phone keys while the bag of sandwiches dangled from her arm. A concept popped into her head while she was on the subway, and the long walk down the placard-lined hallway gave her enough time to draft a quick email of notes. She couldn't afford to let an idea slip away, especially given her current preoccupation with Simon. Regina knocked on the door brandishing the name *Toni Kent* followed by a bunch of letters.

"Hey, Lady." Sleek legs supported a petite frame and vanished under a black pencil skirt. "How are you?"

"I'm good." Regina held out a bag with the name of their favorite deli on it. It was time to pull out all the stops to drop this bit of news on her best friend. "Your lunch."

Toni opened the bag and smiled as she inhaled. "Yes, I'm starving." She twirled on one designer heel and walked further into her office "Come on in."

"I'm lovin' those shoes, girl."

Toni stopped and stuck out one leg. "Thanks. They're my gift to me."

"Alright, now." Regina tucked one leg under her on the sofa. "A queen has to treat herself occasionally."

"Or more frequently." The friends laughed and started eating.

"So," chimed Toni between bites, "What's the reason for this impromptu lunch? She dabbed her lips with a napkin. "Since you don't want Marcus involved, I'm assuming it has something to do with a man." Crossing her legs as she reclined, Toni balanced her drink on the arm of the chair.

Regina's fingertips disappeared between the folds of her sandwich. "Well, I did have someone over last night."

Toni's smile broadened. "It's about damn time. How long has it been?" She tucked hair from her bob behind one ear. "More importantly, who is it?" she inquired before wrapping her lips around her straw.

Regina tilted her head and examined the contents of her sandwich. "His name is Simon." She spied for Toni's reaction over the bread. "We met while working on a project for the center."

Toni swirled the ice in her drink then sat on the edge of her chair wide–eyed. "Wait. Are you talkin' about Simon Young?" The corners of her mouth jerked along with her dainty round shoulders. "You slept with your brother's old college roommate?" She held her sides and threw her head back in a laughing fit. "Are you insane? He's gonna flip."

"Why?"

"*Why?* You know why. Simon's like Marc's main boy. He's the only person who he made sure was at the courthouse for our wedding." Regina recalled the family's partial surprise when Marcus and Toni announced their marriage. She was still at college in San Diego when she got the call. Marcus Kent was not the type to do things on the fly, so everyone knew he'd fallen deep for Toni.

"Your brother can barely tolerate the two of us being so close, and you know how overprotective he gets when you're dating. Now you're bumping uglies with his best friend? Oh, I can't wait to see this." Toni took another sip. "Please, please, tell him when I'm in the room." The armchair practically swallowed her frame as she fell back into it. Regina's napkin flying at her only increased her laughter.

"Thanks for the support." Regina kneaded her thigh. *How am I gonna tell Marcus? Toni's right. He's not gonna take any of this well.*

"Don't worry," Toni said, touching her best friend's knee. "He'll have to come to grips with it."

"Maybe not. It was only one time."

"So, what? You had a one-night stand? That's not like you."

Regina shrugged. "Sleeping with him in the first place is not like me." She rested her arm on the back of the sofa and sighed. "It's probably better if it is only once."

Toni straightened in her chair. "Tell me about last night."

Regina fiddled with her earring. "The sex was pretty amazing. I mean, granted, I haven't had any in a million years." She stared at the swirling patterns in the painting on the wall across from her. "But there was something about the way he touched me—how his lips felt on my skin. It was electric. When he whispered my name, it was like he had to have me, not just have sex, but me."

"I bet he did," Toni broke through.

Regina cast her friend a side–eye. "Maybe I'm reading too much into it. We were probably just both really horny."

"Maybe, or maybe there's more." Toni leaned forward. "You'll never know if you end it now."

"True."

"Either way, you made an excellent choice to end your dry spell. Simon is fine and smooth."

Regina bit her nail and mused over the memories of the last time she saw and felt the man that made her so hot. It was less than half a day, but it felt much longer. "Indeed, he is."

Toni propped her head on her palm and gazed into the air. "I get why you wanted to bed the man. I just hope you practiced safe sex, young lady." She wagged her finger at Regina.

"I'm glad you find this funny."

"I do. I really do." The friends continued to talk and eat. Toni glanced at her watch. "Time to get ready for my next client."

Regina gathered the remnants of their meal into a bag. "Thanks for listening to me, Toni."

"Of course. I'm always here for you. Now, I really have to get ready," Regina obeyed her friend's gentle prod towards the door, "and don't worry about Marcus. The two of us can handle any kind of man-fit he has."

❧❧❧❧

Back at home, Regina rubbed her distended belly and suppressed a burp with the back of her hand. *Time to get to work. I got bills to pay.* The typing commenced. After a while, she scrunched her nose and mouthed the words of the article she wrote based on the email she sent herself. *Nice, and there's still time to have it ready to go live tomorrow.*

Her phone vibrated next to her hand. Her heart jumped a little when she read *Simon* on the screen. She cleared her throat. "Hello?"

"When can I see you again?" His sultry voice drifted into her ear and sent a shiver down her spine.

"I'm not sure."

"How about tonight?" She pursed her mouth, trying hard not to let him hear how hard he was making it for her to breathe. Droplets of sweat formed at her temples as a rush of heat ran up her neck.

"I can't tonight." She grabbed the mouse with her trembling fingers and leaned forward to gaze at the computer screen. "I have plans."

"Unbreakable ones? I can make sure you don't regret it."

Regina's nipples hardened and a warm sensation blossomed between her thighs. She wanted nothing more than to have a repeat performance of last night and feel Simon's hands exploring her hot body. *Control yourself.* "I'm not at your beck and call, Young. I have a life, you know." *Hopefully taking a stern tone will cool things down.* "Would you drop everything and come running uptown if I asked?"

"If it meant I could put my head between those thick thighs of yours, yes. Is that an invitation?" His smooth voice sent messages to all the right places. She was going to have to change her panties after this phone call.

Hell yes. Regina put her thumb between her front teeth and bit hard to steady her nerves. "No."

"Well let me know as soon as there is one. Until then, how about tomorrow night?'

She scanned her calendar with increasing dread at all the colors it hosted. Meetings and interviews spotted her week, and then off to see the parents on the island. *I can't blow them off. I'm not risking the wrath of Adrian Kent for some guy that's hot between the sheets—no matter how great the sex. Shit!* "No to that, Young. The soonest I'm available is Monday."

"Seriously? Aren't you a freelancer? Can't you move your schedule around?" Regina lifted her eyebrow at the new tension in his tone. Did he really think that she was some accessible booty call? It was time to nip that assumption in the bud.

"Yeah, the word *free* is deceptive. I actually have a tight schedule and commitments." She exaggerated a little. There were a couple of meetings she could reschedule, but like hell was she going to be that weak. "I've professional obligations that I can't just toss to the side."

"I wasn't saying that."

"Yes, you were, but no worries, Young." Stretching her legs in front of her, she shook her foot and waited. *He's gonna have to get the message real quick that I'm not going to be his plaything.* "Monday?" She expected a flat rejection. Experience taught her that men didn't take kindly to women not making themselves available. Most wanted an easy lay, something she refused to be.

"Sounds great. How about dinner at my place?"

Hell no. "How about lunch? I've dinner plans. I can meet you downtown so it won't be a hassle for you to get back to work."

"I can do lunch." The corners of Regina's mouth twitched. He was apparently not used to women saying no to him. The heavy sigh she heard over the phone gave her pause. "Whatever you want, Regina." Regret tugged at her heart. *Is this what I want?* Last night was amazing, and her body was still burning from the thought of his touch.

No, I want him, and he's exactly who I'm gonna get. She put Simon on speaker phone and opened her text message app.

Regina: *Hi Damion. I'm going to need to reschedule our meeting tonight. Is there any way we can meet earlier?*

"Do you want anything in particular," Simon continued.

"Surprise me."

Damion: *Hey, Regina. Sure. I'm free at 5, but I can only give you a half-hour.*

Regina: *That's fine. Thanks for understanding.*

Damion: *np*

"Umm, Simon. I just got a cancellation for tonight. Today must be a lucky one for you."

"I guess it is." His tone perked up. "So, it's dinner then? Where do you want to go? Like I said, whatever you want."

The sensation between her thighs stirred again. She leaned her head back and closed her eyes. It's not like she hadn't been flirted with before. There was a steady stream of men approaching her, but she typically swatted them away like annoying flies to focus on her career. She'd planned to do the same with Simon, but, for some reason, that was not possible. She wanted him there, at that moment, in her bed, and nothing was going to stop her. "Nowhere. Why don't you come here? Around 9 good?"

"I prefer 8." The sensual tone returned to his voice; she shifted in her chair. Words on the screen swam in front of her. She silently prayed that he hadn't heard the small squeak that escaped from her throat. The lust stirring inside her demanded satisfaction.

"I can do 8." *And you.* "I'll see you then."

"Yes, you will." Air returned to Regina's lungs. Her shaky legs carried her to the refrigerator. She patted her face and neck with a cold-water bottle. She returned to her seat in front of the computer and tapped the desk with a pen. It was sheer madness to get involved with Simon. Nothing could come of their relationship—not that what they were doing was one. Dinner and a night of hot sex wasn't exactly a testimony of undying love, no matter how good the kebabs and orgasms.

Stop making a toss in the sheets more than it is. She gazed at his contact pic in her phone. The only thing Simon's actions indicated was that he wanted her physically. *No obsessing over what might happen. I'm gonna just enjoy the ride—literally.*

8-Let's Keep This Between Us

REGINA RUBBED HER GLOSSED LIPS TOGETHER and inspected herself in the mirror. The short-sleeved white top contrasted her brown skin and made it shine as did the gold pendant that hung around her neck and rested just above her cleavage, matching the anklets from her friend Hind jingling under her skirt. *It's been a while since I played the seductress role, but I'm pretty sure I can pull it off.* Her stomach fluttered at the sound of the doorbell. She raced out of the bathroom and past the steaming hot pots bubbling on the kitchen stove. She looked at herself one more time in the hall mirror and smoothed the front of her skirt just before opening door with a smile.

Simon balanced bags in each hand. His eyes lit. "You look great."

Regina shifted hers to the floor and pulled at the waist of her skirt. "Thank you." She rested her hands on his shoulders as he wrapped one arm around her waist and kissed her. The toes of her bare feet curled when his lips covered hers. The kiss began soft but quickly increased in desire. Regina turned her head to break it before the two of them ended up tearing each other's clothes off in the doorway. "What's all this?"

"It's dinner." Simon brushed passed her and strode into the apartment. "I figured you might like some Italian." Placing the bags on the counter, he looked over at the stove. "Oh, you already made dinner?"

"Yeah, I did." Regina eyed the steaming pots. "It's okay. We can eat what you brought."

"No, I definitely want what you have for me." Simon smiled mischievously and rested his hand on her behind. "How about I get a reward for bringing all this sustenance?"

"Let me see what you brought first. Then I'll decide on a reward."

Simon began to take the packages out of the bag, announcing confidently what each one contained: "shrimp parmesan, eggplant parmesan, garlic knots, Greek salad."

"Impressive. Someone has been paying attention."

"Indeed, I have," his lips hovering over hers, "and now, for my reward." She grabbed his shoulders and pulled him into her embrace. Their lips met. Hot blood flushed her entire body when he pressed his already hard cock against her leg.

Regina slowly moved backwards, pulling Simon with her until the wall stopped them. She reached down to caress the bulge in his pants. Shivers of pleasure ran through her body as his hand traveled down her back and rested on her bottom. Simon pulled her hips against his groin and crushed his lips harder, deepening the hunger of their kiss. The intensity rattled Regina's core. She wanted to hear him call her name again, to lose himself to her.

She strained her lips away and peered into his eyes. They gleaned with passion as he stared down at her breast. "Regina." Her name passed through his lips layered with lust and aspirant need—both of which she was all too willing to satisfy.

A sharp shriek from the ceiling seeped into her consciousness. A burning smell accompanied a billow of smoke bursting from underneath pot lids, creeping up the wall and fanning out over the ceiling.

"Oh, no. The food." A grey cloud bombarded her as she reached the stove and lifted the lid. It cleared away to reveal tiny dots of black invading the surface of the rice. Scraping the bottom of the pot, a charred layer sticking to it confirmed the futility of even thinking the food she worked so hard to make was salvageable.

"Aww, I'm sorry." Simon stood behind her and held her hips. "Is all lost?"

"Yeah. I guess we're eating what you brought." Regina fanned at the beeping smoke detector with a dish towel until it stilled. She picked up the oven mitts and maneuvered the pot full of now offensive chow at arms distance towards the sink.

"I'll go wash for dinner." Simon disappeared down the hallway.

The pot landed with a crash as Regina jumped at the sound of the doorbell. "Who the hell can that be?" She eyed the closed bathroom door before answering the second chime. "Please, don't be Marcus." She crept down the hall; dread mounted in the pit of her stomach, and every nerve fired at the touch of the cold doorknob. A sigh escaped her lips at the site of Jeremy's bright smile.

"Hey, Regina." His green eyes sparkled behind square glasses. "I'm sorry to bother you, but you left this at the center. He held the crimson crocheted scarf right under her nose. "Everything okay? I smell smoke." Regina stood on her tiptoes and swayed back and forth to obstruct the sight line of Jeremy's craning head. Though a harmless enough young man, if Marcus's acolyte saw Simon, it wouldn't be long before big brother would be harassing her with questions, and she wasn't inclined to have her life unfold like a scene out of a 90's teen melodrama.

"Hi, Jeremy." Regina stepped into the hallway and pulled the door behind her until it was barely cracked. "Aww, thank you. I was wondering what happened to it. I could've sworn I put it in my bag. You didn't have to come all this way to bring it to me."

"It's no problem. I don't live too far."

"Don't you live up in Washington Heights?"

"Right." Jeremy jammed his hands in his pockets. "I meant you don't live far—from the center that is. So, I came here to give you this before heading home." His cheeks were quickly becoming as red as the scarf.

"I really do appreciate that, Jeremy." Regina looked back at the door, grateful that the inside of the apartment was still.

"What's that smell?"

"Huh? Oh, I burned dinner."

"Great. I mean, that's not great. I'm sorry about your dinner." Jeremy stared down at his shuffling feet. "I mean, since you burned dinner, why don't we go get somethin' to eat?"

A sound came from behind her. "I would love to Jeremy," she said eyeing the apartment door again, "but I've a ton of work." Regina backed into the doorway, careful not to open the door too wide. "Now I have to clean up the mess I made. Some other time, I promise."

She returned to the kitchen just as Simon emerged from the bathroom. His shirt once again neatly tucked into his trousers, he combed his fingers through his hair as he peered at the door.

"Someone here?"

"Umm, no. It was nobody."

Simon pulled her into his arms. "I'm sorry about dinner. I was really looking forward to it."

Her nipples pebbled and tingled as they brushed against his chest. She was really beginning to feel like a horny teenager. "It's okay. Can you get the plates?" She slid past him, trying to put some distance between them to keep her head clear. "They're in the cabinet to the right of the sink." Regina began opening the takeout packages when she noticed a small plastic bag. "Hey, what's this?" She pulled out a tall black plastic bottle with the words "Hair + Body Wash" printed in bold letters on the label. "Soap?"

"Yes, soap." Simon took the bottle, grabbed the bag and set it to the side. "It seems that people notice when a man smells like a bouquet of lilacs. So, I'll be using this in the morning."

Regina knitted her eyebrows. "You're that sure you'll be staying the night?" The pitch in her tone probably gave away her excitement at the thought of his warm body against hers all night.

"Yeah," Simon pronounced as he grabbed a plate and fork and headed for the sofa. "I'm that sure." After sitting down wide-legged, he picked up the remote and flicked on the television before jamming food in his mouth.

Regina chuckled and scooped a spoonful of shrimp. This was the first time he appeared completely relaxed, He usually looked like he was constantly gauging the room or guarding what he was doing or saying.

"Okay." She walked towards him, balancing a plate in one hand and two drinks in the other. "You can put it on the sink next to your new toothbrush." Purposefully ignoring Simon's smirk, she positioned herself to fit in the crook of his arm. "No sports. Marcus drove me crazy with basketball games when we were kids."

Simon threw his head back with a hearty laugh. "You have my sympathy. I went to sleep and woke up to sneaker squeaks. If Marcus's nose wasn't in a book, he was watching or playing basketball." Simon consumed another forkful of food and settled his hand on Regina's thigh. "So, what'll it be?"

A warm sensation crept down her leg. She stabbed at the food on her plate. "I'm not sure." The feelings Simon stirred inside her were exhilarating and frightening. Her body longed for him, and she loved the time they spent together, but the nagging truth of their different races pierced at the back of her mind. People were not going to make a relationship between one of their most vocal pro-Black activist writers and an Asian man easy. They won't care that he made her heart skip with a smile. To some, she would be a sellout—another Black person who skipped out on their people to date or marry outside their race. Given the tensions between Asians and Blacks in the country, others may think her dating Simon was worse than being involved with a White guy.

"How about one of these?" Simon pointed at the screen.

"Huh?" A row of movie thumbnails with people at varying stages of decay or screaming for their lives shined on the screen. "The one with the zombies."

"Yes." He leaned and pecked her lips. "My kind of woman." Simon sunk back into the sofa.

"Simon?"

"Mmm?" He kept his site on the blackening screen. Ominous music filtered the room.

She bowed her head. "I think it may be a good idea to just keep—this—between the two of us."

"What do you mean?"

Twirling the fork between her tapered fingers, she watched the mound of spaghetti grow. "I mean, we're just having fun, right? I think if people knew, it would get strange and uncomfortable. They would ask questions that I'm not prepared to answer, and I really don't want to deal with everyone getting all intrusive." She let go of the fork and rubbed her temple. "You saw what happened with the guy in the elevator. So, can't we just keep it quiet, for now?"

He maintained an even tone. "I think you're right." An austere stare contrasted the agreement. "It really isn't anyone's business but ours anyway."

Regina continued despite Simon's deadpan expression. "Are you sure? I want you to be okay with it. I'm not ashamed of being seen with you."

"I'm sure."

"Good." Regina cuddled against him. "Now bring on the zombies." She'd hoped the bubbly tone in her voice would bring down the barrier that suddenly formed between them, and was disappointed when it didn't——not completely.

9-Basketball with Marcus

FLOPPING ON THE COUCH, Simon tucked both his arms under his head and let out a large puff of air. Time was just creaking by. Regina only left the day before to visit her parents, and it was as if it had been ten years. Why he was pining like a teenager was unclear, but it was hard to ignore the desire coursing through his veins at the very thought of her.

He swiped his thumb across the phone screen, passing all of the names of more easily-attainable bed mates, landing on the only person he wanted. *Hey. What're you doing?* It wasn't right. Their affair was less than a week old. Unlike other sexual escapades, where he'd be happy with a single night of ecstasy, He still craved the thrill that feeling and tasting her curves brought him. He wanted more Regina, but here he was—left with texting and looking at a tiny avatar.

Regina: *Hanging with my parents while they banter and make breakfast. You?*

Simon: *Chillin', thinking about the last places I kissed you. If I remember correctly it was—*

Regina: *I remember.*

Simon chuckled and propped on an elbow. *I'm also thinking about new places to put my lips.*

Regina: *Are you now?*

Simon: *Yes. My mind is getting very creative.* Regina's face flashed on the screen under her number. He let out a throaty laugh before answering. "Hello?"

"Okay, Young. No more sexy texts."

He smiled. "You don't like my texts?"

"Not when I'm sitting across from my mom and dad. My mother asked me what could possibly be on the screen to make me smile that way, and who was sending it."

"So, you do like them? I can send more."

"You need a distraction."

"No, I need to sink my teeth into your—"

"Simon." He sensed the excitement under her warning tone. *"Oh, thanks dad. It smells wonderful. I'll be there in a minute."*

The phone beeped in his ear. "Hold on a sec, Regina." He took a deep breath as the name registered. "Hey, Marc." He cleared his throat to try to get rid of the cracking in his voice. "What's up?"

"Nothing much, man. I was wondering if you're up to some ball? I need another player."

Simon sprung from his seat, jammed his hand in the front pocket of his jeans and paced the floor. "Umm, yeah. I can go for a game."

"Thanks, man. How soon can you get here?"

"Give me about an hour?"

"An hour it is."

Simon let out a deep sigh and returned to Regina's call. "That was Marc. He invited me to a game." He bounded into the bedroom.

"See," Regina muffled and chewed, *"there's your distraction."*

"I can think of a better one."

"I'm sure you could, but let's put a pin in all of that, shall we?" Her light giggle was infectious. He chuckled as he grabbed a pair of sweats out of the drawer.

"Okay. When do I get to pull it out?"

"Tomorrow, and Simon. You won't mention us to Marc, will you?"

"Don't worry," he strained to control his tone, "I remember our agreement."

They said their goodbyes. Simon started to change his clothes. Besides the law, basketball was one of the main things he and Marcus had in common. They hit the court right after meeting, and were practically invincible together, each intuitively knowing what moves to make to win. A hard game of one-on-one was also the best time to relieve stress and talk about life. Simon yanked sweatpants over his shorts and zipped the hoodie over his sleeveless t-shirt. He was actually looking forward to racing up and down the court with his best friend and clearing his head.

🎵🎵🎵🎵

Gym bag in hand, he panted as he lightly jogged up the subway stairs and weaved through pedestrians on the street. Marcus was already dribbling between players. He did a wraparound on his opponent and made the ball swish into the basket with a lay in. Simon stood on the sideline and grinned when Marcus's expected smack talk followed.

He pounded a hand against the *Boston College* letters on his sweatshirt. "Yeah! Yeah! That's what I am talkin' 'bout, son!" Marcus jogged triumphantly past the guy he scored on. "You youngins ain't ready!"

Simon raised his hand. "Yo, Marc!"

"Simon!" Marcus waved him forward. "Just in time. We gotta show these scrubs a little som'thin', som'thin' 'bout playin' ball." He slapped Simon on the arm. "This is my man Simon." The men around them gave Simon various forms of side-eye.

"He know how to play," asked a large man, jerking his head towards Simon.

Marcus slapped Simon on the shoulder. "He has some basic skills." He looked at his friend. "You ready, man?"

Simon crossed his arms holding the large man's gaze. "Yeah." The men dispersed from the friends.

"I love when they look at you like that." Marcus elbowed Simon. "They don't know what's comin'."

Simon twisted his mouth into a wry smile. "No, they don't." With no further resistance, the games began.

🎵🎵🎵🎵

The door to Marcus and Toni's apartment swung open. The sweaty duo poured into the entryway. "Yo, man. That was dope." Marcus dropped his ball and bag by the door. "I never get tired of the shocked faces when you play. Idiots forget that there are Asian players in the NBA. Put your bag there." Marcus strode into the kitchen and pulled two beers out of the refrigerator.

Simon let go of his bag and put his hands on his hips. "Yeah, man, but those guys were young. I almost didn't make it." He accepted a beer and took a swig.

"Nah, you had 'em. They couldn't mess with your skills. After all," Marcus playfully jabbed Simon in the stomach, "you learned from the best."

Toni glided into the room wearing slacks and a blouse. "Good game, I take it?" She approached Marcus, who was leaning back on the counter. She stood on her tip toes and greeted her husband with a kiss.

"It was intense." Marcus patted her bottom. "My man never disappoints."

"Nice to see you again, Simon."

Simon sensed something different in her tone. "Hi Toni." She set her full mouth into a half smile and sized him up with a glint in her eyes.

"Would you like to clean up a little?"

"Yeah." Simon slung his bag over his shoulder.

"You know where the guest bathroom is." Toni pointed a delicate finger towards the door. "Feel free to use any toiletries and linens."

"Thanks." Simon followed the direction of her finger.

"And you, my dear," he heard her saying to Marcus, "can hit the shower."

"Yes ma'am."

Simon stepped outside the bathroom a while later and dropped his bag full of sweaty clothes on the floor next to Marcus's. He heard muffled laughter coming from the master bedroom. Toni emerged, adjusting her blouse and pulling her fingers through her hair. "Umm. Marcus will be out in a few minutes," she said with a shy smile,

"Why don't you have a seat?" She walked towards the fridge. "Would you like something to drink?"

"Water, thank you." Simon sat on the overstuffed leather-trimmed sofa. He put his phone on the coffee table and rested his elbows on each leg.

Marcus strutted from the bedroom and into the living room with two beers and a satisfied grin. "Okay." He plopped on the couch next to Simon. "Let's see what's on."

Simon shook his head and chortled. He knew what that meant. There was either a basketball game on or some other sport. Marcus didn't do tv, the news being the only other exception. After a few clicks, the screen filled with players running back and forth on a court. The men reclined on the sofa, and it was as if they were transported back in time to their college apartment, except with better furniture and beer.

"So." Marcus threw his head back and took a large drink from the beer bottle. "I hear you guys finished the grant proposal?"

"Yeah. My assistant is having it proofed. It should be ready when I get to work on Monday."

"Good." The room fell silent save the squeaking sound of basketball sneakers streaming from the television. Simon slid further down. Hanging out with Marcus always gave him a chance to relax. He didn't have to be on guard around his friend, which was always a relief. The two fixated on the players. Simon put the bottle to his lips. The cold brew tingled as it passed down his throat.

"How was it working with Gina?" Marcus broke the silence. "I know how demanding she can be. I hope she didn't ride you too hard."

Simon sprang straight. Air and liquid sputtered from his mouth. He braced his hands on his thighs and coughed uncontrollably. He turned to his friend. Marcus suspended his beer bottle just in front of his lips. Simon shifted in his seat as his friend scrutinized him, one eyebrow arched.

"You okay, man?"

Simon raised his hand. "I'm fine." He sat back and rubbed his hands on his thighs, trying to appear relaxed despite his racing pulse.

"No, she isn't," he cleared his throat, "riding me too hard. We work just fine together." A warm feeling crept through his neck and face. "What's the score?" He purposefully concentrated on the screen, avoiding Marcus's gaze.

"10 to 2." The tiny hairs on the back of his neck stood at the steely tone in Marcus's voice. He was one of the few people that could read Simon like a book, and things were going to get tense very fast if he couldn't manage to not look guilty as sin. Marcus was traditional about his masculinity. He vested a lot of it on protecting and caring for the women in his life, which meant he would be very defensive of Regina and hard on any man circling around her.

Simon tried to keep his foot from tapping on the floor. "Good, good." His cell phone chimed on the coffee table and lit Regina's name. He snatched the phone and glanced at Marcus. *Did he see her name?* Fortunately, Marcus was back to watching the game and emptying his beer bottle. The phone rang again. Simon shut it off.

Toni approached with a platter full of crudité and cut fruit. "Are you staying for dinner, Simon?"

"Huh?" He shoved the phone in the leg pocket of his cargo pants and rubbed the sweat from his forehead and palms.

"Yes," Marcus answered before Simon could, "he is." Their gazes met. A plastered smile contradicted his piercing stare. "I owe him a meal after his performance on the court today."

Simon swallowed back the bile bubbling from his stomach and turned his attention to Toni. "Yeah, thanks, Toni."

"Good. I took an extra steak out when I overheard Marcus talking to you on the phone earlier. I figured you'd be hungry. When will the grill be ready, hun?"

Marcus groaned as he rose. "I'm on it." He glared down at Simon. "Come on, man."

He joined Marcus on the balcony. Marcus rubbed the top of the grill. "Let's get this baby started." It took a few tries, but the flames eventually sprang from the grill. Marcus backed away to stand next to him, admiring his accomplishment with primal satisfaction. "I guess the proposal will be ready for the review committee Monday?"

"It should be. I can bring it by after work."

Marcus clapped his hand on the back of Simon's neck. "Excellent, but that's not necessary. The deadline isn't for a few weeks, and we have an advisory board meeting next week. Why trudge all the way up here? You got other business?"

"No." Simon hunched his shoulders to his ears and looked at his shoes. *Well, actually, yes. I'll be taking care of a few things with your sister.* Even in his head, Simon realized how creepy the idea of him and Regina dating will be to Marcus. "No other business. I'll bring it to the next board meeting."

"Cool. Listen, man." Marcus held Simon's gaze. "You know, I may come off as overprotective about Gina, but that's just me bein' an older brother. It never turns off, no matter how old we get."

Simon nodded his head a little too vigorously. "Yeah, I get it. She's your sister." He fell off balance under Marcus's shake.

Marcus smiled and dug his fingers into Simon's skin. "Yes, and I'm always ready to do whatever I have to do to make sure no one messes with her."

"Yeah, man. Definitely."

Marcus laughed and punched Simon's arm. "I knew you would. Let me get those steaks on the grill," he announced before disappearing into the apartment.

Simon braced himself on the balcony and blew air into the Harlem landscape. Marcus's warning reached him loud and clear. Hands off his baby sister. Except, it was too late. Simon's hands and everything else had already been all over every inch of Regina's voluptuous brown body, and he didn't have any intention of keeping them to himself and ending their torrid lovemaking. The only reason he wasn't in her bed at that moment was because she was way out on Long Island with her parents. Otherwise, he would be busy flouting his best friend's veiled warning. *Another night of passion with her is definitely worth the risk.*

Simon crossed his arms and kicked the top of his shoe at imaginary rocks on the ground. *Look, idiot. Marcus has been a great friend, and you're going destroy your friendship because you like rolling around in the sheets with Regina? He's going to kick your ass for touching his sister.* Marcus was capable of taking a man down in seconds. Although no slouch in the fighting department, the last thing Simon wanted was to brawl with his best friend. "What am I going to do?" He asked the sky.

"About what?" Marcus appeared holding a plate full of raw meat.

"Nothing. Just thinking about a case."

"You wanna run it by me?

"Nah, thanks though, man. I really don't want to talk shop right now."

"I can dig that." Smoke billowed from the grill as Marcus laid the steaks on the grate. "I just checked out the score. Knicks down by 10." He poked at the meat.

"Of course, they are. I don't know why you constantly hope they have a chance in hell of winning."

"Hey, what's wrong with having faith in people?" Marcus stabbed at the meat sizzling on the hot grill. The two laughed and the tension evaporated.

As fool hearty as it was, Simon decided that he couldn't give up what he started with Regina or his friendship with Marcus. *If things become more serious between us, I'll let Marcus know about Regina and me. Preferably when he isn't brandishing a pitchfork.*

10-JAMAICA STATION

SIMON SCOOPED ANOTHER SPOON OF FOOD into his watering mouth. He felt his mother's warm hand on his shoulder, and a sense of comfort enveloped him. It had been so long since he sat at her table, eating to his content. Although they lived in the same city, her home in Queens was a distant place to people living in and closer to Manhattan. She might as well live upstate or on Long Island. Consequently, visits were rare, but Simon decided to take the train ride. Besides, he had other people to meet.

He flipped his buzzing cell phone, curling the corners of his mouth as he dropped the fork and read Regina's text message.

Regina: *I am catching the 4:56 train, so I should be home about 8. Do you want to grab something to eat?*

Simon's groin tingled. *I most certainly do.*

Simon: *Good. I'll meet you at your place.*

Regina: *I'm looking forward to it.*

"Who's that?" Alice placed a tall glass of water on the table in front of her son and descended on the chair next to him.

"Huh?" Simon slipped his phone into his pocket. "A friend I'm meeting for dinner tonight," Simon rubbed his belly, "but I think this delicious meal just spoiled my appetite." He enjoyed watching his mother's shy grin spread. It was nice being in his childhood home with her. Things were hectic at work, and his personal life was getting crazy now that he was sleeping with his best friend's little sister. *This is the calm I needed.*

"I can pack some for you to bring home." Alice balanced her fork in her delicate hand.

"No, I've some errands to run, so I won't be able to carry it around."

"Suit yourself. So, what have you been up to? How are things at work?"

"Fine." *Other than the fact that I'm surrounded by a bunch of bigots, things are terrific.* "How are things going with you?"

"Well, how much time have you got?" Simon spent the afternoon listening to his mother talk about her social life while he mapped his route and timed which train he needed to catch to meet Regina at Jamaica station. When the alarm buzzed, alerting him that it was time to leave, Simon hugged and kissed his mother before rushing to the subway. Once on the train, he pulled out his phone.

Simon: *Did you make your train?*

Regina: *Yes.*

He chastised himself for being so corny, but he wanted to see her as soon as possible. Simon pounded his feet on the steps as he bounded up the stairs two at a time. He hiked his jacket collar around his ears and peered down the open platform. The monitor blinking in front of him showed that the trains were running on time. He dialed Regina's number.

"*Hi,*" Her sultry voice sent tingles through him. Her bed in Harlem was too far away.

Simon pressed his free ear. "Hi. How's your ride?"

"*Fine,*" he heard her yawn into the phone. "*I'm not too far from Jamaica.*"

Simon's heart skipped as the train approached and screeched into the station. He looked up and down as it ground to a halt. "That's good. Just let me know when you pull up to the station."

"*Actually, it just stopped.*" The doors flew open, and a small stream of riders poured onto the platform. "*Why?*"

"Because I wanna make sure I'm getting on the right train." Simon bent to help a mother get her stroller onto the noisy platform. He nodded and smiled when she thanked him.

"*What? You're here?*" Simon stood straight. The deep breath he took stayed in his chest when he saw Regina poke her head out of the train and curve her lips into a radiant smile. "*You're insane, Young.*" Her mouth moved while her words floated into his ear from the phone.

"Get back in the train. I'll come to the car you're in." He rushed between cars, flying each door open until he saw her standing across from him. Coils spilled from under a black linty hat and swept across her thick, arched eyebrows. Regina's lush eyelashes beat against her raised cheeks as she blinked at him. Hips tightly wrapped in denim peeked out between the opening of her fur-lined jacket and swayed with the train on top of long legs that tapered from luxurious thighs. Had she grown she more beautiful than before? Finally reaching her, he cuddled her face in the palms of his hands and covered her mouth in a series of small kisses. "Hi."

Regina laid her hands flat against his back. "I can't believe you met me here."

"I couldn't wait to see you." A lump formed in Simon's throat. He'd meant it, but he had no intention of letting her know that she was so irresistible to him. "I mean, I was visiting my mother anyway. She lives in Queens, so I decided to meet you."

Regina knitted her eyebrows and scrunched her lips to one side. "Okay." She sat in the seat next to her bag. "Well, it's a nice gesture, anyhow."

Fantastic, now she thinks she is an afterthought. Simon slung the bag in the seat across from them with a grunt. "I thought it would be nice to take you out to eat," he explained as he claimed his place next to her, "before we head to your place." *And I get a chance to peel those pants off of you.* Laying his arm across her shoulders, Simon guided her mouth to his by gently pulling her chin. "I missed you." She tilted her head and slowly lifted her eyes. The electricity was definitely firing both ways.

"Me too," she sighed between her parted luscious lips, inviting him to get lost in them—which he did. Their kiss lasted until they reached Penn Station and resumed during the ride uptown. He groaned when Regina pushed him away. "I need to breathe some, Young." She nuzzled next to him.

"So, how was visiting your parents?" Simon tried to will the bulge in his pants down. He couldn't wait to get her in bed.

§♥§♥§♥§♥

Regina fumbled the keys in her trembling hands. With Simon caressing her hips and kissing her neck behind her ear, her composure was almost completely undone. He'd barely given her a moment to breathe on the train and in the hired car, which she loved, but she needed to focus. *Key in—yeah right there—hole. Get key in hole.*

"Having trouble?" Simon whispered in her ear as he gently squeezed one breast, "I can get it in for you."

She closed her eyes, and her knees went soft. Simon snaked his arm around her waist and lifted her against his body. *Damn, he's strong.* He pressed his stiffness into her. *And hard.* "I can do it. I just need you to back up a little."

"No way." He bit the back of her ear. The sound of his breath blended with the clicking of the lock tumblers. "I waited days to get near you. I'm not backing away now."

Simon's tight grip kept her from falling as they tumbled into the apartment. "Wait." Regina moaned, twisting in his arms and pushing her hand against his chest. She heaved for air as she took a few steps away and leaned against the wall. "Get the suitcase out of the hallway." She lifted her leg and yanked at the heel of her boot. Space now between them allowed the haze in her mind to lift. Spending the weekend on The Island should've helped her control the hormones Simon had bouncing through her body, but it proved futile. She'd spent three days thinking about what she would do to him when she got back.

Regina let the second boot drop to the floor, watching Simon walk towards her. She tugged one corner of her mouth into a half smile.

"What's so funny?" Simon shrugged out of his coat.

"You're all red." Regina playfully tugged at his ears as he closed the space between them.

"That would be because of you." His boyish smile made her insides quiver. Simon smoothed his hands down her sides. Hot jolts of desire pulsated between her legs. Coat falling to the floor, Regina felt shaking muscles under her hands as she slid them across the top of her lover's back and brushed her lips on his neck.

Simon groaned and pushed her away. "Bed." He grabbed her wrist and pulled her towards the bedroom.

She spun on socked feet and giggled, following behind him. The light from the hall glowed on his light tan skin. Back muscles rippled as he pulled his shirt over his head. His sneakers were next. She'd missed and wanted him so much that it created a turmoil in her that only he could settle. One person having that much power over her emotions and body was terrifying. She usually had more control over both, but Simon made her reckless. She slowly pushed the door closed behind her. Darkness overtook his glowing taut butt and muscular legs as he pushed down his jeans.

෪෪෪෪

Regina stretched her legs and cracked opened her eyes. Simon sat on the edge; his back contrasted the room's darkness.

"How did you get my number?" The acidic tone in his voice brought Regina out of her groggy state.

"Simon?" She saw his back straighten. "What's wrong? What time is it?"

"Everything is fine, babe." She felt his tense lips peck her forehead before the bed shook more vigorously. "Go back to sleep."

Light flooded the bed and blinded her then narrowed into a slit emanating from a crack in the door. She blinked at her phone. *Who's calling him at 2 am?*

He continued to talk in the hall. "That's none of your business."

Rolling over, she closed her eyes and tried not to listen. *I should respect his privacy. Maybe I should close the door.*

"Damn it, Samantha. I'm not interested in anything you have to say, ever. Lose my number, and stop calling my office."

Regina opened her eyes and peered into the darkness. *Who the hell is Samantha? Is she another woman Simon is messing around with? Are there more?* She clenched the pillow and shifted under the covers. He didn't seem like the type to be a player, but then again, she really didn't know him that well. *If I confront him about it, he'll know I was listening in on his conversation. Besides, it's obvious that he doesn't want anything to do with her.* Her muscles tightened under the blankets at the sound of Simon's footsteps.

The bed dipped under his weight. She tried to control her rapid breathing until her chest ached. She waited for his touch, for him to pull her into his warm embrace, but it never happened. Even though he'd only slept in her bed a few nights, Regina's body craved feeling him. It was denied.

ᔕ ᔕ ᔕ ᔕ

Regina strained her legs and arms to their brink and formed large 'O' with her mouth. The sounds of cabinet drawers opening and closing, dishes clinking and running water reverberated through the apartment and drifted in a muffled huff past the closed bedroom door. She rubbed an eye with the bottom of her palm while smoothing the cold bed sheet where Simon's body once laid. *Already up?*

She lifted her rebellious muscles out of bed and headed into the kitchen. Tying the front of her robe, Regina smiled at the sight of Simon, furrowed eyebrows and lips set in a determined line as he bent in front of the coffee maker.

"Good Morning."

"'Morning." He only glanced at her quickly before returning his attention to the machine. "How do you work this thing? There are like a million buttons."

Regina rounded the counter and reached from behind him. "It's set to start in an hour." She pressed the appropriate buttons. "You're up early."

"Yeah," he said, pulling her towards him. "I tried not to wake you. I need to change at work before my day starts." She welcomed the delicious series of endearing kisses.

"It's okay. Are you hungry?" Regina slipped her arms from around Simons waist and shuffled to the cabinet in her slippers.

"No, I found some oatmeal. It hit the spot." He stared at the coffee maker and patted his belly. "Oh, and I cleaned the mess."

"Thanks."

"No problem." Simon flashed a smile before striding around the counter. "Be right back."

Folding her arms and staring off into space with a broad smile, she took his place as sentinel in front of the machine. A warm feeling filled her. It was really nice waking with Simon there. She wanted more mornings like this. *I have to ask him what he likes for breakfast.* She pulled a pad and pen from the drawer. The sound of Simon's phone made her jump and drop them on the counter. She stared at the device as it quaked and pulsated a buzz into the air. She stepped closer to it. *Could it be that woman from last night?*

Regina looked towards the bathroom and then back at the phone. A lump formed at the top of her throat. She'd have to turn it over to read the screen. She inched her hand towards the vibrations and chimes. *No.* She snatched her hand away from it. *I'm not going to be that insecure.* The phone stopped, and Regina moved back to listening for the last hisses and bubbles that signaled the coffee was ready. *If there is another woman—or women—that'll come out, and I'll decide what to do at that point. It's not like Simon is exclusively mine anyway.* Although she wasn't the type to date multiple people, she was unsure if he was. She'd have to broach it, but not by shaking his phone at him in her bathrobe like some jealous girlfriend.

"Coffee ready?" Simon took his jacket off the hook and shrugged it over his wide shoulders.

"Just now. You've got good timing, Young." Errant drops fell from the spout and sizzled into evaporation on the hot plate. Regina filled the mug, noticing Simon reading his phone screen out of the corner of her eye. "It just stopped ringing'." She offered him the morning libation. "I hope it wasn't urgent."

Simon's face remained cheerful. "Nope. Just someone from work." He grabbed the mug and pulled Regina towards him. "See you tonight?"

"I can't. I'm goin' out with some girlfriends. Tomorrow night?"

"I'm probably gonna be workin' late preparing for a case."

"If you don't mind the train ride," Regina smoothed his tie, "I won't mind the lateness." She laced her fingers in his silky hair, drew him into a long, hot kiss, and softly blinked, waiting for a response.

Simon's eyes smoldered. "I'll be here."

Regina kissed his nose. "Good. Now go." She teasingly pushed him away. Hearing the door close behind Simon, she poured some coffee and perched on a stool, cradling the hot mug in her hands. Only gone for a few minutes, she already yearned for his presence. There was no denying that Simon Young was under her skin, and she was going to make sure he stayed there.

She hopped off the stool and shuffled to her desk. It started to ding a series of notifications as soon as she raised the laptop open. She skimmed through a list of articles, stopping and cringing at a headline:

Can you be Pro-Black and Marry White?

She scanned the article, which contained the usual arguments for and against Black activists and celebrities marrying interracially. Regina focused her attention on the comments section and the plethora of derision, which included words like "internalized racism," "color struck" and the same "sellout" the guy in the elevator shouted at her.

She pushed in the squishy belly of the kitty-shaped stress reliever stuck on her desk. She couldn't deny that many of her followers might have the same criticisms about interracial dating and marriage as the ones on the screen. Some may be accepting, but others will eviscerate her and jeopardize her blog. She couldn't lose everything she worked for—or Simon.

11-SAMANTHA

REGINA SQUINTED AND BLINKED her eyes at the humongous screen before her. Simulated sonic booms and screeches billowed through the movie theater, washing over the audience. She shrugged her shoulders in defense of the cacophony assaulting her ears. The ticket for the summer blockbuster proved a good buy, at least for one of them.

Simon's eyes filled with youthful wonder at the umpteenth explosion on the screen. He sprang in his seat, and the popcorn jumped in the tub he held, matching his excitement. A bunch of pieces splattered on the theater floor. The light from the screen glowed on his chiseled jaw and broad smile of delight. This was a new side of Simon. Usually, his demeanor was calmer, stoic even at times. But now, her date bordered on downright giddy. It was nice.

"Oh, Man, did you see that, Gina?" He scooped a handful of popcorn and crammed it into his mouth. Cheeks puffed out, he chomped the snack. In between mouthfuls of popcorn, Simon made lively responses to the action unfurling in front of him.

His bounding oohs, ahhs and laughter was more entertaining than the movie. She sat, soda in hand, furthest away from her excited date. *Look at him. It's hard to believe this big kid is the same cool, calculating attorney who helps make million-dollar deals happen.* His suit jacket laid neatly folded on the empty chair beside him, he'd loosened his necktie and rolled his sleeves. Reclining in the theater seat, Simon happily munched on what was left of the tub of popcorn and looked back and forth between her and the screen. "What?"

"Nothing." The corners of her mouth twitching, she bit her bottom lip.

"Come here." Simon drew Regina into the crook of his arm and brushed a light kiss on her forehead. "This is fun, right?"

"Definitely, I couldn't wait to see...umm...what's the name of this explosion fest again?"

Simon bolted upright at another flurry of bullets. The couple, popcorn, and soda jolted, and more popcorn scattered on the floor. Figuring it was best to finish it before it ended up all over her green silk maxi skirt and white blouse, Regina took long sips of her soda. A car pile-up on the screen, and some popcorn spilled over her legs. *Oh, no. I agreed to an action movie, not an evening of scrubbing out stains.* She took the tub before all was lost. There was nothing left for her to do but watch Simon's animated reactions and wait for the final blast signaling her release from the action-packed melee.

Once the hero shot his last bullet and the credits rolled, the couple spilled into the lobby along with their fellow movie goers. They walked down the hall lined with illuminated posters. The smell of imitation butter filled the air. Sneaking downtown for a movie and a bite to eat was a pleasant treat. Simon placed an arm over her shoulders, drew her closer and used the other to throw his jacket over his shoulder as he navigated them towards the main entrance.

"You didn't like it, Gina?" His impish grin and the gleam in his eyes tugged at her heart. They settled onto the sidewalk. Streams of chattering people rushed by them. Simon's bulging forearms disappeared as he unrolled his sleeves. He shrugged his broad shoulders into his suit jacket before wrapping his arms around her.

A warm feeling radiated through her as she placed her hands on his chest. She wasn't sure, but somewhere during the months they dated, Simon started using her family nickname. She liked the way it sounded coming from him. It felt right—all of it did. Regina gently brushed a tiny piece of popcorn from the corner of Simon's mouth. "I thought it was an excellent piece of cinematography. Nothing says entertainment like watchin' a man have 800 bullets shot at him without getting' hit once."

Simon's muscles struggled against his tailored dress shirt as he threw his head back to let out a laugh that shook them both. "I'm sorry." He kissed her lightly with his buttery lips. "I'll make it up to you."

"You bet you will." Regina laced her fingers behind his neck. Normally, she was not a fan of public displays of affection, but it had been over a week since they were together and even longer since he was in her bed. She was not going to let the opportunity to be close to him for as long as possible pass. "But how?"

"For now, you pick the place for lunch."

"It won't be cheap, Young." She shot him a playful look and smoothed his shirt over his chest. "I intend on making you take me to the best halal cart downtown."

"Really, what would you know about downtown halal carts?"

"Hey, I come down here, sometimes."

"All right, so where are we heading?"

Regina squinted and searched around her. Truth be told, she had no clue where they were. She grew up on Long Island and never really left Harlem after she moved to the city, but she wasn't going to let him know that. *Hell, just pick a cart. The city is full of them.*

Simon's eyes sparkled with mischief as he mimicked her. "You don't know where to go, do you?" His smugness made her even more determined to find a place. Her heart ratcheted when his warm breath caressed her ear. "I tell you what—"

"Simon?" Someone called out from the city crowd. Simon went stiff. His warm dancing eyes narrowed into a cold stare. Regina squirmed at his tightening grip before his arms fell from her waist and air rushed between them.

A petite, beautiful woman carrying an assortment of high-end store shopping bags approached them. She wore a short burgundy ruffled skirt, printed tank top, and a pair of knee-high boots that added irony to her ensemble given the current heat. "Simon, I can't believe it's you. How are you?" Simon's body remained rigid as the woman stood between them. The nameless person laid her hands onto Simon's shoulders and stood on her tiptoes with her lips puckered. He wrenched his head and swept her arms away.

Bags hit Regina on the leg, and tension mounted at the base of her neck. She stepped back and crossed her arms, resisting the urge to grab the hair falling down the woman's back. *Who is this woman? It's obvious Simon knows her, but how?*

"Samantha." The woman flinched at the ire in Simon's tone. The name clicked in Regina's head. She had to be the woman that he argued with on the phone the other night. Simon's head was visible over blond tendrils. Jaw clenched, he stared daggers at her.

Samantha shifted her weight to one leg and put a hand on her hip. "Why so mean?" She turned and sized up Regina with a critical glance. "She's a big one, isn't she?"

"Excuse me?" Regina put her hands to her hips and stood with her legs apart. "Simon, who's this person?"

Simon circled past Samantha and hooked an arm on Regina's waist. "Nobody." He gently prodded her to walk. "Nobody at all." She slid her arm through his and rested her hand on his hip. They began to meander through the crowd.

"So, it's like that?" Samantha's shrill tone wafted over the street sounds.

His eyes fixed straight ahead, Simon raised his hand and sent a dismissive wave towards his back. Regina jumped a little when he slid his hand to her bottom and squeezed. She glanced over her shoulder and sneered at Tiny Barbie's scowl. "Bye, Samantha," Regina said blandly. Samantha took a few steps forward in her high-end boots, but then stopped and disappeared behind a rush of pedestrians.

Simon's pace quickened. It was all she could do to keep up with him. Regina remained quiet and rubbed Simon's back as they walked, hoping it would stop his arm from shaking.

"Everything okay?"

"Fine." He didn't look in her direction. They were forced to stop at a traffic light. The childlike joy was gone, swept away by a brief encounter and replaced with hard, icy bane.

Regina bit her bottom lip. *Should I ask him about her?* Her feelings for Simon grew strong, and they had developed a real connection. *I want to know if someone is hurting him, but I don't want to risk what we have over curiosity about someone he obviously can't even stand.* "So, lunch?"

"Yes." He released his grip on her waist. "Actually, there's some work I need to get done today."

Rubbing the vein at the top of his forehead, she tried to find warmth in his cold, steely eyes. "Simon."

He took her hand and placed it at her side. "I really need to get back to work. Let me get you a car." He looked down at his phone and stepped away.

The distance between them grew with every passing moment and all because of some blonde in a bad outfit.

Simon opened the door to the car when it stopped. "I'll call you." Once Regina was settled inside, she rolled down the window and opened her mouth to say something, but she didn't get a chance. Simon spoke to the driver and handed the bearded man a large bill. Then he hit the roof of the car and strode away.

᯾᯾᯾᯾

Simon walked through the boardroom doorway and scanned the room. As usual, it was filled with advisory volunteers clustered in klatches of conversation. His gaze fell on Regina sitting and writing. *Of course, Jeremy is planted right next to her.* He stretched his neck and lifted his shoulders. It was foolhardy, but he was going in.

He took a deep breath and strode to Regina. "Hi, Regina. I was wondering if we could talk for a minute about somethin'?" He managed to calm himself at his office earlier, and realized how terribly he treated her after their run-in with Samantha, foolishly allowing his rage to cloud his judgment.

"Hi, Simon. How are you?"

Waves of irritation permeated across Simon's shoulders. "Hey, Jeremy." His eyes never diverted from Regina. "What do you say, Gin—Regina? Just a couple of minutes." Simon stared at the blossom of coils hiding her face, resisting the urge to lose his fingers in their softness and apologize profusely for his foolishness.

Regina flicked her pen and turned her head. Starting at his feet, she scanned him from toe to head. Face neutral, her eyes flamed with anger. She opened her mouth. *Here it comes.* Simon tightened his stomach, preparing to get it with both barrels.

"Okay, everyone," Marcus announced as he walked in the room, looking down at a stack of papers, "let's get started." Marcus took his usual place of authority at the head of the table. "We have quite a few things on the agenda today."

His voice faded from Simon's mind and thoughts on what to do to get Regina's attention took its place. He pulled out his phone. *I'm sorry.*

Regina flipped her phone and shot Simon an annoyed glance before tapping her manicured fingers on the screen. *You certainly are.* She returned her attention to Marcus.

Simon: *Are you gonna stay mad at me forever?*

Regina: *Stop texting me.*

Simon: *I will, once you give me a smile.*

Regina read Simon's last message and stared directly at him, or rather, through him. Then she turned her head back to her brother. *She's very mad.* He put his phone in his pocket and turned his chair towards Marcus. It was going to take a lot to get her to hear him out and forgive him. `

"Next, we're scheduled to have a booth at the upcoming street fair. I think it's important for a few of the advisory board members to join the volunteers and help collect petition signatures." The room went still. Regina and Simon made eye contact as they simultaneously raised their hands. Marcus smiled. "That's good to see. I'm sure your presence will encourage our volunteers to do their best. Any questions? Thanks. Meeting adjourned."

Simon hurried through the crowd herding from the room. He spotted Jeremy's head bobbing over everyone else's. He tailed it, sure that Regina couldn't be far away. Simon continued down the hall. Everyone spanned out in the entryway and out the door; Simon caught sight of Regina craning her neck and listening to Jeremy while he chattered. *Doesn't this guy have anything else to do than hang around my girlfriend?* The word rolled easily from his mind and into his heart. Afterall, she had a hold on both. Hardly a moment went by that Simon didn't think about Regina, and her smile alone could make his entire day.

"Simon," Marcus called out from his office. "I need to talk to you, man." Simon slumped his shoulders and walked into Marcus's office.

There was no way I'm going to catch her. I may have totally blown it.

12 - Am I Forgiven?

SQUEEZING HER HANDBAG STRAP, Regina tapped the side of her leg. *Come on. I hate this friggin' elevator.* She turned and saw Jeremy grinning down at her. She couldn't help but smile back. "You didn't have to keep me company, Jeremy. I'm fine, really."

"No, Regina." Jeremy raised his hand. "It's my pleasure. Besides, we can do some planning about the street fair."

"Do we have to?" She stifled a yawn with the back of her hand. "I'm beat."

"Whatever you want."

I want to bop Simon Young on the top of his thick head for shoving me in a car. "Movie? I have popcorn."

"That sounds great."

Regina swung the door to her apartment open and dashed straight to the air conditioner. She fanned both her hands in front of her face and surveyed the room. Satisfied it was suitable for company, she bade her guest inside and walked into the kitchen, grabbing a packet out of the cabinet. "You pick the movie, I'll make some popcorn. Water or soda?"

"Soda, please. How about an action movie?"

"Hell no." Regina passed a can to Jeremy and sat next to him. "I'm in the mood for somethin' where the arrogant jackass boyfriend—who doesn't appreciate what a fantastic girlfriend he has—gets it in the end." She unscrewed the cap with more gusto than necessary.

"That's specific."

"I'm a specific gal." She braced her bare feet on the edge of the coffee table and drank.

She turned her attention to Jeremy. He groped the remote with his long fingers. "This one looks good." A bead of sweat traveled down his light skin, and he kept rubbing his hand on his jeans. "This looks good too."

"How about we just watch the news or somethin'?" A muffled buzz emanated from her handbag on the counter. "Excuse me." She retrieved the phone, and a nervous pit formed in her stomach as she read Simon's name on the screen.

"Hello?"

"Hi, Gina. Look, I'm sorry for cutting our date short."

"Who's this?" She fiddled with the zipper of her handbag.

"I deserved that. Please understand, I just needed to be by myself for a while."

She leaned over the counter. "Oh, I understand. Everyone needs some solitude. So why don't you stay alone?"

"You're going to be mad for a while, aren't you?"

"You have no idea."

"Come on, babe, don't be like that. I'm really sorry." She twirled a coil around her finger and smiled. She loved to hear him beg.

"Everything okay, Regina?" Jeremy's question reminded her that she was not alone.

"Fine, just give me a minute." She bowed her head and held her hand near her mouth. "I'm not interested in talking about this right now."

"Is someone there with you?"

"Jeremy came home with me to keep me company." She maintained a hushed tone. *"He seems to enjoy it."*

"Jeremy? Why am I not surprised?"

"What's that supposed to mean?"

"Nothing. I'm going to have to talk to him about trailing behind you all the time."

She heard a familiar ding and slow grind in the background. "Wait a minute. Where are you?"

"*I'm getting into the elevator.*"

"Of your building, right?"

"*No, yours.*"

She squinted into the peephole. "What makes you think I'll even let you in? You assume too much, Young."

"*I think it's fair to assume that you'll give me a chance to explain. Besides, I've got something to say to that overgrown puppy dog.*"

"No, you can't. He'll shoot his mouth off to Marc and start a whole mess." Her stomach churned at the silence. She was aware of Jeremy's fondness for her, but Simon had to consider the trouble a confrontation over a harmless crush might cause.

"Regina," Jeremy called out. "You said you wanted to watch the news?"

"Yeah, the news is good," she shot over her shoulder. "Simon?"

"*Fine. I'll take the stairs, but I'm heading up, so you better get rid of Lurch.*"

The soft disconnect click denied her any chance to respond. "Why that—"

"Regina, I think the popcorn is done." Jeremy stood his full height and went to the kitchen. "I can get it if you want."

"Umm, Thanks, Jeremy. You know what?" She massaged her forehead with her fingertips and reached for his jacket. "I'm startin' to feel a bad headache coming on. I think it would be better for me to just go lay down." She handed the young man his coat.

Jeremy drained the soda can and slammed it onto the counter, crushing it, He looked at her and smiled. "I'm sorry to hear that. I was lookin' forward to us hangin' out. He shrugged on his jacket and turned once in the hallway. "Do you want me to get you somethin'? I can run to the store if you need me to."

"No, no, thanks. I just need to rest." She began to slowly shut the door. "Good night, Jeremy." She slumped against the wall, letting out a huge sigh. *I hope he doesn't run into Simon.*

A few minutes later, a key clicked in the door locks. Simon stormed in with his fists clenched. "Is he still here?" He flung his backpack into the side chair and spun in a circle in the middle of the apartment. She half-expected him to start peeking in the closets.

Regina crossed her arms and fought the smile twitching at the corners of her lips. "No, he left." *Unbelievable. He's working himself into a tizzy about Jeremy of all people.*

Simon's fists relaxed, he hung his suit jacket. "Good. We need to talk about how Jeremey is always—"

"No. We don't need to talk about Jeremy. We need to talk about you." Regina pointed at Simon's face. "You got strange blondes approaching you in the street and turning you all broody. I won't let you make this about some kid with a schoolboy infatuation. You got some balls comin' here after leavin' me on the street like that." She turned off the TV and prepared to listen
to his reasons for ditching her.

"I know Gina." Simon looked inside the refrigerator and grabbed a can of his favorite soda sitting between bottled water and Aloe vera juice. "I was wrong." He stared across the room. She was perched on the edge of the sofa, legs crossed with one arm resting on the back. A pearl headband surrounding coils made her look especially regal.

Taking a swig of soda, Simon prepared to do some fast talking to charm his way back into her good graces, but he remained uncertain about how much of the truth and past pain to reveal. He settled next to her. It was hard to tell if the chill diffusing through his limbs was from the cool air blasting by him or her cold stare as his gaze met hers.

"Who's this Samantha?"

Let the inquisition begin. Simon took her hand and pressed his lips against the soft inside of her wrist. "No one."

"You sure as hell didn't act like she was no one."

"She's an ex." He inched closer and placed a hand on her lap.

"An ex?"

Simon heard some shakiness in her voice. *She can't possibly be worried about Samantha, can she?* "Yes, an ex. It didn't work out."

"That's obvious, but why were you so angry, and why in the world did you send me on my way?"

"I needed to be alone." He placed his hand on Regina's cheek and leaned forward until his forehead was on hers. The tension that sat at the base of his neck loosened. He needed to be with her, to forget the hurt eating away at him. "She did somethin' really horrible that caused me a lot of pain." Simon watched his hand as he caressed Regina's leg. "It took me a long time to forget about her. Seein' her again just brought it all back."

"I-I'm sorry you were hurt, but that doesn't give you the right to mistreat people. I don't know what this woman did to you, but she did it, not me."

The anger washed away from her eyes, replaced by a softness that pierced through his heart. *I was a damn fool this afternoon. Gina deserves so much better.* "You're right." He brought his lips close to hers. "Do you know," he said grazing his lips against hers, "I thought I wanted to be by myself. That's how I usually deal with things, but all I could think about was you." He gazed into her eyes. "Gina, you mean a lot to me. I feel so relaxed and happy when I'm near you. I was an idiot to allow anything or anyone to keep me from treating you as special as you are for even a second. His heart burst with relief when she encircled her arms around his neck and brought him closer. "I never want to hurt you, Gina. If I ever do somethin' stupid again," he ran his hands up her back. "Please remember that."

Simon relished the sweet, intense kiss from her. Her soft lips sent a charge through him that surged down to his toes. He drew her legs onto his lap and showered her neck with kisses, breathing in her sweet scent. "So, am I forgiven?"

"Mmm. I guess I can let you off the hook. Do you think that she'll bother you again?"

"Who?"

"Samantha."

"What do you mean?"

She pulled the knot out of his tie. "Well, don't you think it's kinda strange that in this big city, your ex-girlfriend was passin' by the movie theater at the same time you were leavin'?"

Simon stared at the humming air conditioner. He hadn't thought about how incredible a fluke it was running into Samantha. Was that because she was now keeping tabs on where he went? "I'm sure it was just a coincidence. What would she get out of followin' me around?"

"You?"

Simon resumed smooching Regina's neck. "Not a chance." He moaned when Regina pushed him away and settled her head on his chest.

"Well, that's good to know." She handed Simon the remote and stretched her arm across his torso. "I just hope she got the message today that you're taken."

He buried his chin in her hair and turned on the tv. Being taken was nice.

13 – Strap on a Helmet

S IMON INSPECTED THE TABS as he flicked files on the shelf with his fingertips. He pulled one out, dropped it with a soft thud on top of stack on his desk and begrudgingly prepared for a late evening at work. "Corella?" The soft clicking sound drifting into his office ceased.

A moment later, she stood at the other side of his desk, sliding her hand up and down her tablet. "Yes, Simon."

"I'm sorry to interrupt your work." He scratched the back of his head and scanned the table before having the courage to gaze directly at her. "I need you to arrange for a paralegal to come to my office and help me. I am assisting Rameez Baig in court tomorrow.

"Okay."

I was also wondering if you could stay late today?" He tried to make sure not to behave as if only his time was valuable like some of the other attorneys, so he kept requests like this infrequent. "This case is proving to be very challenging."

"Shall I order dinner?"

His gaze fell on the bright eyes, full lips and soft round cheeks in the photo on his desk and a wistful sigh escaped his lips. "Not for me. I'm going to try and have a late dinner at Gina's, but order for yourself."

"Thank you." Corella returned to her desk.

He couldn't suppress the smile demanding to shine at the mention of Regina's name. Their schedules didn't allow them to be together as much as he wanted, so careful planning was essential and difficult, but worth it. Things were going very well. They'd weathered their first argument with no scrapes. Regina thoroughly forgave him for his insensitive actions that night, so much so that talking about Jeremy slipped his mind.

By the time he remembered to tell her how angry knowing that Jeremy was not only hanging around her but was in her apartment made him, it was best to just let it drop. He'd botched things enough already on his own; there was no sense in putting her on the defensive, particularly since she was being cool about the whole Samantha debacle.

Knowing he would have a chance to talk and laugh with her fed his resolve to finish. During the nights he spent alone in his apartment, everything about Regina—her beauty, delightful laugh, wit and charm—flooded his mind. Phone calls weren't enough. He wanted to be next to her, hearing about her life and sharing his. Eyeing the piles of paperwork on his desk, Simon pressed his lips together and released a sharp snort. *I'm making it to Harlem tonight.*

"Excuse me, Is this Simon Young's office?" A knot formed in his stomach at the familiar voice drifting through the doorway. *What in God's name is she doing here?* He closed and opened his eyes. Being overworked must be causing hallucinations—no such luck. Hands on hips and one leg sticking out, Samantha stood in front of Corella's desk in her usual contrived pose.

Corella peered over her glasses, lips pursed at the sight of Samantha's clinging dress that was so snug, it made one wonder if breathing was even possible. "Do you have an appointment?"

Samantha shifted her weight and pressed her shoulder back, obviously ready to serve Corella a stinging retort, but after making eye contact with Simon, she flicked her long, polished nails at the seated woman. "Oh, never mind. Simon." She waltzed on eight-inch stilettos into his office, closing the door behind her.

"Son of a—." Simon jumped and leaned his knuckles on his desk. "What the hell are you doing here?"

Samantha whisked a lock of hair behind her back and sighed. "Well, you refuse to have a friendly conversation on the phone or in the street. So, I decided to come here, where I know you'll behave. Samantha looked around at her surroundings. "Nice office." She pushed the pencil holder on the desk to the side with on finger. "Very—sparse."

"Get out." Simon crossed his arms. *Why does she refuse to get the message that I have nothing to say to her? I'm in no mood to entertain any of her bull.*

"Now is that nice?" She started to round the desk towards Simon but stopped when he shot her a warning glare. "I don't know what happened to you. You used to be so charming."

"You happened to me."

"Me?" Simon rolled his eyes at the phony look of surprise and chagrin. She batted her mascara-laden lashes over her blue doe eyes. "I don't know what you're talking about."

There'd been a time that he would have been fooled by her, but he knew behind those eyes worked a sociopathic and manipulative mind. "You need to leave," he hissed through gritted teeth. White-knuckled and heart pounding, he turned on his heel and approached the window. There needed to be as much distance as possible between them. He wanted to grab Samantha by her arm and fling her out of his office. Violence against a woman never crossed his mind before, but she was an exception.

"I will not. Come on, Simon. We had good times together."

He stormed back to the desk. "Are you crazy?" The contents of the pencil cup splayed across the surface. Regina's photo fell face-down with a soft thud. "You tore my life apart."

Samantha rolled her eyes and sighed. "You're still angry about that? Damn it, Simon. We were young, and things were getting too serious." He scoffed. Samantha continued, "I was terrified of the feelings I had for you, and besides, it was my decision to make, and it was a hard one."

"I don't think it was hard for you at all. Choosing daddy's money and the ability to walk around without having to justify having me on your arm was quite easy for you."

"It wasn't," her tone softened, "That's why I'm here. You've been on my mind lately."

"Too bad."

"Simon, you can't expect me to believe you've gotten over what we had."

"Had—past tense. Let it go and move on, I sure as hell have." He set Regina's picture aright. *As usual, she's trying to act like all of her cheating and lying was no big deal. She's never to blame for anything.*

Her eyes narrowed. "Oh, and I guess you've moved onto Miss Kinky Hair?"

"I'm warning you, Samantha."

"Come on, Simon. You can't be serious about her."

"So that's why you're here? You saw us together, and it bothers you that I'm with a Black woman? You're pathetic."

"I'm not pathetic; I'm concerned. I mean, I knew I banged your heart a little but not bad enough to make you wind up messing around with someone like *that*."

"Her name is Regina, and she is more woman than you can ever imagine to be."

"It's one thing to indulge in a little, what do they call it—swirl, but you'll never get anywhere in life with her on your arm. You could never take her around important people. How do you expect them to accept someone like her and—" Simon glowered. She stepped back and turned her head towards the door.

Racist Bitch. Samantha didn't finish her vile statement, but Simon knew exactly what she meant. How does he expect good White people to have an Asian and Black together at their dinner parties? Minorities were better tolerated in bits and pieces or at least as a matched set. It was one thing for him to be accepted, but he didn't have the privilege for them to allow Regina in their circles with him.

It was bad enough that he worked with people who clutched onto their Whiteness and ignorance for dear life, but Samantha and her ilk were worse. They deluded themselves into thinking they were somehow progressive by cuddling with minorities and "slumming," while all along their minds worked with the same racist motivations as someone with a white hood in the closet.

I'm not about to allow this shrew to malign the woman I love. Love? Yes, damn it–love. "You're done. Don't come anywhere near me again."

Samantha lifted her chin and sneered. "Be as mad at me as you want, but you know I'm right, Simon. As long as you're walking around with that Black Lives Matter poster girl, you'll be stuck in this tiny office working twice as hard for attorneys making ten times as much." Samantha slipped her dress off her shoulder, she fondled her cleavage along its neckline. "Let me know when you're done eating fried chicken and want to come back to prime rib."

Simon looked down at what Samantha was offering and leaned in until his lips barely touched hers. He stared deeply into her sultry eyes, halting her breath. "I wouldn't touch you if you came dipped in gold." He pushed the intercom button on his phone. "Corella."

The door flew open within moments. "Yes, Simon?"

"Please, show this woman out." He turned and stared out the office window at the city, trying to even his breathing.

"I guess you're done here?" Hearing Corella's voice, Simon looked over his shoulder. She and Samantha stood right outside of the office door. His assistant's disdain was apparent from across the room. He moved in the direction of the two women, stopping at a safe distance and crossing his arms. *This is gonna be good.*

Samantha, claws ready, opened her mouth to speak. Corella raised her hand. "Before you get all distraught, I suggest you fix your dress." Corella looked back and forth down the hallway and let her glasses dangle from their chain. "People may get the wrong idea about the kind of business you came her to conduct." Retrieving a small book from her desk, she asked the wide-eyed Samantha, "Shall I validate your parking?"

"You know, I could get you fired." Samantha narrowed the small distance between them. One corner of Simon's mouth twitched at her attempt to intimidate a woman who didn't scare easily. Corella made quick work of people unwise enough to step to her, and it looked like his ex-lover was about to join the ranks of "fools" as she called them.

"Maybe, but what you can't do is get that man in there to give you the time of day." Corella continued to stare at the furious blond, waving the pad back and forth in front of Samantha's crinkled nose. "Well?" Corella leaned back just as Samantha flung her hair at his assistant's face.

A small laugh escaped Simon's lips. Samantha's dressing down helped diminish the rage heaped inside him. The burning around his ears and twisting sensation in his stomach subsided.

"Corella." He motioned for her to come to him with his finger.

Corella walked to him. "Yes, Simon?" she looked confident and unapologetic about her decision to take Samantha down a peg.

"Would you sue the firm for sexual harassment if I hugged you?"

She laughed and opened her arms. Simon rounded the desk. "Thank you." His muscles relaxed further as Corella patted his back.

"You're welcome. Now get to work so you don't miss your late dinner with Regina."

"Yes, ma'am." He reached back and pulled his chair underneath him.

"Oh, and Simon." She retrieved a black card out of the trash can and held it in front of him. "It's important for you to go to this one. You can't avoid them all. The partners forget associates quickly, and a brilliant legal mind like yours shouldn't be stuck in this office."

He accepted the card. "I understand."

"I knew you would. You should bring someone with you."

Simon rubbed the back of his neck and looked at the photo on his desk. "I don't know. This is not Regina's type of crowd."

"But it's yours. You can't keep your professional and personal lives separate all the time. Every so often, they will collide. Strap on a helmet, and ask the woman already."

14 -REGINA MAKES BREAKFAST

SIMON ROLLED HIS HEAD, rubbing the twisted muscles at the base of his neck. Limbs resisted movement, and it was a struggle to keep throbbing eyes aching to be closed opened.

Triumphantly, the last folder was placed in the bulging knapsack, and Mr. Young had all the exhibits needed for court. *Now for the long ride home. I hope she's still awake.*

The empty corridor stretched to the elevators too far away for his sore legs to carry him. He traversed his way out of the empty offices. Reaching the subway entrance, he had a choice of destinations. The big comfortable bed in his apartment beckoned him from across the East River. The ride home was shorter than the one uptown, and the commute back to work would be far less arduous—but she wasn't there. The choice was easy. He adjusted the garment bag over his aching shoulder and headed down the stairs.

᭡᭡᭡᭡

Simon gently closed the apartment door. Guilt poked him at the sight of Regina lying on the sofa. She stretched and yawned as she sat. "I'm sorry, Babe." The clinking sound of keys hitting the counter joined his hushed tone.

"You're late, Young," she said in a sleepy, sexy drawl as she shuffled towards him.

"I know. Sorry, I finished work later than I expected." He used the blue light falling on the wall to find the hook for his jacket and garment bag. He'd planned every detail to make sure he could spend the night. He nuzzled her neck and breathed in her essence. Sliding his hands down her sides and drawing her hips to his, a new ache overtook him.

Regina put some distance between them. "Did you eat?" The soft swishing sound of her slippers stopped at the refrigerator. The light shone on her tank top, shorts and silk head wrap, highlighting her gently jiggling breasts as she pulled out a foil-covered plate. Simon couldn't decide which he wanted to satiate more, his appetite or hunger for her. An insuppressible yawn escaping his lips helped him decide.

"No, and I'm starvin'." He skirted passed her, reaching into the cabinet for the *gochujang*. "Thanks, Babe." He made a few small circles on the round bottom he'd trekked up Manhattan to be near. It'd become that he couldn't end the day without her, and when he was forced to, it was tortuous.

"No problem," she said between yawns, "sit down. I'll heat it up for you."

She isn't saying anything about eating hot sauce so late? She must be tired. "I got it. You go to bed. I'll be in." There was no protest, only the weight of the plate in his hands and a soft kiss from Regina before she shuffled into the bedroom. Once the hum of the microwave assured his stomach that a longed-for meal was coming, Simon reached in his jacket pocket for the folded cocktail party invitation Corella gave him and balanced on a stool.

It's important for you to go to this one. Flipping the invitation back and forth in his hand, Simon recalled Corella's words. A flurry of reasons not to ask Regina flooded his mind. *She'd have to be around Vince Deckland and his ilk, ready to spew a bunch of microaggressions all over her. Does what we have include Gina fulfilling girlfriend duties like going to work cocktail parties? She may say no. Not that I would blame her. I don't want to go to the damn thing.*

His stomach rumbled at the beeping sound and even more when the aroma of Regina's cooking drifted into his nose. Simon devoured the delicious fare and used the little energy left in his aching carcass to drag himself out of the kitchen. After brushing, he expertly navigated the now familiar bedroom to his side of the bed with only silver rays spilling through the window to light his way. Having relieved himself of an article of clothing with each step, only boxers were left as he crawled into the bed he'd coveted being in all week. He found Regina's warm, soft body among the cool sheets and drew her into the curve of his, soothing away the stresses and strains of the day. *Definitely worth the trip.* Burying his nose into her silk head wrap, he breathed in the scent of her, falling asleep to the sound of her soft snore.

໖໖໖໖

Regina yawned and stretched under the sheets, batting her eyelids and smiling when her gaze focused on Simon's sleeping face. She barely remembered him coming to the apartment, but it was nice to wake up with him there, especially since he could've just taken the train home. *He deserves a nice breakfast.*

She wiggled her hips and gently pushed Simon's leg trapping her to the bed. She sidled towards the edge, but his hand tensed on her breast. He drew her back into the curve of his body and pressed his morning wood against her. She sighed when it relaxed and deep breaths continued. *Unbelievable, he's even horny in his sleep. I better get up before he wakes, or we're not going to get out of this bed.* She slipped out of Simon's embrace, swung her legs over the side of the bed and scrunched her toes in her cool, furry slippers. Her legs jutted out of the front of her robe as she headed to the kitchen.

The sputtering sound of the coffee maker welcomed her along with the aroma of fresh brew. Regina grabbed a mixing bowl from the cabinet and reached for the carton of brown organic eggs in the refrigerator. She tapped an egg against the edge of the bowl and opened it with one hand. The yellow and clear contents spilled and swirled against the white ceramic vessel, settling at the bottom. Preparing breakfast for Simon before he left for work almost made her feel domestic, which she never pictured herself being. She was not the Suzy Homemaker type, but it was nice anticipating how much he would enjoy eating what she made for him—once he managed to tame his massive erection and get out of bed.

She hovered the next brown orb over the bowl and stared at a black card next to her hand. After reading it, she began to slightly freak out. *It's an invitation. Does he want me to go? Maybe that's why he left it on the counter?* Regina swallowed a lump in her throat. "I need to talk to Toni. Where's my phone?" Careful not to wake Simon, she tiptoed into and out of the bedroom then dialed.

Toni answered. "*Wow, Simon's got you up early.*"

"Where's Marc?"

"*Don't worry, he's out for his morning run. What's goin' on? You were talking so much about finally gettin' to see Simon, I figured the two of you would still be...um...busy.*"

"You're too hilarious." Regina rolled her eyes at the sound of Toni's giggling. "We need to talk."

"*What is it?*"

"I found an invitation to a cocktail party at Simon's firm."

"And?"

"It was on the counter." Regina returned to cracking eggs in the bowl and lit the flame under the pan on the stove. "What do you think it means?"

"I think it means that someone at Simon's firm is throwin' a party."

Regina poured the eggs in the pan and jumped at the clicking sound of the bedroom door. Clutching the front of her robe, she allowed breath to flow in and out of her chest again when the bathroom door shut. "Simon's up." She stirred the eggs and watched them puff in the pan. "I can't talk for long."

"Well, has he even asked you?"

"No. He's been asleep." Steaming eggs bounced on the white plate. Regina wrinkled her nose at the few tiny specks of brown invading the yellow mounds. *So much for the special breakfast I planned.*

"Oh, so you're panicking over nothing then?"

"Basically."

"I'm gettin' in the shower."

"Come on, Toni. What should I do?"

"First, wait and see if the man asks. If he does, you're going, of course. That is what one does in a relationship, my dear."

Regina popped her head as vigorously as the bread in the toaster. "I'm not sure if this is a relationship."

"Really? Let me ask you something. Simon's apartment is much closer to his job than yours, right?"

"Yes."

"But where did he go late last night after working all day?"

"Here."

"Mmm-hmm. Which means he wanted to lay down next to his woman, and nothin' was gonna stop him. And, pray, tell, how did he get into your apartment?"

She rubbed the key on Simon's keyring on the counter. "He has a key."

"Of course, he has, and does our dashing attorney also have any of his suits and toiletries there, so he can go straight to work?"

Regina eyed the garment bag hanging on the entry wall and thought about the two drawers in the bedroom she cleared out to make room for his clothes as well as the brand-new tie hanger in her closet. "He has one or two things here."

"*Yeah.*" Toni's tone sent the message that she knew Regina's answer was an underestimation. "*Are some of his favorite foods in your cabinets and fridge, and did you buy any of them?*"

She spied the bottle of *gochujang* sitting on the counter. She'd made a special trip to the Asian market for it. "Damn."

"*Exactly,*" Toni said in a triumphant tone. "*So, accept the fact that you are in a relationship with this man and buy a dress for that party.*"

"I'm not sure I can do that. You know how I can get. I'm not the one to suffer fools lightly, especially ones blinded by their own privilege."

"*Of course, you can, Gina. It's the same as one of those things your mom used to drag you to at the college, but instead of a bunch of professors full of themselves, you'll be surrounded by a bunch of lawyers full of themselves.*" Toni laughed, enjoying herself a bit too much for Regina's liking. "*How much time do you have?*"

Regina scanned the invitation while her stomach proceeded to toss. The seamless way her and Simon's casual thing evolved into a relationship scared her down to her slippered toes. Relationships came with responsibilities such as boring-ass cocktail parties. "Three days." *Things are happening so fast. First a new man, and now I have to deal with a new circle of people, who I'll probably not like so much. What if someone recognizes me from me blog? That could open the very can of worms I tried to keep firmly sealed for months.*

"Oh, we have to get to work," chimed Toni. "*You want to meet after my last client?*"

Simon emerged from the bathroom and took his garment bag from the hook before traversing to the kitchen to offer Regina a minty kiss. "'Moring. You snuck out of bed." He tugged the sash of her robe.

"I had to." Regina scanned down Simon's glistening body with nothing covering it but a towel. "You were primed to keep us there for a while, and you have court today."

Simon grunted "So, I do." He pecked her cheek. "Hello, Toni," he called into the phone before rushing into the bedroom.

Toni laughed. "*He's gettin' to know you really well. Now, back to findin' you a dress.*"

ಶಿ ಶಿ ಶಿ ಶಿ

Simon sat at the counter and smiled at the spread before him. "Thanks, Gina. This looks fantastic."

"You're welcome." She leaned back against the kitchen counter with a mug of coffee. Her chest swelled with satisfaction as he stuffed a mound of eggs and toast in his mouth before gulping down some coffee.

He cocked his head and slid the black invitation from underneath the mixing bowl. "Did you see this?" Simon left his seat and stepped around the counter.

"Yes." Regina tried to maintain a nonchalant tone. "Are you going?"

"Yeah, it's one of those unavoidable things." He flipped the invitation and circled his arm around Regina's waist. "I think it might be fun for us."

She dabbed a napkin at the tiny red nick on his tan chin. "Us? I never agreed to go to some stuffy party."

"Of course, us. We can dress up and eat fancy hors d'oeuvres. It'll give me a chance to show off my lady."

Regina laced her fingers behind his neck. "Oh, you're good."

"What'd you say, Gina? Are you going to make me beg?"

All her resolve dissolved. She straightened his tie knot and looked into his eyes. "I do love it when you beg, but if it's important to you, I'll be happy to go."

"Thanks. It also might be a good idea," he said while tugging his suit jacket over his shoulders, "that we stay at my place after. It's probably gonna end late, and my apartment is closer."

"Ah-hah." Regina poured coffee into the thermos. "This is not about some party." She pointed her finger as she glided to him. "It's a ploy to get me to stay at your place. I see right through you, Young."

He chuckled and took the thermos. "I can't get anything past you. You're way too smart for me." His arms wrapped around her again.

She straightened his jacket lapels. "Yes, I am." They rocked back and forth, relishing the moment of domestic serenity. *This is nice. I don't know about the rest of the world, but I think I'm more than ready for this new change.* Simon's phone notifications popping in his pocket signaled the end of their time together. Her arms tingled in protest when his fell away.

Simon grabbed his backpack. "Well?" He looked so darn cute and hopeful.

"I'll pack an overnight bag."

"Two nights. I'm keeping you there all weekend." He closed the space between them. Regina gasped as he pulled open her robe and slid her tank top upward. One breast bounced from underneath the white cotton, its nipple immediately hardened by the rush of air.

"What are you doing?" A surge of pleasure pulsated through her body from the nipple Simon licked and sucked. She arched her back and slid her fingers through his hair. Her body shook when he lifted his head and pulled her shirt over the throbbing breast.

He winked. "Just what I need to start my day." Before any protest could escape her mouth, he kissed it and shot her a naughty look before disappearing out of the door.

15 - COCKTAIL PARTY FROM HELL

THANKING THE DOORMAN, REGINA pressed her hand against her queasy stomach as she walked through the glass doors. The pianist's tune joined the pulse pounding through her ears. Nervous wasn't the proper word for how she felt. She smoothed at the African print skirt of her outfit. The pendant of her gold necklace fell just above the beginning of her cleavage, protruding from the sweetheart neckline of her top; the cuffs of the form-fitting sleeves disappeared behind bangles. She rubbed her hoop earrings between her fingers as she typed on her phone.

I'm here. Where are you? She searched across a sea of suits and cocktail dresses, noticing that hers was the sole dress with any type of elaborate "ethnic" pattern. *Well, I guess my plan to blend is shot.* She startled at the sound of a voice.

"Can I help you?" Her gaze fell on a small man who'd appeared behind the podium. He looked up at her, curling his top lip. She clenched her evening bag, knowing that question very well and the meaning conveyed through the curt tone he used when asking it. He was more interested in finding out how she thought she belonged there than wanting to actually help.

Regina wrenched her shoulders back. "Perhaps," she said in a pointed tone. "My name is Regina Kent. I'm a guest of Simon Young."

The maître d' squinted and looked down at his ledger. "Let me see if your name is here. What was it again?"

"There's no need, thank you." Regina's body quivered at the sound of Simon's voice. He approached her side and gently massaged the small of her back. "Gina, did you have a hard time finding the place?"

She met his gaze. His full grin made her heart flutter. "No. The car you sent dropped me right in front."

He offered her a loving peck on her lips. "I'm so glad."

She flashed a smug smile at the maître d'. He dropped his head and started flipping through pages.

Simon slid the mint green bag from her shoulder. "I'll take that. Excuse me." He turned and dumped the bag on the podium. "The lady needs this put away until we're ready to leave."

"Absolutely, sir," the maître d' grunted as he lifted the bag, "My pleasure."

"Thank you." Simon took her wrists in his and raised her arms. "You look stunning." His eyes flickered with a mixture of admiration and desire as he gazed up at her.

A small rush of heat passed over her. "Thanks." She put her phone in her purse and grasped her necklace. "I'm sorry. I didn't realize that I would be taller than you if I wore heels." She caught one side of her bottom lip between her teeth. She grew up the "tall girl," peaking at 5' 11". They were usually eye-to-eye, which was a relief. With heels on, she only had him by a couple of inches, but she never felt more gargantuan than that moment.

Simon's shoulders shook with a small laugh. "Don't worry. I'm not a man whose ego fades because a woman is taller." Her breath quickened as he drew closer. "Besides, I like it." A warm rush of air tickled her ear. "You can leave 'em on when we get home later." He nipped her lobe before steering her towards the party. "Come on. There's someone I want you to meet."

Regina ignored people's gapped-mouth stares as she walked into the hall on Simon's arm. She towered over the surrounding women sipping from glasses and whispering to each other while they moved through tall, round tables with half-finished drinks, plates of mini quiches and brass-trimmed votives on them.

They approached a woman standing in a pair of laser-cut black embellished court shoes wearing a black tuxedo blazer, black slim pants, and a black silky camisole. The French twist in her hair finished of the sleekness of her look.

Corella?" Simon virtually shined. "This is my girlfriend, Regina Kent." She held her breath. It was the first time he referred to her as his girlfriend. Things were definitely changing. "Regina, this is Corella Banks, my assistant."

"It is nice to meet you," Corella said in a warm tone as she raised a hand with a huge diamond ring on one finger.

"Nice to meet you too."

"Regina's a writer." He slid his hand around her waist and brought her against his side."

"Really?" Corella smiled. "Anything I might have read?"

"Well," Regina fiddle with a bangle. "I do occasional freelance writing for different publications, but I also have a blog, *Blackness of Kent.*

Corella partially closed her eyelids and focused on her drink. "Mmmm. That sounds familiar. Did you write an article about the politics of Black women's hair and the shaming of Black girls in school?"

"I did."

Corella smiled. "My daughter and I loved that article."

"I'm glad to hear it."

"Why don't I get you ladies some drinks?" Simon reached for Corella's empty glass.

"Thank you, Simon."

He touched Regina's arm and smiled. "Shirley Temple?"

She tucked her lips between her teeth and glanced down. "Yes, thank you."

"I have to tell you." Corella moved to Regina's side. "That article was a big help for my daughter. She went natural four years ago, and has been getting flack ever since."

"I understand. It's a problem globally. I wrote that article after reading story after story of young Black girls being told that their hair is unkempt and being threatened with suspension.

The women's voices faded. Simon continued to glance back at them as he approached the bar. Things were going well.

A bartender stood opposite Simon. "What can I get you, sir?"

He placed his order. Dread seeped into him at the sound of a familiar and unwelcome voice.

"Si." His back smarted where Vince slapped it. "How are you doin'?" Vince leaned an elbow on the bar. "Give me another," he said, tilting the nearly empty glass at the bartender. "So, I saw you talkin' to that hot Black chick over there." Vince jerked his head in Regina's direction. "I noticed her as soon as she walked in the room. Is she with you? Because she if she isn't," he sneered, "I know what I'll be doing with the rest of my evening."

"She's with me." Simon surveyed the women through the mirror. Regina glowed as she chatted with Corella. He shot Vince a cool look before returning to admiring the women.

"You're shittin' me." Vince's laughter garnered a few glares from people seated at the bar. "That tall drink of hot chocolate is with you? I don't believe it."

Simon squeezed the edge of the bar. He altered his weight, peering down each end.

"I mean that," Vince leered, lifting his finger from the glass in his hand to point at Regina, "is a fine-lookin' piece of ass. She looks like she could break a man in two if he isn't careful." He adjusted his tie's knot with his free hand, lifting his jaw in the air. "Now, of course, I could handle all that woman, but I have to say, I'm impressed, Si. I didn't think you had it in you."

"Watch it, Vince."

"You must be getting all kinds of lovin'. You know what they say about the *sistahs*. They like it any way you give it and all the time." Vince playfully jabbed Simon's arm. "No wonder you've had a smile on your face lately."

Simon straightened and balled his fists. "I said watch it." Eye to eye with Vince, he plastered a fake grin for the benefit of the people around them but seethed through gritted teeth. "You'll show some respect for my lady, you understand?"

Vince raised his palms and propped his back on the bar. "Alright, Si. I'll say no more." He leaned to one side and ogled Regina with a smirk. "I thought you were just taking a walk on the wild side. I didn't know she meant somethin' to ya."

"She does."

"My apologies, man." Vince offered his hand.

Simon relaxed his hands at his sides. "Here are your drinks." The waiter placed four glasses on the bar in front of the men. "Will there be anything else?"

Simon squeezed Vince's hand and continued to stare for a moment before he reached for a tip in his wallet. "Thank you." He balanced the drinks in his palms "You'll understand if I don't introduce you, won't you, Vin?"

Vince drained the last of the drink he was holding and grabbed the fresh glass. "Yup. I gotta go mingle anyway." He strutted back into the party, careening away from Regina and Corella, who's glare was just as menacing as Simon's.

Simon walked slowly back to his date and assistant. "Here you go ladies." As he passed out the drinks, a few of drops fell near his wrist, almost touching a white shirt cuff. Corella immediately dabbed at the liquid with a cocktail napkin. "Thanks." He smiled and tipped his glass to his mouth. Two important women in his life hitting it off made it easy for him to forget Vince's stupidity. Corella was the only person in the room whose impression about Regina mattered, so them chatting and laughing was quite satisfying, even though it meant he became invisible.

"Simon." Corella took Regina's arm and jutted her chin towards the alpha pack of men standing under a chandelier and talking as loud as the damn well pleased while drinking straight from beer bottles. "Why don't you go schmoose so Regina and I can talk a little more?"

Simon started to decline but Corella's expression demanded that he complied. Networking was the primary reason for them being there, so it was best for him to get on with it. He squeezed Regina's hand. "You're okay?"

Regina ran her fingers through the top of his hair and smoothed down his tie. "Yes. Go impress the higher ups. I'll be fine." Her full lips spread and pearly teeth peeked out from behind burgundy lipstick that he desperately wanted to smear.

He kissed his date's soft knuckles, tilted his head back and set the empty glass on a nearby table. "Here we go." A few handshakes later, Simon had a cold beer in his hand and was busy impressing the pack.

Every so often, he would sweep the room and see Regina talking to people; there was always a cluster around her. Everyone was drawn to her personality and beauty, not that he blamed them. Regina was an amazing woman, and he felt truly lucky to be with her. "Will you gentlemen excuse me?" Too much time had passed since he got to be near his stunning girlfriend.

Catching Regina proved a challenge. As soon as he managed to come within five feet of her, she was brought to another small crowd of people. "She's very popular." Corella appeared at his side.

"I know." He laughed when she poked his arm. "Thank you, for being so nice to her."

Corella treated Simon to one of her rare, unguarded, smiles. "You're more than welcome. I really do like her, Simon." She looked in Regina's direction, and her grin shifted downward. "Uh-oh."

Simon followed Corella's gaze. Three pair of eyes stared upward at the coils atop Regina's head. Women, all a few inches shorter, circled her with their hands outstretched to touch her hair. One even stood on her tiptoes. Regina backed away from one, but then there was another reaching to fondle her crown. "What the hell are they doing?"

"Treating her like an animal at a petting zoo," Corella sighed. "It happens to Black women daring to wear their hair natural a lot. People lose their inhibitions and start acting like it's some kind of sideshow attraction. You'd think they knew better."

A small knot twisted at the base of Simon's neck. The humiliation on Regina's face made his gut wrench with rage. He could bear all the low-key racism thrown at him by his coworkers, but seeing her subjected to it was intolerable. He started towards the appalling scene.

"Hold up, Simon." Corella's small frame intercepted him. "I'll handle this. You get your coats." Her protective tone ebbed at his anger. She spun on the ball of her stiletto and glided across the room. As soon as she reached the group, Corella stood in front of a shell-shocked Regina and said something that made the handsy women immediately disperse into the crowd. She then tilted her head to Regina's bent head and stroked her shoulder. Simon walked towards them, but Corella's hand stopped him. She turned and guided Regina away from him.

"Simon." He reluctantly looked over his shoulder, shifting his attention from the two women walking to the restroom. Rameez Baig stood at the center of the pack, signaling Simon to come. Unable to ignore the junior partner, he yanked down the front of his vest and straightened his shoulders before making his way back to the pack.

❧❧❧❧

Regina stopped dabbing her eyes. "Can you believe those bitches?" Her voice bounced off the bathroom's marble walls and floors as she paced between the sink and stalls, gulping air between sentences. "No manners. No respect for personal space."

Corella leaned on the sink and passed another tissue from the box behind her. "I know. They were definitely out of pocket, but it's a common thing at these kinds of occasions. I think once people get all liquored up, it loosens their lips and conduct."

Regina took the tissue from Simon's assistant. "Thank you." She stared at the web-like veins in the white wall and blew her nose. "I nearly lost my cool when I specifically asked them not to touch me and they completely ignored me—talkin' 'bout 'but it's so interesting and exotic. How do you get it to stand like that? I love how plush it is.'" Regina curled her lips and spoke in an exaggerated nasal tone.

She moved closer to the mirror to inspect her eyes. *Thank God for waterproof mascara.* "It took hours to get ready for this dumb-ass party. I'm not letting that brood of hens make me look like a fool."

She opened her compact to freshen her eye shadow. "I didn't even know what to say because I was afraid to embarrass Simon."

Corella reached behind her back for another tissue. "Yeah, one of the things many of the spouses and significant others like to do the morning after these parties is gossip about who did what. Making a scene would've created a lot of fodder for them." She brushed a fingertip just below the hair of her brow. "You missed a spot. It'll probably not affect Simon. The attorneys usually don't let stuff like this interfere with taking care of business, but they'll be the same people you'll run into at other events, and things could get uncomfortable." Corella reached at some errant coils at the top of Regina's hair and offered a motherly smile. "You handled it very well."

Regina relaxed her shoulders and let out a gust of air. "I tried. Normally I'd—" She clamped her lips together when she heard the huge wooden restroom door squeak open. Two women came in prattling away. "Hi," chimed the one with soft blond curls that spilled over the front of her green lace backless party dress. Her companion dashed to the stalls. She took the empty space in front of the mirror next to Regina.

Regina stopped brushing the color across her eyelid and knitted her eyebrows. "Is there a problem?" Green dress suspended an open tube of lipstick in the air and stared at her through the mirror.

Regina tightened her lips and peered sideways. She'd had her fill of impudence for the night and was folding all filters to let anyone fool enough to bring anymore nonsense have it.

"I know you." The youthful partygoer put the cap on her lipstick and straightened her back. "You're Regina Kent, right? You do that blog, *The Blackness of Kent*. My boyfriend reads you all the time." She moved her mouth closer to Regina's ear. "He's Black," she whispered.

"You don't say." Regina glanced at Corella, who wore an uneven smile and twitched her eyebrows. Regina examined her visage in the mirror. "Yeah, I get that a lot." She snapped the compact shut and straightened. "Sorry," she said as she dropped her eyeshadow in her bag and barely glimpsed at the blond, "you've got the wrong person."

Regina held out her hand. "Good night, Corella."

"Good night. It was really nice meeting you."

Regina slowly blinked and grinned when she opened the restroom door and saw Simon leaning cross–legged against the opposite wall with her overnight bag slung over his shoulder. His face brightened when he saw her. Simon pushed off the wall and offered Regina his arm. "I hope you don't mind if we leave now?"

She hooked her arm in his. "You read my mind." Chin in the air, she swung her hips and shoulders towards the tall clear doors that were the gateway to their freedom. She silently celebrated the sound of car engines, horns and hundreds of feet shuffling on the pavement replacing the drone of music and chatter inside. Simon pulled her with him to the curb and raised his hand to hail a cab.

It was such a relief to be out of there and not have to force any more smiles or conversations. A pit of anxiety formed in her stomach as she recalled Corella's words. *They'll be the same people you'll run into at other events...* She hugged Simon's waist and made small circles with her foot. *How am I gonna tolerate any more drivel like tonight? It wasn't completely bad, but I don't think I'll be able to control my temper next time someone is stuck on stupid.* The feeling of Simon's lips against her forehead, although brief, made her grin. Her head bobbed against his shoulder. It'd been a rough evening, but Simon was worth it.

"Finally," he grunted. Simon opened the cab door and put his hand under Regina's elbow. "Let's go home."

16 - SIMON'S PLACE

LIGHT BOUNCED OFF THE PRISTINE WHITE MARBLE entryway floor. After leading Regina into his apartment, Simon turned on a ceiling light and flourished an arm in the air. "I present my humble abode to you, my lady. I hope it's to your liking."

"Impressive," she said as she walked into the great room.

"Indeed, it is," quipped Simon, enthralled with her bouncing bottom. Whenever she moved, he paid attention. "I never tire of admiring it. Can I get you something to drink?"

"No, I just want to go to bed." Regina stretched and released a sultry yawn as she turned to Simon. "I'm exhausted." Her arms fell on his shoulders. Smiling sleepily, she caressed the back of his neck.

"Thank you, for doing this. I know it wasn't easy." He pulled her closer, still in awe of how well she handled herself—poised and controlled among so much obliviousness.

"Simon, I know this is an important part of your life, and I want to be there when you need me. But, you're right. It was damned hard. When those heifers kept tryin' to touch my hair, I just wanted to tell 'em off, but I didn't want to cause trouble for my man, or I would have read each one of them."

His smiled at the sound of the soft twang that crept into her voice. It only appeared when she was around close friends and family—people that made her feel safe. "Am I your man?" His heart filled with content.

She pressed her forehead against his. "Of course, you are. I wouldn't have been in that den of causal racists if you weren't." Warmth infused every nerve at the brush of her lips against his. Having her there felt so right. Regina balanced a hand on his chest and took off her shoes. "Now where's the bedroom?"

"That anxious, are you?"

"For sleep, Young."

He caressed her hands with his thumbs and moved backwards to the bedroom. "Right this way, my lady."

Once they reached the bedroom, Regina assessed her surroundings. Simon walked to the far side of the bed. Smiling, he motioned for her to join him.

She fixed her gaze between the floor and bed. Her heart raced when he took her hand and touched her back, guiding her to sit. He slowly pushed her skirt to the top of her quaking thighs and kneeled between them.

Simon cupped her face. "You're breathtaking." His eyes simmered with passion. She lowered her gaze to her jittery hands. Being in his bedroom was exciting and terrifying. This was uncharted territory. Not knowing what to do, she didn't move and watched Simon open the top draw of the nightstand. "Here you go. I figured I hole up enough of my stuff at your place." He reached in and dangled a bronze key on a silver ring with a round fob. "This is for you." He turned it until the engraved words "Simon's Place" shined in the hall light.

Regina twitched her eyebrows upwards and held a palm against her chest. "Is that a key to here?"

"Yes. I already have one to yours. I want you to feel at home here. I know I do when I'm at your apartment." He dropped the key back in the drawer. "Now, to get you in bed." He tugged her earrings and held out his palm. "Take those off, please."

A nervous laugh barely made it passed her throat. "You don't like them?" she pulled at the clasps.

"Very nice, but they and the rest of what you're wearing will be better off." She quivered at the desire and demand in his voice. He placed the earrings in the drawer then reached around her neck, holding her necklace between his fingers. "Now this." It joined the earrings. Regina held her breath as Simon clasped her wrists and made circles under the bangles with his thumb. She parted her lips and let out passion-filled breaths. "And," he said kissing one wrist, "these," and then the other. The bangles clinked as they hit the drawer. He took a small blue packet out and closed it.

Simon pressed his lips to hers. He pulled her top from the skirt and tucked his fingers under it, gliding them back and forth. She wriggled on the bed and let out a soft giggle. "I keep forgetting how ticklish you are." She detected a slight bit of anxiousness in her lover's voice. She rested her hands on each side of his square jaw and glided her thumbs across his cheeks. There was an intense hunger in his eyes. Perhaps she wasn't the only one who found this moment different from all the other times they had sex. Something changed, making her feel like she never had before.

Simon pulled her top over her head and dropped it on the floor next to him. An electrifying sensation burst all over her skin. He ran his fingertips down her arms and rested them on her hips. "You're so beautiful." His warm breath rushed into her ear. "I can never get enough of you." He cupped one hand behind her head and brought her mouth to his. A tingle rushed down her breasts as he released them from the bra with the other. The straps dropped down her round shoulder. Simon lifted it away and let it join the top.

Regina wrapped her legs and arms around him and moved to the edge of the bed. She felt his muscles tighten under her hands and between her thighs. She burned and creamed between her legs. Her nipple pebbled and throbbed incessantly when he rubbed his thumb against it. Simon broke their kiss and stared at her. His eyes burned with desire and a mandate that she give more of herself to him. He didn't have to say anything. She sensed it deep inside. It made her heart beat so hard that it felt as if it was going to explode from her chest. He wasn't the first man she'd been with or even serious about, but he was undoubtedly the only one to drive her passion and lay her soul bare. "Simon." His mouth reclaimed hers before another word was uttered.

He pushed her shoulders. It was as if she was falling for an eternity. The comforter caressed her back. A rush of air escaped her kiss-bruised lips. Covering her body with his, one leg teased at her wet panties and what lay beyond them while the length of his hardness pressed into her leg. Simon clasped her breasts with his hands; her nipples ached in exquisite pain between his fingers. She spanned her palms and fingers down his back and rested them on his tight behind. Simon moaned. His breath and hot kisses emblazoned a trail down her neck and between her breasts. He held one nipple between his teeth before encircling it with his lips. She arched her back, demanding more.

Her belly shuddered as he continued his kisses downward. Simon slipped off her wet panties and made her legs tremble as he passed his fingers up and down her full brown thighs. "These are glorious." He nipped the inside of each, stopping just close enough for his breath to pass over her outer folds. "All of you is, Gina." Chest heaving, she widened her eyes and then fluttered them closed, running her fingers through his hair.

She tightened her buttocks and closed her thighs on either side of his head. Her long legs cascaded down his broad back. Bursts of light flashed behind her lids. Her breath was no longer hers to control. Nothing was. She floated, helpless against the waves surging through her body. She grabbed the blanket to keep her arms from flaying then braced herself on her elbows and spun her hips as Simon's tongue worked her into a frenzy.

She pushed at his head to stop the impending release, but he wouldn't cease flicking and rolling his hot tongue. She looked down and saw him watching her. He stilled her hips in a steely grip and closed his them, exploring her deeper and more intensely. "Simon, please." She tried to slide away from him on her elbows before she exploded, but he jerked her back to the edge of the bed and ecstasy. Everything was spiraling out of control. Throwing her head back, only a small squeak escaped her closed throat as her insides spasmed. She fell back against the bed, gasping.

She slowly opened her eyes to see Simon raise onto his knees, wiping under his self-satisfied grin. His weight forced more of the little breath she had out of her body. "Gina," he panted in her ear. "You're the most wonderful thing I've ever tasted. Did you like that?"

Regina swallowed hard. "Yes. But you didn't finish."

He rose, every muscle in his chest and torso heaved. "Oh, I intend to." He turned her on her stomach and pulled her hips until she was on all four quaking limbs. He pushed her skirt and kneaded her buttocks. She held her breath and throbbed in anticipation at the sound of the packet ripping. She wanted to feel him inside her and satiate the naked lust he uncovered. She moaned as her longing insides stretched to fit him.

Simon's hands gripped her hips. He pushed and pulled out of her, gradually increasing the intensity of each exquisite thrust until he dug his fingers into her flesh and slammed so hard it rattled the bed to its coils and Regina to her core with a wonderful union of pleasure and pain. Once again teetering at the brink of ecstasy, she tightened around him. "Oh, Gina." His voice shook. He bent over her and strapped her to him with his arm. Her muscles shuddered, supporting both of them as they convulsed with pleasure. Satisfied that Simon was spent, she allowed her aching arms and legs to buckle and collapsed on the bed.

They laid there staring at the ceiling. "You know," Regina breathlessly chimed into the silence, "I think I can get used to your way of getting ready for bed."

Simon laughed and brushed his brackish lips against hers before bouncing off of the bed and going into the bathroom. Regina followed and leaned against the doorway. She watched Simon's muscles ripple as he washed her way from his lips and chin. He glanced at her through the mirror, reached inside the medicine cabinet and pulled out toothpaste and two toothbrushes.

"I got this for you. I also got you some flower-scented shower gel so you don't have to smell like a man tomorrow."

Regina accepted the little gift. *He's really trying to make me feel at home.* "Thanks." She bit her bottom lip and fiddled with the brush between her fingers. "That's sweet." Simon placed a dab on his brush and then hers. She stood next to him and passed the soft minty bristles over her teeth while watching Simon sway in a lull of mutual comfort with each other's presence. She rinsed her mouth and took a few steps away from the sink. He was so cute standing there butt bare. "Can you brush your teeth like this whenever I'm around?"

He finished and tickled his refreshing tongue against hers until her knees threatened to give way. "You got it." He patted her on the behind. "As long as you do the same for me. Now, come to bed." Regina calmed her breathing. He knew how easily he threw her off kilter and was clearly enjoying it. She followed him into the bedroom and watched him slip underneath the blankets *au natural*.

"Let me guess." Regina approached the side of the bed and stared down at Simon with her hands on her hips. "You have me to keep you warm?"

Simon tucked his arms under his head. The sheet fell across the bottom of his waist. "That's the plan."

"Okay, let me get my bag."

"That won't be necessary." He flipped the sheet back on the other side of the bed. "*You* have me to keep you warm."

Regina tilted her head and looked at his obvious arousal bulging through the linen out of the corner of her eye. "We're sleeping, right?"

Simon's eyes glinted. "Maybe."

Regina sighed. He was too damn irresistible. She took off her skirt, settled in the curve of his body and rubbed her cheek against his arm. Her buttocks bumped against his erection, which jerked in response. "Down, Young," she commanded despite the sensation between her legs.

🙥🙥🙥🙥

Simon had been up for a while but remained in bed, unwilling to end the pleasure that lying next to Regina brought him. He turned on his side and propped his head in his hand. Mesmerized by her breast he traced circles around the dark areola slowly moving closer to the inviting nipple. The late-morning sunlight filled the bedroom and bathed them in a soft, warming light. She opened her lids and pulled the corners of her mouth into a sultry grin. Simon continued, becoming more excited the closer he got.

He groaned at the sound of the phone buzzing on the nightstand. Regina braced on her elbow and slid the sheet over her chest, snatching the prize from his eager finger. She let out a heavy sigh then answered. "Hi, Marc."

17 – KIMCHI

*D*AMN. SIMON'S STOMACH TIGHTENED with dread. Marcus still didn't know that his best friend and baby sister were seeing each other, and the threat of him finding out constantly loomed over them.

Regina's once dreamy eyes narrowed. "What are you doing in my apartment?" Her full lips thinned. "No, I was not home last night. Is that really any of your business?"

He slid a finger along her bare arm. *I know we agreed to keep things about us quiet, but it's been months now. How much longer does she think we can keep this a secret?*

"The maintenance man is coming next week to fix that. Stop fiddling with my faucets. Just leave the food in the fridge, and thank Toni for me." She rolled her eyes. Simon held her hip and slid closer. He began to kiss her neck. "Yeah, yeah. Dinner at your place tomorrow." She pushed him away and shot a warning glare. Her eyes shifted back and forth in their sockets. "Simon? How would I know? Why don't you ask him yourself? Bye, Marcus." She returned the phone to the nightstand and let out a long breath.

"I take it that was Marcus?" His hand itched to pull back the sheet and finish what he started.

"Yup."

"He asked about me?" He gathered her in his arms.

"He did. I think he's catching onto us. He keeps asking me if I've seen you or if I'm gonna see you. I just want to punch him."

Simon laughed and kissed her forehead. The two of them acted like adolescents whenever they dealt with each other. "Yeah, he's been playing detective with me too. He's no dummy."

"He needs to mind his business."

He caressed her shoulder. "Yeah, but so what, if Marcus knows about us? Would that be so bad? I mean, I could understand not telling him when this began. You didn't want your big brother in your business, and Marcus is a good friend to me. I didn't want to jeopardize it for some casual sex, but that's not what we are now."

"I don't know," she sighed. "I'm thirsty. Is it okay if I get something to drink?" She sprang onto the floor searching for her clothes.

Simon swung his legs over the side and sat. *Does she ever want to tell anyone about our relationship? Maybe she's ashamed of me. Afterall, having me in her bed jeopardizes her pro-Black rep and is probably why she doesn't want to take the risk of going public.* A familiar anxiety crept into his gut, but he willed it away. Massaging the tight muscles at the base of his neck, Simon swallowed the hurt and passed her his crumpled dress shirt from the floor. "Here, put this on." He flashed a look to send a clear message that he expected her to listen.

"Thanks." Although the slim fit shirt was big enough to accommodate his broad shoulders and muscular chest, Simon noticed with delight how it barely covered Regina's taut, voluptuous bottom peeking out from underneath it as she strode out the bedroom. The corner of his mouth twitched. *I have to make sure she wears more of my shirts.* Taking a small blue packet out of the nightstand, he followed the direction of the wiggling orbs.

He bounded out of the bedroom in his pants and bare feet and headed towards the kitchen. Stopping to cross his arms and rest his chin in his hands, Simon enjoyed the truly delightful scene before him. Regina's booty stuck out from behind the opened refrigerator door. She shifted her weight from side to side then glanced over. "Is soda all you have here?"

"Water's on the door."

The shirt rose slightly higher, revealing more of her firm round buttocks. "Got it. What is in all these little containers?"

Simon's cock stiffened with the movement of Regina's foot up and down the back of her leg. "*Kimchi*" He brushed past his inquisitive guest, trying desperately to refrain from tossing her onto the kitchen counter. "It's Korean."

"I've heard of it. What's in the other jars?"

He chuckled and bent next to her. "They're all *Kimchi*." He tapped each lid. "*Baechu, Oi Sobagi, Baek*," he called off the names while caressing her backside. "That is *Kkakdugi*." He placed his hand over hers. "My favorite."

"Is it the best thing you've ever tasted?" She smirked.

"No." Simon gently sucked her bottom lip. "That would still be you. Do you want to try?" His question carried a challenging undertone.

She swallowed hard. "What is it made of?" Her throaty tone caused sparks of desire to flicker deep inside of him. He still hadn't learned how to keep from being so disarmed when she was close.

"*Mu*, it's a Korean radish. I grew up eating it."

She walked around the kitchen island and tucked his shirt tail under her as she perched on a stool. "Maybe some other time. Is that all you have?"

He gave her a playful glance and half smile. "Well, I've been spending a lot of my nights in somebody else's bed. So, I haven't had much time to shop. Come on." He flipped the lid open and presented a small, white cube covered in a red sauce on a fork. "It may be another Asian thing you discover you have a hankering for."

"Really, I'm good."

He closed the distance between them, pressing his hardness against her thigh and hovering his lips over hers until they barely touched. "Then can I taste you?"

She wrapped her arms around his neck and one leg around his thigh. "You're insatiable."

"For you, yes."

"Well," she flicked the tip of his nose, "if you expect me to have any energy to keep up with your libido, we'll have to get something to eat." I'm taking a shower. Then you can bring me to that soul food restaurant you've been raving is just as good as the ones in Harlem." Regina slung her overnight bag over her shoulder and disappeared into the bathroom.

Simon's question buzzed in Regina's mind as water rushed from the shower head and down her body. She may have thought she was ready for things between them to get more serious, but Simon's revelation that he wanted to reveal their relationship set her nerves on end. *So, what if Marc knows? How's he going to just throw that out there and expect me to react? If Marc finds out about us, he'll probably demand that Simon make a choice between their friendship and his relationship with me. I can't take a chance that he'll choose Marc instead of me.*

She stepped out of the shower and stood in front of the mirror, twisting large sections of her damp coils around her fingers into a braid down the back of her head. *Simon is clearly comfortable with the world knowing about us, but am I?*

She ran her hands down the sides of the towel and over her hips. She wiped the mist from the mirror and peered at her hazy reflection. "You know he's everything you've wanted—-smart, funny, successful and sexy as hell." Feelings of affection radiated through her from memories of how wonderful it was to be near him, washing away the hesitation and fear. "You're always tellin' readers to be unapologetic and strong against haters, but you're going to continue to hide your feelings for a good man? Stop being such a fuckin' coward."

Taking in as much air as her lungs would allow, she waltzed out the bathroom with the confidence of a warrior heading into battle—a half-naked one. *Right, no dreamy bedroom eyes or sensual distractions. We're gonna sit and have an honest discussion about where we're heading as a couple.* "Simon, I think we should talk." She gasped and scrunched the top of the towel over her racing heart. Her body shivered from the sudden rush of cool air and two sets of eyes gawking at her.

One pair was Simon's, the other belonged to a petite, well-dressed older woman standing next to him. "Oh, ummm, hi," she said with a quaky voice. "I didn't know there was someone else here." Suddenly aware of how little it covered, she tugged at the bottom of the towel while her fearsome warrior retreated like a big ass chicken. She felt about ten sizes smaller but still too big to crawl under the arm chair beside her.

"Hello." Regina's entire body began to burn with embarrassment under the older woman's piercing gaze as she sized her up. There was no missing the judgment on her face. She was clearly displeased by the presence of the semi-clad woman dripping water onto the waxed hardwood.

The woman raised an eyebrow. "Well, aren't you quite the surprise. I've apparently interrupted, something." She folded her arms across her chest and shifted her weight to one leg. "Don't be rude, Simon. Introduce us." Both of them turned their attention to a beet-red Simon rubbing his chin.

18 - Regina Meets Alice

SIMON CLOSED THE DISTANCE between him and Regina. "Ma, this is my girlfriend, Regina Kent." He put a protective arm around her shoulder and pulled her against his side. "Regina, my mother, Alice Young."

Well, at least she'll know I'm not a hooker. "It's nice to meet you." She started to offer Simon's mother a hand, but decided it was best to keep them securely on the towel.

"Girlfriend?" Alice's face remained stoic save one raised eyebrow. "Inter-resting. This is news. How long have you two been dating?"

Simon squeezed her arm and glanced reassuringly. "A few months."

Alice scoffed. "I find that hard to believe, Simon. All these months, and you've never even mentioned—I'm sorry what was your name again?"

"Her name is Regina, ma."

"Re-gee-na." Alice stretched out the name like it was the strangest thing she'd ever heard.

I guess my Black ass isn't even in the room? Regina looked down and wiggled her toes in the tiny puddles of water at her feet. *Damn it. Not enough to drown in.*

Simon cleared his throat. "My mother unexpectedly stopped by, Gina."

"Yes. I'm sorry for arriving unannounced. I had no idea Simon would be entertaining." She elevated the cluster of high-end store shopping bags dangling from her forearms. "I just came to drop off new bedding. Clarissa said you needed some. It looks like I arrived just in time."

"Ma," Simon snapped.

Regina winced at the critical undercurrent in her statement. *I can't believe this is happening.* She tried to turn and high tail it out of the room, but for some insane reason, Simon kept her at his side.

"What? I apologized for intruding, but you have to admit— this," she said motioning her hand towards them, "is quite alarming. I'm not certain how to respond. How did you and my son meet?"

Regina was not sure if the astonishment Alice expressed was due to her lack of clothes or abundance of melanin. Either way, it was apparent that Simon hadn't revealed her existence to mommy dearest, and she wanted a damn good explanation why. "Simon and I both volunteer on the board of my brother's community center."

Alice wrinkled her nose. "Community center?"

"Yes, in Harlem."

Simon's mother let out a disgusted sigh. "Oh, you're one of those people."

"Those people?" Bile stung in Regina's throat. She crushed her tongue between her molars and pierced Simon's profile with her eyes. He ran his fingers through his hair, visibly flustered by the situation. Unlike a courtroom or deposition—where he had full control—he probably didn't know what to say to her or his mother.

"Look ma," Simon began.

Alice raised her hand and a cool stillness flooded the room. "No need for theatrics, Simon. I'm quite sure your *girlfriend* would like to put on more clothing." She placed the bags on the floor before gliding to the sofa and crossing her legs. "Now, how about you make your mother some coffee while, Rene was it, finds something to wear?"

Regina feverishly batted her eyelashes. There was so much she wanted to say at that moment, could have said to cut a woman like Alice at the knees, but she couldn't. Just like the party last night, her feelings for Simon denied her the ability to make use of her verbal arsenal. If she was going to be in his life, she would have to rethink her usual bitch-batting strategies. She pointed towards the bedroom. "I'm gonna go get dressed." She padded into the room at record pace, resisting the urge to slam the door.

"Seriously?" Her entire body quaked with rage. "How in the world did I end up in a mess like this? It's all like something out of a bad movie." Mumbling drifted into the room. She sneered. "Mama is probably discussing the naked Black woman in her little boy's bedroom." Being in the middle of a *Guess Who's Coming to Dinner?* moment made her stomach turn. "I gotta split."

She dropped to the hardwood floor and crawled on her hands and knees searching for the clothes Simon peeled off her the night before. It was easy to spot the billowing skirt on the far side of the bed, but it took squirming under it to find the top, bra and panties. She tried to shake as many wrinkles as possible before donning everything and preparing to take her mini walk of shame out of Simon's apartment. Once dressed, Regina squeezed her shoulder blades and stuck her chin in the air. She strode into the great room. "I'm sorry. I just realized that I'm late for something. I have to go." She made a beeline for the bathroom and started throwing her scattered beauty supplies into her overnight bag.

"No, Gina wait." Simon followed her into the bathroom.

Alice rose from her seat and glided towards the kitchen. "Simon, do you have any sugar?"

Simon glanced back "Yeah." Regina flapped her hands, trying to subvert his efforts to hold them. He sighed and grabbed her shoulders. "Look, don't go. Maybe the two of you can get to know each other better."

She rolled her eyes to the ceiling and crossed her arms. Are you friggin' kiddin'?" She maintained a low voice but one filled with ire. "You expect us to sit and share a cup of coffee or somethin'? The woman didn't even know I existed until 10 minutes ago."

"I can explain that."

"No, nothing to explain. This is just fun, right? No strings and sure as hell no explanations."

"Damn it, Gina. You know that isn't true." He moved closer but she stepped further into the bathroom.

"Where is the fresh cream?" Alice's voice wafted in and created a wedge between them.

Regina shoved Simon's arms off her shoulders. "Tell me somethin', Young. How am I supposed to know that's not true? You looked like a wounded deer because I'm not so sure I want to let the world know about us, but you've been just as quiet. You didn't even allude to your mother that you were seeing someone. Hell, at least my family knows your name and that you walk the earth."

Simon closed the door and brought his face close to hers. "Yeah, they know me as Marcus's old college buddy, not your boyfriend." His eyes sparked with anger. "Tell me, who in your family knows that we've been dating? Are any of them aware that I've been sleepin' with you for over three months? If memory serves, you're the one who wanted to keep things just between us."

She wagged her finger between his eyes. "No. Don't you dare." She poked his chest between sentences. "You're not gonna use my words against me. You don't want to tell Marcus either, and we both know why—'cause he'll freak. Now, inform me, counselor, why you have no problem bringing me around your coworkers but haven't found the time to tell your mother slash personal shopper about the Black girlfriend whose bed you've been hopping into? Is it because I'm one of *those people*?"

He opened his mouth then turned to the soft knock interrupting him. "Simon? I asked if you had any fresh cream." Alice continued to knock.

Regina sneered and folded her arms. "Go ahead, Simon. Get your mother her cream. She doesn't even like her coffee black."

Simon squinted. "Nice, Gina." He shot out of the bathroom, passing his mother's critical sneer. "I don't have any cream, ma."

Alice trailed her son. "How about some of that vile non-dairy creamer you always have in your cabinets." She gazed over her shoulder at Regina. "Why you're so determined to go low-rent despite me raising you to appreciate quality, I'll never understand."

Fury streamed through every nerve, sticking Regina to the floor shaking. It was time for her to get the hell out of there before saying or doing one of the regretful things surging through her mind. She zipped her bag and dashed by the kitchen where Simon was getting a container of creamer out of the cabinet.

"Gina." Simon placed the it next to three black coffee mugs and approached her near the entryway. "Please, stay."

Perched on a stool, Alice poured white powder into a mug and stirred. "Yes, please stay."

Regina closed her eyes and rolled her head from side to side to tug at the ball of tension sending a shooting pain up her neck. *Don't be snide. Don't be snide. This is Simon's mother. Don't be snide.* "No, thank you Mrs. Young. I really do need to be somewhere." She jerked her arm away from Simon's touch and glared daggers at him, who trudged back towards the kitchen.

"That's unfortunate." Alice looked at the huge diamond ring on her finger and cuddled the mug between her hands. "I think we could've had a nice conversation now that you are properly attired."

Don't be snide. Don't be snide. "Yes, that is sad." Regina nudged the shopping bag on the floor with her shoe. "Well, you can just spend the rest of the afternoon helping Simon change his bed sheets." *Fuck.* She ignored the clamoring sound and sauntered to the door. She didn't want to match Alice's rudeness, but the woman's stunned expression brought some satisfaction to a humiliating morning. "It's been a pleasure." She swung it open and stepped into the empty hallway.

She tapped her foot as she waited in front of the elevators, occasionally looking back to see if Simon was coming after her—he wasn't. When it arrived, she stomped in and fell against the back wall. As the doors closed, she watched the hallway and probably her relationship disappear.

19 – Subway

REGINA THANKED THE ELDERLY WOMAN and took her clipboard back. She smiled triumphantly at Jeremy. "That makes another full signature sheet, Regina."

"Yes, it does. We're on fire." She smacked his raised hand just before rubbing at her sore neck.

"I agree." Toni hooked her friend by the arm. "That was also the last one, so our work is officially done. How about a reward for the team boss?" She tugged Regina's arm. "Hey."

"Huh?" Regina stopped searching the crowd. "Yeah, that sounds good. Wait, what did I just agree to do?" Before she knew it, she was passing over her card to a concession stand vendor with one hand while balancing a huge chocolate waffle cone in the other. The afternoon was getting late, but the fair was in full swing. Multi-colored pennant streamers hung zigzag overhead. Booths were packed with vendors selling everything from custom crafts to jerseys and mugs with team logos on them. People bustled between them carrying their purchases or entertaining themselves by trying to win prizes.

The entire team of volunteers scoured the fair for petition signatures. Their fearless leader, Marcus Kent, split the ragtag operation of teens and adults into two groups. Regina led one while Simon led the other, which meant that there wasn't a chance for them to talk. She could only watch him take directions from Marcus and then walk away with his crew. *He barely acknowledged that I was even there. It's not like I don't kind of deserve it. I was pretty awful to his mother, which she completely deserved.* She tripped as Toni whisked her away from the others. "Wait a minute, girl."

"Sorry. We've done our duty, now I want to do some shopping. I saw this cute lingerie shop down the street."

"For real, Toni?" Regina passed her tongue across drips of brown sweetness sliding down her cone. "I'm not in the mood for that. Let's just go find Marcus." *And Simon.* She'd almost crashed into a few people thinking about and combing the fair for him while trying to get signatures.

"I *am* thinking of Marcus. I plan on making his tired eyes pop out of his head tonight. You might want to consider picking up something yourself." Toni crushed a napkin in Regina's hand and pointed to a garbage can. She defiantly shoved the rest of her cone in her mouth and cringed at the pain shooting through her head. "How lady like." Toni dragged her into the shop with scantily-dressed mannequins posed in the window. They immediately began browsing the racks. "Aren't you meeting Simon after?"

"I'm not sure. We haven't spoken since I called his mother a racist and left his apartment. It was terrible. She kept making sarcastic remarks, and not only did I rake him over the coals for it, I was rude to her before I stormed out."

"Whitney Houston?"

"Angela Bassett."

Toni held a gown against Regina's chest and leaned back. "So, you definitely want something to make him forget all of that."

"I don't think a gown will cut it, Toni. Besides, I don't even know when I'm seeing him again. He was pretty mad when I left. We both were. I accused him of being afraid to tell his mother about his Black girlfriend."

"That doesn't sound like the Simon I know." Toni lifted a ruby-tipped finger. "Excuse me." The clerk who had been hovering around them approached. "We want to try some stuff on."

Regina followed salesperson and best friend. "So," Toni's voice drifted between the dressing rooms a few minutes later, "you were right there tussling right along with Simon's mother. You kinda left him in the middle."

"I know." Regina grunted and let the satin fall over her hips. "I could've handled things better. I should've left it to Simon to put his mother in check." They stepped out of their dressing rooms and gave each other approving glances.

"Nice. Trust me, Gina, Simon will be coming around as soon as possible and is most likely just as anxious as you to resolve things. Just be a woman about it, and apologize." Toni placed her hand on her chin. "Do it wearing that, and he'll be especially inclined to accept." Toni turned her back to the mirror. "I think we'll have to cancel dinner for tonight."

"All right." Regina examined her image in the mirror. The peach satin complemented her brown skin and accentuated her hips. *Better to play it safe and get it.* They tried on a few more outfits then left the store with their seductive purchases.

The fair crowd had thinned, and vendors struggled to pack their remaining wares against a breeze carrying a cornucopia of aromas from the food trucks. Regina's phone beeped followed by Toni's. "I bet that's my taskmaster husband trying to track us down."

Regina slumped her shoulders. The text message on the screen was not from who she'd hoped. Instead, her big brother was ordering her back to the rendezvous point with her *partner-in-crime*. She and Toni dashed through the horde of fairgoers with their bags jostling behind them.

Marcus spotted and shot them a disapproving glare while continuing to talk to those surrounding him. "Everyone did a great job today. The advisory committee will review the information at the next meeting. I'd like to thank our board members Regina and Simon for joining us today." Marcus smiled in Regina's direction.

"Anytime, Marcus." Simon appeared at her side, so close that his body barely touched hers. She tugged at the bottom of her top to keep from throwing her arms around him and fixated on his profile while he continued to talk. "This work is important, and all the volunteers were fantastic. It's really motivating to see so many of our youth working hard for their community. Wouldn't you agree, Gina?"

Regina's heart jumped at the sound of her nickname and beat at top speed when he touched her shoulder and flashed a brilliant smile that seemed like it was just for her. "Yeah," was the only thing she could get out of her mouth before looking down, attempting to hide the obvious affect him being so close had on her. He may have been trying to be platonic, but her body flushed and trembled as if he was being anything but.

"Okay." Marcus's face grew pensive. He bit his lip but then offered his wife a muscular arm. "How about we all enjoy the rest of the fair? Thanks again, guys." Toni's head barely reached the top of the shoulder she leaned on as they walked away.

A thrill of excitement surged down Regina's spine when Simon's fingertips traversed downward from her shoulder and pressed the sensitive spot at the small of her back that only he knew made her quiver. Still looking in Marcus's direction, he leaned until his bottom lip grazed her ear. "I'll meet you at the station." Her brother turned his head just when Simon walked away.

Marcus stopped and watched Simon's back with a suspicious gaze then shifted it to her. She grinned and waved a little too brightly than the situation called for. "Yeah, he's totally catching onto us." She walked in the direction opposite from Simon and collided into a tall, slender torso.

🙂🙂🙂🙂

"Regina, wait up."

She stepped off the last step onto the subway platform, releasing a loud huff of air and groan from between her lips. There was no shaking Jeremy. She looked back. His head bobbed above everyone else's descending the stairs. Not able to resist his endearing smile, she put a hand on her hip and waited for him to reach her.

"I told you that you didn't have to come with me, Jeremy." She swept her gaze up the stairs for Simon. *He must be keeping out of sight because of Jeremy. As nice as this kid is, I need him gone.*

"It's no problem, really." Jeremy shoved his hands in his pocket and heaved in big gulps of air. "I wanted your advice on a few things." He dipped his head and tilted it to one side. "If you don't mind. I wouldn't want to bother you."

Just say no and find Simon. "Wouldn't you prefer to talk to Marcus?" She put the back of her hand to her yawning mouth. "I'm really beat, and he'd probably give you better advice anyway."

The corners of Jeremy's mouth dropped. "Marcus told me earlier that he and Toni were goin' out right after we finished at the street fair. You know what?" He raised a hand and backed towards the stairs. "You're right. It can wait until I get to talk to him. I'm sorry to bother you." He bobbed and weaved through the people and disappeared into the sunlit street.

"Great, Now I'm a bitch," Regina mumbled and turned on her aching feet. Simon still hadn't showed up and there weren't any notifications. "Seriously, Young?" She dialed and pressed her phone to her ear.

"Hello?"

"I thought you wanted to meet at the station. Where are you?"

"Why don't you turn around?"

The tension in Simon's shoulder blades eased at the sight of Regina's radiant round cheeks and eyes. Her brilliant smile confirmed that her anger had waned since yesterday's drama with his mother. He dangled her key to his apartment from his finger. "You forgot this."

Regina's eyes lit up. "Thanks." She dropped it in her purse and took his hand. "I was afraid you might've bailed on me."

He closed the space between them. "Sorry, but I was waiting for your lost puppy to go frolicking off."

"He's sweet. He just could really use some friends."

"I agree. Then he can stop hanging around you."

She glanced sideways at him with a smug smile. "Are you jealous, Young? You really have nothin' to worry about."

Simon caught his bottom lip between his teeth and squinted in the direction where Jeremy disappeared. "You know what, let's forget about him." He wrapped his arms around Regina's shoulders. "Come here." His heart raced as she snuggled against him. He let out a big sigh and twitched his nose at her coils tickling it. They swayed back in forth in silence. It was so nice when it felt like it was just them. "I hate when we fight."

"Mmm, me too." Regina rubbed her nose against his neck. "I'm sorry that I barged off yesterday, but I was really embarrassed." He held her tighter. "I guess the whole time we've been together, I never thought about how *your* people would react."

Simon sighed. "I know, Gina. My mother was rude, and I spoke to her about her behavior."

She raised her head. "Thank you, but it's more than that. Yesterday reminded me that what we have is not just between us. We have family and friends. They're gonna react, and we'll respond. It might not be all positive." She stepped back and stroked the back of his neck.

"I have a friend from college, Elliott. He fell for his now wife, Bree. I mean really hard. He'd talk about her all the time and try to be wherever she was. It was so obvious that he was deeply in love with her. They dated; then he introduced her to his family, and they seemed to like her too—until Elliott asked Bree to marry him. As soon as they saw that ring, his parents, siblings and relatives went ballistic."

"You see, they're the kind of White people, who are perfectly fine with havin' *People of Color* over for dinner, and could even tolerate Elliott sleepin' with a Black woman, but no way in hell were they gonna let one climb their family tree. They'd say stuff like, 'Do you know how hard things are going to be for the two of you?' and 'What about your kids? They'll grow up confused.' It was terrible."

Now, Bree's family wasn't thrilled about Elliott either. They asked her why she was trying so hard to lighten their family blood. Fortunately for her, they came around once they got to know Elliott and realized how much the two of them were in love.

Elliott's family never accepted Bree and nearly destroyed their relationship. His mother told him not to bring 'that woman' to family gatherings and refused to go to their wedding. The only person that would even talk to Bree after they got married was his little sister. Elliott split from everyone but her.

Last year, they had their first baby, and she was the only one to see that beautiful little boy. Elliott's parents won't even acknowledge their own grandson's existence. Elliot lashes out and says things like 'screw 'em,' but when he talks to me sometimes, I can hear the pain in his voice. He really misses them."

Simon kissed her and drew her back into his arms. "It's not like that with us, Gina. Please try to understand. My mother spent years planning my life, trying to make sure I'm as successful as possible. She's imagined the career and family she thinks I should have. You're not what she pictured—not because you're Black. In her mind, my wife ought to be a socialite of some kind that'll help me ascend the ladder of success—a woman more interested in social climbing than social justice. Basically, you don't fit her equation for my life." He lifted her chin and gazed intently into her eyes. "You fit mine, though. You're actually the only person that really has."

Regina's hand smoothed across his jaw. "You've come to mean so much to me, Simon, but I can't become a person that you have to choose over your mother. I couldn't live with coming between the two of you."

"You won't, Gina. We just need to be truthful with everyone about us."

She opened her mouth but then closed it. Her eyes narrowed at something behind him. "It's not that easy," she said taut-lipped. "People can be pretty damn ignorant and cruel." Simon peered over his shoulder. A frowning woman ogled them as she walked pass.

He tilted his head. "I always assumed you didn't care what people thought?"

"Usually, I don't, but I have my blog and employee. I've gotta consider her. Havin' a bunch of people trollin' and discrediting me can affect my traffic and revenue. They won't like the idea of a me not bein' with a Black man and will want to rake me over the coals."

He pressed his forehead to hers. "I don't wanna ask you to risk everything you've built. How about we just tell our families? I'm tired of hiding it from them, especially Marcus." He raised his head and squinted at the approaching train lights. "I've been feeling guilty about keeping our relationship from him. Our friendship is usually open and honest. It's time that it is again."

"You're right." Regina pressed her mouth to his ear as the roar of the train filled the station. "I'll text him and see if he and Toni are available for dinner tomorrow. We can talk to him together." She leaned back and looked at him. Her hopeful smile filled his heart with the same.

Simon gently squeezed Regina's hand as he guided her through the jolting subway car. He had no clue how to ease any of her fears about how the world was going to react to them, or his either. That came along with interracial dating. No matter how two people feel about each other, almost everyone around them has an opinion about why they shouldn't be together. Since most of his past relationships didn't go further than the third date, none of that really bothered him before, but Regina and her happiness was now an imperative. They had a connection that meant what scared her, concerned him.

They found seats. Regina rolled her head from side to side. Simon instinctively reached out and kneaded at the tension in her muscles. "You okay, babe?"

She let out a soft moan. "Yes, I just can't wait to lay down." He kept his naughty retort to himself. Motivated by the feeling of being watched, he scanned the train. His gaze fell on a pair of eyes staring at him. An Asian man was seated directly across from them. He held an opened newspaper but apparently found Simon and Regina more interesting. The man blinked furiously over his glasses and wavered his gaze between them. He then held Simon's gaze with an accusatory glare, making his displeasure crystal clear.

Simon briefly broke eye contact to look at Regina, who was busy tapping at her phone. "There, I texted Marcus. I hope you're ready for this, Young."

He put his arm over her shoulders and slid her closer. "More than ready." He pressed his lips to hers and explored his love's mouth. The sweetness of ice cream lingered on her silken tongue and increased his hunger for her. The world fell away. She was all he wanted, and his mind buzzed with ways to tell her how much he loved her for the rest of their lives.

She broke the kiss and panted. "Wow." She raised the brows over her dilated pupils. "You realize we're on a crowded subway?"

He glanced sideways for a moment. "I do."

Understanding flashed in her eyes after she gazed at the old man across from them. "You alright?"

Simon covered her hand with his and put it to his lips. "Fine, babe." He slid down in the subway seat and pecked her forehead as he laid her head on his shoulder. He pulled up one corner of his mouth and looked down his nose at the Asian man. "Just fine.

20 – INSTAGRAM

SIMON LUMBERED INTO THE APARTMENT and tossed his keys on the counter. "Man, it's gonna be nice to spend the evening alone with my woman."

"Agreed, and I can't wait to hit the shower." Regina arched her back. Her shoes fell from her feet in a small thud on the floor.

He climbed a stool and stretched at different angles. "Do you want me to order somethin' for dinner?" He held Regina's hands. "How about I cook? I don't want you caught up in the kitchen."

Regina's thighs grazed his and the shopping bag hanging from the crook of her arm swung against his side. "I don't want you in the kitchen either. Not tonight." She leaned her body against his and reached over his shoulder to get a stack of menus from the mail organizer. "So, takeout it is."

"Anything in particular?"

"Surprise me." She disappeared behind the bathroom door.

White noise from the running shower filtered into the room. Simon undid the buttons of his Henley shirt and flipped his fingers through the restaurant trifolds. "Chinese is good." After ordering their meal, he opened the music app on his phone and selected the playlist he constructed for their first weekend at his place.

He noticed Regina coming out of the bathroom and stiffened—everywhere. Her hair was pulled into a small bun that spanned across the back of her head. A head chain spread a garland of tiny pearls from the center of her forehead. A small pearl hung from a white gold chain and settled at the beginning of her cleavage. Peach satin waved open, revealing glistening brown thighs. "I thought you said you wanted to relax?"

Regina smiled and averted her gaze. "I do."

He scanned her full body again and shook his head. "Not looking like that. Those aren't your usual comfortable clothes."

"Shall I change?"

"Hell no. No one's taking that gown off of you but me. I just don't understand how you expect to relax looking so sexy."

Regina held up a finger. "Control yourself, Young."

"Do you really want me to?" He pushed play. Sexy bass and trumpet sounds drifted from the speakers.

Regina began to swing her shoulders. "This is nice."

"I was hoping you'd like it."

"I do." Torso and hips soon joined the arms in obeying the musical spell.

Simon fixated on the shimmering gown against Regina's breasts and along her rotating hips. One leg peaked out from the slit in front and peach swished around her ankles and bare feet. He couldn't imagine anything more beautiful. He danced towards her and touched her waist.

She opened her eyes and side stepped with a coquettish grin. "Shoes." Her body continued to tease him.

"What?"

"Shoes."

Simon sighed. He propped himself against the chair, hauled off and dropped each sneaker on the floor. He included the socks for good measure. "Would you like me to take off anything else?"

She laughed and opened her arms. "Thank you. I didn't want to risk getting my feet crushed."

He wrapped an arm around her, splayed his hand on her back and extended his arm along hers. He entwined their fingers and brought her arm against his chest to graze each knuckle with his lips before drawing it around his neck. Touching his forehead against hers, he brought her closer, slipping one leg between hers until their hips met and rotated in unison. The singers' smooth voices floated around their dancing bodies. Simon's heart flooded with content. Nothing felt so right.

"Wait a minute." Regina lifted her head and stared off to the side. "Do you speak Spanish?"

"*Sé lo suficiente.*" He dropped his hips and bent his knees, bringing her down with him. He straightened them with a smug smile to match her impressed expression. "I know Marc speaks it. Do you too?"

"*Mamá insistió.* She strongly believed that her kids should be at least bilingual."

"I agree. I decided that if I was gonna practice law in New York, it would be a good idea to know some." He continued to lead the swaying of their bodies. *I love surprising her.*

"So, you understand the lyrics?"

"I do. That's why I chose the song." He pressed his lips to her bare shoulder. "It reminds me of you. You captivate me just by walking in the room." Feeling her shudder, he gazed into her glossy eyes while she grasped the nape of his neck. "Something burns inside me when I look at you, Gina. It's more than desire. It's like I can't breathe—not fully—until I have you near. I've never even said anything like this to anyone. You awakened these feelings in me."

She brought her palm around to his jaw and stroked his cheek with her thumb. "I feel it too."

Simon crushed his lips to hers. An intoxicating rush washed over him. He wanted all of her—body, mind, and soul. He would be willing to give her the same, but she already owned his.

Regina stilled her hips and backed away from Simon. "Let's sit down."

"Huh?"

"Didn't you order takeout?"

He tightened his hold and dipped his head to nibble her neck. "Yeah?"

She pushed him away again and pat his surging chest. "Well, if we continue like this, we'll be in the bedroom when it gets here."

"I can live with that." Simon leaned in for a kiss, but received a disapproving glare. "Fine." *Amazing. I'm getting cock blocked by takeout.* Every nerve in his body urged him to satisfy the lust surging through him. Waiting for some sesame chicken was not an option. He peeped sideways to the living room and got a brilliant idea. "Come here."

Regina followed him to the sofa, where he sat and tapped his lap. "Sit. Then we'll be *here* when the food comes." *But still naked.*

She turned to her side to lower herself on his lap.

"No." He clasped her hips and turned them towards him. "Like this. It's much more comfortable, and I want to be facing you while we—talk."

Regina towered over him with her fists on her hips. "You think I'm buying that line, Young? You're truly relentless. We're waiting for the food to arrive."

He made a half smile. "Yup, just waiting."

She opened the front of her gown at the slit and straddled him. "Since we have some time, I want to really apologize for my behavior yesterday."

"I forgive you." He concentrated on the two beautiful orbs bouncing before him. They cried for him to free them from their pastel prison.

"No, for real." Regina rubbed her thighs, causing the bounce to progress to a charming jiggle, making him more determined to liberate the hypnotic brown spheres. "I was disrespectful to your mother."

"She'll live." He hooked a thin satin strap with his finger and moved it down Regina's shoulder. The top of the bodice fell until it was caught on a hard nipple, revealing the dark brown areola. *To hell with delivery.*

"Simon." He dismissed the warning tone in her voice and followed the trail from the strap across his lover's chest to caress her skin right at the hemline of the garment obstructing his view. She trembled. He caught his bottom lip between his teeth. *I guess she isn't worried about takeout anymore.*

"Enough talk." Regina planted a hungry kiss on his lips. She lifted her head and dropped the side of her peach gown, freeing the hard nipple trapped underneath.

Simon moaned and drew the it into his mouth. Her sweetness permeated all senses and sent him into a frenzy. A soft knock cut through the melodic sound filling the room. He ignored it, yanked the satin gown up her hips and slipped his eager hand underneath her panties. He stroked where the top of her buttocks met with a fingertip. The low moan and her quivering signaled the effectiveness of his touch. He filled his palms with supple flesh and drew Regina's hips forward.

She ran her fingers through his hair and moved her hips to the rhythm. "Oh, Simon, I—"

The knocking increased to a bang. The splendid weight, scent, feel, and taste of Regina vanished. Simon's entire body shook in frustration. For the second time, cold water was splashed on his flaming passion. *Aww, hell. What's it gonna take?*

"There's the food." She pulled her clothes down and turned to the door.

"Who cares?" He dropped his head on the back of the sofa and moaned. "Don't answer it. I'll take you out to eat later. Wherever you want to go, you name it." He lurched forward and tried to regain his lost prize by holding the bottom of Regina's gown. but to no avail.

She pinned his hands to his sides on the sofa then clasped his chin in between her thumb and forefinger. "Stop pouting, Young. I'll grab the food." She fixed her bodice. "Then you can get back to grabbing me."

All that was left was her perfume lingering in the air and an ache in his chinos. "My wallet's on the counter." He adjusted his pants and rested one ankle on the opposite knee. It was going to take a minute before he would be able to leave his seat.

"Megan?" Regina's voice drifted from the entryway.

Her assistant swept into the apartment with her fingers furiously plugging away at her phone. "OMG, Regina. I can't believe this is happening." Megan pushed her glasses further up her nose and strode to the side chair. She stopped in her tracks when she saw Simon on the sofa. "Oh, hi, Simon." She surveyed the room until her face turned the appropriate shade of red. "I'm sorry to interrupt."

"Megan." He forced a smile. They'd met when Regina hired her. She kept things organized, and even made sure that he got to be with Regina, so he tried hard to hide how unwanted her presence was at that moment. "How're you doing?" Simon went to turn off the music, his plans for the playlist thwarted—again.

The brunette turned and raised her head to Regina as she approached. "What are we gonna do?"

Regina hunched up her shoulders and turned her palms to the ceiling.

"You don't know? You haven't seen all the notifications?"

"No, my laptop is in sleep mode and my phone is on silent. What are we going to do about what?"

Megan floated the phone before her boss's face. "This."

Regina's mouth fell open. She snatched the phone from Megan. The light glittered in her eyes darting in her head. "No, no." She stomped in and out of the entryway. "This can't be happening." She grabbed her forehead. "Not now." She changed her pacing direction to across the apartment. Megan joined her.

Simon reached for his phone. As soon as he turned off the music, Marcus's name and image flashed on the screen. "Hey, Marc." Regina stopped in front of the small hallway leading to the bedroom and bathroom. Holding the device against her chest, she huffed wildly as tears spilled from her anxiety-ridden eyes. *What the hell is happening?* "I'm in the middle of somethin'. What's up?"

"Where're you?"

Simon bowed his head. Something about Marcus's tone indicated that he already knew. "I'm home." It wasn't a total lie. For him, Regina's apartment was his other home. He had more than enough stuff in it to be comfortable for an extended period of time and already planned to stay the week.

"Really? Are you sure you're not somewhere messin' around with Gina? I mean, from the looks of these pictures, the two of you have gotten pretty damn close."

Simon gaped at Regina. "What pictures?" She flew across the room and held up Megan's phone screen. A pit of dread grew in Simon's gut. An image of them in a passionate embrace, in the clothes they had on that day, shone on the screen. She slid her thumb across the screen, and there was another picture of them gazing into each other's eyes with his hands clearly groping her backside. Her thumb passed again. They were kissing in the last picture. It was already a meme with the captions *WHEN A SISTAH SWEARS SHE'S PRO-BLACK* at the top and *BUT GOES OUT FOR CHINESE* at the bottom. "Fuck."

Marcus's voice streamed from the phone so loud that Simon was sure Regina heard. *Yeah, fuck. That's a good word. Tell me, bro, how long have you been fucking my little sister?*

21 - Be a Man About Yours

S IMON STEPPED TO THE LIVING ROOM WINDOW and moved the geometric-patterned curtain to the side. The phone's heat burned in his ear along with the Marcus's enraged words.

"This is bull, Simon. You couldn't even be a man about yours and tell me that you were—I don't even want to know what you've been doing."

He rubbed his forehead and peeked over his shoulder. Regina emerged from the bedroom in a pair of sweats and one of his white tanks. She descended onto the edge of the chair in front of her laptop and rolled her head. He wanted to fix things so badly. All of it was his responsibility. He desired, pursued and fell in love with a beautiful person, and it was wrecking their lives. It would only be natural if she bolted, but he was going to do whatever was necessary to make sure she didn't.

"Yo, man."

"I'm here, Marc." He cleared his throat and stuffed a hand in his pocket. "I'll explain everything."

"Oh, damn straight, you will. Not over the phone, though. You'll meet me and explicate the reasoning that made you decide it was a good idea to start fooling around with my sister."

There was a bang at the door. Regina and Megan remained engrossed by whatever was on the computer. He retrieved his wallet before opening the door. "I'll come to your place now." He passed the delivery person a one-hundred-dollar bill and kicked the door closed behind him.

"You don't want to do that. I'll be expecting you Friday. How about you stay out of my sister's bed until then?" It was more of a demand than an inquiry.

He dropped the bag on the counter and closed his eyes. Marcus's anger was completely justified. Some may consider his behavior a little strange, but Simon knew the values Marcus's parents gave him. Even though she was a grown woman, his sense of duty to protect his sister was very strong. *I shouldn't have snuck around behind Marc's back with Regina for so long. I have to straighten things out.* "Yeah." The phone disconnected. He was a fool for agreeing to stay away from Regina until they spoke, but he couldn't risk damaging their friendship more by stomping on Marcus's manhood any more than he already had. It meant too much to him, and if he was going to be with Regina, her brother's approval was important. She might kick and scream about Marcus's butting in, but she deeply valued her brother's opinion. The situation required diplomacy, finesse and giving into Marcus's demand.

Simon braced himself on the counter and glanced at Regina clicking away at her keyboard. A cold, deep longing settled inside him at the thought of staying away from her. He wanted nothing more than to turn off everything, hold her in his arms and shut out everyone trying to keep them apart, but that was no solution. They couldn't ignore the world's reaction to their love. *I'm not able to shield her from this professional Armageddon, but I can make things right with Marc.*

He started unloading the food and filling plates from the cabinet. Megan offered a tense grin and walked around Simon to the coffee maker. "This is a disaster." After filling the coffee pot, she accepted the plate Simon offered her.

"That bad?" Regina's keyboard made a rapid succession of clicks.

"Yeah. She's writing a reaction piece now. Black Twitter is on fire. Every hotep, misogynoirist and Black separatist is raining down on her." Megan rested against the sink and popped a broccoli floret in her mouth. She obviously learned a lot about Black social media during her brief employment. "It would've been better if the two of you went public on your own. Now, people are accusing Regina of hiding it because she knows she's wrong for dating you. She has to defend herself on multiple fronts."

"Do you think we can get her to stop for dinner?"

"Not now. She's on a mission."

Regina stretching her long arms in the air caught his attention. She dropped her arms and rolled her head from side to side. She wrote until the wee hours when her writing flowed. A few times, He'd go to bed with her poised at her desk and get up for work to find that she hadn't moved much. There was little to no conversation at those times, and definitely no hot breakfast—just a peck on the cheek and brief goodbye as he headed out the door.

She bit her bottom lip and squinted at the computer. A forefinger started attacking the mouse scrolling wheel as she leaned closer to the screen. Simon skirted past Megan and took a tall silver thermos from the top shelf of the slender cabinet over the coffeemaker. "Megan, can you get me the half-and-half?"

"Here you go." She passed the tall carton to him along with the glass sugar pourer.

"Thanks." Simon added just the right amounts of everything, twisted the cap closed and shook the contents as he rounded the counter. The bottom right corner of the computer screen strobed with notification pop-ups accompanied by incessant dinging. Fingers shot across the keyboard at an impressive speed as the blank whiteness filled with black letters. "Here, babe." Simon bent to kiss the soft, brown cheek closest to him.

"*Mmm.*" She hardly acknowledged his presence, not that he expected her to. He grabbed a plate of food from the counter and flopped on the sofa. She was in the trenches now. *It's gonna be a long night.*

🙚🙚🙚🙚

"Simon?" Regina gently shook Simon's knee. The plate smeared with what was left of his dinner teetered in his hand. He lifted his eyes and the corners of his mouth pulled into a groggy smile. He was so handsome, even when she had to scrape dried duck sauce from the corner of his mouth. Hell would freeze over before she gave him up.

Simon stretched his legs. "Gina." She secured the plate and put it on the coffee table before it toppled on the rug. "What time is it?"

"It's nearly two." She ran her fingers through his hair and tugged at both his arms until he rose.

Simon staggered on his bare heels. "Are you finished?"

Not even close. Her stomach rumbled. She'd spent the entire night sustained on coffee and skirmishes with a bevy of haters, bigots and racists about her audacity to have a love life. "Tonight, I am." There would be more in the morning, but for now, all she wanted to do was curl up next to Simon and feel his strong arms around her. With boyfriend in tow, she trudged towards the beacon spilling on the hallway floor from the bedroom. It was the only safe haven they had.

"Where's Megan?"

"She left about an hour ago. I managed to get a response article posted, but I don't think it's enough. Some people are just plain hateful."

"You got that right," Simon drawled between yawns. "I expected some stupidity, but Megan said it's pretty bad."

She stopped and slumped against the wall. The tears she'd kept at bay for hours demanded release, but she restrained them with deep breaths. "She's right." She let Simon lift her aching body and take her in his warm embrace.

"It's gonna be okay, babe." She rested her head on his shoulder. The wonderful caress of his strong hands on her back eased a little of the tension, which would probably be replaced by more come sunrise.

"Yeah. Let's just get in bed." She continued to lead him closer to the beam of light. Normally, those words would make her feel better, but this time, they simply didn't. The real possibility of all her hard work spiraling into a drain of narrow-mindedness and fanaticism sank her spirit like a stone. *What the hell am I going to do? This took me years to build. I'll talk to Elliott for advice. There has to be some way that I don't have to choose between my work and the man I love.*

She stopped and turned inside the bedroom. Simon stood in the doorway framed by darkness, scratching the back of his head. "I think I'm just gonna head back to my place."

"What are you talking about? Why would you leave now?" She passed her hand over the waves at the top of her head. "Are you dumping me?" Her arms folded, she tilted her head until she was able to peer into his red-streaked eyes. "Is all of this too much for you?"

"No." Simon slouched his shoulders and picked at a sauce stain on his shirt. "Nothing like that. I just thought-"

Regina dropped her head back and moaned at the ceiling. "Please. No more thinking. I can't think another thought." She skimmed his body and leered. "Well, maybe just one." She hooked the waist of his pants and walked backward until her legs met the blanket scraping the wood floor. "What do you say?" She lingered her lips close to his and swung her hips to the memory of the music. "Why don't we pick up where we left off before all of this mess started?" Their lips touched. He groaned and covered her mouth. The sweet, pungent taste of his lips made her empty stomach growl and set a fire between her legs. "Take these off," she ordered while fumbling with his belt buckle. She yearned to feel him on top of her and wrap her legs around him.

Simon stilled her hands and stepped back. A rush of air shot between them and shocked her burning senses. "Regina. We need get some sleep."

She closed her eyes and then opened them to the blackness of the hall. "Sleep?" She spun.

Simon was on the other side of the bed tossing the large pillows on the floor. "Yeah. We both have long days tomorrow, and only a few hours before they start." He bounced on top of the covers with his back to her.

She dropped her jaw and gawked at the scene before her. "You're not changing?"

He squirmed. "No need. I'll have to change in a couple of hours anyway, so why bother?"

"And you're sleeping on top of the blankets?"

"I'm in my street clothes."

"Seriously?" She shifted her weight. There was something funny going on, and she planned on finding out what.

Simon let out a heavy sigh. "I'm exhausted. We can talk more tomorrow. 'night."

She turned out the light. Sitting on the edge of the bed, she glared at his back, trying to control her breathing and growing rage. Things had been running hot and cold between them all day. His behavior signaled that things were once again cool. Her body, however, had not received the memo. She inhaled deeply and stared into the darkness beyond the doorway, trying to subdue the tingling between her legs. It was an exercise in futility. No meditation was going to work—only one thing would.

She eased over to Simon. Mashing her breast against his back, she curved her arm over his side and caressed his chest. He shuddered and his breath quickened. *So, I guess you're not all that tired after all, hmm counselor? Let's see how awake you are.* She moved her palm down his body, enjoying the way her touch made him quiver. She nibbled at his ear. "Are you asleep yet?" She scooched her hips against his tense buttocks. Their breaths joined in a frenzy of passion. "Babe," she whispered.

Just as she reached the top of his pants, he halted her progress with a firm grip. "Damn it, Gina," he panted, "you have to stop now." He pushed her hand behind him and writhed to the edge of the bed. "Go to sleep."

She propped on an elbow, reeling from the rejection. He'd never denied her before. Even when he was exhausted, Simon manage to summon the strength necessary for at least a quick romp to send them both over the edge. Things were beyond cool; they were frozen, and he laid there like a block of ice. "This is bull." She wasn't going to allow him to just roll over and not explain himself.

She smacked his back. Simon winced, but the strike had no impact beyond that. Neither did the second and third ones. She filled her hand with hair and yanked his head back.

He yelped and grabbed her wrist. "What're you doing? Let go."

"No." She jerked his head while she spoke. "You expect me to believe you're too tired for sex? I know you better than that. You were ready to give up eatin' 'cause you couldn't wait to get busy." She released her grip and kneeled on the bed with her hands on her hips. "What the hell is goin' on, Young?"

"All right." Simon turned over, rubbing the top of his head. "When I was on the phone with Marc before, I sorta agreed not to be with you until I had a chance to explain things to him."

She scoffed, waiting for some indication that he was joking. "Excuse me?" *He better be freakin' kiddin'.* Regina jumped onto the floor. The lamp on the night stand rattled as she paced between it and the end of the bed. "Let me get this straight. My brother ordered you not to have sex with me, and you agreed?"

His face became stoic. "Yes."

She raised her hands in the air and slapped them against the sides of her thighs. "Unbelievable. What is this? Are we in 15th Century North Africa or something? Did he threaten to take back his goats?"

Simon rose and approached her. "Listen. He was angry, and I didn't wanna make things worse."

She punched his chest. It barely made him move, but it felt damn good. "No, you listen. Nobody decides who fucks me but me. I spent half the night in front of that computer fighting people who were tellin' me not to be with you. My entire brand is in shambles, but I'm standing up to them to keep you in my life. Now you tell me one word from my brother sends you scurryin' for the hills?"

"I'm not."

"Then what the hell would you call it?" She pushed at his chest with both hands and stormed to the bedroom window. *I'm the only one fighting. If he isn't willing to stand firm against Marc for us, what about his mother or the world?* She closed her eyes and swallowed the pain welling inside her throat. "I thought I was important to you."

"You are."

"Obviously not as much as my brother's hurt man feelings. She folded her arms. "You know what? I think it *is* a good idea for you to go back to your place."

"Babe."

She heard Simon's bare feet padding the floor. "No." She turned and glowered. "Marcus didn't give you permission to touch me, right? So, you should leave." Regret choked at her throat, but no way was she apologizing. She was weathering a ferocious storm while he ate Chinese, napped and arbitrarily decided to deny her any solace in his arms.

Simon lumbered out of the bedroom. Tears started streaming the moment the sound of the front door slamming reached her ears.

She turned off the lights and found her way under the blankets. Simon's side of the bed was still slightly warm. She buried her nose in his pillow. She felt so alone and fought the urge to call him back to hold her. Everything was slipping out of her grip, and knowing how to stop it was lost to her.

ᔕᔕᔕᔕ

Regina staggered out of the bedroom. She balanced on the mahogany desk and searched with throbbing eyes for the source of the ring piercing into her ear and making her head pound. "Hello?"

"Hey, lady."

"Hi, Toni." She leaned against the bedroom door. Her heart sank at the sight of the empty bed.

"I'm calling to check on you. How's it goin'?"

"Not good." The tears renewed and streamed down her cheeks. "Simon's gone."

22 - Marcus Confronts Simon

S IMON WAS NO STRANGER TO BEING IN PLACES where he was less than welcome. It didn't take too long for him to figure out at the Young family gatherings that he was definitely the odd cousin, with his tan skin, "exotic eyes" and dark features that clashed against the white skin, and light eyes of the other children. None of the adults said anything directly, but it was clear that his was not the most wanted presence in family photos.

It was never like that when he hung out with Marcus. Wherever they were, Simon was sure of his place and value. He wasn't so much anymore. He shifted his weight in front of his friend's door. He'd fouled up things majorly. A bunch of pictures circling the internet of him and Regina pawing each other was one of the worst ways for Marcus to find out about their love affair. He was so enraged that he kept Simon waiting to talk to him. *I need to cool off from this* was as the only response Simon got after asking multiple times for them to meet. He finally decided to just show up at the apartment.

Swallowing, he winced at the sharp pain shooting at the back of his mouth. He rubbed his throat. Stress-induced exhaustion from arguing and worrying about Regina and fighting with Marcus was already taking its toll. The new pain surging down his esophagus meant he would soon have to struggle with some kind of nasty sickness. Just one more thing. *I'm so tired.*

He wrapped his knuckles on the door, waiting for the storm. He dropped his arm to his side and released an achy sigh when he saw Toni's open-hearted face.

"Hi, Simon." Her smile comforted his frazzled nerves.

"Hi, Toni. Is Marcus in?"

"No, I'm sorry, he went to play basketball. Why don't you go meet him at the court?"

"Yeah, Thanks." He started down the hall when Toni's voice stopped him.

"Hey, Simon. Why don't you wait for him here? You aren't dressed to play, and I wouldn't want you just standing around."

"Okay. Thanks." Toni offered him a drink. He flopped on a stool and massaged his throat while his hostess went into the kitchen.

"Here you go." Toni said with a forced lightness in her tone.

"Thanks." Simon stared into the mug. "How is she?"

Toni sighed. "Stressed. Social media has been brutal."

"I've seen." Simon sipped his coffee. "She won't talk to me. I want to be there for her, but—"

"She's barely talking to anyone." Toni touched his hand. "She's trying to focus on how to handle this. It's all complex. Neither Marc nor their parents can even get in touch with her."

"Yeah, but, I think there's a special silent treatment just for me. She never answers my calls and only responds to text messages and emails with a single word like "fine," "okay" or "busy." She's really mad about the agreement I made with Marcus."

Toni's spoon rattled on the counter. "I don't blame her. I mean, what the hell were you thinkin'? How could you give into that asinine demand?"

Simon dipped his head and rubbed his thigh. "I thought I was doing the right thing. I didn't want to make Marc any angrier. I know it sounds stupid."

Toni rolled her eyes and folded her arms. "Sounds stupid? It was beyond idiotic. Listen," she rounded the kitchen island, tucking her bob behind her ear, "normally, I wouldn't even talk to you after the stunt you pulled on my girl, Gina, but I can see how hard you two have fallen for each other, so I'm gonna help you out." She crossed her legs on the sofa and pointed to the overstuffed armchair. Simon obeyed the petite woman and moved to the seat. "I'll attribute your foolish behavior to you not having any sisters and thus being clueless about women beyond how to get between their legs. Marc, on the other hand, knew better and played you foul."

He squinted at her sideways. "What do you mean?"

She stuck out her index finger and held his gaze. "You should've told him to go to hell. Do you have any idea the message you sent Gina by agreeing to that juvenile bro-pact? You basically made how Marc felt more important than her, and at a time when she needed you at her side the most."

He slammed shut and rubbed his throbbing eyes. "Damn it."

"Yeah, and you caved into him while she was struggling against a whole army of people condemning her for being with you. So, you basically told her that you aren't willing to fight for her—she's not worth the hassle."

"That's not true."

Toni straightened her posture and pulled at the hem of her top. "Maybe, but I'm not the person you have to prove it to. Gina needs to know that she's the most important person in your life."

"She is, Toni. All I want to do is hold her and let her know how much I love her."

"Then you've got some work to do." The door locks clicked. She looked over his shoulder. "Starting now." She got up and walked into the kitchen.

Simon inhaled and stood like a warrior. It wasn't only Regina he'd have to convince about her importance.

"Sweetness," Marcus pronounced in a booming voice, "Your man has returned triumphant." His gleeful smile faded. He snarled and lunged, seizing Simon by the front shirt and pinning him to the wall.

"I came to talk, man." Simon's feet almost dangled in the air. He tried pushing Marcus away, but the man was like a stone pillar. There was no way of escaping his steely grip without starting a fight. "You told me to wait until the end of the week."

"It wasn't long enough. I'm still ready to bash your face in."

"Marc, just listen to him." Toni fruitlessly shoved between the two men. "This isn't helping anybody, least of all, Gina. How do you think she'd feel knowing the two of you are fighting?"

Marcus looked at his wife and loosened his grip, but nudged Simon on more time before stomping towards the kitchen.

"Look, Marc, I wanted to tell you." Simon braced himself on the counter.

Marcus let out a wry chuckle as he opened a bottle of water. "You wanted to tell me that you were fuckin' my baby sister?" He jerked the bottle at Simon. "I knew something was goin' on when you were acting all funny that time I mentioned her. But, no, I convinced myself that it couldn't be possible." Water sputtered out of the top of the bottle. "Simon would never do something so slimy as to hook up with his best friend's sister. I can trust him. Maybe not other guys. Them I have to watch, but I can trust Simon!" Water sprung around Marcus, splashed his shirt and sprinkled his beard as he slammed the crushed bottle on the counter.

"I know what you must be thinkin'."

"Yeah, what's that?" Marcus crept towards Simon like a lion stalking his prey.

"That I'm just usin' Gina." He managed to control the shakiness in his voice. He put his hands to his side and stood fearless to Marcus's approach.

Toni positioned herself in front of Simon just as Marcus reached him. "Come on, Marc. Cool down." She held her hands against her husband's hulking chest. Marcus stopped, gently lifted her at the elbows and set her on her feet behind him.

"That sounds about right." He bumped Simon's chest with his. "Toni, I need to talk to my *friend* alone."

"Do you really expect me to leave the two of you like this?"

"Please." Simon's heart leapt into his throat when he heard keys rattling but he remained firm.

"Only if you promise not to bust each other up or anything in my home."

"I won't break anything." He turned his head briefly when the door clicked closed and then peered back at Simon. "What the hell are you playing at?"

"Marc—"

"You think you can get away with treating my baby sister like one of your string of hoes ready to jump on your dick when you call?"

"I'm not."

"Oh, Come off it, man. Remember, I was your roommate. I saw how you treated women. You'd pick 'em up, bounce 'em in your bed and then right out the door. You barely even knew most of their names."

Simon scoffed. "Like you were lonely until Toni came along? Besides, I was honest with them. I let them know I wasn't lookin' for anything serious."

Marcus formed two formidable fists at his sides. "Were you honest with Gina? Did you run the same lines on my sister? Did you let her know that she was just a piece of ass?"

Simon groaned and paced a small distance. "I'm tellin' you, it's not just a sex thing, man. I care about Gina. She means something to me."

"Please," Marcus spat. "You're lying to me and yourself. You've been screwed up about women ever since Samantha."

Simon glared at Marcus. "She has nothin' to do with this." It was messed up for Marcus to mention the woman that tore through his life and heart.

Marcus sneered. "Oh, I think she does. You never got over what she pulled, and now you're draggin' my sister into your bullshit and crappin' up *her* life."

Simon closed the distance between them. "And how, exactly, am I doing that?"

"Well, she was just fine before you. She had a successful blog and a powerful voice. Now, her career is in jeopardy. People are attacking her and she won't even talk to me—all because she got involved with you."

"Are you seriously takin' the side of a bunch of close-minded bigots who—wait." He took in Marcus's frame. "Do you agree with them? Are you mad because Gina's with me, or is it that you can't stand the idea of your sister with someone who isn't Black?" Rage charged between them in a way it never did before.

"Get out." Marcus's voice quaked with anger.

"Yeah, but get this in your head, man. Gina and I are together. No matter how mad you get, I'm not letting her go." He bumped Marcus's shoulder as he passed. "She's in my life, and she's staying there." He stormed out of the door. *It was a bad idea to try and talk Marcus into accepting my relationship with Regina. I think I just made things worse. We've had our strains, but our friendship may not survive this one.*

꙰ ꙰ ꙰ ꙰

Simon lumbered on aching legs up the subway stairs. Beads of sweat rolled down his forehead and stung his burning eyes. The fight with Marcus racked his throbbing head. The harsh words they exchanged wrenched his gut. *How can I make things right and keep my best friend?*

Wiping away rivulets with the back of his hand, Simon braced himself on the wall of the small elevator in his building. Everything hurt. Even the small jolt as the elevator moved upward made pain ripple through him. He tried to dial Regina's number as he trudged down the hallway, but everything swam on the screen. *I need to talk to her. She has to listen. We can make this work.*

He fell against the open apartment door. The pain in his eyes faded in the darkness. He kicked off his shoes and dropped each article of clothing as soon as he managed to shrug or pull it off. He bumped the kitchen counter, knocking over a stool before stubbing his foot on the armchair. His pants fell onto the hallway floor. The cool sheets made him shiver more violently than before. With only his boxers on, he wrapped the blankets around his body and over his head. Pale blue light filled the impromptu tent. Unable to stop shaking or thinking, Simon stared at Regina's smiling image. *What will I say to her?* His usual razor-sharp wits dulled from the pain surging through him. Limbs and head became too weighty to lift. Soon, he was out cold.

23 - HEART TO HEART

YOU'VE GOTTA BE KIDDING ME. Regina peered through the peephole. "Go away, Marc. Now." Exhausted from another night at the keyboard, she shuffled back to her desk. It was not the time for him of all people.

"Let me in. You're being a big baby." The door locks started clicking.

"I'm a baby? You're the one stompin' around havin' tantrums." She dropped in her seat and rolled the leather pencil holder Simon gave her between her fingers.

"Whoa." Marcus ducked his head. The cup whizzed by and crashed into the wall. Pencils and pens splattered around his feet to the floor. "Very mature. Was that necessary?"

She smirked and took the cold stapler in her hand. "It's the least you deserve, you busybody. Give me my key. I don't want you havin' any more access to my life."

He shoved the keys in his pocket and rounded the wall to the refrigerator. "Toni made me come here with food and to talk." He stacked oblong containers inside then sat on a stool. "I take it that you're still pissed?"

She raised the stapler. "I plan on remaining pissed."

He scowled and pointed. "Put it down.

"You told my boyfriend to stay away from me."

"Hey, before he was your boyfriend, he was my best friend. God Regina, you're already best friends with my wife. Why the hell do you gotta have Simon too?"

She dropped the stapler and rested her head on the back of the chair. "You said he would impress me. Well, he did."

"Funny. Look, Gina. I can understand you bein' upset, but you aren't the only one. Do you know how traumatic it was to see pictures of Simon grippin' your ass on the internet?" He hunched his shoulders and shivered. "I still have nightmares."

"Oh, please. You're being way too over-dramatic." Regina spun in her chair and frowned at the numbers on the computer screen. The anticipated pattern was happening, which was not good. She switched tabs and clicked the send button for her email to Elliott. *Time for an exit strategy.*

"Am I?" He rose and sat on the arm of the side chair. "The two of you worked damn hard to keep this from me because you knew I wouldn't approve."

She rolled her eyes into her head. "We don't need your approval, Marc."

"Then why all the sneaking around, Gina? Toni tells me that you've been dating Simon for months. You could've just told me."

She braced herself on the arms of the chair and leaned forward. "I didn't because I knew you would be juvenile about it. Look at the way you acted when Toni and I got closer. You couldn't stand it."

"Yeah, and you know why? 'Cause I have to worry about you two fighting. Then I'd be in the middle of a whole mess and have to choose sides."

She got up and popped a container from the refrigerator in the microwave. "We wouldn't ask you to do that," she pounded the buttons, "and you know it."

Marcus chuckled. "Neither one of you would say it outright, but you'd expect it." He stood across from her at the counter. "Now you're with Simon. He's like a brother to me. What happens if you two fight, split up or he hurts you? I'd have to hurt him, and then I'm out a friend."

Regina used a fork to stab at the food in the container, ignoring the sense he made. Now was time to stay mad. "Well, you're the one who hurt me, Marc."

"Me?"

"Yes, you." Food flung off the fork, landing on the pristine countertop. "You made this about your ego and manipulated Simon's respect for you to get him out of my life."

"I was tryin' to protect you, Gina. I know a lot of things about him that concerned me when I found out he was involved with you."

She jutted her chin to the ceiling. "Like what?"

"That's for him to tell you."

"Oh, no, Marcus Kent. You don't get to wiggle yourself in my business and keep information from me. Spill it, or else I bring this to The Island."

His eyes widened. "You wouldn't."

She raised her eyebrows and chewed victoriously on her food. If necessary, she'd pull all the stops to get her brother to come clean, even if it meant bringing her parents into the situation. Adrian Kent was the only person walking the earth that Marcus truly feared. It would only take a few baby sister tears to get their mother to force every bit of information out of him.

Brother and sister stared each other down while the computer hummed. "Simon liked to go through women when we were in college, and he showed no indication that he changed his ways."

"How many?" *Why was I stupid enough to ask that? I don't want to know the number of bodies that have been in his bed.*

Marcus held up his hand. "You don't want to know. Suffice it to say that he didn't spend many nights alone, which is another reason why the thought of the two of you bothered me."

"Was he careless?"

"No. He practiced safe sex and let every partner know that he was not looking for anything past a few kicks that night. It was just sex. I minded my business then, but I won't stand by and let my sister be treated that way." He sat on the sofa. "Now, can you at least understand why I was so mad?"

"I guess." She took her meal with her back in front of the computer. "But you need to understand what sending Simon away did to me. I needed him that night. I was reeling from everything, and he was the only person I wanted by my side. I still do." She wiped at the tears blurring her brother. "I miss him so much, but I'm so mad that he wasn't there for me. You did that."

Marcus's mouth dropped open. "You're in love with him."

She screamed at the ceiling. "Yes, I'm in love with him, and you took him away from me, jackass. What if I tried to convince Toni to leave you?"

"I got it. I'm sorry. I was wrong."

"Yes, you were." She turned the chair and smeared more tears across her cheek. *His heart was in the right place. I'll forgive him eventually.* She blinked at the throng of problems in front of her bigger than a meddling brother.

Marcus's hands rested on the chair's high back. "How's all of that?"

"As expected. There's been an initial bump in my blog's reach since I posted some responses to the photos, but that's just short-lived interest because of the scandal. I expect to start losing more subscribers within the month."

"So, all is lost?" Marcus went to the doorway and began putting pencils and pens back in the holder.

"It doesn't have to be, not totally. I could work my ass off for the next six months trying to get people to forgive me for loving someone."

He reached over her and set the cup between the mouse pad and keyboard. "Can you stop saying that? I'm gonna puke."

She swung her fist backward. Anger and melancholy washed away when it contacted Marcus's nose. "Stop makin' this about you, Marc." She let him spin her around.

He sat on the coffee table, rubbing his nose and laughing. "Okay. So, you apologize?"

"No, I move on and do something else. I don't want my professional life dictating my personal one. People don't have the right to tell me who I can love. No matter what happens with Simon, I'm planning on a transition."

"So, you're just giving up *The Blackness of Kent*?

"No, at least not all of it. I still want to write, it's what I do. So, I won't be building myself as a brand anymore. I'll go back to focusing on writing. Elliott knows an online media company that'll probably be interested in adding *The Blackness of Kent* to their blog lineup. They've approached me before, but I wanted to stay independent. It may mean a smaller audience, but I get to keep my privacy."

She refreshed the analytics page and sighed. "He's also arranging for an editing job interview. So, I get to feed myself. I'll have to let Megan go, but she'll find something quickly; she's very talented."

"What about Simon?" Regina glowered at her big brother. He raised his hands. "I'll stay out of it."

ᔔᔔᔔᔔ

"*Simon Young's office.*"

"Hi, Corella? It's me, Regina." She checked the screen.

"*Hello Regina.*" Corella's upbeat tone was a welcome change from Simon's voice mail. "*How are you doing?*"

"I'm good, thanks. I was trying to get in contact with Simon. I've been calling and texting since yesterday."

"*He called in sick,*" she said over soft clicking in the background. "*He forwarded his phone here.*"

"Thanks."

"*You're welcome. Bye.*"

ᔔᔔᔔᔔ

Regina stood in front of the door, rubbing the shiny key between her fingers. *I'm not even sure I have the right to use this. Are we broken up? What do I say when I see him? Does he even want to see me?* A whirlpool of uncertainties swirled in her head and shot down her body, leaving her unable to get past staring at the doorknob. She shook her head. "Ah, the hell with it. I'm goin' in."

She crinkled her nose and spied the sink full of dishes as well as mugs and glasses sprawled across the counter. "Simon?" She put her bag next to the cluster of mugs and ventured further into the dim apartment. She pressed her hand to her chest and raced past the man's rambling head on the screen towards the sofa. "Oh, babe."

He was laid out, half-covered by a blanket and with a throw pillow tucked under his head. She touched his burning forehead.

Flushed, Simon fluttered his eyes open. "Gina." He raised a hand but it quickly fell to his side. "You're here."

"Hi." She pulled back the blanket and rested her palm on his abdomen. *His entire body is on fire.* "Corella said you were sick, but I didn't think you would be this bad."

"I'm okay." He groaned, sitting up and flopping his head back.

"You definitely are not okay. Have you been to a doctor?" She tucked her legs under her and settled next to him. "You're burning up. Are you taking anything?"

"Nah, I'm good." Simon smacked his parched mouth and turned his closed eyes in her direction. "I'll just sleep it off."

She rose. "I'm taking you. Where is your doctor?" she asked, walking into the bedroom.

"Queens, since I was a kid."

"I'm not takin' you all the way to Queens. I'll bring you to an urgent care."

"Okay."

Simon was hot and heavy. Regina struggled to change his clothes and get him into the car. She smiled when he tried to walk completely on his own accord in front of the facility but ended up leaning on the car and laying his head on the roof.

"Come on, Hercules." She swept herself under his arm, her shoulders aching from their burden. Regina squinted at the beams bouncing off white walls and floors attacking her eyes and sat Simon down before approaching the reception counter. "Hello. My friend is very sick." A pang of guilt stabbed at her heart. Just calling Simon a friend didn't feel right. He was so much more, but after the way she treated him, he probably didn't consider her even that. "He has a really bad fever."

The nurse perched on her chair and feigned a look of concern before shooting a series of questions while scavenging her desk for papers. "Has he been here before?"

"No, I mean, I doubt it."

"Does he have a rash?"

Regina closed her eyes to remember if she saw anything while dressing him. "No."

"Has he recently been out of the country?"

"No."

The nurse tucked a pile of papers into a clipboard and handed it to her. "Fill these out please, and return them to me. He'll need to sign them."

"Thanks." She slid down the counter. Rubbing her head, she scanned and started scrolling the pen above the inadequate lines demanding information. Pride seeped into her chest when she realized she was able to complete a lot of the form from her knowledge about Simon. It faded when she got to the insurance section. *I have no idea what insurance he has.* She searched her bag, glad she grabbed his wallet before leaving the apartment.

Regina rubbed the soft, worn black leather. *How long has he had this thing?* She gasped at her smiling face greeting her when she opened it. Tucked behind clear plastic was a printed copy of a photo he must've taken with his phone. Her heart leapt. She held the wallet against her chest with her trembling hands and gazed at Simon's slumped body through glistening eyes. Blinking rapidly, she continued to complete the form.

"Gina," Simon weakly moaned and shifted in the chair.

She gathered her things and walked towards him. "Yeah, babe?" She tried to soothe his restlessness with her soft tone. "I'm here. What do you need?"

He lifted his head and smacked his cracked lips. "Thirsty." He pivoted from leaning on the back of the chair to her legs.

Regina stumbled at the sudden weight. The clipboard slipped down her side. "Okay, babe." Jamming Simon's wallet under her chin, she grabbed a bottled water out her handbag and unscrewed the top. She struggled to push his limp body back and sat next to him. "I have some right here."

She managed to get him to take a few sips before his head lulled like a ragdoll. Regina stood to go back to completing her task, but Simon pulled at her. "No. Don't go." She returned to her seat, and he laid his head on her, loosely wrapping his weak arms around her legs. *How the hell am I going to complete this damn paperwork now?*

She turned towards laughter in the room. An older woman in a stylish hat and coat giggled and winked at Regina. "Big babies when they're sick, aren't they?"

"Tell me about it." Regina packed the bottle and wallet in her bag and balanced the clipboard on Simon's shoulder. She looked down a while later and wiped sweat from his forehead. Her heart prodded her to sit there and not to disturb him, but she had to give the stuff to the nurse. "Simon." She tapped him gently. "I need to get up." She lifted his limp head and shoulders and propped him on the chair.

Regina passed the clipboard to the nurse and thanked her. She then poked in her purse, searching for her buzzing cell phone. "Hi, Elliot. What's up?"

"Gina. I have some great news. They're interested in adding *The Blackness of Kent* to their blog roster. I'm going to need you to come to D.C."

24 - You Can Go Now

REGINA LET OUT A RELIEVED SIGH. "That's fantastic, Elliott. This transition will help me get more control over my private life."

"They also want you to take an editing position and be a paid contributor to some of their major platforms. Quite a few of the managing editors there are fans of your work. Only thing is, they want you to come to D.C. for an interview."

She pushed identical pens around in the cup on the counter. "I can do that."

"Tomorrow."

"Tomorrow?" She looked at Simon's slouching body. "It's kinda late to make travel plans. How about next week?"

Elliot's tone became more authoritative. "Regina. I had to do a lot of finagling to arrange this. You said you were ready to move as quickly as possible."

"I know, and I am. I just need a more time to get down there." As soon as she reclaimed her seat, Simon rolled his head onto her shoulder and flopped his arm across her waist. "I really appreciate what you're doing for me." She switched the phone to her other hand and stroked his scruffy jaw. "Friday. I can get there Friday, and I'll spend the weekend with you and Bree. I'll even babysit Daniel."

"Are you using my wife and son as leverage?"

"A little bit."

Elliott sighed. "You're shameless. I'll call you back."

"Can you text me?"

"Can I what?" His displeasure oozed into her ear. They may be close friends, but he was not a man to be put off, and she owed him big for extending so much time and energy to help her.

I'm really pushing my luck, but I can't leave Simon now. "Text me. I'm in the middle of somethin'." She wiped the sweat trickling past her ear. *I'm clearly not thinking straight, otherwise, I'd be flying down the I-95 saving my career.*

"Young?" The nurse stood at the doorway. "Simon Young?"

"Right here." Regina raised her hand. "Please, Elliott."

"You know, you're one of the few people I would go to such lengths for, right?"

"I do, and I love you for it. Well? You got this for me?"

"I'll text you."

"Thanks Elliot."

"Simon Young?"

Regina pulled Simon to his feet, and dragged him to the nurse.

ୋ ୋ ୋ ୋ

"I can do it." Regina wrapped her arms around Simon as he clumsily attempted to climb the examination table.

"Come on, Young. You have to let me help you." The doctor walked in just when she got him seated.

"Simon Young?"

"Yes." The scale rattled as she backed into it before dropping into the seat in the corner.

After introductions, a series of questions and some poking and prodding, the doctor sat in front of the computer screen and started typing. Regina resumed her place next to Simon at the examination table. "It's a good thing your girlfriend brought you in, Mr. Young. Your tonsils are infected."

Simon smiled and squeezed Regina's hand. "Yeah."

"I'm going to call in a prescription for antibiotics to the pharmacy you provided." She clicked away at the keyboard. "You can take something over the counter for the pain. Get plenty of rest, and drink lots of fluids. Any questions?"

"No, thank you." Simon pulled Regina closer and dropped his head on her shoulder.

The physician flashed a combination of humor and sympathy at Regina. "Good luck."

᭶᭶᭶᭶

Regina closed and fell against the bathroom door. Despite repeated propositions, she was able to get Simon in the shower without joining him. Rubbing a shoulder, she walked across the bedroom and began searching the draws for pajamas. After tossing a pair of sweats on the bed, she took off her soaking top and stretched a red Boston College t-shirt over her head. She then chose one for the sickly horndog in the shower.

"Gina." A steam burst followed a slump-shouldered Simon into the bedroom, who was naked save a towel he held in front of his groin. "I feel a little better."

She took the towel and patted at his glistening body. "Of course, you do, and clothes will make you feel magnificent." She squatted and passed the towel over Simon's rump and thighs when she was confronted with his noticeable arousal. She gazed up. "Really, Young? Even when you're sick?"

A weak smile spread under his droopy eyes. "Sorry, I can't help it. You have that effect on me."

Regina stood. "Well, I can." She snatched the sweatpants off the bed and opened them at the hips. "Here. We're getting you in bed— to rest." Maneuvering past more advances was necessary, but she eventually gave Simon his medicine and lay the overstuffed comforter over the feverish law man.

"Thanks, Babe," Simon yawned. The fluffy white pillow framed black locks, and a content grin. "I'm so glad you came."

Regina slowly blinked and smiled. "Yeah, I am too." He was not as hot as earlier. She leaned forward and pressed her mouth onto his moist lips. She'd missed them so much that even a light kiss brought with it a plethora of feelings. *It's so good just to be near him.* "I'll get you some more water."

Regina took two water bottles from the fridge and surveyed the great room. Cleaning the messy apartment passed her mind a few times while she was at the doctor with Simon. Mercifully, Simon's cleaning lady returned it to its usual orderly state while they were gone. *Thank you, Clarissa.* Carrying Simon's heavy carcass around the city had every muscle in her body singing for a break, and she was going to take one lying next to her big man baby.

Retrieving the phone from her purse and strolling towards the bedroom, Regina huffed at the daunting number of notifications on the screen. *I'm not even in the mood. I'll deal with this mess later.* She stopped and frowned at the door. She closed and rolled her eyes as Simon's mother glided into the apartment. *Are you kidding me? Haven't I been through enough today?* "Hello, Mrs. Young."

Alice dragged her gaze over Regina while flipping her keys in her hand. "Hello, Rebecca."

"Regina."

"Yes, that's it. Re-gee-na. Well, it's nice to come into my son's apartment with you fully dressed."

Don't be snide. Don't be snide. "Yeah, it must be a real comfort."

Alice cast a sideward glance at Regina's chest. "Where's Simon?"

Regina looked down at the distended *Boston College* letters across her chest. "He's in bed." She turned, grinning at the sound of Alice's gasp behind her. Eyeing the shocked woman over her shoulder gratified her further. *I know exactly what's she's thinking, and I should let her keep thinking it.* She continued down the hall. "Sick. He's in bed sick. I just brought him back from the doctor."

The shopping bag landed on the floor next to her. Regina jumped to the side on one foot and hit the wall trying to avoid Simon's mother ramming into her. Alice was already on the bed stroking his hair when Regina leaned against the doorway and crossed her ankles.

Alice drew a few tissues from the box on the nightstand and dabbed his forehead. "How long as he been sick? What has he been taking?" Beautiful dark eyes sparkled with irritation at Regina. Alice Young was truly a stunning woman—albeit acidic and condescending—and she plainly cherished her son. "You didn't let them give him penicillin, did you? He's allergic."

"I found him like this earlier. I think he's been sick all weekend. The doctor said his tonsils are infected." Regina pushed from the jamb and placed a hand on her delicate shoulder. She was hard as nails for someone with such a tiny body. "I told them I wasn't sure of his allergies, so they didn't give him penicillin. The doctor said he should start feeling better in 24 to 48 hours. He needs rest and fluids. I was just about to check on him." *I was also going to lay next to and hold him because I missed him so much, but you messed that up for me.*

Alice flicked the hand off her shoulder and swiped the water bottle. "Thank you for all of your help." She rose from the bed and shoved Regina towards the door. "I can take care of Simon from here."

Regina staggered. "Umm, I'm not leaving him, Mrs. Young." Simon squirmed on his back and let out a heavy sigh. "I want to make sure he's okay."

Alice glowered and prodded harder. "Are you implying that I can't care of my own son?" The two women stumbled into the hall. "You've known him for a couple of months. I've seen to his health all of his life. I know what he needs."

"I'm not saying that. I just want to be with him." Her leg bumped a stool, making it wobble.

Alice let out a wry laugh. "Well, there will be time enough for that when he's better. You can go now, and do whatever it is you do. I'm sure there's a protest somewhere."

Regina felt the heat surge up her neck and out of her ears. *She's throwing me out? Who does she think she is?* She clenched her teeth and glared as she towered over Alice. *It's time to set this woman straight.* She opened her mouth to spit one of a list of venomous retorts her mind formulated in the time it took her to inhale, but then she glanced across the apartment at the hall. Simon was sick and did not need the two of them bickering. If she stood her ground, that was exactly what would happen. There was so much they had to talk through; adding a fight with his mother to the list was not wise. She'd have to bow out of this verbal brawl—this time. "All of his medicine is next to the bed."

Alice half smiled. "Thank you." The expression of gratitude was more appropriate for the help and not anyone significant to Simon's life.

Regina lifted her handbag from the hook and let the weight drop on her shoulder. She opened it and dipped her head as she walked into the hallway. The contents jostled in front of her until she saw the worn leather bi-fold. "Here's his wallet." She reached in again and handed Alice a bunch of folded papers. "Oh, and these are from the urgent care visit."

"Excellent. Goodbye."

Tears began to wet the front of Simon's red shirt. She'd been dismissed before, but this rejection tore at her heart. Clenched fists shook to pound on the brown door blocking her from the man she loved. Instead, she relaxed them at her side, resting her throbbing head on the molding and staring at the intricate carpet pattern until it swam around her aching feet.

There's no winning by battling his mother. I'm too exhausted to fight anymore. After a few deep breaths, she raised her head and wiped the tears away. Her phone vibrated in her pocket.

Elliott: *Sorry. I couldn't get them to wait until Friday. You have to be here by noon, Wednesday.*

25 - I NEED TO FIND HER

OR THE FIRST TIME IN DAYS, Simon was able to raise his head without it feeling as if it weighed a ton. He opened his eyes to the dimness of his bedroom, flipped the blankets back and sat on the side of the bed. The wonders of modern medicine were kicking in. Simon stretched while faint memories of the past few days trickled into his mind. It was all very foggy, but one thing stuck and filled his heart with happiness. Regina was here.

He'd never felt as much delight as when he opened his eyes and saw her radiance. *She took such good care of me.* Her touch lingered on his body. "Gina?" He trudged out of the bedroom. Smells from his childhood awakened his senses. His wobbly legs still needed help. "Gina?" He pushed his palms towards the ceiling and arched his back while searching the great room through half-opened eyes for the person he yearned for the most.

"Good morning, Simon." His mother's cheerful voice drew his attention to the kitchen. The huge pot in front of her billowed steam when she lifted the lid and stirred. "How are you feeling?"

Despite his disappointment, Simon mustered a smile and kissed his mother's soft cheek. "I'm feeling a lot better." He grabbed a water from the fridge and relished the cool sensation down his dry throat.

"That's good. I made you some soup. Sit down."

"Thanks, ma. It smells awesome." His grumbling belly confirmed it. "I was out of it for a while, huh? There's probably a ton of work on my desk."

"I would assume so." Alice placed a steaming bowl on the counter along with a spoon and chunk of fresh brioche. "Eat."

"Thanks." His nasal passages opened to the scrumptious aroma and steam. Simon glanced around the apartment again before diving in. "Where's Gina? Wasn't she here?"

Alice briefly paused her stirring then continued, lifting her chin. "Who?"

"Gina, ma." Steam from the soup tickled his scruffy chin. "Regina, my girlfriend. Where is she?" Simon concentrated on the swirling broth with chunks of vegetables and meat floating in a centric pattern around the bowl. *Did I dream her? I wanted her here so bad; maybe I just imagined the whole thing?*

"Oh, her. I sent her away."

Simon dropped the hand poised at his mouth with a spoonful of soup. Broth sprayed from its container onto his wrist. He stared across the counter, barely registering the stings from the array of tiny burns on his skin. "You did what?"

"I told her to leave. You needed your rest, not to follow some girl in a tight t-shirt around."

Simon slammed his fist on the counter and sprang from his seat. "Damn it, ma."

Alice blinked rapidly then frowned. "Simon Young."

He raced to the bedroom. Battling his sore muscles, he ripped the blankets from the bed, then combed the floors and rifled his night stand draws. He stopped to gaze at the golden bangles on Regina's side before rummaging through the rest of the apartment.

The sofa was next. Pillows and blankets flew in the air. "Where the hell is my phone?" He overturned books and magazines, finally hitting the coffee table with his palm. "Shit."

"Is vulgarity necessary, Simon?"

He stood and rubbed the back of his neck. "I'm sorry, ma, but you have no idea what you've done." It was hard to suppress the fury and desperation in his tone. He loved and respected his mother but just wanted to yell at the top of his lungs at the rashness of her actions. "I've been trying to talk to Gina for over a week. She finally comes to me, and you kick her out? She already thinks you don't like her because she's Black, and then you go and treat her as if she's nothing?"

His mother scoffed and folded her arms. "That's nonsense. I don't care that she's Black. Now, her being one of those social justice warriors *is* a problem."

"Yeah, well that's what she thinks, and that's the only thing that matters." He propped his aching body back on the stool and massaged his forehead. "I wanted her to open to the idea of making this her home, of it being where we share our lives." Simon sighed and relaxed a little as his mother's fingers passed through his hair.

"How serious are you about this woman, Simon?"

He met his mother's gaze. The concern in her eyes chipped away at his anger. She meant well, in her way. "I'm very serious about her, ma." He went back to the bedroom and set an engraved silver ring box on the counter when he returned. "I love her."

Alice stared in wonder at the box and then him. She opened it, revealing a platinum engagement ring with a huge diamond surrounded by French pavé-set round diamonds that also ran along the band. "Nice ring. I've taught you well. I'm sorry. I didn't know you cared so much for her."

Simon touched his mother's hand. "I didn't tell you, and that's my fault, but you had no right to put her out, ma. She's my life. You have to show her more respect."

Alice nodded. "I will, Simon. I have to admit, she did take good care of you." His mother grunted when he caught her in a bear hug. "Okay, okay. Can I breathe now?"

"Yes." Simon kissed her cheek and dashed out of the kitchen. "Now I've gotta go find her."

"What?" Alice followed her son. "No, Simon. You're still sick," her muffled voice floated through the bedroom door.

❦ ❦ ❦ ❦

Marcus swelled his chest and sauntered to his beautiful wife lounging on the sofa. "Here you go, sweetness." Toni's smile made the trek to Brooklyn well worth it.

She took the box and marveled at the assortment of small pies. "You went all the way to Abu's Bakery for me?" She yanked at her husband's tie. He bent to receive a loving kiss. "Thanks, Marc. You spoil me."

Marcus settled next to his wife and gathered her small frame in his arms. "That's my job. I know the past few of weeks have been especially hard."

"Tell me about it," Toni mumble with a mouth full of sweet potato pie. She set the box on the wood coffee table and proceeded to the kitchen. "We need milk."

Marcus removed his tie and sank further into the sofa. "Any word from Gina?"

Toni walked towards him with a carton of milk in one hand and two glasses in the other. "Yes, she's safe and sound." They both furrowed their eyebrows at the knocking on the front door.

Marcus peered at his watch. "Who the hell can that be?" Because their schedules became erratic at times, he'd established a strict policy against uninvited guests. Everyone knew not to just pop by the Kent's or there would be consequences. Of course, Regina ignored that rule, but she was long gone.

Toni stood on her toes at the peephole. "Simon?"

Marcus shot off the couch and was at Toni's side in seconds. "What's he doing here?"

"I'm not sure." Toni held Marcus's chin and glared. "But you be nice. Remember, your sister loves him, and so do you. It's about time the two of you make up anyway."

He grunted. That was the best she was going to get out of him.

Toni continued to look back at him as she glided past the kitchen.

He cracked the door and jutted his head into the hallway. "What? I'm trying to be with my wife." Marcus stopped his tirade when he noticed Simon's sickly appearance.

Simon slowly blinked, standing with his hands jammed in the pockets of his hoodie. "Sorry, man, but I need your help."

Marcus opened the door further and stepped to the side. "You look like shit."

Simon chuckled. "That accurately describes how I feel. Hi Toni."

Toni flew her hand to Simon's forehead. "Why are you wandering around the city with infected tonsils?"

Simon looked over his shoulder at Marcus, who shook his head. "They tell each other everything."

"Shut up." Toni guided Simon's ragged body to the side chair. "You should be in bed."

"I'm doing okay. I just need to find Gina. She was at my apartment last night."

"You mean until your mother told her to leave?"

Marcus up held his hand at Simon's shocked gape. "You'll get used to it."

"Yeah, I want to talk to her," replied Simon, shifting under Toni's clinical scrutiny.

Marcus met Toni's gaze as he pulled her down on his lap and stroked her leg. "And you came here?" His wife ran her fingernails along his scalp, making him instantly relax. They fixed their attention on their feeble guest.

"I was just at her place."

"Why didn't you call her?" Toni inquired.

"I can't find my phone."

Marcus tilted his head. "Let me get this straight. You can't find your woman or your phone?" He chortled and rubbed the back of his head to soothe the sting of his wife's slap. "Hey, why you hittin' me? I didn't lose 'em." *Simon's never this disorganized. Maybe Gina is something special to him. I'm gonna vomit.*

Toni sighed. "Regina isn't home Simon. She took a shuttle flight to D.C. this afternoon. You must've just missed her."

"D.C.? Why is she goin' to D.C.?"

"Job interview." Marcus tapped Toni's behind and stood. "Some media company is in love with her writing, and she decided to make a career change." The glasses clanked in the custom-made cabinet. He removed one and held it to the room. "We were just havin' dessert. Want some?" The invitation contained just the right undertones of irritation.

Simon's head dipped down. "I can't believe she's thinkin' of leavin' New York."

Guess he's not too sick to jump to a big ass conclusion. "Actually, she's—," Marcus began to explain to his lovelorn friend that the job was not in D.C. but spied Toni's shaking head and glinting eyes. "Yeah, go figure." He shot her a look. *What are you plotting, woman?*

"They were excited to be bringing her on board," chimed Toni. "They couldn't even wait until Friday, which is when she wanted to leave." She touched Simon's knee. "Gina tried to buy more time when you guys were at the clinic, so she could take care of you," she sat back and crossed her legs "until she was tossed out like garbage."

Brilliant. Marcus beamed at his wife's keen skill to manipulate the hell out of someone. Fortunately, she only used her powers for good. Toni was working the perfect emotional angles to make Simon realize that he'd better act fast or risk losing his lady love. Marcus's stomach churned. *I'm still not completely all right with the thought of the two of them together, but I guess I have to get used to it. I'm definitely gonna vomit.* He leaned against the sink and waited for his friend's reaction.

Simon's hand was on the front door almost instantly. He stepped back and looked at Marcus. "We cool, man?"

Marcus nodded. "Call me when you get back. We'll play some one-on-one." He reached on the wall and pulled down a chrome key ring with the word "Charger" and a fob. "Here." Simon snatched the key out of the air. "I'll call the garage to let them know you're taking my car."

Simon smiled. "Thanks man." That was all that needed to be said between the two friends. Things were settled.

"You got it. Can I get back to *my* woman now?" Relieved of one love-sick fool, Marcus made a quick phone call then rejoined his wife and their pastries. "So." He eased down on the couch and wrapped his arm around Toni. "Will you be tellin' your girlfriend she's got 5'11" of infatuation comin' for her?"

Toni curled her legs on the couch and nestled against Marcus. "I hadn't planned on it." She put a forkful of pie into her mouth. "You," she mumbled.

"I was told to mind my business." He brought his mouth close to hers. "Now, let me taste some of that pie."

§❧§❧§❧§❧

"Yes, Corella. I'm feeling better, but I won't be in the office for a few more days." Sandwiched between a pickup and mac truck, Marcus's black muscle car protested every time Simon stopped on the packed Belt Parkway instead of releasing the machine's true speed potential. Despite wanting to hit the road as soon as the garage released his friend's car, he'd decided to give his recuperating body some sleep before the four-hour trip to D.C. He also found his phone, but all his calls to Regina went straight to voicemail.

"*Okay, Simon.*" Corella's voice rang through the car speakers. "*I cleared your schedule for the rest of the week, but Rameez was looking for you this morning.*"

"I noticed." Simon gripped the steering wheel tighter and peered at the brake lights of the pickup with the gun rack and Conservative sticker. "I'll call him back right away. Thanks, Corella."

"You're welcome, Simon. Bye."

Maybe he wants me to assist him in court again. It took a few transfers, but eventually Rameez's voice filled the car. "Simon, I'm glad to finally get a hold of you."

Simon tilted his head from side to side. "I apologize for the delay, Rameez."

"No need for apologies. I heard you were sick. I hope you're feeling better."

"I'm coming around." The pickup truck's bumper sticker got smaller as traffic loosened. The car's huge engine roared.

"Glad to hear it. I'm putting together a team for a case that hit my desk, and I want you on it."

"Absolutely, Rameez. Whatever you need." Simon cut the wheel and shifted gears. He half smiled at the petite woman in the pickup truck with long blonde hair. The irony was not lost on him. He followed the sign for the bridge.

"That's what I wanted to hear. Now, I need you to get ready to come with me to Singapore. There'll be a lot of investigating and negotiations. Your acumen when it comes to international law will be an asset."

"Thank you."

"I'm flying out tomorrow night. I know it's short notice, but things are moving quickly on this one. I can brief you on the plane."

Already half-way across the bridge, Simon inhaled and bit his lip. "Is it possible for me to fly out on Friday? I'm having a personal emergency." *I'm trying to keep the woman I love from leaving me. That's one hell of an emergency.* He might have been ruining a major opportunity to advance himself, but Regina was more important.

"That's acceptable, but I need you there no later than Sunday."

"You got it, Rameez."

"See you on Sunday."

26 – D.C.

REGINA MASSAGED THE BASE OF HER NECK with her fingertips. She shifted and rested her elbows on the arms of the overstuffed hotel lounge chair, which was an improvement from the myriad of office seats she'd bounced in and out of all afternoon. It'd been a stressful day.

"You did great, Gina." Elliott's biceps strained against his designer dress shirt as he pulled down the edge of his vest. His forearms bulged from the rolled-up sleeves, something that was not lost on the waitress, who made sure to serve their drinks as close to him as possible.

The young woman bent directly in front of the blond hunk. "Here you are, sir." Her masculine uniform didn't give the server the chance to display her assets, but that didn't stop her from trying to get Elliot's attention.

"Thank you." Elliot leaned back, pulling his black card from his wallet and dropping it on the disappointed waitress' tray. "Now all that is left is to sign the contracts tomorrow." Regina bit back a smile. Though many tried, there was no chance another woman was opening his nose. Bree Grey had him on lock.

The cobalt tie highlighted a pair of twinkling blue eyes that always made Regina feel like things would be okay. He really came through for her, and the way he sat straight like a peacock proved that he knew it.

"Thanks, Elliott, but I can't help feeling like I could've avoided getting bounced around shuttles and cabs. Why did they need me here? It's obvious they'd made their decision before I arrived."

"They did, but some of them wanted to meet you. There's some hard crushing on you in that company." Elliott sat back and swirled the ice cubes in his drink. "Curiosity most likely played a role as well. Some of them probably wanted to make sure that they wouldn't be working with the stereotypical head bobbing, finger snapping angry Black woman." He sipped his drink and bared his teeth. "You know how we White Liberals can be."

"No comment." The friends laughed. Elliot's dimples lightened the stress from Regina's neck. It was really good to see him.

"Don't worry. I'll make sure to usher you out of there once the contracts are signed tomorrow, so you can hang out with Bree and me this weekend." Elliott's eyes flashed. "Then you can get back to New York and your other new venture."

Regina stared at the round art deco lighting fixture shining down on them. "I was waiting for you to bring that up."

"Yeah, it was a given. How serious is it with Simon anyway?"

"I don't know." She met Elliott's skeptical gaze. "Really, everything is all convoluted. When it's just the two of us, it's all good. We talk and laugh, but then the rest of the world gets involved, and it's a mess."

Elliott grinned. "That sounds about right. I read some of the comments under the pictures of you two. Pretty harsh."

"Yeah, if people aren't calling me a traitor for being with an Asian man, they're questioning why a handsome eligible Asian attorney would want to be with a kinky-haired Black woman."

"I hear ya. Everyone and their mother thinks they can have an opinion on whether or not an interracial couple should be together."

"Including *his* mother. The woman can't stand me." Regina squeezed the lime into her bubbling glass of mineral water and told Elliott about being tossed out on her butt.

"Simon just let her throw you out?"

"Please, would I be talkin' about him now if he did? He was passed out in the bedroom sick at the time. I haven't spoken to him since because I was hot tailing it down here. Normally, what she thinks wouldn't matter but—"

"You're in love with her son?" Elliott hiked in the chair on his elbows.

Regina crossed her legs and adjusted the folds of her skirt while trying to bite back a smile. She really couldn't hide much from him. They've had entire conversations through facial expressions, so it wasn't surprising he could see right through her. "Is it that obvious?"

"You haven't stopped beaming since I mentioned his name. I get it though."

"Well, nobody else does, and I'm certain his mother sure as hell doesn't. *She's* definitely not crushing on me. I already told him that I didn't want to come between them."

"That was stupid, and you couldn't."

"Come on, Elliott. Look at the relationship with your family since you married Bree."

Elliott knitted his eyebrows. "You got it backwards, Gina. Bree never came between me and my family." He smoothed his pant leg. "I wouldn't allow my family to get me to toss the woman I loved aside. She never demanded I stay away from them, but they sure as hell commanded me to leave her. If anything, that's what would probably happen. His mother might become hell-bent on getting you out of his life." He squeezed her hand. "Bree is everything to me. I wake up happy knowing I get to spend another day with her. The thought of losing her is unbearable. My family doesn't understand that, which is their problem. I'm not letting go of the most important person to me because of their hang-ups."

"But I've noticed how much you miss them."

"Maybe," Elliot shrugged, "but I would miss Bree and the life we've built even more. Trust me, if Simon feels for you even half of what I feel for her, then he won't allow anyone to interfere with the two of you being together—not even his mother." The sides of Elliott's eye's wrinkled. "Considering how he looked at you in those photos, I strongly suspect that he does."

Regina smiled so wide that her cheeks hurt. The idea that Simon would fight for them filled her heart with hope. He was going to be the first person she saw when she got back to New York. "It'd be great if you were right, Elliott."

"I think I am. The ice in Elliott's glass rattled as he pointed to her. "Don't be surprised to find out that he's been looking for you when you get home."

An icy chill shot down Regina's spine. She squeezed the cold glass as her jaw dropped. It couldn't be real. She gawked at Simon, standing a few feet away, legs spread and arms crossed with an icy stare that bored into her. He strode closer, fists closed and nostrils flared.

Simon stood directly over Elliott. "Gina." He didn't acknowledge her companion's existence. She sat on the edge of her seat. *Why is he so angry? I'm the one that got put out like a call girl.*

"Let me guess." Elliot's voice pierced between them. "He's right behind me?" The tall blond rose. "Simon Young?" Elliott shot out his hand. "It's nice to finally meet you. I'm Elliot Grey, Gina's friend from college. She's told me a lot about you."

Simon sized up Elliott with a steely gaze. He shook hands but remained silent.

"Please, join us."

Regina swallowed hard. She wanted to fly in his arms, but the way Simon glared at her as he approached kept her pinned in her seat. He straddled the chair with his arms and leaned over her. "Hi, Simon." The kiss that kept her from speaking further filled her body with a glorious sensation. He pressed harder; the intensity caused her to sink backward. She laced her free fingers in his hair, not allowing the shock of his unexpected appearance or any onlookers to keep her from reveling in the joy bursting through her.

Simon tore his lips away. The anger had somewhat faded, but it lingered behind the passion in his eyes. "Hello." He walked around and took the seat next to her. A large warm hand replaced the cold glass she was holding and fingertips boldly caressed the back of her quaking knee.

What the hell am I supposed to do now? Regina turned her pounding head to Elliot, who sat back with an ankle on a knee, watching the two of them through half-lowered eyelids. Their gazes met, and Elliott jutted his eyebrows up before his smirk vanished behind his drink. She scowled and turned back to Simon. There would be plenty of time later to make sure he paid for his smugness.

"Simon, what are you doing here?" She couldn't help but grin when he smoothed his lips on the back of her hand.

"I'm here for you."

"I told you," Elliott murmured between sips.

Regina shot him a menacing glance.

"Marcus said you came down her for a job interview," Simon resumed, squeezing her knee. "I wanted us to talk before you made any decisions."

Elliott chuckled. "Oh, he's got it bad."

Regina twisted her body away from Simon. "Are you done?"

"I think I am." Elliott drained his glass and stood with a grunt. He adjusted his vest and pushed his shirt sleeves over his elbows. "You two lovebirds need time alone, and I need to get to my wife and son."

Regina walked into her friend's arms. "I'll be strangling you when I get a chance," she whispered in his ear.

"I'm not scared. Besides, it looks like Mr. Young will have you busy for some time." Elliott stepped back. "I'll see you tomorrow to sign the contracts. You're still spending the weekend with us?"

"Definitely."

"It was a pleasure meeting you, Simon." Elliot strutted down the sunlight-bathed lounge.

Regina shivered at Simon's touch on her arm. She stroked his cheek. "You look better than the last time I saw you."

"Yeah, I had a good nurse." The toughness vanished. Simon blinked slowly and grinned. "Thank you for taking care of me."

"You're welcome." Strong arms surrounded her waist and made space between them nonexistent.

"When I woke up and found you weren't there, my heart sank." He stroked the small of her back. "I thought I dreamt you for a moment, but the reality was worse. I'm so sorry, babe. My mother had no right to—"

"Shh. I don't want to talk about her." She pulled the hairs at the back of his head. "I can't believe you're here." She tried not to giggle like an infatuated high schooler, but it couldn't be helped. "Am *I* dreaming?"

Simon graced her lips with a gentler but equally passionate kiss. "No. I drove down here to beg you not to leave New York—to stay with me. I know it's selfish, but I can't imagine my life without you."

She moved her head back. "Leaving? I'm not leaving New York. I'm only down here because the company is based here in D.C., and they wanted a face-to-face interview. I'll be home by Monday."

A hearty laugh boomed from his throat. "I would've come anyway. I couldn't wait that long to be near you. I just want to be where you are." He glanced over her shoulder. "Is there somewhere we can be alone?"

"I'd like that. Do you have a room here?"

"No. I didn't think I would need one." He pecked the tip of her nose.

"Oh really." She didn't know whether to hug him or punch him for making assumptions about her bed. "What if I decide to send you out into the cold, cruel world?"

"Now, would you really do that to me, Gina?" His playful grin made her heart sing. There was no denying him or herself of what they obviously both wanted.

"Come on." She lifted her bag off the carpet and pulled him by the hand down the wood floors leading to the lobby. It felt like she was floating. The past two weeks were filled with longing to be near the man trailing behind her. *I finally have a chance to block out the whole rotten world and just be with him. Just be.*

Simon stopped their progress at the lobby's revolving doors. "You know what? Since I'm here, let me run and get my bag out of the car first. What's our room number?"

"701. You can't get it later?" Every body part was protesting any potential delay in feeling Simon. Just holding hands caused tingling between her thighs. The bag could wait. She could not.

"Don't worry. I'll be quick."

Regina sighed. "Okay, here," She scrounged through her bag and retrieved a plastic card from a small envelope, "take the second key."

"Be right up." He kissed her cheek and dashed out the revolving door.

🙚 🙚 🙚 🙚

Regina's full lips creased and spread under the makeup wipe she smeared over them until she was sure that every bit of burgundy lipstick was gone. "He just showed up, Toni. I couldn't believe it." She peeled off her top and brought the phone out of the bathroom with her. "He went to get his bag from the car."

"We knew that's where he was heading when he left the apartment." Toni's voice sprang from the phone's speaker. *"When he found out about your interview, he flew like a bat out of hell."*

Regina's breast bounced out of the bra. "Why did you let him think that I was taking a job down here?" She tossed the bra in the suitcase on the hotel stand. Her partially-taut nipples shook as she searched through the contents. An evening of seduction was not in the game plan for this trip, so she'd have to work with the limited options available.

"I wanted to make sure he was properly motivated. He already was on the hunt, but a long drive down I-95 requires a certain amount of urgency."

Back in front of the bathroom mirror, Regina slipped the open-back cream tank top over her body. The sides swished at her hips. Her white panties peaked under the front. *No, not white.* "Well, he looked urgent and angry. He was not pleased to see me talking with Elliott. He stormed up to us like a jealous boyfriend."

"Well, it sounds like that's exactly what he was, with every intent of claiming the woman he loves."

Regina stretched orchid lace panties over her hips and assessed the sexy level of her outfit. "He never said he loved me."

"Are you kidding? Does he really need to? The man barreled down the interstate while recovering from an infection." Toni's laugh echoed off the bright walls. *"Don't be one those desperate women who has to the hear the words to know the feeling exists. Have more confidence. Besides, if he hasn't said it yet, it won't be long."*

"You're right, Toni."

"You know, Gina, it wouldn't hurt for you to tell him."

Regina released her afro puff, fluffed her hair and shook her head. *Lips bare, hair out, scarcely dressed, just the way he likes it.* "That's exactly what I plan on doing, girl. Simon Young is not leaving this hotel room without knowing exactly how I feel."

"I'm sure he doesn't stand a chance."

They laughed "Girl, you need to stop." Regina gasped at the door knob click. "He's here. Bye." She pressed the phone screen and stared out of the bathroom doorway holding her knotted stomach. "Here we go."

"Gina?" Simon rushed by.

She gripped either side of the door jamb and crossed her ankles. "I'm here, Simon." He spun; the bag fell from his shoulder. Breathing through his gaped mouth, he repeatedly ran his gaze over her body. Regina felt an explosion of goosebumps covering her.

He shook his tilted head and raced towards her. Breath rushed from her when he took her in his embrace. Everything she wanted to tell him remained caught in her dry throat, held back by a torrent of emotions. How much she loved him, wanted him, needed him. She pulled his shoulders and pressed her mouth to his. He groaned and swung them around.

The closet's cold glass against her back and buttocks did nothing to cool the heat surging through her. Simon kissed at her neck. Regina yanked his belt open. She wanted him inside her, now. To hell with everyone trying to keep them apart. He was hers.

He raised his head and pinned her gaze. "I love you, Gina. You're the most precious thing in my life." He hungrily rained kisses on her lips and jaw, running them down her neck, shoulder and heaving body. "I feel actual pain when I think I can't be near you. You've been in my mind since I first saw you and my heart from our first kiss."

His hands grasped her bottom. She gasped as her feet left the ground. Her heart soared. Simon loved her as much as she loved him. She looked down at his face, tears falling from her eyes onto his cheeks. "I love you too, Simon. You're everything to me."

He laughed. and walked backward until she straddled him on the bed sprayed with rays from the setting sun. "I won't let anyone or anything come between us. Do you hear me? I'll fight day and night if it means we get to be together."

Regina pulled Simon's shirt over his head and then her own. She explored his chest and torso with her hands while relishing the wondrous taste of his shoulders. "Every piece of me missed you. Wanted you for so long. Just agony." She pushed him back and rolled his body on top of hers, wrapping her legs around his hips. Simon's skin glowed in the light bathing them from the window. "Make love to me, Simon. It's been forever."

Both the sun and moon set before they tired.

27 - CONDOM BREAK

SIMON OPENED HIS WEARY EYES. The rest of his limbs rebelled against any movement as he rolled and saw his love's beautiful shoulder and back. He lifted on his elbow, traced down her spine and caught his lips between his teeth as goosebumps spread across her brown skin. So lovely. Nothing was going to keep him from having her always. He braced Regina's hip and aligned his body near hers. "'morning, babe." Half-aroused, he nibbled at her shoulder. "Are you awake?" They'd spent the night with their bodies entangled in bouts of erotic frenzy until sheer exhaustion required them to rest. But the little sleep he'd gotten only refueled his desire for her.

He reached around Regina's stretching body and cupped her breast. His thumb went to work on the nipple. The sensual sigh and snicker escaping her lips fanned the flames of his lust. "Obviously you are, Young." The warm fingers surrounding him made his stiffness jerk and harden even more. "After all we did last night, what does it take to satiate you?" she asked with ragged breath.

Simon lined his stiffness along the cleft of her plump rump. "You, and it's a new day." He stroked her hair down and caught her ear lobe between his lips. It was so satisfying to know that he was the reason for its puffiness. Each sweat-shrunken coil testified to the numerous times he made her tremble, moan and cry out. "When do you have to leave for your meeting?"

Regina reached for her phone. "Not for a while. It's early."

"See, even time is on our side." Her stomach shuddered under his touch. He wanted more of her, so much more. Simon reached his hand into his dearest's soft folds. "I want you, Gina."

Regina sucked air through her teeth. Her thighs clamped around Simon's fingers. "I'm a little sore."

He gently pulled his hand away, fell on his back and exhaled. "It's okay. I don't want to hurt you." The notification chime caught his attention.

Corella: *Hi, Simon. I emailed you the itinerary for your flight. You're scheduled to leave JFK tonight at 11:30 pm.*

He put the phone face-down on the bed. *I just got Regina back in my arms. How can I tell her that I have to leave?* It was insane to think about letting this chance slip through his fingers, but the thought of being a world away from her was unbearable. He hated when the East River separated them, let alone oceans and continents.

"Hey." Air rushed out of his lungs. Regina dropped her chest on his and glided her fingers along his shoulder. "I said I was a little sore." She covered his mouth and held him again. Everything hurried out of his mind but her. "I just need you to be gentle."

"I can do that." He dashed across the room and rustled through his bag sitting on the hotel dresser. He took out a string of small packages and the silver ring box. *Do it now. You have to do it now.* He turned and faced Regina, hiding the box behind his back. She was balancing on an elbow, watching him lovingly. *We don't have a whole lot of time, and there is no way I'm crossing the Atlantic without this ring on her finger.*

Regina shook her head and laughed. "Damn, Young. How many of those do you have?"

"Enough for the amount of making up I had in mind." He laid the string across the night stand and slipped in under the blanket she held up for him. Her afro tickled his cheek as she cuddled on his chest. Simon closed his eyes and sucked in a deep breath through his teeth. Her hand was already under the blanket touching all the right places. *Get a grip and ask her.* "Gina?"

"Mmm-hmm?"

He took the roaming hand in his. "I love you so much."

"I love you too, Simon."

He touched her back with the box. "I want to ask you something."

She squirmed and wrenched her head to her shoulder. "Wha-What's that?" Her eyes shined and glistened when he held the box before them. "Oh, Simon."

"I bought it just before the firm's party." He opened the box. "I knew from the moment I saw you that I wanted to share everything with you. It didn't take long before you became my everything to me, Gina." The diamonds glistened in the morning light. Simon slipped the ring on her trembling finger and kissed her knuckles. "Will you marry me?"

"Yes." She pulled his lips to hers.

He ripped a packet off the string on the night stand and turned to hold his fiancé. He glanced down for a moment then caught her gaze and gently filled her soft folds until her eyes fluttered closed.

Regina bent her head back, allowing Simon to feel the moan echoing through her throat with his lips. One leg hooked his hip and a heel pushed him deeper inside her warmth. "Yes, Simon." He grazed her lips with his thumb. Regina closed her mouth around it and sucked so hard that it shot down to his toes.

Thinking about her soreness, Simon read cues from Regina's body to determine how fast and hard he would go. Eventually, slow, determined strokes became harder, and their hips crashed together until they both cried out in ecstasy.

Their limbs entangled, he spiraled back down to reality, holding the woman he loved. Simon closed his eyes and smiled while Regina wiped the sweat off his forehead. Things were the way they should be. His breathing had just steadied when the alarm on his phone chimed. He groaned as he moved from the magnificent embrace that filled his heart with joy. "I've got to take my medicine."

Regina settled under the billowing blankets he flipped over her. "Hurry back."

He shuddered when the cold tiles prickled his bare feet. Turning on the light, Simon ran the sink and opened his palm. *Shit.* A chill shot through all his extremities. *No, this can't be happening.* Tan skin peeked through the tip of the torn white latex condom. The shocked face staring back at him in the mirror was little help. He looked at the hair and skin care products strewn across the vanity. *I've gotta tell Gina.*

He returned to the side of the bed. Regina was breathing softly, neck-deep in bleached linens. "Gina," he whispered and sat on the bed, putting a hand on her hip.

She raised her eyebrows and snuggled a little deeper under the blankets. "What's up, Young?" Her languid tone made him even more hesitant to share his discovery, but she had to know right away.

He took a deep breath. "The condom broke."

Her lids flew open. Dilated pupils of wide brown eyes stared at him. "Are you sure?" She raised on her elbows and slammed them shut. "Yeah," she shot through clenched teeth, "it did."

Her brown bottom jiggling away was the last thing Simon saw before the bathroom door slammed and the hum of shower water drifted into the room. "Is there anything I can do?" Simon leaned against the door jamb and kneaded his tense shoulder muscles. Here was yet another thing for them to contend with as a couple. God was keeping them on their toes.

The air rushed past his naked body. Regina clutched a towel around her "All right." Wet coils dripped on her shoulders as she paced in front of the hotel window sliding fingers across her phone screen. "I'll need to find a pharmacy and buy one of those emergency contraception pills."

Wow, she's working damn hard to prevent pregnancy. I wonder if she even wants my baby? Simon shook his head. The irrational thoughts coursing through his mind weren't helping the situation. He strode into the bathroom. "Okay, let me get ready."

"Leave the door open." Regina pulled a pair of black slacks over her hips. "I need to do my hair."

🐾🐾🐾🐾

Regina let Simon guide her through the crowd while she studied the arrow on her phone. "We need to make a left," she announced at the stop light. His arm rested around her shoulders, Simon looked pensive as his head oscillated with the cars whizzing by. It was understandable. The thought of a baby terrified her too. Things were

~ 210 ~

already at lighting speed for them and with a ton of accompanying drama. *Where the hell is this pharmacy? My nerves can't take much more.*

Ironically or luckily, the pharmacy was on the same block where she had to be to sign her contracts. Cool air washed over her as she stepped through the automatic doors. She had a little over a half hour to meet Elliott, and the summer heat already had her crisp, white blouse with black trim wilting. "Can you get me some water, Simon?"

"Sure." His lips formed a tense smile. He disappeared down an aisle. *What's eating him?*

Regina bit her lip and scanned her surroundings. "Where's that pharmacist?" Big red letters at the back of the store led her way. She approached the counter and a tall, young redhead in a lab coat. "Hi," She tried to sound as matter-of-fact as possible, "I'm looking for emergency contraception."

The technician offered a friendly smile and bent slightly over the counter. "Sure, they're right over there."

"Thanks." Regina was already skimming the package directions when she met Simon at the front of the store.

"Hey, why didn't you wait for me to go with you?"

She continued to squint at the tiny print on the thin slip of paper. "Because, I prefer that we not look like two guilty teenagers the morning after prom."

His laughter bloomed around them. "I can respect that." He took the package and paid for it.

Regina shoved the paper in her pocket and retrieved her phone.

Elliott: *You almost here?*

Regina: *I'm in the pharmacy across the street. Don't ask.*

Elliott: *Oh, but you know I will.*

It was going to be good to talk to Elliott and Bree about it. They'd be able to put a light spin on one of the most harrowing experiences of her life. *A bunch of internet trolls pale in comparison to trying not to get knocked up by my boyfriend.* She gazed at the sparkling diamonds on her finger. *Fiancée.*

Regina continued to drink the cool water long after the pill washed down and their feet hit the sidewalk. She waved back at Elliott, who stood across the street. "There's Elliott." She hugged Simon's waist. "This shouldn't take long. Do you want to meet back at the hotel and then do something?"

"Actually, Gina." Simon caressed her cheeks and kissed her. "I have to head back to New York."

"What? Why so soon?"

"You remember me talking about Rameez Baig? He asked me to join him on another case."

"So, of course, you accepted." She smiled brightly despite the pain gripping her heart. *Stupid Rameez Baig.* "It sounds like a great opportunity. I'm happy for you." She hugged him tighter.

"It is, and I'm sorry to just drop this on you."

"It's okay." She leaned back. "I'll just see you when I get back."

He stared down at the pavement. "The thing is, I have to get back to catch a flight to Singapore."

"Excuse me? Did you say Singapore?"

"Yeah. I have to be there by Sunday."

She rested her head on his shoulder and squeezed harder. *It's important to be mature and supportive.* She resisted the urge to kick and scream and demand he stay with her. "I understand. How long will you be gone?"

"Eight weeks."

Eight weeks? Oh, hell no, Young. I'll miss you way too much. How can you just leave me? You just said you loved me, and now you're flying off to the other side of the world? This is bullshit. "That's such a long time." She splayed her hands on his back. "But, we'll make it work." *Please, don't go.*

"Excuse me," Elliot's voice came from behind. "I hate to break up you two love birds, but Gina and I have business to settle."

She lifted her head and claimed her fiancé's lips. Salty tears mixed with the sweetness of his mouth. It was too soon to say goodbye. She ripped her lips and turned towards her friend's voice, but Simon drew her back in his arms.

Yearning sprung inside her from his kiss and plunged her heart into an abyss. How was she expected to live or even breathe without him? His forehead touched hers. "I'll be back as soon as possible. I won't let a moment pass that'll keep you from me."

Air and sunlight swept over Regina. Heartbreak wrapped her in a cocoon of sadness. She stared at the throngs of people hurrying past her sides. She jumped at a hand touching her shoulder and spun. A confused Elliot towered over her. She caught his gaze. The crinkle in his nose softened. She let him wrap his long arms around her and laid her head on his massive chest. She needed her friend now more than ever.

28 – BOARDROOM

RIGHT, I THINK WE CAN SETTLE EVERYTHING this evening." Balancing his weight on one leg and hands on his hips, light from the window behind filtered around Rameez's tall frame and brightened his pale blue dress shirt. "Simon ran some great ideas by me last night that I think just might satisfy all with a vested interest in finalizing this deal."

Simon inhaled. He'd spent over two months working to show the junior partner that he had what it took to be one of the firm's top attorneys, and it was paying off. Rameez asked his advice more and allowed him to lead some of the meetings. He walked to his boss, who then sat further down the long boardroom table. "Thanks, Rameez." Simon sat and flipped open the black folder in front of him, cuing everyone else to do the same with theirs. "There're just a few sticking points that's keeping us from closing this deal. Let's start with page 127."

All heads sprang up and eyes fell on Simon. "Sorry." He leaned back into the soft leather and reached into his pant pocket to stop the familiar ringtone. "It's my fiancée in New York. We'd planned to talk at this time." Heat rushed through his neck and face. His gaze landed on Rameez, who nodded and slowly blinked. Simon held his finger up and flashed a sheepish smile at the parallel rows of suits. "Excuse me for one moment." He bent his head. "Hi, Gina."

"Simon. It's so good to hear your voice. I've missed it."

Her honeyed drawl awoke parts of him inappropriate for the present setting. "Yeah, me too. Can I call you back?"

"What? Why? Isn't this the time I was supposed to call?"

"Yes, but I'm in a meeting that's running a late." He looked to confirm his suspicion that he had everyone's attention. "We should be done in about an hour."

"Oh, I understand. You finish your meeting. I'll just lay here in your bed and wait for you to call back."

Clearing his throat, he turned the chair away from his audience and rose. "I'm sorry, can you repeat that?" he asked in the most professional tone he could muster.

"Your bed. I missed you so much that I came to your place. I hope that's okay."

"Of, course." Brilliant rays streamed between tall buildings and bounced across the skyline. It was beautiful, but he longed to be in a different city—the one where the woman he loved was lying in his bed.

"Good. I didn't think you'd mind. I also put on one of your shirts so I could have your scent near me."

"That's fine."

"Wanna see? I sent you a picture."

The phone buzzed into his ear. A warm sensation ran down his body. Regina's slightly-parted lips and dazzling eyes made him need air. She'd rolled the sleeves of his white dress shirt to her elbows and left the front unbuttoned, revealing a glimpse of her breasts and torso before puddling at her long, crossed legs. *Damn.* She was spectacular. He had to have her soon. He closed his eyes and brought the phone back to his ear. "That's good. Thank you."

"You like it?"

"Very much." He glanced back at the table. All eyes were still on him. "I gotta go."

"Yeah. You're busy. I've distracted you too much." The sound of Regina stretching and yawning drifted from the phone. *"Maybe I should just get dressed. Being in this bed, thinking about you, just makes me hot and bothered. I don't know what to do with myself."*

"No, no need to do that. Just wait until I call back."

"If you think that's best, Simon. I want to make you happy."

He stretched his neck. She was using her "obedient woman" tone to drive him crazy with desire. She wasn't making it easy to hang up, something she'd become skillful at doing over their extended time apart. "I do. I'll take care of everything."

"Okay. Bye."

Simon returned to his seat. "Again, I'm sorry for the interruption." He set his phone on the table. Heart racing, Regina's sensual image dominated his mind while he flipped through the papers. "Let's return to page, umm—"

"127." Rameez caught his gaze and then looked down with a smirk. "Are you sure you don't want some water, Simon?"

Simon continued to turn the pages. "No, I'm good. Now, page 127." His phone buzzed and another suggestive image appeared.

A small grunt emitted from the man sitting to his right, who'd caught sight of Regina lying on her back with the shirt fallen to her sides, barely covering her nipples. His eyes opened into spheres, and he grabbed the phone before Simon had a chance. *"That's* your fiancée?" He lifted his glasses to his forehead and held the phone close.

"Yes, sir." Simon stretched his hand It was ignored. "Please, may I have it?" He almost snatched it out of the pervert's grip, but there was his career to think about.

"Oh, yes. Here you go." The man smiled until his eyes were slits. His body shook with a chuckle, chair squeaking as he turned to the others. "Let's get this young man back to his phone call." The entire room exploded with laughter.

Simon peeped sideways at the gray-stripped carpet and shoved the phone in his pocket. The abundance of ceiling-to-wall windows behind him and along one side of the room didn't keep it from closing in on him. The idea that another man ogled even a picture of Regina, his Gina, pricked at his nerves—as did being the butt of the room joke.

The situation even garnered a smile from Rameez, who reclined in his seat and watched his acolyte squirm. He eventually straightened and flicked a pen he took from the table in his hand. "Shall we let Mr. Young off the hook and allow him to give us his suggestions?"

Everyone complied with Rameez's recommendation. The room stilled, and Simon returned everyone's attention away from his half-naked fiancée and to the business at hand.

The rest of the meeting went well. Simon and Rameez worked seamlessly as a team. It wasn't long before all parties were satisfied and ready to move forward. The two of them then spent some time talking with people as the room slowly emptied.

"You did a great job, Simon." Rameez walked around the row of abandoned leather swivel chairs and patted him on the back. "How about dinner? Oh, wait." He rubbed his long-stubble beard. "You have an important call to get back to, right?"

Simon crossed his arms and shifted his weight. "Thanks, and I'm sorry about that."

Rameez filled the room with a bout of laughter. "Hey, it broke the tension, didn't it? So, glass half-full." He prodded Simon to the door and down the hall.

The two men entered the empty elevator studying their phones. "How long have you been engaged?"

"How long have I been here?" Simon leaned against the back of the elevator and scanned his surroundings. Longing clenched his chest. He was lucky Regina hadn't thrown the ring back at him right there on the D.C. streets when he told her he was leaving. They'd been engaged less than three hours before work separated them. A project expected to be eight weeks turned into more than ten. Fortunately for Simon, she was bearing everything a lot more patiently than he.

"Seriously? You got engaged and then flew here?" Rameez continued pushing at the screen of his phone.

"Basically. I was on my way to propose when you called. That's why I needed another day."

"I didn't know. I appreciate how hard that must've been. *As salam Alaykum.*" He walked towards the front of the elevator and continued his phone conversation in Urdu. The tone in his voice made it clear that it wasn't a business call. His smile when he turned confirmed it. Simon couldn't understand a word of the language, but he recognized a few English ones like "engaged," "New York" and "unbelievable."

Simon's phone grabbed his attention.

Regina: *Almost done? I'm falling asleep.*

Simon: *Can you hang on a little longer? I'll make it worth your while…and mine. Btw, no more sexy pics. Someone saw one.*

Regina: *I guess you better be more careful about who has access to your phone.*

The notification light flashed in the corner. Simon couldn't help but smile and open the latest piece of titillation. Like the others, it didn't disappoint.

Simon: *Continue to be naughty, and I'll have to punish you.*

Regina: *Promise?*

He raised his eyebrows. She was not usually the type to send sensual pictures or be so suggestive in her texts, but their time apart changed that. The things she normally reserved for when he was front, center and rock-hard took the form of erotic messages. He responded in-kind, but it increasingly made it harder to be apart. Any more time away from her would kill him.

"*Wa alaykum salam, jaan.*" Rameez tucked his phone in his dress shirt pocket and swayed with the halting elevator. "Well, my wife has ordered me to let you leave for New York immediately." He disappeared into parking garage.

Simon's shoes clicked against the concrete as he lightly jogged to catch up to Rameez. "I'm sorry? Your wife what?"

"She wants me to let you go home. She thinks I'm a monster for keeping two people in love apart for so long."

"It's my job." A message notification binged.

Rameez stopped and turned. "And you've been great at it, which is why I chose you, but I can handle things from here. Besides, there's some ground work for another case I want you to do in New York before I return. So, you can catch a flight back to your fiancée and make my wife happy." He opened the rental car trunk and dropped his message bag inside.

Simon set his backpack next to it. "Really, Rameez, I can stay and finish whatever work needs to be done."

"You don't miss—-Regina, right?"

"Yes, and very much." Another ding.

Rameez shut the trunk and fumbled with the fob. "Then it's settled. You go to Regina, and Dilshad will come here." The usually stoic attorney's face lit when he mentioned the name.

"Your wife's coming here?" Simon peered over the black sedan. Things were getting more confusing.

Rameez swung the door open and shot his eyebrows upward. "Yup." He leaned against the roof of the car with his hands. "I've been trying to get her to visit for weeks, but she didn't want to leave the kids and overwhelm the nanny. I told her your lovesick sob story, and she demanded I let you go, which means I have stay longer," Rameez held his hand against his chest, "all alone." He shot his finger at Simon. "You were just what I needed. She's booking a flight as we speak."

They settled into the car. Rameez started the engine, grinning at Simon. "You get your fiancée. I get my wife." He pulled out of the parking stall. Sunlight filled the car as he drove into the Singapore street.

Simon read the thread of messages from Regina, each expressed an increasing irritation.

Simon: *I'm sorry. Something came up.*

Regina: *Everything okay?*

Simon: *I need to talk with Rameez. I think you should go to sleep. I'm sorry.*

Regina: *You owe me, Young.*

Simon: *More than you know. I love you.*

"I'm telling you, Simon," Rameez shifted gears, "I plan on keeping her to myself for as long as possible."

"Huh?" Simon closed the message app. "Yeah." The car went silent, and he busied himself checking flight times for New York.

29 - RED LINE

"NO, MA." REGINA CRANED HER NECK over the refrigerator and yelled at the phone on the counter. "Simon and I don't want a big wedding." Her stomach growled and then churned at the sight of the *kimchi* jars. *Why did I decide stay here?* The apartment made her feel closer to Simon while he was in Singapore, but the food selection left a lot to be desired. Exhaustion overwhelmed her the past few weeks, so shopping was out of the question, until now. *Eggs. I want eggs.*

"I understand, Regina. Your father and I want you to be happy, but ever since word of your engagement got out, a lot of people have hinted about wedding invites."

"I'm sure they have, but dad's business associates and your colleagues will have to simply deal with the disappointment of not attending." She eyed the bottle of water after drinking from it. This must be old. "Except Professor Murphy. I like her."

"She's on the list. I really think you need to reconsider the venue."

"Sorry. I've wanted to get married in the gazebo since I was a little girl. It's were I had my first pretend wedding with Mateo." Memories of Mateo's wet kiss on her cheek flooded her mind. Simon, of course, would give her a better one. "Besides, things are complicated enough with you demanding Reverend Banes officiate with Judge Kelly."

"Reverend Banes is our family clergy. He baptized you. How could you expect him not to marry you?"

"And Judge Kelly was Simon's father's best friend who watched over him after his dad died. We've been over this, ma, and you both get what you want." Regina leaned back and scrutinized each cabinet as she opened them. They didn't offer any way to curb the hunger or nausea. "What I want is to keep things as modest as possible. The backyard is over an acre. You can certainly fit more than enough people."

"I'll do my best. Simon's guest list isn't very long, so we can take from his side."

Regina went into the bedroom and pulled one of Simon's sweatshirt over her head. She'd developed a habit of wearing them the past few days. "Yeah, he didn't invite many of them. Most of his mother's family lives outside the country and as for his father's," she jumped and pulled to clasp her jean's over her bulging belly, "let's just say that Simon closed the subject." *I haven't even been eating. How the hell am I gaining weight?*

"Subject closed. I'll send you the list to finalize before it goes off to the caterer."

Regina left the front of her jeans open and pulled the sweatshirt over them. *It's time to arrange some visits to the gym with Toni or else Simon will come back to more of me than he expects.* "Sounds good, ma."

"Now, did you two decide on the honeymoon?"

She grabbed the keys off the counter. There were eggs to be had. Her stomached demanded them. "Yes, we wanna go to the Caribbean, but the dates are shaky. They may need him at the firm right after the wedding, so we'll have to save the honeymoon for later." She strode out the apartment door, pausing to brace herself against the wall before trudging down the hall.

"Just make sure you schedule it around your period. You don't want your honeymoon ruined."

Regina stopped halfway to the elevator. She swallowed hard and panted as fast as her racing heart. *My period? When was the last time I even had it?* She was never one to put little dots on a calendar, and with everything swimming around her—haters, a new job, a wedding, and her fiancé an ocean away—keeping track of her monthly "friend" was not on the agenda, until now. "Okay, ma. I'll make sure." She tried to control the trembling in her voice.

"Is everything all right?"

She gripped her forehead and swung back towards the apartment. "Umm, yeah, ma." *It couldn't have been that long ago.* Regina bit her lip and switched directions back to the elevator. "I have to go." Nerves, nausea and plain fear made her head spin. She fell against the wall and dropped the phone by her side. Squeezing her eyes shut, she back tracked over the months of making love to Simon and times she couldn't. The reasons were few, Instagram, Marcus, illness, Singapore. The last time she'd remembered having to turn her amorous lover down because of biology was a few days during the week of the cocktail party. That would mean... She stared at the ceiling as a myriad of calculations and dates swished inside her head.

She pushed off the wall and braced herself back against it, waiting for everything to stop spinning. "You're being dramatic." The hall and empty elevator became her audience. "You used condoms every time." She closed her eyes. "Oh, no. The last time we were together the friggin' thing broke, but I took that pill." Regina's earrings hit the sides of her shaking head. "Just take a test and get back to being scared about real stuff."

ରଙ ରଙ ରଙ ରଙ

The pink box landed with a tiny thump on the marble bathroom counter. Regina tilted the long slip of paper towards the overhead vanity lights and held a bunch of coiffed coils in her fist. For the second time in some months, she squinted at fine-print instructions from a package that held her life in the balance. "Put the tip in urine for five seconds," she mumbled while holding one corner of her bottom lip between her teeth, "wait three minutes?" Things rattled inside the bathroom draws she flew open while searching for something to pee in to find out if everything was about to drastically change. She slammed the last one shut and leaned on the vanity holding the pregnancy test instructions in one hand and the tortuous white stick in the other. "Nothing. I shoulda went back to my apartment."

She raced into the kitchen. Her chest panged with guilt as she took a sparkling square drinking glass from the complete set of Simon's pristine cabinet. Casualties were necessary. After counting the required time, she capped the test and swiped her phone to set the timer for three minutes. It wasn't necessary. Two red lines appeared in the tiny window before the app opened on the screen. She set the phone down next to the test.

The stick rattled on the vanity, shaking from her weight as she braced herself on it and stared at the matching tile floor. "Son of a bitch." She glared at the two lines mocking her then jumped at the buzzing doorbell and the phone's vibration resounding through the bathroom. Hairs stood on the back of her neck at the words on the screen.

Simon: *Hey, babe. It's me. Open the door!*

Her astonished face gawked back at her in the mirror. "You gotta be kidding me." She slowly walked towards the door.

"Gina?" Simon's muffled voice passed into the quiet apartment.

She squealed and rushed to unlatch the door. "Simon?" She threw her arms over the pillow around his neck. "You're home?"

Simon dropped his bag and grabbed the door jamb. "I'm home." He balanced and drew her closer. "Rameez took pity on me," he said between kisses, "and asked that I get some work done in New York." Strong hands pressed her against her beloved's chest. "So, I booked the next flight back and got the hell out of there." Regina's heart quickened as soft lips tickled her neck and her fiancé's hands squeezed her round bottom.

Her head swirled with a befuddling mix of disbelief and passion. "But, why didn't you let me know?"

Simon dragged the large suitcase into the apartment on its wheels with one hand and carried shopping bags with the other. He left everything in front of the closed door along with his coat and gathered her back into his arms. "Surprise. Now," he lifted the hem of her sweatshirt while walking deeper into the apartment, "I've been waiting for months to get you in bed." The sweatshirt fell to the floor. He pecked the soft mounds of her breasts. "And if I remember correctly, you are in line for some punishment." He seemed determined to keep his lips on some part of her body. Lips, face, neck, shoulders and breast all tingled from his intoxicating caresses and nips.

Giggling each time he led her into another piece of furniture, she finally stopped their progress. "Why don't I just turn around?"

"Or," he lifted and straddled her thighs around his waist. "We can do this." He strode into the bedroom and fell with her on the bed. Clothes cascaded to the wood floor, and the two were soon entwined in a long-awaited embrace. Simon stroked her coils. "I've missed you so much."

Regina closed her eyes and reveled in his caresses. "Me too."

He turned to the nightstand and opened the drawer. "Ah, no condoms?" He kissed her shoulder. "I think there are some in the bathroom. I'll be right back."

Regina's eyes flew open. The test! "No." She bolted straight and pulled a confused Simon back down on the bed. "No," she smiled and rubbed his chest, "I can get them. I want to freshen up a little more anyway." She slid off the bed.

He pulled her hips. "No, Gina," he moaned burying his forehead in her abdomen, gliding his nose from side to side, "I want to smell and taste you, not a bunch of perfume."

She clutched his shoulders and leaned her head back. He could make her forget everything with a few words or a single touch. She pushed away and backed into the hallway. "Don't worry. You won't." Once in the bathroom, Regina looked at the two red lines. *Maybe I should tell him now? Oh, we don't need condoms. You already knocked me up.*

Her heart jumped at the sound of creaking from the bed and Simon's footsteps. "Gina? Is everything okay?"

"Yeah, everything's fine." She shoved the test and instructions in the box and buried them in the back of the bottom draw, ironically on the huge box of condoms. She pulled a few out. *I can't tell him now. All I want to do is be in his arms.*

"Let's go, woman."

She pointed at her reflection. "Shut up." She dashed out of the bathroom. "I'm coming."

ૠૠૠૠ

Regina shivered and wiped the drops of water cascading down her neck from her wet hair. She tied all but the front mass of coils in a tight bun and tucked them under a silk scarf and cap. Simon stirred in the bed. She let out a sigh when he stilled and his chest rose and fell. She'd managed to arrange meeting Toni for breakfast and couldn't risk waking the slumbering ball of libido. He'd insist that she return to bed, an offer she would be hesitant to refuse even with morning sickness.

I gotta get out of this bedroom and somewhere I can think. Regina grazed her lips against Simon's cheek and slipped away.

ૠૠૠૠ

Ten minutes later, she slumped against the diner's door. Aromas greeted her nose and caused renewed waves of nausea that had waned when she got off the rocky subway. She closed her eyes and pressed her head against the cold glass. Life sucked.

"Gina." Toni waved at her from a booth all the way at the other end of the diner.

The black and white tile pattern on the floor added dizziness to the nausea. She trudged between people perched on padded chrome stools at the counter and eating at booths, shielded from the morning sun by a blue-striped awning outside the row of windows. "Hey." She plopped on the burgundy vinyl and closed her eyes.

"I hope this breakfast emergency is urgent enough to justify leaving my warm bed and hot husband." Toni's spoon clinking against the steaming mug assaulted Regina's ears.

"Yeah, thanks for coming." Regina scanned the table for the offending odor making her empty stomach roll. "I need to eat something." She raised her hand then massaged her aching shoulder. A result of some creative positions the previous night.

Toni reached across the table. "Are you okay?"

Regina held Toni's hands and leaned forward on her elbows. "I'm pregnant." She looked at the waitress. "I'll have eggs, scrambled, toast, no butter and coffee, thank you."

Toni shot straight and blinked repeatedly. "Are you serious?"

"I took a test, and it came out positive. So, yeah, pretty serious." Regina thanked the waitress and stirred the coffee with her shaky hand. "On top of that, while I'm reading the damn thing, Simon arrives back from Singapore and starts knocking on the front door."

"You're kidding."

"I wish I were. They let him come back to New York to do some work here. He decided to surprise me by taking the first possible flight home." The shaking mug rattled against her teeth. She wrinkled her nose at the metallic taste the coffee left as it washed past her tongue and down her throat. Her stomach wasn't too thrilled with the brew either. "Excuse me." The young waitress approached the table. "Is this coffee fresh?"

"Yes, ma'am."

"Well, is it okay if I have a fresh cup?"

"Sure." The waitress swooped up the vile drink and walked away. Regina massaged her temples. The flashes of light behind her eyelids were harbingers of a major headache, one she was not prepared to deal with or anything else for that matter.

"Did you tell him?"

Her shoulders slumped and mouth fell open. "How, girl? How was I supposed to tell him? I'd just found out myself. Besides, he was too busy carrying me into the bedroom and trying to get me naked as quickly as possible."

"I'm sure he was." A chuckle escaped Toni's lips just before she sipped tea from the mug held between her delicate hands. "He was gone for three months. That's a lot of sexual frustration."

Before any semblance of a comeback came to mind, the waitress returned and set down their breakfasts. She placed a new mug of coffee before Regina. "Here you go, ma'am. I made a new pot."

"Thank you." Regina sipped and curled her lips. *It tastes as gross as the last one. I don't know how I'm gonna live like this for months and not starve to death.* "May I have a glass of water with lemon?"

The waitress smiled. "Absolutely." She spun on the heels of her white slip-resistant shoes and walked behind the counter with so much pep that her pony tail bounced.

Regina poked at the puffy mounds of yellow with a fork. "It can't be right." She immediately regretted holding a forkful of eggs under her nose and clamped her hand over her mouth while her abdomen convulsed. Body and life were completely out of her control. Peace, security and a decent plate of eggs were all unattainable. "Excuse me." Regina raised her hand and pushed the offensive fare to the middle of the table. She maintained Toni's gaze. "I must've taken it wrong or something. We used protection every time." She gazed at the waitress with doleful eyes. "I'm so sorry, but may I have eggs without pepper in them?"

"I don't think there's pepper in the eggs, ma'am." The strain of impatience in the waitress voice was apparent. "But, I'll ask the cook."

"No." Regina wiped her forehead. "Can I just get some oatmeal? Just plain oatmeal with nothing in it."

The eggs jumped in the plate as it was snatched off the table. "Right away."

Toni turned her head to follow the waitress stomping away. "Yeah, it could be wrong, but they rarely are." She bent her head over the cup of tea. "I've learned that over the past year."

Regina jammed her hands between her thighs and stared out the window. It was the only safe place to look. The floor pattern and food on the table along with the guilt gnawing in her gut from Toni's hurt expression threatened her ability to keep from hurling. "I'm sorry, girl. I shouldn't be talking to you about this."

Toni's forced smile only made thing worse. "Of course, you should. Who else would you tell? Your mother?"

Regina closed her eyes to the flurry of pedestrians on the other side of the window. Adrian Kent was not going to be pleased at the news that her only daughter was becoming a statistic. Her mother and father had strong convictions about children being raised in two-parent homes. Marriage was an automatic, especially when a baby was involved. "Shit."

"Exactly, or would you tell Marcus?"

She raised her hand in defeat. "Okay, point taken. I'm not ready to tell any of them about this. At least not yet."

"I know you aren't." Toni reached for her hand. "Don't worry about me. Marcus and I had long conversations after the last treatment failed. He's content with not having children, and eventually, I'll be too."

Regina sniffed and wiped the drops escaping her eyes. "I'm glad to hear that. I couldn't bear it if you guys broke up."

Toni handed her a napkin and took one for herself. "Well that's not happening. I can't let a possibility ruin the wonderful sure thing I have with him."

"Good, because as much as I love my brother, you're the only reason I can even deal with him." The friends sniffed and laughed then sat quietly for a few minutes.

"When will you be ready to tell Simon?"

"Not today. First, I'll make an appointment to confirm that I'm in fact pregnant."

"Then?"

Regina glanced at the steaming oatmeal laid before her and then the waitress standing with one hand on her hip.

"Damned if I know."

30 - Skinny Girls' Pill

REGINA RUBBED HER GOOSE PIMPLY ARM as she glared at the pregnant woman blissfully standing in a meadow, appearing content in her maternity. Dr. Algiers's office wall was full of similar posters hanging between shelves of books and small photos of happy new mothers. *Lying bitches.*

Her introduction into the world of motherhood had been less than delightful. After the obstetrician confirmed that the little red lines were not a result of factory malfunction but a bona fide pregnancy, she endured a slew of tests. Vials upon vials of blood drawn, breasts squeezed. Her torture ended with the mother of all pelvic exams. Dr. Algiers was obviously making her pay for missing the last annual checkup.

Balancing the stack of pamphlets and information sheets the nurse with an irritatingly bright smile passed off to her, Regina instinctively crossed her legs, remembering the intrusive instruments passing into her nether regions. There was so much to learn. *How am I gonna make it through this pregnancy? How am I gonna tell Simon?*

"Okay, Regina." Dr. Algiers entered her office. The striking woman in the lab coat glided across the room while reading the contents of a manila folder with color codes and letters running down one side. "Given the information you provided us about your last menstruation," she continued and pulled out a small paper wheel from her lab coat pocket, "I would say you are about 13 weeks, almost 14." Dr. Algiers's smile did nothing to perk up Regina's somber mood.

Why is everyone in this Goddamn office smiling? Don't they know my life is careening off a cliff? "I'm still not sure how this happened."

"I'm pretty sure you know how it happened." Dr. Algiers shot Regina a sardonic glance. "Perhaps if you hadn't missed your last annual, we could've discussed birth control methods." The obstetrician's ability to remain professional while sticking it to her was both admirable and infuriating.

"That's the thing. We did, my fiancée and I, did use birth control, condoms. One broke once, but when we realized, we went to the pharmacy for one of those birth prevention pills."

"You took the pill within 24 hours?" Dr. Algiers began reexamining the contents of Regina's file.

"Yes, right away." Regina wiped the sweat from her forehead. *How was it possible to be cold and sweating at the same time? Nothing happening makes any sense.* She leaned towards the desk, tapping her foot to the sound of rustling papers.

"Um, Regina. I understand you're perplexed, but I've determined why you're currently pregnant despite your precautions. No birth control method is 100%, and the pill you took is only 95% effective under the most perfect circumstances. The pill's effectiveness lessens for a variety of factors, one of them being weight."

"Say what now?" Regina sat erect. "Are you implying that I'm obese?"

"Now," Dr. Algiers stretched her arm and patted the desk, "I'm not saying you're overweight. You're within the normal range for a woman of your height and build. Unfortunately, the pill you used won't work for a woman your weight."

"Are you telling me it's a skinny girl's pill?"

She folded her hands over the chart. "Basically, yes. There're a lot of women for whom the pill will not work. I'm surprised the instructions didn't indicate that."

"Yeah, go figure." Regina's gaze shifted to the information packet in her hand. The picture of yet another serene pregnant woman in profile pose mocked her for her carelessness. "Maybe I didn't read all of the instructions."

"I see." Dr. Algiers's tone softened. "Look, you need to concentrate on having a healthy pregnancy, which means a healthy diet, rest, moderate exercise, and coming to your appointments."

"Yes, Dr. Algiers." It was like sitting in the principal's office. She took a prescription for prenatal vitamins, and vaguely heard the doctor say something about the softening of stool. Reality crushed her like a load of bricks. A baby was coming, her baby, and the father had no clue about it.

ᔑᔑᔑᔑ

The busy city street gave no solace for Regina's racked nerves. People scurried around while her stomach turned as a mixture of street cart food and exhaust fumes invaded her nose. She answered her phone. "Hey, Toni."

"*Well?*"

"13 going on 14 weeks. Turns out, I'm a bit too much woman for that type of pill to work."

"*Oh, boy.*"

"Or girl. What the hell am I gonna do? How am I gonna tell Simon? He thought everything was handled that day in D.C. He doesn't like loose ends, and now I have to inform him that not only is the end loose, but it's weaving into a baby blanket."

"*Gina.*"

"Then there is Ma and Dad—Marcus. I just started a new job, and I'm planning a wedding."

"*Gina.*"

She managed to walk into a bodega and grab a bottle of water and box of crackers. "The wedding. I guess Ma will demand that get pushed up—to like yesterday." She swiped her debit card.

"*You're freaking out. You need to calm down. Is there someplace you can sit?*"

"Yeah." Regina walked into the park across the street and sat on a bench. Children played while their moms chatted with each other

~ 233 ~

or on cell phones. As she slowly munched on the saltines, the waves of nausea ebbing and flowing in her belly eased.

"Better?"

"Yes. I gotta hide this pregnancy from social media as long as possible."

"Don't think about that now."

"I have to, Toni. Do you remember how things were when the pictures of Simon and I kissing came out? What do you think will happen when the trolls find out I'm having a baby with him?"

"Yes, with him. You're having a baby with Simon, the man you love. That's what you need to concentrate on, not a bunch of internet idiots."

The diamonds on her engagement ring glistened in the little sunlight filtering through the trees. "You're right." She let out a sigh. "Why am I allowing the potential musings of small-minded people taint this moment? Why am I so scared to tell Simon? He asked me to marry him. He wants a life with me. This baby is a part of that."

"That's better."

"I need to tell him. Tonight. Can you and Marcus come to his place for dinner? I need you there."

"I'm texting Marcus now."

"This may sound silly, but I think I want to get him a gift. It must be the hormones."

"It doesn't sound silly at all. I know just the thing."

꙰ ꙰ ꙰ ꙰

The problem with unanswered questions is that often the questioner makes the mistake of trying to think of the answers. Simon glared at the small white stick on the coffee table. He'd decided to surprise Regina by coming home early and got one himself. He noticed the pregnancy test box while searching in the bathroom for—something. He no longer remembered because what he found in its stead rocked his world.

Regina's pregnant? Why the hell didn't she tell me? He leaned over to re-inspect the test. His lunch rolled in his stomach. As he glared at the two faint red lines, rage mounted from deep inside. *She must not want the baby. She may be planning to get rid of it.* Simon ran his fingers through his hair. "I won't go through that hell again."

It took over a year for him to function after Samantha's betrayal nearly destroyed his life. His love for her was one-sided. She'd left him broken-hearted for a guy she could bring home to daddy. The realization that he was nothing more than a fulfillment of a sick Asian fetish for her devastated him. To then discover that she'd aborted their baby, his baby, from a "well-meaning" source without even telling him delivered a crushing blow to his heart.

He didn't eat, sleep, or concentrate. If Marcus hadn't been there for him, Simon would have just deteriorated into an empty shell of a human being. Marcus led him through those dark days of rejection and despair, and the thought that his best friend's sister could be pulling the same cruel stunt was unbearable.

"No." Simon sprung from the sofa and marched back and forth across the apartment. "Regina isn't Samantha. Samantha is an opportunistic bitch that used me for sex. Regina loves me. She wouldn't hurt me like this. She's gonna tell me." He grabbed the pregnancy test. *Then, why hasn't she? Is she afraid of how I'll react, or other people? She already paid a heavy price for loving me. Maybe she thinks having my baby will cost her even more.*

The sound of Regina's key unlocking the door brought Simon out of his musings. She walked in carrying two cloth shopping bags. "Hey. What are you doing here, my love?" She made a beeline to the kitchen, and began unpacking.

"I left work early." Simon cupped the test in his hand, and sat on a stool. She had to clear things up before his imagination got the better of him.

"Aww, that's so sweet." She leaned over the counter beaming. Simon kissed her puckered lips. "I'm sorry I wasn't here. I had an appointment, and then I decided to run some errands. Did you get my text about Toni and Marcus coming over for dinner?"

"I did."

"Great. I got you and Marcus beers and even some of those horrible orange chips you like." She laid each item on the counter, and grinned with her chest out. "Don't you just love having such a thoughtful fiancée?"

"I do." The small plastic stick felt like a ton in his hands under the counter.

"Damn straight, Young." Regina spun around and continued packing away groceries.

"I do have a question for my thoughtful fiancée."

"Ask away." Simon dropped the stick on the counter while Regina closed the refrigerator. Her eyes widened. She blinked at it and then looked at him. "Si—"

"Are you pregnant?"

31 - I NEED SPACE

REGINA GRIPPED THE BOTTLE against her chest. "Yes," her voice shook like the rest of her. "I—"

"And you didn't feel the need to tell me?" Simon sprang from the stool and stormed across the great room. "I'm gonna be a father? Didn't you think that would be something I'd wanna know? When did this even happen?"

"D.C."

Simon blinked and raised his eyebrows. "D.C?" He spun on his heels and stalked back towards her. "No, not D.C. You took a pill in D.C. to make sure this wouldn't happen." *What is she playing at?*

"It didn't' work."

"What the hell do you meant it didn't work?" Each simple answer she gave plucked at his nerves. *There must be something she's hiding.*

Regina grabbed the stick and met him in the middle of the living room. "I mean it didn't work. Apparently, the damn pill is made for women built like this," she said, waving it. "I guess it's a shame you weren't fucking a smaller woman. Then you wouldn't be saddled with a kid." She went into the bathroom. A small thud of the test hitting the bottom of the trash can drifted through the door.

Simon grabbed a beer off the counter. *What the hell is happening? Regina's pregnant? The pill didn't work? She conceived in D.C. before I left for Singapore?* "Wait. D.C. was over three months ago," he yelled at the bathroom door. "How long have you known?"

She emerged, leaned on the doorway and twisted a lock of hair around her finger, avoiding direct eye contact. "Three weeks." Everything about her demeanor confirmed the irrational fears rattling through his mind.

"Three weeks?" Simon strode to the end of the small hall and back. "You knew all this time and said nothing?" He stopped. Toe-to-toe, he stared at her. "What, were you weighing your options? You took that pill pretty damn quick, so you must've been pissed when you found out it didn't work."

Regina pushed past him. "You know you're talking crazy, right? You were at the pharmacy with me. You bought the damn thing."

"You wanted it. So, what? Now you're pregnant but you couldn't be *thoughtful* enough to let me in on it?" Simon stood behind her and sneered. "Were you trying to decide if having a biracial baby was worth the hassle? Were you concerned it would taint your pro-Black image? Were you worried about your followers, haters or whoever? Everyone but me?"

She gasped and spun. Tears welled over the pain in her eyes from the sting of his words. She opened her lips to speak, but nothing came out. Simon shut his eyes and tightened his lips. "Gina, I'm sorry." Full of regret, he reached for her, but she backed away and walked into the kitchen.

She stood in front of the sink with her head bowed. Simon rubbed the back of his neck and headed towards the kitchen. He just hurt the woman he loved, the mother of his child. "Gina, babe, listen." Desperately wanting to ease the hurt he caused, he tried to hold her, but Regina was not having any of it. She shoved his arms away as if he had the plague.

"Just leave me alone." The crackling pain in her voice made him feel even worse. There was a knock at the door. Regina attempted to walk past him.

He squeezed her shoulders. "Listen, I'm sorry. I shouldn't have said that."

"I have to answer the door."

"Please, just hear me out."

"Move." She thrusted past him.

Simon reached for a beer and leaned against the counter. He'd bungled things badly. Normally, he knew exactly what to say to get back into Regina's good graces. Now, he was at a loss as his turbulent emotions overtook his ability to be calm and charming.

"Hey, girl." Toni's voice wafted from the hall. Regina's head fell on her best friend's shoulders as soon as the petite woman entered. Sobs sprung from her shaking body. Toni rubbed her sister-in-law's back and shared a confused glance with Marcus. "Gina? What's wrong? What's going on?"

Marcus hung their coats. Fists clenched, he stormed straight up to Simon. "Yo, man." He scanned him from head to toe.

"Hey." Simon managed to keep a calm tone despite his thumping heart. The chances of him getting out of this encounter unscathed didn't look promising. Considering how he treated Regina, he certainly deserved a good thrashing.

Marcus relaxed his hands and stepped back. "You got another one of those?"

Simon passed a green glass bottle to his friend while Toni walked Regina into the bedroom. He took a few steps towards them. "Gina, please." Toni raised her hand and scowled at him over Regina's hair. Simon bent his head and re-settled his backside on the counter.

Marcus balanced his muscular frame on a stool and glanced over his shoulder as the bedroom door muffled Regina's cries. He pressed the bottle to his tight lips and took a drink. "What the hell, man? I came here to eat, not beat your ass."

Simon released a derisive snort and scratched his shoulder. "I fucked up, bro. I found out Regina is pregnant, and didn't react well."

"She finally told you, huh?" Marcus kept looking at Simon as he tilted the bottle at his mouth.

"Of course, you know."

"Look man, my wife and sister are best friends. There are things I wish I didn't know."

"Well, she didn't tell me."

"What do you mean?"

"I found the pregnancy test jammed in a sink drawer and flipped out."

Marcus descended the stool and erected to his full height. "Describe flipped out."

Simon surveyed Marcus's stance. They were at one of those perilous moments Marcus warned about when he found out that his sister and best friends were involved. Usually, it was Marcus who Simon would talk to about situations like this, but how much could he disclose without the Marcus's big brother instincts kicking in? "I confronted her with it."

Marcus scoffed. "Dumb-ass move, man." He placed his arms akimbo. "She's pregnant, which means she's all hormonal and emotional. Never confront or argue with an emotional woman. She'll destroy you."

"Yeah." *At least he doesn't want to kick my ass anymore.*

"What else?"

"When she told me how long she knew," Simon took a swig of beer and braced himself on the counter. "I accused her of thinking about getting rid of it."

Marcus slapped his thighs and paced along the kitchen island. "Enough. For real, man? What a fuckin' idiot."

"I know. I tried to apologize."

Guttural laughter echoed off the walls. "How did that work out for you? You accused her of hiding her pregnancy just in case she wants to get an abortion behind your back."

Simon tilted his head and looked at the floor. "Well?"

Marcus got right into his face. "No. You don't compare my sister with that harpy you warmed your bed with, you understand? Regina loves and has battled the world for you. Start appreciating that."

"I do, it's just that when I saw that test, I didn't know what to think. I drew the worst conclusions even though I knew deep down they were wrong."

"You're letting that bullshit Samantha put you through affect things between you and Gina," he spat while backing away, "and it's costing you a chance at a good life with a good woman." He strode to the bedroom door and knocked gently. "Toni? We need to let Simon and Gina talk."

Marcus returned to the counter and slammed back the rest of his beer. "Look man, I wouldn't be in your business like this, but you chose to have a relationship with my baby sister."

"I know."

"Well, you need to come clean with her about Samantha and beg her to forgive you. Trust me, knowing my sister, it's gonna take a lot of begging. She's not used to and will not tolerate being treated like shit. I won't allow it either. You got me?"

"Yes."

"Good." Marcus shrugged on his coat and filled the entryway with his large frame. "The woman you love is in there crying. Fix it."

Toni emerged from the bedroom smoothing the front of her tear-stained shirt. She tucked a lock of hair behind her ear and walked towards Simon like a lioness. "Tell me something, Simon. Just how self-destructive do you plan on continuing to be?"

"Toni." Marcus suspended his wife's open coat in front of himself. "Let's go eat. They'll work this out."

Simon crossed his arms. He wasn't accustomed to so much accountability in a relationship. Regina's tight family meant that he had to hear criticism from a line of people, all of whom he respected. Censure from Marcus and now Toni dug deep and set in his mind just how badly he wrecked things this time. "Yeah. "Listen, Toni, I love Regina."

"You've got a funny way of showing it." She wrenched her neck and frowned up at him while pointing a finger behind her. "She was fragile about this pregnancy before. Now she's falling apart because of your thoughtless accusation."

"Toni. Let's go. Don't worry, he's gonna handle it." The future in-laws left, and the apartment went silent.

Handle it? How the hell am I supposed to do that? Simon stared at the closed bedroom door. *Everything I've done so far has been wrong, wrong, wrong.* There was so much to lose by making things worse. Regina was his life, carrying a new life created from their love, and he allowed his past to taint it. *Beg. Marcus said to beg.* He squared his shoulders and walked to the bedroom. "Gina? Please, let's talk."

Regina opened the door. The streaks from her eyes left Simon mute. Her tears did that to him. She barreled out of the bedroom. "I think you've said quite enough." She went back to unpacking the groceries. "Do you know where I was earlier today? I went to the doctor's office to confirm that I was pregnant because I couldn't believe it."

He approached but stayed on the opposite side of the island when She scowled at him. The level of anger on her face was unprecedented.

The cabinet slams got louder as she continued to speak. "Something must've been wrong with the test, and I didn't want to worry my loving fiancé unnecessarily." Regina paused and bore into Simon's soul with her stricken eyes. "The doctor told me that not only was I pregnant but I'm just entering my second trimester, so the rest of the afternoon involved a bunch of tests. Do you know what I was thinking of when they came at me with needles and cold torture devices to thrust into every orifice of my body?" She closed the distance between them until her breath sprayed his lip. "How will tell Simon? He needs to know he's about to be a father."

Simon remained still on the stool. *Never confront or argue with an emotional woman. She'll destroy you.* Her countenance made it clear that she was ready to annihilate him with prejudice.

"All I thought about was you. Your feelings were the main thing on my mind all these weeks. From the time I saw the lines on that test, every time I tried to play down how sick and tired I felt and even in the doctor's office—Simon, Simon, Simon was all that ran through my mind. As a matter of fact, do you know where I went right after I left the doctor?" She disappeared behind the counter. "I trekked across town to a specialty baby store and got this." The white tissue paper sticking out of the shiny black gift bag shook on the counter.

Simon closed his eyes and dipped his head. Guilt choked at his throat. Regina was wonderful, and he'd treated horribly. He brought his gaze back to hers. Instead of laughing and celebrating about their baby, she was holding back tears of anger. "Gina."

"Open it."

Simon tilted the bag in his hands. Its lightness contrasted the heaviness in his heart. He pulled out and unfolded the tiny white short-sleeved body suit and let it fall across his large palms. The colorful words *my daddy is a lawyer* branded the chest. Scum was not the proper word to describe him at that moment. "Oh, Babe."

She stormed to the entryway and snatched her coat off the hook. "I've only thought about you all this time. Now I need to concentrate on the baby and me."

Simon dropped the garment and jumped off the stool. "No, don't go." He dashed between her and the door.

Regina buttoned her coat and threw her purse straps over her shoulders. "Get out of my way." She wasn't teary any more. Her countenance was blank. Her cold eyes peered through him. "I need to be away from you."

He drew her unbending body in his arms. *She can't be leaving. We love each other. This can be fixed.* "Gina, give me a chance to apologize and explain."

"You apologized. I'm just not accepting it, and I don't want to hear any explanations. I'm not focusing any more energy on what you think, feel, or want to do. I'm going home to take care of myself and my baby."

"Our baby, Gina. Stay, and let's talk about this."

"No."

"No?"

"No. Let me go."

"Please, babe, please, just stay." He grasped her shoulders and covered her lips with his. Her body remained rigid and lips limp. He searched her eyes for the spark of love and desire that flashed whenever he was near. Nothing. Just emptiness and pain.

"Are you finished?"

Simon dropped his hands to his sides. Regina bolted to the door. It was as if the passion and tenderness between them never existed. *No, she's just angry. She still loves me.* "Gina. When can I call you?"

She gripped the jamb of the open door and looked back at him over her shoulder. "I need space. Don't try to contact me."

"What if you need something?"

"The only thing I needed was for the father of my unborn child not to be a jackass." The door softly closed.

Simon sat at the counter. He opened a fresh beer, took a long deep swig and set it down. Despair built in the pit of his stomach. He repeatedly slammed his fist on the counter. The beer bottle teetered and fell with a clank. Amber liquid spilled from the small opening and splashed on the body suit. "Great." Simon brought it to the sink, squeezed a few drops of dish soap on the stain and held the small garment under the faucet until it was clean. "This isn't over. I can't let Regina walk out of my life with
our baby. I'm gonna get her back."

32 - REGINA AND JEREMY

REGINA WALTZED TO HER BROTHER'S DESK and pirouetted in her silver ballerina shoes. The royal-blue chiffon of her empire waist gown wisped around her ankles. "I believe I'm presentable, dear brother."

"I love it." Toni slid her hands down Regina's arms, stopping at the end of the lace middle sleeves. "You're stunning."

"As are you, my queen." Marcus came from around his desk and stood between wife and sister. He wrapped one arm around each woman and gently kissed Toni's cheek. "I'm a lucky man to have the honor of escorting such a beauty." He looked at Regina mischievously, "and my sister."

Regina jabbed him in the side. "Very funny."

"Come on, you two." Toni straightened Marcus's bow tie. "Behave, and act like you've been somewhere. This is a big night." Tonight's fundraising gala was an annual event that brought out important donors who made it possible for the center to stay open. Everyone vested in keeping things running dressed to impress and charm money out of some heavy wallets, Marcus was usually that most successful.

Toni passed her hand over the front of Regina's dress. "See, I told you that cut would keep your condition a secret. Although, I don't know how much longer you think you'll be able to hide it."

Regina clasped her hands and looked down at the folds of her dress, relieved that it covered the bulging abdomen underneath it.

She was not ready to answer questions about her pregnancy, especially since she wasn't sure what was happening between her and the father. It'd been over three weeks since she left Simon's apartment after their last argument. It seemed like forever. "Yeah. I can barely fit anything, and remember when I was sick all the time? Now I'm hungry day and night."

"That is to be expected when you're expecting." Toni fell back against Marcus's chest and laughed at her own whit. "We'll have to go shopping."

Marcus rolled his eyes. "Oh, Lord."

"You can zip it, Marc." Toni smiled with excitement and stretched out her hand. "Did you bring the sonogram? I can't wait to see my little niece or nephew."

Regina slid the picture out of her evening bag. "The doctor said the baby is healthy." She used to be hesitant about discussing her pregnancy with Toni, considering the fertility issues her friend was struggling with, but Toni insisted on being supportive and loving. "The right size and with all fingers and toes accounted for."

"I'm so glad." Toni scanned the black and white image while Regina examined her friend for signs of pain. "Beautiful. When are you showing Simon?" Toni held the picture in front of Marcus, who looked at it quizzically then his sister. "He should be at the gala," she continued, "and he'll want to see it."

"I haven't thought about it." Regina purposefully avoided eye contact. Simon was the only thing on her mind lately.

"Mmm-hmm." Toni crossed her arms. "I can't believe you're still being so pigheaded. The poor guy's been bugging Marcus and me every day, asking how you're doing and if you need anything. Just call him already." Marcus sighed and closed the office door.

Regina tucked the sonogram back in her clutch and laid it on the desk. "I don't know how to, okay." She began to fiddle with a tab sticking out of one of her brother's law books on the huge book case against the wall. "I was so mad, and now I'm not, and I can't even think of what to say if I'm in the same room as him."

Marcus sniggered. "You got that right. You two were pathetic at the last advisory board meeting."

Toni glared at her husband and stood next to Regina. "You know I'm always in your corner, but you're being plain foolish right now. Simon is hopelessly in love with you and that baby, and you just have him dangling."

"I do not."

"Oh, yes you do, my dear sister-in-law. I was on your side the first week that you wouldn't talk to him. What he said was hurtful, but you have to think past that and to the future." She caressed the distension in Regina's abdomen. "He'll come running if you asked."

Regina laid her hand on top of her friend's. "I guess."

"Simon committed himself to you before the baby. Do you really think he's going to just walk away? No. It's you who's pushing him away, and you better get your act together before he's gone." The two women turned in Marcus's direction.

He chortled. "Yeah, right. Like either of you is really interested in what I have to say about this." He rested Toni's coat on her shoulders.

"Come on, Marc." Toni turned and looked at him. "You're a man."

"Nope. You're always telling me that Gina is a grown woman, not my little sister." He began typing on his phone. "Well, let her work it out with the father of her kid. We gotta go." He stopped in the doorway. "Damn it. We need more pledge forms, but I can't be late. Gina, can you make copies and meet us there?"

"Sure. Where's the original?"

"Right on my desk. Thanks, sis." Marcus placed his hand on the small of Toni's back and guided his wife out of the office.

"Call the man," Toni commanded over her shoulder.

Regina took the pledge form off her brother's desk and wobbled to the copy room. Soon, she was following the small light peaking under the lid of the machine back and forth with her eyes. The whirring sound cut through the silence of the empty office and lulled her into deep thought. Now in her second trimester, there was so much she was experiencing alone. Her heart hurt yesterday when she looked at the baby fidgeting on the ultrasound screen and Simon wasn't there holding her hand. She wanted him so badly, but for some reason, she was stuck as to what to do to get him back in her life.

She was so cold to him that night, and refused to even return a text message. *Toni is right. I'm being a fool. I should just call him.* A little flurry of movement inside her made Regina smile. She circled the belly bump with the palm of her hand. Simon had the makings to be a great father; he was loving, kind, patient, and strong. The little person growing inside her needed him. She needed him too. No matter how mad she was before, her love for him did not fade one bit. He was still hers. She peeked down at the blue front of her dress. "Let's get daddy."

Regina grasped the door jamb and swung out of the copy room. She threw her hands in front of her and let out a small shriek as she slammed into a bony chest. "Oh, Jeremy. I'm sorry. What are you doing here?"

"I never left." Jeremy held Regina arms. A white evening scarf swung from his neck. "I was in my office. I'm just about to leave for the gala. What are you doing?"

"Marcus asked me to make more copies of the pledge forms. Can you keep an eye on them?"

Jeremy smiled. "Sure. I'll wait for you, and we can go together."

"That sound's good. Thanks." Regina dashed to Marcus's office. "I just have to make a phone call." Her hands shook as she hit speed dial.

"Regina?" The sound of Simon's voice made her weak in the knees. She braced her legs against the desk.

"Hi. How are you?" She fondled the clasp of her evening bag. That was about all she had.

"Is everything okay?" The clicking sound of the subway filtered into her ear.

"Yeah." She wiped liquid beads from her forehead and put her hand on her hip. "Yeah. I just wanted to let you know, that you should know, that I went for my first ultrasound yesterday. I mean, I thought that maybe you might wanna know." *Get a grip. You sound like a blithering idiot.*

"Really? Thank you for letting me know." His tone was distant.

Maybe Toni is wrong. Simon may not care about the baby or me for that matter. He hasn't called in all these weeks, after all. He might have decided to move on with his life. Idiot. He didn't call because you told him not to.

"I wish I could've been there with you." The strain in his voice shot straight to her heart. He was hurt that he missed such a special event in his unborn child's life.

Regina's eyes glistened. She sniffed and swallowed hard. "You do? Of course, you do. I should've told you. I'll make sure you know next time."

"Thank you. Listen, Gina. I've been trying to respect your space. I haven't called, even though it's killed me not to. We need to talk. What I said to you was horrible. I regretted it the moment it left my mouth and ever since then. You're the best thing that's ever happened to me, and my life has been one big empty hole since you left."

"I don't understand why you would say something like that."

"Because it's happened to me before." He told her everything about Samantha. "But that's in the past. I know you would never do anything like that. I love you and the baby." She heard the subway screech in the background.

She took in a deep breath. "I love you too, Simon. I'm sorry, for everything."

"I'm sorry too, babe. I don't want to lose either of you. I want to be with my family."

Tears breached her eyelids. "Me too. I was angry and hurt, but as that started to fade, I wanted you so much. I was just being stubborn. When can we meet and talk? I'm at the center now, but I'm heading to the gala soon. Are you going?"

"I know you're at the center. I should be there in about 5 minutes."

"How did you know where I was?"

"Marcus texted me. He said I should get there in a hurry."

She laughed and reached into her handbag. "I guess he decided to be an intrusive big brother after all."

"I guess." The train is coming to the stop. "I'll be there soon."

"I'm glad. I've missed you so much." Regina pulled out the small square of paper with the image of their baby. "I have the sonogram. I can't wait for you to—" She gasped as fingers dug into her shoulders and spun her around. A sharp pain shot through her eye, and everything went blurry. She stumbled backwards into the desk and fell to the ground. Her phone made a cracking sound, skidded crossways and slammed into the wall. Pledge forms fluttered to the floor around her.

"Gina?" Simon's voice drifted across the room from the phone. "Are you okay? What's happening? Gina?"

Regina tried to brace on quaking arms, barely making out the black loafers with her throbbing eye. She shook her head, trying to stop the room from rocking.

She grabbed at the hand on the back of her head and cried out in pain. Jeremy hauled her from the floor and propped her against his body.

"I can't believe," he seethed, "that after everything that's happened, you're still fucking that Chinaman!"

33 – EMERGENCY

A SHARP PAIN SHOT across Regina's back. Jeremy laid over her body splayed across the wood desk and wrapped his tendril-like fingers around her neck. "Jeremy? What are you doing? Stop." She choked out the words and slammed her fists against his narrow chest, but with no effect. He was so much stronger.

Jeremy thrusted his knee between her thighs. "No matter what I do, you keep runnin' to spread your legs for Simon." He pinned her arms underneath her and put his full weight on her body. Pain radiated through her abdomen. "I thought posting those disgusting pictures of the two of you pawing each other on Instagram would make you realize how wrong screwing him was." He snatched his evening scarf from around his neck and flung it to the floor. "Not even your fans checkin' you on your nasty behavior made you come to your senses. You still went crawlin' underneath him."

He jabbed his fist into her lip. Blood oozed into her gaping mouth. "Please, Jeremy." The sound of Simon screaming something streamed from the phone. "You don't want to do this. We're friends."

Jeremy scoffed. "When were we ever friends? You treat me like a pet. I spent so much time waiting on you, trying to get you to think of me as more than a lap dog, but you never even noticed."

"What are you talking about?"

"Don't act like you didn't know. I hate teases like you. We used to hang out all the time. You'd smile and twirl your hair." The rage in his eyes faded. Jeremy buried his nose and sniffed. "Your hair is so pretty, Gina. All of you is." He peered into her eyes with renewed anger. "Then Simon came along and you sniffed around him like a bitch in heat."

"I'm sorry, J. I didn't know. I always thought of you like a brother. Please, I'm pregnant. Don't hurt my baby." The adoring baby face she thought she knew so well screwed into maniacal disgust.

Jeremy growled and grabbed fistfuls of her hair, slamming her head over and over again against the hardwood. The room spun out of control. "You stupid, selfish cunt. You think I give a shit about some mongrel you're breeding? Another confused child that doesn't belong?" He rammed his fist over and over into her sides. Screams burst out of her constricted throat. "You're just like my father. Your own race isn't good enough," she cried out after another blow, "so you lay with anything else and make a bunch of mixed-up, mixed-race mutts, and it's the kids who suffer. Where do you think your kid is gonna fit in, with its dark skin and chinkie eyes?"

Agony streaked across her torso and down her body. She could only think about saving her baby, an innocent life that shouldn't be snuffed out.

"I don't know what's wrong with bitches like you. What? a brotha isn't good enough?" Jeremy tore away the blue chiffon and tugged at his pants. "A Black man's too much for you?"

"Get off me."

Jeremy lifted his head and snarled. "I'm not getting off you." She rocked her head back and forth to avoid his mouth touching hers. He slid his tongue along her cheek instead. "I'm about to get in you. Let you know what a real man feels like." His stiff penis pushed at her thigh and the feeling of long skinny fingers rubbing violently at her panties made her back arch in convulsions and her heels kick at the back of his long legs.

This wasn't happening. It couldn't be. Jeremy was a friend. *Simon is coming. I have to keep him talking.* "You? A real man? Sneaking up on a woman and sucker-punching her, is that what makes you a man? Just let me go J. You don't want to do this."

"Shut up, cunt. Don't tell me what I want. Are you afraid, Gina? You can't handle some Black dick? Is that it?" He smashed his lips against hers. She tried but couldn't move her head away. Bile burned her throat with trapped screams as Jeremy's tongue invaded her mouth and sloshed around spit and blood, churning her stomach along with his stale breath and cheap cologne. "I knew you tasted good," he said with a sleazy moan. "Now to taste those." The delicate chiffon and lace yielded to Jeremy's grip and tore back, laying one breast bare.

Regina screamed and bucked at the searing pain of teeth cutting into her. She yanked her arm. Her hand flew from underneath her. "I said get the fuck off me!" She buried her nails into the soft flesh of Jeremy's cheek and dug in hard.

He howled, jerking his head from side to side, but Regina dug in her nails so hard that they wouldn't budge. She cut four red streaks across his fair skin and started punching his cheek. "Get off! Get off!"

Jeremy grabbed her wrist and shoved her arm back underneath her. He touched his cheek and then looked down. She stared into his hard, enraged eyes. He was always smiling and happy, but now Regina saw raw killer instinct. He roared over her. "I'm gonna fucking kill you!"

Long fingers cut into her neck. Her lungs burned for air. Thrashing limbs slowed and went limp. *Baby. Simon.* Jeremy and the world became increasingly black.

"Hey!" Simon's voice cut into the blackness. A rush of air ripped through Regina's lungs and washed over her body, replacing Jeremy's crushing weight. Legs kicking into space, she stared at the ceiling, gasping and coughing, her chest heaving to take in more air while shattering glass and cracking wood from the other side of the room reached her ears. Regina rolled on her side. She saw Simon delivering a series of blows. "I'm gonna break your neck, you piece of shit."

Regina slid off the desk. She wobbled a bit. A sharp pain pierced through her abdomen. She sank to the floor, holding her stomach. *The baby.* "Simon, wait," she grated despite her burning throat. Her words were futile. Pain overwhelmed her torso. Tears and fear for the tiny life inside her made it impossible for her to say anymore.

Jeremy wedged his forearm under Simon's chin and pushed until they rolled on the floor and he pinned and punched his foe. "She's not yours. She's mine."

Simon hooked a jab into Jeremy's temple, and the two tumbled again. He straddled the tall attacker and bashed his face over and over. "You're out of your mind. She never wanted you, and if you touch her again," Simon spoke between punches, "I'll kill you." He continued to pummel Jeremy until police uniforms stormed the room.

The officer pinned Simon's arms behind his back. Fiery pain seared through his shoulder. "What's goin' on here," asked a burly policeman. "Someone made an emergency call."

"I'm the one who called, officer," Simon panted. His heart was still thumping from the moment he heard Regina's screams on the phone. Fear welled in him when he realized she was in danger, and he ran from the subway. "I was on the phone with my fiancée, and she screamed." He craned his neck to view the less than gentle police officer holding him. "I called 911 and ran here to find that man assaulting her." He lunged towards the similarly-restrained Jeremy, who just stood with his hands behind his back staring at Regina. "Stop looking at her, scum."

When he saw Jeremy on top of her, Simon's rage controlled him like never before. He yanked the assailant by the neck and threw him on the floor. He was just about to break the gangly rapist's neck when the police arrived and pulled him off the slime. Just a few seconds later, and they would've needed a body bag.

"Hold your horses, buddy," warned the officer restraining Simon. "There'll be no more fighting."

Simon took a few deep breaths. *I'm no good to Regina blinded by fury.* "My name is Simon Young, I'm an attorney admitted in New York."

The cop behind him tugged at his wrists. "Then you really need to cool off." He looked at his partner with Jeremy towering in front of him, already in handcuffs. "Take that one out of here," he commanded, jerking his head towards the door. "You alright, ma'am?"

Simon's heart sunk. Regina was shaking on the floor, surrounded by a pool of blue. She leaned on one arm and splayed her hand across her belly. Their gazes met, and the terror in her tear-soaked eyes filled his gut with dread. "I'm calm now, officer," Simon spoke in a forced collected tone. "Please, let me go so I can help my fiancée. She's pregnant." Simon dove onto his knees the moment he was free from the cop's grip and wrapped his beloved in his arms. "Gina, Gina. Are you okay?"

Regina crushed Simon's coat lapels in her hands and held his gaze. "The baby," she said through bloodied, quaking lips. "Something's wrong—pain." She laid her head on his chest. Tears soaked his shirt. Breathing became harder than when he was fighting Jeremy. *Please, let the baby be okay.* Just a few minutes before, he was excited about seeing a picture of his unborn child. Now it was possibly dying while its mother sits beaten.

Simon stroked her hair. "It's alright, I'm gonna take care of you." He pressed his lips just above her salty eyebrow. He looked at the police officer. "I need to take her to the emergency room."

"Don't worry, buddy. We'll get you there. I'll call for an ambulance." The cop craned his neck and hovered his mouth over the device on his shoulder.

"No." Regina brought her face in line with his. "They won't let you on it with me. I want to stay with you."

"No, thanks. We'll take a cab." Simon started to rise from the floor, but Regina tugged at his coat. He grabbed the desk to keep from falling on her.

"Don't leave me, Simon." She pushed her arms under his coat and clutched his waist.

"Okay. I'm not. I'm right here." He sat and propped his back on the desk. Regina rested her head on his chest. "I'll order a car." He retrieved his phone and searched small dots on the app screen. He selected one and put the phone on his lap. "It's coming." He squeezed tighter. "We're gonna be alright, babe. We're *all* gonna be fine." They stayed that way until the notification ding announced the arrival of the car. "It's here, Gina. Can you stand?"

"I think so." They struggled to their feet. Regina shook and gripped her belly. "It hurts so bad."

Simon yanked off his coat and laid it across her shoulders. "Just lean on me. I got you." He kicked the papers and fallen furniture out of their path. The corridor stretched in front of him. They moved to the door, stopping occasionally for Regina to gather enough strength to bear more pain. "Where almost there."

Frigid wind whipped around them and cut straight through Simon's evening jacket. He closed his coat closer to Regina's hunched body. His teeth clenched so tightly that his jaw ached. He raised his hand to the black car at the curb.

The driver jumped out and jogged around the car with a grin. "Simon?" It faded when his eyes fell on Regina. "Is she okay?"

"Yes. No." Simon shook his head and grunted. "Yes, I'm Simon. No, she's not okay. Open the door, and get us to the nearest hospital." He supported Regina's back and helped her onto the seat then lifted her leg into the car and shoved the flowing dress under her. He wiped at the tears on her anxious face. "We'll be at the hospital soon. Please, hold on."

"I will." She extended a shaky hand towards his cheek and traced the cut on it with her fingers. "Are you okay?"

Simon closed his eyes and winced. Staring into his love's eyes, he saw her concern for him overshadow her own agony. He kissed her hand. "I will be, once you are." He closed the door and climbed in on the other side, sliding over until he could hold her again. The car veered into the busy street. Motors and horns became background music for their tense ride.

The smile he offered Regina fell as he peered into traffic. He rested his hand on the small mound poking from her stomach. It was the first time he'd touched his baby—ever. The two most important people in his world were in crisis, and everything that made him happy was in jeopardy.

34 - SHOWER

SIMON GENTLY SLID HIS COAT from Regina's shoulders. "Would you like something to eat, babe?"

"No. Not now." She shuffled towards the hallway, her hands remained protectively covering the small bump in her lower abdomen. "I just want to take a shower."

Simon hung the coat and evening jacket before walking into the kitchen. He rolled up his sleeves. "Okay. I'll put something together while you're in there." He bent into the refrigerator. There was an assortment of fruits in a large container, and a platter of vegetables. Next to stacks of yogurt were three dozen eggs. He spotted a pot from the bottom shelf. He took it out and lifted the lid. His stomach released a huge growl. *I guess I found dinner.* A mound of food on a plate started spinning in the microwave.

"Simon?" Regina appeared and extended her arm over the counter. "Can you cut these off?"

Drawers clanged until one presented a pair of scissors. The blades cut between the names "Regina" and "Kent" on the hospital bracelet, which then fell to the counter, revealing purple bruises. Simon kissed the precious wrist and held her hand. "Done. I'm heating up the beans and rice you made."

"Toni made them." She shivered, holding one side of her torn dress at the breast. A purplish-red mask surrounded both her eyes, searching his face for something. What it was, he didn't know. "I don't think I can eat. My mouth is pretty sore." She looked down and pulled her hand away, walking back towards the bathroom.

"All right." He pushed over the counter and raised his voice. "I can make something else."

"No." The bathroom door creaked but didn't click shut.

Simon exhaled and got the food from the microwave. He left the kitchen with the hot plate and a fork in hand. Stretching his head to glean the inside of the bathroom, he saw Regina with her hands under the stream of water running from the sink. "Are you okay, Gina?"

"Fine."

His favorite spot on the sofa welcomed him back. He massaged the tender spot on his side where Jeremy punched him and reclined into the soft leather rotating a sore shoulder. The forkful of food he slammed into his mouth filled it with savory flavors. It was strange how easily he felt at home after such a long time away.

Simon examined the contents of the coffee table. There were quite a few books with babies and pregnant bellies on the covers. He smiled and flipped the thickest one with colorful tabs sticking out along all the sides. No surprise, Regina was being thorough about the care of their baby. Toni already told him how serious she was about eating and doing all the right things. *I have to make sure tonight doesn't derail all of her hard work.*

The bathroom door squeaked. "Simon?" His heart wrenched at the sound of her tremulous voice. He tossed the book on the table and placed his plate on top of it. Regina was holding her shoulders and staring in the mirror, the pain evident in her profile. The creaking sound of the bathroom door being fully opened reverberated down the hall. "I'm here, babe."

She looked at him through the mirror. "I can't reach the zipper. It hurts too much."

"I'll do it for you." He tried to restrain the fury building at the sight of long red marks on her neck left by Jeremy's fingers. The opened zipper exposed even more. Another, faint purple discoloration spanned across her lower back. *I wish I'd killed him.* He let the gown drop. "Do you want me to unhook your bra?"

She sighed and nodded. he held his breath and maneuvered the clasps. Regina's arms flew to hold the garment. She turned and buried her head in his chest, sobbing. Fear and concern joined his anger as he hovered and shifted his hands trying to find a spot to hold her without irritating the contusions branding her body. She was so fragile. He gazed down her body in the mirror. "Where are your panties?"

"They kept them." It was as if every bit of her physical and emotional strength was spirited away from her.

He laid his hands on her back. "Come on, take your shower, and I'll get you something to eat."

He started to leave the bathroom, but Regina gripped his shirt at the sides and cried harder. She pressed him against the wall. The bump where their unborn child was nestled pushed against his abdomen and ripped at his insides. "I won't leave, Gina. How about I help you?"

"Okay," she sobbed. She wrapped an arm around his waist. She wouldn't let go, so he moved them to the bathtub and turned on the water. Steam filled the room. They had so much hope earlier. A chance to finally be content was stolen. It was time to try and get some of it back.

Simon pushed his shoes off at the heels and stepped on each sock until they lay at his feet. The shirt, undershirt, and belt joined the other clothes. "Let's get in." Pants still on, he drew Regina under the warm water with him and shivered when his back touched the cool tiles. He kissed her forehead and rocked from side to side until her sobs eased and his tears—hidden by the flowing water—ceased.

"I'm ready to get out." Regina lifted her head and stepped a shaky leg in a puddle on the floor. Simon steadied her at the hips, noticing the water dripping from the bra against her chest. He lifted a towel from the rack to wrap around her shoulders. "Thank you." She let the soaking garment fall to the floor and wrapped the towel around her body.

Light chased the bedroom shadows away and familiarity hugged Simon. It'd been months since he was in the lilac room and laid under the soft blankets talking with and holding Regina. He pulled out a pair of pajama pants and a t-shirt from the dresser then reached over to Regina's side and opened a bottom drawer. She stopped next to him and placed a hand on his back. "You're cold."

"I'm fine." He warmed away the bumps prickling her arms. "What would you like to put on?"

Regina clenched the front of the towel with one hand and touched his shoulder. "I can dress myself I think." She stretched her arm to select from the bottom draw and winced, closing her eyes tight and baring her teeth. "Maybe I can't."

"How about you tell me what you want, and I get it?" Simon stroked her chin with his finger. She was going through so much. "Then I'll get changed in the bathroom." His soaking dress pants scratched his legs when he bent and opened the drawer. Every muscle tensed against the increasing cold sensation running down his body, but that didn't matter. He had to get Regina resting.

"No stay. I'm gonna need help. It's just that—"

Simon got her favorite plush pajama bottoms from the drawer and stood to search her face. There was clearly something she wasn't telling him. "What is it?"

She turned her head to the bedroom window. "I didn't want you to see." A tear trickled down her cheek.

Simon couldn't help but gasp when she opened the towel and he saw a wet white bandage with a spot of blood covering her right breast. *Fucking animal.* "What happened?"

"The son of a bitch bit me," she shot through chattering teeth. She snapped the towel shut. "I'm glad I scratched him. I wish I coulda clawed his eyes out. I can change the bandage, but I'm not going to be able to put my clothes on by myself. It still hurts to breathe."

He hugged her. The anger in her words actually loosened a knot in his gut. She was still a fighter—down but not out. "We're going to get you dressed and then you need to be in bed."

Once he got both of them dried and garbed, Simon darted around the apartment getting everything necessary for Regina to settle. He eventually towered over the bed with his chest puffed out watching her snuggled between blankets and pillows and sipping tea from a mug with a list of Black women historical figures on it. "There, sure you don't want me to heat up some of the food Toni made?"

"No, even drinking this tea is a struggle." She held her side and pressed the back of her hand against her mouth. "Anyway, I'm too tired to eat."

Simon took it and set it on the night stand. He shifted the blankets and pillows around as she slid deeper under them. "That's fine, but you definitely have to eat in the morning."

"I promise. Oh." Regina's swollen lips stretched upward.

"What?"

She reached her arms under the blanket. "The baby's moving. I can finally feel it again."

"Good." It was a wonderful sign. She'd stressed since the attack that she couldn't feel any fluttering. The doctor assured her that it was probably because of the trauma. Even though they both saw the little one kicking around on the ultrasound screen and heard the heartbeat, Regina still worried. Now she didn't have to, which meant neither did he.

"Can you make eggs? The baby likes eggs."

He smiled. "Is that why there are dozens of them in the refrigerator?"

She yawned again and grimaced. "Yeah," she answered with increased drowsiness, "a little salt and no pepper and butter not oil."

Simon eased next to her and sighed when she pulled his arm across her stomach. "You got it." He closed his eyes and buried his nose in the silk scarf on her head.

"No brown. If I see brown, I get nauseous."

"Not a speck."

ॐॐॐॐ

Simon's eyes flew open. He slipped his numb arm from under Regina's slumbering body, praying the pounding at the door wouldn't rouse her. *Who the hell? I just got her to sleep.* Bumping between walls and furniture, he managed to traverse the cold apartment floor on legs, rickety from a night of tribulation and squinted through the peephole. More thumping ensued.

"Would you stop trying to beat the door down, Marc. They're probably asleep." He caught sight of Toni yanking her husband's burly arm away.

"I don't care. I can't believe y'all kept this from me."

"No one kept anything from you, man." Simon peered at Marcus through one eye, rubbing his finger into the other. "Can you please stop banging on my door?"

Marcus raised his eyebrows. "Your door?" He scowled and barreled passed Simon. "Regina? Where is she?"

Simon jerked Marcus's arm to keep him from going any further. "Keep it down," he shot with a strained whisper. He became a barrier between Marcus and the hallway. "She just fell asleep."

"Why didn't you tell me?" Marcus peered at Simon. He was in his usual overprotective brother mode, but this time, Simon wasn't backing down.

"I told Toni. Gina didn't even want me doing that, but I decided that you should know. I asked Toni not to tell you until the gala was over."

"So, you think I care more about raising money than family?" Searing pain shot through Simon's tender shoulder where Marcus jabbed it.

Tension mounted at the base of his neck. Not Marcus or anyone else was going to interfere with Regina's recovery. The ER doctor said that stress could trigger contractions. He wasn't going to let that happen. "I was a little too busy to give a damn about what you think. Gina didn't want anyone coming to the emergency room, and she wanted you to focus on the gala. He fixed his stare at Marcus. "Take that up with her, after she's feeling better. Right now, you have to leave."

"Oh, I'm not going anywhere until I talk to Gina."

Simon folded his arms. "You can't. She doesn't want you seeing her."

"What? That's bullshit." Simon steeled his muscles, preventing Marcus from plowing past him. "God damn it, Simon, she's *my* sister."

"Well, she's *my* fiancée and she's having *my* baby. I'm looking out for both of them." Simon reared his shoulders and lifted his chin. "You're not seeing her." He moved in closer until his forearms came into contact with Marcus's heaving chest. "Now, you can be mad about that, but take your yelling and screaming into the hall."

"Both of you need to stop acting like idiots." Toni stepped next to Marcus. "I'm in no mood to try and keep you two from tussling. When two bulls fight, it's the grass that suffers." She gazed down at Marcus's pocket. "Answer your phone, Marc."

"It's Ma." Marcus put it to his ear and swerved away from Simon. "Hi, Ma. No, Simon won't let me." Toni caught Simon's gaze and rolled her eyes. Marcus was trying to stoke the mother bear in Adrian Kent with his simpering tone. Marcus smirked and hovered the phone under Simon's chin. "She wants to talk to you." It obviously worked.

Simon snatched the phone and whispered, "punk." He bowed his head and shifted from leg to leg with one hand on his hip. "Hi, Mrs. Kent."

"Simon. You know, you're about to make me a grandmother. So, how about you call me Adrian?" His future mother-in-law's pointed speech intimidated him as much as everyone else who crossed her path."

"Hi, Adrian."

"That's better. Tell me about my daughter." Everything in her words sent the message that she wanted to know all the details with no holding back.

"She's in a lot of pain." Simon paced the living room. "At first, we thought she was losing the baby, but the doctor ran a bunch of tests and did an ultrasound. The baby is fine. He said the pain is from sprained muscles. She also has two bruised ribs. They monitored her for a few of hours. Fortunately, she didn't have any contractions.

"That's good to hear."

"Very. The doctor wanted to keep her, but she refused to stay." He crossed the living room and stopped at the bedroom doorway. Regina's soft snoring did his nerves good. *She must be exhausted to sleep through all of this.*

His muscles relaxed at the sound of Adrian's laugh. *"That sounds like her."*

"I tried to convince her to let them observe her overnight. I would've stayed too."

"No, she hates hospitals. I blame Marcus and all those horror movies."

Simon chuckled as he turned off the light and closed the bedroom door. Toni was holding Marcus's arm. The finely-dressed couple stuck in their places. He looked at them while he continued to talk to Adrian. "Well, the doctor released her, but he said she needed rest and no stress, and to come back if there is any cramping, bleeding or anything. She's hasn't had any. I have to take her to the obstetrician tomorrow."

"Has she eaten?"

"No, but she promised to in the morning if I made her eggs." Toni let out a small laugh and sniffled. Simon strolled to her and took hold of her slender fingers, presenting a reassuring smile. They all loved Regina as much as he and were just as worried.

"You're doing a splendid job, Simon," said Adrian. Her reassurance strengthened his resolve.

"Thank you. She showered and is sleeping. I want to keep it that way."

"As you should. Can you put me on speaker phone?"

"Yes."

Can everyone hear me?

They all confirmed.

"Good. Sounds like Simon has everything under control. We should give him and Gina some space and quiet. They've been through a huge ordeal."

"Yes Ma'am," the three replied in unison like school children.

"Simon, will it be okay if Gina's father and I call tomorrow?"

"Of course."

"Then we'll do that, and don't worry. None of us will attempt to see her until she's ready." Adrian sent the clear message that no one is to interfere with how Simon was caring for her daughter—including Marcus, who practically pouted.

"Yes, Ma'am."

"Good night."

Simon dangled the phone in front of Marcus. He allowed his twitching lips to draw back into a full grin of vindication. "Here you go, man."

Marcus yanked the phone and glowered at him. "You're enjoying this."

He grabbed Marcus by the back of the neck. "Immensely."

Marcus plopped on a stool and scratched his head. "I can't believe this is happening."

Toni positioned herself behind her husband and massaged his shoulders over his coat. "I find it impossible to believe that Jeremy hurt Regina."

Simon exhaled and sat on a stool next to his friend. "Well, he did." He put his elbow on the counter and massaged his temples. "When I ran into the office and saw him on top of her, I wanted to kill him." He held his palms in front of himself. "I had his head positioned just like Quinn taught me, but the police stopped me."

"That's good. You belong here with Gina, not in a jail cell." Toni stepped from behind Marcus and hugged Simon. "You go get some rest. We'll call tomorrow afternoon to check on you guys."

"Yeah." Marcus stood and extended his hand. "You keep them safe."

Simon accepted the hand and hug that made his shoulder sting again. "Okay, man." He definitely had a big responsibility to handle and wouldn't have it any other way.

35 - Eggs with Alice

ALICE LET OUT A SIGH and pulled the keys from the lock to her son's apartment. She opened her Michael Kors bag and let the ring fall to the bottom. *That habit has to go.* There was a new woman in Simon's life, which meant mama was now a guest, and guests knock. She hooked the purse in her arm, shifted her weight on one of her three-inch designer heels and poised her fist. *What am going to say to her?*

Simon called and asked her to visit Regina, who she hadn't seen since pushing the shocked woman into the very hall in which she now stood. *She's going to slam the door in my face.*

Please, Ma. I have to work and I don't want Gina alone all day. Her heart tugged at the memory of the strain in her son's voice. It hadn't been long since Regina was attacked by some horrible man at that awful little center, where Simon insisted on volunteering. Regina did not want any visitors, and their tumultuous past made it easy for Alice to avoid talking to her, but Simon's request made it impossible to stay away any longer. It was past time that she comforted and got to know her son's fiancée. Alice chuckled into the empty hall.

It seemed like yesterday when she first saw a half-naked Regina dripping water onto the hallway floor. She thought the tall, beautiful Black woman was just another fling. *Now she's inside with an engagement ring on her finger and a baby in her belly.* Simon was usually reserved, so the speed at which he took on the roles of boyfriend, fiancée and father made her head spin, but he'd made his feelings for Regina clear when he rushed to find her while he was still sick.

Since he was not easily besotted, she was pretty sure that Simon loved Regina, which meant she had to make nice with the woman who possessed her son's heart and carried her grandchild. Facing the door again. She knocked and braced herself. Things were going to be bumpy.

The door swung open. Regina was already walking away from it. "Hello, Mrs. Young." Her voice oozed ire.

"Alice, dear, please." *She's not going to give me an inch. I can handle that.* Alice retrieved the shopping bag she'd set down earlier and glided into the kitchen. "You're about to be my daughter-in-law." She peered into the dimness. "Why is it so dark in here?"

Regina's dark skin soaked the glow of the screen in front of her. "It helps me write better."

"Nonsense. You'll go blind." Alice tugged the thin white cord hanging on the side of the window frame and let in a burst of afternoon light. "There. That's better." She opened her mouth slightly when her gaze fell on Regina holding one hand against the brightness. Blackness surrounded one, and blood clots reddened the outside corners of both squinting eyes. "Oh."

Regina curved her back over her protruding belly and brought her forehead to her fingers. "Don't, okay. I've had enough oh's for a lifetime, and I can't hear them from you of all people." She cast a suspicious glance at Alice. "Simon's not here, so why are you?"

Alice took a sponge from the sink and approached the counter. "Your rudeness is more than warranted after the way I treated you. I apologize for my behavior. I was worried about my son and didn't know how important you were to him." She made purposeful circles along the marble, gathering errant crumbs. "I could pretend that I thought it might be nice to pop in for a visit, but I won't insult your intelligence."

"I appreciate that."

"Simon sent me. He's concerned about you," she stopped her task and concentrated on Regina, "and now I fully realize why. Are you okay?" The women became locked in a stare. Alice's question was ridiculous, but she couldn't help asking it. There was no reason for Regina to even speak to her let alone divulge her feelings.

"Fine."

"Really?" Even with a scowl and bruises, there was no discounting her loveliness. *No wonder Simon fell so hard, so quickly.*

Regina finally lowered her eyelids and shifted on the stool. She started clicking at the laptop. "I'm hungry."

"You haven't eaten?"

"I got swamped with work. I'm in high demand with the writers at my new job."

Alice spied a silver coffee thermos. She picked it up and teetered it between them. "But you had time for this?"

Regina batted her eyelashes. "It's tea."

Alice raised her eyebrows. "Tea, huh?" She started to unscrew the top.

Regina raised one hand. "All right, it's coffee." She put her elbows on the counter and caught a thumb between her teeth. "Don't tell Simon. He worries enough."

Alice lifted the cap and scrutinized the contents of the almost-empty thermos. "How many have you had?"

"Just one. I swear."

"Well, I read somewhere that a little coffee, once in a while won't hurt a pregnant woman." She reached the sink and poured the remaining coffee down the drain. "Now, what would you like to eat?"

Regina moved her head closer to the screen. "Nothing. I'll eat later. I have to finish editing this article."

Alice opened the cabinet and got a white dinner plate. She set it on the counter before bending over the thermal shopping bag and pulling out a container. "Simon told me you've been eating eggs day and night." She took the lid off and allowed the aroma to permeate the air. "I thought you might like something different."

Regina glimpsed away from the screen and eyed the plate of chicken, rice and vegetables. "That smells good."

Alice pushed the dish across the counter and stuck a fork underneath the fluffy rice. "It does, doesn't it?" By the time she got a glass and water, Regina was already digging into the fare. *Now to get her away from that blasted machine.* "Why don't you sit on the sofa, dear?"

Regina licked her lips and took a sip of water. "Because that was not made for a pregnant woman. I can't believe how hard it is to get out of it. Ma said it'll only get worse."

She handed Regina a napkin and laughed. "She's right. I can help you when you're ready."

Regina bared all her teeth as she chortled and stroked her belly. "You're going to lift all this?" Her hand covered the mouse. "Thanks, but I really gotta send this back to the writer."

"Suit yourself." Alice busied herself in the kitchen. It was too easy. The one thing Regina needed after all she'd been through was a little mothering, and the fact that she was so likeable made it pleasant to care for her. *It's a shame that such an awful thing led us to getting to know each other.* Alice kept an eye out to make sure the food continued to disappear from the plate while she straightened the kitchen and put the rest in the refrigerator. She searched a bottom cabinet. "Regina, do you know what Simon did with the empty *kimchi* jars?"

Her question unanswered, she looked over the counter. Regina was staring at the computer. Tears welled over and soaked her lashes. "What's wrong? Regina?"

Regina shook her head violently. "Fucking bastards." She swiveled the stool and climbed off. "They won't leave us alone." She pounded her bare feet across the floor. "Why can't they just let us love each other?"

Alice read the source of the current upset. *Jeremy Stacks is a hero. Two bad he didn't kill that coon-ese mongrel inside you. You betraied your ansestors and womm by fucking that chink. Sellout bitch.* "Who are these people?"

"Assholes with nothing better to do. They call me a coon and him a nigger lover. What the hell is wrong with them? We get it from all sides, you know? Blacks, Asians, Whites—all of them trying their hardest to scare us into tearing our family apart. That's not going to happen." Regina pounded her fist against the wall and screamed in the air, "Fuck all of you!" She slumped and sobbed.

Alice led the distraught woman to the sofa. "Why do you read such hateful nonsense?" She went to the kitchen and got her a fresh water bottle. *How long have she and Simon been dealing with this?* "Stay off the computer, okay?" She stopped and looked at the buzzing phone on the counter. "It's Simon."

Regina's body heaved. She straightened her back and signaled Alice to hand her the phone.

"Are you sure?"

"Yes," she said between sobs and wiping away tears with her sleeve. "Give it to me."

Alice passed her the phone. Regina cleared her throat before answering. "Hey, Babe. What's up?" She continued to convulse and tears flowed, but there wasn't a hint of distress in her voice. "I'm fine. Working. No, just editing articles. Your mom's here. Okay." She pressed the screen.

"Ma?"

"Hello, Simon." Alice wondered at Regina. Her hands shook and tears continued to flow, but she was trying her hardest to hide the pain gripping her from Simon.

"You're taking care of my girl?"

"Yes." Regina stared at Alice, slowly shaking her head. "We're just chatting."

"That's great. I have to work late. Can you stay? If not, I'll bring it home."

"Come on, Young. I'm not a baby," Regina chimed. "As a matter of fact, I'm having one. Your mom brought tons of food. Let her go home, and you finish working at the office."

There was a brief silence. *"All right. I'll see you later tonight. Bye, ma. I love you."*

"I love you too, son."

"You're gonna eat and rest, right, Gina?"

"Yes, I am. Now get back to work."

"Love you."

"You better, bye." She dropped the phone on the sofa and rested her head in her hands.

"Why didn't you tell him about that awful email?"

"Because there's always an awful email or social media post. I arranged to stay off social media for my job, but I still have to check emails."

"Don't you think he should know?"

Regina rubbed her abdomen. "If I told him, he'd worry and rush home. There's nothing either of us can do about it. We have to wait until the trolls find someone else to go after. It sounds horrible, but that's the way it is."

Regina sat crossed legged. "You know what Simon had to do the night I was attacked? He fought my attacker and took me to the hospital. After that, he brought me home and climbed in the shower with me because I wouldn't let go. He tried to hide it, but I saw the pain in his eyes when he looked at my bruises. It was the same pain I felt when I looked at his. That night was not only hell for me but for him too. He stayed strong and protected me. I must be strong and protect him."

The room blurred in front of Alice's tears. "Can I hug you?" It was the closest they'd ever been to each other. Simon was marrying a strong and amazing woman.

ᔥᔥᔥᔥ

"Babe? Babe?" She stretched over the sofa and opened her eyes.

Happiness filled Regina's heart. Her love was back. She rested her hand on his shoulder. "Hey." The feel of his lips caused a surge of excitement to run through her. "I thought you were workin late?"

"Nah, I decided I missed you too much." Simon straightened and helped her to a sitting position. "How are you and this little one?" he asked sinking next to them and smoothing his palm over her abdomen.

She rested her head on his shoulder and tilted it to accept more of his magnificent kisses. "We're fine. Where's Alice?"

"She wasn't here when I came in. I guess she went home or had another engagement. Her social life is busy most of the time. Did you have a nice visit?"

She chuckled "Visit? You're stickin' to that story, Young? You sent her to babysit me."

He nuzzled her neck. "Guilty. Forgive me?"

"Yeah, it was actually nice, and I didn't know she was such a terrific cook. I was pleasantly surprised. I figured she had chefs or somethin'."

"Nah, she owns the kitchen. What did she make?" He grunted and slid the knot out of his tie as he walked to the refrigerator. He disappeared behind the door. "Yes. That's what I'm talkin' about. Ma does it again. You want some, Gina?"

"Yes, please." Alice taking care of her was nice, but it was even better to have Simon around.

It didn't take long for the microwave to start humming. Simon clanked a fork on the counter and tossed his tie next to the computer before turning it on. "So, you wanna tell me what upset you earlier?" He lifted the screen and started tapping on the keyboard.

"Wha-What do ya mean?"

"I mean," he said clicking until blue light reflected off his shirt and tan skin, "I know when you're hiding somethin' behind that super-proper, extra-sweet tone of yours, *Ms. Kent*."

"Are you breaking into my computer?"

"Yup."

"That's an invasion of privacy, Young. Aren't you supposed to uphold the law?" She wiggled on the sofa like an upside-down turtle. The baby, obviously in cahoots with daddy, tumbled inside and demanded that mommy stay put. *Why did I let him have my damn password?*

"Sit there, Gina. You sounded like a customer service rep. on the phone. You only do that when you don't want anyone knowing how pissed you are."

"Simon. Don't. It's just nonsense."

He narrowed his eyes as he read. After closing the laptop, he retrieved their dinner from the beeping microwave. "You shouldn't hide things like that from me. I can handle it." He stirred the food while walking back to the couch.

"I know you can. I just don't want to worry you all the time. It'll blow over soon." She opened her mouth at the food he offered.

"That's what happens. When two people love each other, they worry." He took a bite and then presented more to his future wife. "You know, Gina. I realized a long time ago that loving me has cost you a lot. It endangered your career, peace of mind and physical safety." He set the food aside and cradled her hands in his. The fear of losing her twisted his heart and had to be purged. "I wouldn't blame you if you left. I'm just glad you haven't. I love and need you so much."

She ran her fingers through his hair. "The slurs and hate are stressful, and the pain from what that monster did to me is not going away any time soon. You didn't cause them though, and being without you would only give me more anguish. I'm not going anywhere."

"Then that makes me the luckiest man in the world."

36 - COURTHOUSE

EGINA'S SCREAM PIERCED through every corner of the dark apartment. "Don't hurt my baby!"

Simon flung the blankets over the back of the sofa and bolted. Papers fell from his lap and drifted onto the floor. He groaned and rubbed his shin where it hit the coffee table and stumbled towards the screeching.

Regina was sitting in the bed yelling and tearing at the air. "No! No! Please!"

Simon knelt next to her and held her head between his hands. "Gina, Gina. babe, it's okay. It's just a dream." She stared into the shadows, tears flowing from her eyes. A flailing arm struck his mouth. He jerked back and pressed his hand against the stinging sensation and metallic taste oozing into his mouth. He dodged another swing, locked her arms and let her fists pound his back. "Regina, it's me." The night terrors started after a process server appeared at their door with subpoenas for them to testify at Jeremy Stacks' trial. He'd endured quite a few punches since that day. The bed creaked while he rocked and waited for her arms to fall at her sides.

"Simon?"

Her palms spanned his back. "Yes, it's me. You were having a nightmare."

"The baby?"

"The baby's okay. Here, lay down." He drew her trembling body into the curve of his and caressed her belly. It soon quivered from the inside and there was a tiny poke under his hand. "See, she's fine." They'd learned they were having a daughter at the 24-week ultrasound. They basked in the joy of their discovery and the wedding that soon followed. The guests donned coats, and the Kents had a huge tent erected with high-powered heaters so their daughter could have the gazebo wedding of her dreams. Their teeth chattered as they uttered their vows. They were ecstatic then, but now, apprehension hung in the air.

Going back and forth to court drained both of them. Simon didn't want his wife to come to hear him testify, but she insisted. Tomorrow was her turn. *She's gonna have a hard time testifying on such little sleep.* Another tiny kick from his daughter jolted his attention. He grazed his lips against Regina's ear. "There she is again."

Regina put her hand over his. "I feel her. She's okay?"

"She's perfect. He slowly drooped his eyelids closed. "Sleep. We have a big day tomorrow."

ᔍᔍᔍᔍ

Simon paced and stared at the bathroom door while people darted behind him through the large courthouse hall. Sharp retching sounds drifted from inside every time someone opened the door. His stomach turned in sympathy for the agony his wife was going through.

Testifying about the sexual assault took all the strength Regina had, and he was forced to watch helplessly as the defense attorney reamed her. Marcus and he tried their best to get her ready, but sleepless nights made her vulnerable to having an emotional breakdown when cross examined. He paced in front of the bathroom door. *At least it's over.*

Jeremy's attorney pulled no stops in trying to discredit Regina as a mental wreck, but she stayed strong. She answered every question and made it clear that the young man sitting across the room attempted to rape her and kill her and the unborn child she was carrying.

"I think she did very well." Marcus stood with his coat draped over his arm, his head following Simon as he walked back and forth on the marble floor. "Did you see the jury. They appeared sympathetic towards her."

"Yeah." He never took his eyes off the door. Toni emerged with her arm around Regina's shoulder. She made eye contact with Simon. The usual serenity in his sister-in-law's brown eyes was gone. Instead, they were anxiety-ridden. Things were not good.

Regina shuffled along holding her panting chest with one hand and rotund abdomen with the other. The dark circles around her red eyes were a mainstay lately. She looked at Simon and flew towards him, throwing her shaking arms around his neck. "Please, take me home."

"Okay." Simon swallowed back the pain jammed in his throat and drew her closer. "Do you want to get something to eat first?"

"No," she sniffed, "I just want to go home."

He desperately wanted to take away her anguish. "You got it."

The group turned. Everyone stopped in their tracks. Down the hall, Jeremy Stacks towered over his attorney, bending while the shorter man craned his head up and talked. He was the epitome of calm in his tailored suit and clean haircut. He appeared placid, almost serene, as if he wasn't the one on trial. He erected and turned his head in their direction.

Simon flinched at the pain from Regina's nails digging into his side. Her eyes wide, she blinked uncontrollably as Jeremy met her gaze and curled his lips into a boyish grin. Then he flashed his perfectly straight white teeth with a smile that stopped at his cold eyes. He taunted her with his baby face, which may convince a jury that he is not so bad after all.

Simon saw it before. A good-looking criminal getting off because of their ability to charm a jury. As confident as Marcus was, he maintained some doubt that Jeremy being convicted was a given.

"Son of a bitch." Marcus approached and stood beside Simon.

"More like a manipulative sociopath." Toni rubbed Regina's back. "Don't worry. They're going to put him away."

"Come on, Gina." Simon tried to turn her in the other direction, but she remained stagnant, staring right back at Jeremy. Her breath quickened like she'd just finish running and her eyes jumped in their sockets. Regina's body convulsed and she bolted for the bathroom holding her mouth. "Gina."

"I got her." Toni swung the bathroom door open and disappeared behind it.

Simon stomped towards Jeremy. He ached to wipe the floor with the gawky creep who took so much from his wife. It was his photo that almost completely destroyed her blog and irreparably damaged her career. Now that the trial began, instead of enjoying her new life and happily planning for the arrival of their baby, she was a bundle of nerves jumping at every sound. She barely tolerated anyone's touch anymore, and she constantly locked herself in the bedroom, where Simon heard her muffled cries through the door. Jeremy did all of that while presenting himself as the picture of innocence.

"No, man." Marcus appeared in front of him, blocking Simon's view of his target. "You don't want to get locked up for assault."

"Marcus." Simon pushed against his friend's hand and met steely resistance.

"I'm serious. Gina is hanging on by a thread, and you're the one that is keeping her from completely falling apart. Care and security, that's what she needs from you, not to throw down with that scum." He yanked Simon's arm and put greater distance between him and Jeremy. "You don't think Quinn and I weren't ready to take care of him?" he whispered into Simon's ear. "Believe me, we were tempted, but we're lawyers. We have to let justice do its work."

Simon looked down the hall. Jeremy stared at them. "I just want to bash his—"

"You have a career, a wife and a baby on the way. He's not worth risking any of that. Get a hold of yourself and be there for them."

Regina emerged from the bathroom and leaned against the wall holding her round belly. She slid slowly down. Simon rushed forward in time to catch her before she hit the floor.

"I think you should take her to the emergency room, Simon." Toni stroked Regina's braids. "She's very weak."

"No, I want to go home," Regina drawled and bowed her head.

"Don't worry, Babe, we're going home." *Right after we go to the emergency room.* Simon braced his wife in his arms. He took a moment to look back at the still smiling Jeremy before getting her as far away from the maniac as possible.

৬৯৬৯৬৯৬৯

Simon laid his exhausted wife on the sofa. "Here you go, Babe." He tucked a pillow under her head."

"Thanks, hun." Regina rolled on her side and fluttered her eyes closed.

Maybe I should try to get her in the bed. What had once been a retreat for them now hosted some of Regina's worst nightmares. It was understandable why she wanted to avoid it. *Nah, starting a petty argument about where she sleeps will only upset her more.*

Regina moaned and struggled upright. "I have to go to the bathroom."

He grasped her arm and elbow as she rose. "It's no wonder; they pumped you with so much fluid through that IV." He chuckled to mask his concern. The emergency room doctor diagnosed Regina with dehydration and put her on a drip. He wanted to keep her for observation, but of course she didn't cooperate. While signing herself out, Simon listened to all the doctor's instructions—plenty of fluids, water, Gatorade or something similar. He stored it with all of the other instructions from Regina's obstetrician to keep his wife and baby as healthy as possible.

"Gina?" Simon placed one ear close to the bathroom door. "Do you want something to eat?"

"No." She opened the door and sidled past him. "I'm not hungry."

Simon followed behind her. *When was the last time she ate?* He'd started checking the trash for empty containers and the sink for dishes. There was rarely anything there. "Come on. The doctors said you need to drink and eat. Just a little. You have to think about the baby."

She stopped and balled her fists. "Don't you think I've been thinking about the baby?" She walked around the side chair, eyebrows furrowed. "Every waking hour, I think about the baby," she spat through her bared teeth. Her brows softened, and she began to cry. "I'm sorry."

He put his arms around her. Toni told him to expect mood shifts, but they still jolted his heart. "It's okay," he soothed, rubbing her arm. "I'm just worried about you."

"I know."

Simon reclined on the couch and rested Regina's head on his chest. *If only there was a way to make all her suffering disappear.* He squeezed her trembling body, willing all his strength and love to her, hoping it would help her find a way out of all the misery tearing them apart. "Listen, Babe," he said when she calmed down. "I really need you to eat something. I'll go and get you whatever you want."

"All right. Eggs?"

"I figured you'd say that." He jumped to his feet and soon, the pan was crackling on the stainless-steel stove. He laid a napkin over her lap and presented a fluffy, yellow mound. "Toast?"

"No." Regina sniffed over the plate and took a few bites. "I guess you're getting kinda tired of cooking these for me?"

"Not at as long as you're not tired of eating 'em." It was wonderful to see her chewing. "Would you like ma to make some of that chicken and rice you like?"

"Yes, that would be nice." She poked at the pile of eggs. "Do you remember how he smiled?"

"Who?"

"Jeremy." Her face became blank as she stared off into space. "When he smiled at me in the courthouse today. Do you know how many times he smiled at me like that—at a meeting or when we talked in the hall?"

"Regina, please, don't." Simon put his hand on her leg. "He's not worth it."

"It's the same smile he had while he was choking me and trying to rip off my panties." She looked at Simon. "It's what I see in my nightmares."

He put his plate on the coffee table and moved closer to his wife. *I just got her to eat. She can't go back.* He touched her forehead to his. "Please, forget about him."

"That's never gonna happen." She pulled away and sighed. "But, I'll work harder to keep what he did from eating away at me. I was getting better before. I can do it again." She stabbed some eggs on the fork. "These are good. I didn't realize how hungry I was. Oh." Regina rubbed her stomach and laughed. "Apparently she is too."

The rest of the evening went well. There were a few times when Regina smiled and even laughed, and it felt like it used to be between them. Maybe they were turning a corner. Regina yawned, and stretched before she laid her head on Simon's lap. "You wanna watch so'in?" Her relaxed New Yorker accent crept out.

Simon reached for the remote and turned on the TV. "Sure." Yawning and rubbing his wife's belly, he flipped across the tiles on the screen. By the time he selected something and looked down to ask her opinion, a soft purr drifted out of her nose. He smiled, shifted his weight, and put his feet on the coffee table. It was the closest to normal they'd been for a while.

ࢗࢗࢗࢗ

Holding his shoes in one hand and backpack in the other, Simon padded to the front door in his socks. He turned the knob and spied over to Regina, who was sound asleep for the first time in weeks. She'd slept on his lap all night. The leg cramps and knotted neck muscles were totally worth her sleeping without night terrors. He spent the morning trying to be as quiet as possible while getting ready for work.

Satisfied that he'd accomplished his objective, Simon stepped through the doorway and watched Regina's beautiful face disappear. A fluttering pink slip stuck to the door caught his attention. Tension pinched the back of his neck. The slips were a product of the building co-op board. They frequently decorated apartment doors with warnings for countless and often tedious infractions. He pulled down the paper and read. "What the hell?
An eviction notice?"

37 - GIVE IT TO VINCE

I DON'T BELIEVE THIS. Simon folded the paper and headed to work. Once on the train, he sat down and started to read it. He'd barely got past the first sentence when his phone rang. "Hi, Toni."

"*Hey, Simon. How's Gina?*"

"She's doing better." Simon folded the paper and returned it to his pocket. "The ER doctor said she was dehydrated and exhausted."

"*That's not good.*"

"No, but she did eat and drink last night."

"*Great.*"

"And she didn't wake up in the middle of the night. She was still sleeping when I left."

"*I'm relieved to hear that. I was really worried about the effects of long-term sleep deprivation. It's only one night, but hopefully it is a sign that she'll go back to a normal sleep pattern in the near future.*"

"I hope so." He rolled his neck and arched his back in the seat. Every bump of the subway was a reminder of how tense and tender each muscle was. The couch was taking its toll. *I can't wait to sleep in my bed with my wife cuddled next to me again.*

"*Maybe I should stop by to see her after my last patient.*"

"How about this weekend? Thanks Toni. Bye." Simon leaned his head back and closed his eyes. It soon bobbed to the swaying motion of the train as the click clack lulled him. He bolted upright after he opened them just as the subway doors closed and the train crawled away from his stop. "You've gotta be kiddin' me."

𝄡𝄡𝄡𝄡

Simon wiped the sweat from his forehead with the back of his hand and paced in front of the elevator doors, occasionally looking at the lit numbers above them. His little detour took valuable time from an already tight schedule. It was important to get everything done and get home at a decent hour. He took the co-op notice from his suit jacket pocket.

Notice: The Co-Op board has received several complaints of nightly disturbances coming from your apartment...

"Sons of bitches," he spat under his breath. As unbelievable as it was, he and Regina were potentially about to be homeless because the people living around them lost their patience with her night terrors. He continued to re-read the notice until the elevator dinged. Simon balled the paper into his fist and shoved it into his front pocket before storming between the opening doors. *Like hell am I gonna allow them to kick us out of our home. Not after everything we've been through.* He clenched his teeth and fumed. Regina's already raw nerves couldn't handle any more stress—neither could his. He shoved passed people and down the hall to his office.

"Good morning, Simon." Corella's warm smile did not incite his usual charm. He rushed past her into his office, barely mumbling a response.

Slamming the door, Simon sat at his desk and repeatedly pounded his fist on it before bracing his head between his thumb and fingers. He ignored the knock on the door and concentrated on massaging his throbbing temples, contemplating possible approaches to prevent the insensitive jackasses at his building from tossing them out. Regina smiled back at him from a silver-framed photo. He traced around her image with his forefinger. She had to be protected from all of this.

"Hey, Si." Vince Deckland strutted through the door pulling his cufflinks.

Simon didn't even bother to look in his direction. "Not now, Vince."

"You got a minute to help a colleague? I have this-"

"I said not now, Vince." Both Vince and Corella at her desk behind him popped up their heads. Simon placed his fisted arms on the desk that shook from his violently tapping his heel.

Vince stopped in his tracks and stared like a deer in headlights. His hand kept pulling his cuff taught. For a moment, each man was motionless, then Vince started to back towards the door. "Okay, got ya, Simon. Sorry for disturbin' you." He did an about face to the door, closing it and returning to Simon's desk. For the first time, he didn't garner an obnoxious sleaze ball grin. "Look. I know that you've been going through some stuff lately, with that guy on trial for attacking your wife."

Simon loosened his fists and let his shoulders relax, but he kept his lips tight. *I've no patience for Vince or one of his dumb comments today.*

Vince looked down and tapped the desk. "Let me know if there is anything I can do to help." He met Simon's gaze. "I've got your back."

Simon took a deep breath and pulled his chair under him. "Thanks." Vince lifted the corners of his mouth into a smile that exposed his professionally-whitened teeth. Simon shook Vince's outstretched hand and answered his cell phone. "Hi Marc."

"Hey, man. How is Gina doing?"

"She's fine." Simon watched Vince's back as he headed for the door.

"There is something I need to tell you. I just got a call from Faisal at D.A.'s office. He wanted to give me a heads up. Jeremy accepted a plea deal: fourth-degree aggravated sexual abuse."

Every muscle in his body shook with rage. "What the hell do you mean plea?" Vince jerked and pivoted on his shoes as Simon shot out of his seat. "He won't even get 5 years. The ADA said—"

"Man, fuck the ADA. You know they're going to take a plea instead of risking a jury verdict."

Simon rubbed his neck muscles. "So, Regina testified, when she didn't have to? She went through all of that and made herself sick for nothing?"

"Yeah. I think Jeremy was gonna plea out anyway but waited until Gina testified just to be in the room with her again."

Vince, jumped back into the door as Simon barreled past him. "I have to get to Gina before anyone else tells her." Blasting past Corella, he stopped and went back to her desk. "Corella."

"I'll reschedule your appointments for the day." She tried at another warm smile.

Simon sighed. "Thanks, Corella." Everyone in the hall moved to the side, clearing a path for him. A knot twisted at his empty stomach.

"Simon." Vince came racing up to him.

Simon kept moving. "There's no telling what will happen if Gina is alone when she finds out about Jeremy."

"Simon, wait." Vince grabbed his arm. "Is there anything I can do?"

"No, but thanks." Simon squeezed through the opening elevator doors. Vince started to walk away. "Hold up." He pressed his arm against the elevator door and jammed his hand in his pocket, ignoring the huffing coming from the other passengers. "Can you help me with this?"

Vince unfurled and read the paper. He squinted and met Simon's gaze. "What the fuck?"

"Yeah," Simon said tight-lipped. "They're trying to threaten eviction because my wife has night terrors. You heard the scum that assaulted her just copped a plea? I have to be the one to tell her."

"Go." Vince folded the paper and stuffed it into his suit with a smug look. "I got this. You take care of that tall drink of hot chocolate," he shot over his shoulder, strutting down the hall.

Shaking his head, Simon let the last statement slide. "Thanks, Vince." The blond lawyer flicked two fingers in the air. Simon backed into the elevator. "I need to get to Gina and fast."

ട♦ട♦ട♦ട♦

"Gina?" Simon tossed his keys on the counter. Smells from the kitchen wafted into his nose. Last night's dishes laid in the dish rack and a half-eaten slice of toast sat on a plate next to a mug of tea. He smiled and put them in the sink. *She's eating and cooking.* Regina's belly bumped his back. Her arms wrapped around his waist.

"Hi." She laid her head on his back and Simon's heart soared. "You snuck out this morning."

Simon turned and his heartbeat quickened. The dark circles had faded from around her eyes and they glistened with a light that hadn't been there for a long time. "You were so peaceful. I didn't want to disturb you. Forgive me?" He pressed his lips to hers.

She pulled him as close as her belly allowed. After their glorious kiss, she stepped away. "I think I will. Why are you home so early?" She waddled to the stove and swirled a large wooden spoon in the steamy pot.

"I had some extra time, so I decided to spend it with my wife." He nipped the back of her neck and stroked the expanse of her stomach with both hands. His nose captured her intoxicating scent, sending waves of desire through him. He backed away and circled the kitchen island, adjusting his pants as he sat. Any indication that he wanted her sexually heightened Regina's anxiety, so it was important to hide his obvious state of arousal. "Smells good."

"It's for dinner, so it won't be ready for a while." Regina's bounteous curves jiggled and swayed as she turned and settled one hand on the counter with a spoon protruding from it and the other on her hip. "So, you just had all this extra time?" She clearly wasn't buying his story.

"Yes." He purposefully set his gaze to her face, fighting the urge to stare at the glorious cleavage popping out of her top. Black braids splayed from the intricate cornrow pattern on her head and cascaded over her shoulders, drawing lustful attention to the brown globes sitting right below them.

She shook the spoon at him, causing her breasts to jiggle. "You just wanted to check up on me."

They offered too much titillation. "Guilty." Simon bolted out of the chair and strode to the sofa. "Can you get me some water?" He flopped down and inhaled the air around him. Shifting in his seat, Simon concentrated on controlling his body's responses to Regina. He'd longed for her these past months, but any kind of intimacy was out of the question. She was healing, and he accepted that, but times like these were torturous.

"Here you go." Regina handed him a bottle of water and held the back of the sofa, settling onto it. "Since you're here, you can help me with something." She reached for a book on the coffee table.

"What?" Simon put the bottle on his lap. His entire body shivered, but the cold sensation was doing a good job at suppressing others.

"Baby Names. There are like a million of them."

Simon twirled a braid around his finger while she flipped through the pages of the book. "You look so beautiful."

"Mmm, thank you. You're kinda good lookin' too." She held a pen and pad in front of him. "Are you gonna help me name your daughter or not?" Her raised eyebrows and the smile twitching at the corners of her slightly pursed lips lit his spirit. She hadn't been this casual for so long. He would do anything to keep her content.

Simon kissed her tenderly on the mouth. "Of course."

Regina's beach-ball-sized belly bobbed as she slid down the couch. She propped a pillow behind her back and placed her feet on Simon's lap. "Look at those, Young." She pointed to her puffy ankles, wiggling her plump toes.

He smiled and began to caress her swollen feet. "How about I rub them for you?"

"It's the least you can do, since you're the one responsible for me being in this condition."

"Wouldn't that be the fault of a defective condom?" Simon made sure not to look in her direction for a response. He focused on pressing his thumbs at the bottom of the chubby brown feet and managed to maintain a straight face until a pillow crashed into his head.

"For real?" She let out a soft giggle. Finally, the air around them was not filled with tension and dread.

He leaned and kissed the portly tummy. "I'll happily take full responsibility for our daughter. Although, you were just as excited as me that morning."

"Baby names, Young." He massaged his wife's feet while she called out names. Occasionally, he would go wash his hands and stir the pots on the stove as directed and was delighted to bring Regina whatever snacks she requested. Elation washed over his heart at the sight of her biting an apple as she thumbed through the book of baby names. She was eating and laughing. Telling her about Jeremy's plea would potentially destroy the fragile serenity filling their home. *I'm gonna hold off telling her.* The peaceful moment with his family also soothed his fried nerves—he wasn't going to just end it.

Noise from the evening rush-hour traffic filtered through the windows. He put the last of the dinner dishes in the dishwasher and turned it on before collapsing on the couch.

"Delicious, babe," he announced while stifling a burp. "It's been a long time since I ate like that." So busy monitoring Regina's diet, he'd neglected to eat properly.

"I'm glad you're satiated, counselor." Sitting with her legs crossed on the couch and caressing her tummy, Regina continued to scour the book. It was their second round because she wanted to make sure she hadn't missed the perfect name. "Jordan?"

"Didn't we say no to that name last time?"

"Yeah."

"I still like the name Justice."

Regina peered at Simon over the book. "Justice Young, and her father's a lawyer?"

Simon draped his arm around Regina's shoulder and laid his hand on her stomach. "Hey, maybe she'll be a lawyer too."

She rested her head on Simon's chest. "Then you definitely don't want her name to be Justice. Imagine, the first Black, Asian American woman on the Supreme Court—Justice Justice Young? That's corny as hell."

"Fair enough."

Regina sat straight, her eyes alight with excitement. "Hey, how about Justine? It means just and upright."

Simon smiled. "I like it."

"Put it at the top of the list." Her phone rang as Simon reached for the pad and pen. "Hello? Yes, this is Regina Kent."

Simon's stomach twisted. He turned to her. "Gina." Regina raised her index finger.

She met Simon's gaze. "Jeremy Stacks took a plea? No. I have no comment." she stared down at the phone screen.

He held her shaking hands. "Gina."

"Does this mean it's over?"

Initially mute, he searched for the right thing to say. More than anything, the calm that settled around them needed to be preserved. The wrong thing might send Regina spiraling back down. "The DA will probably want you to make a victim impact statement at sentencing."

"I don't want to."

He lifted her head by her chin. "Then you don't have to."

"Good. I'm finally feeling a little like myself again. I woke up and wasn't consumed by visions of that day or his face. I was able to just breathe, you know? I think if I have to be in a room with that monster again, it'll all go away."

Her phone rang again. Her eyes narrowed. "Not one of my contacts."

"It's probably another reporter."

She held down her phone's power button. "Can you text Marcus, Toni, and my parents and let them know to contact me through your phone?"

"Will do."

Regina leaned back onto Simon's chest and opened the book. "Now, what letter were we on?"

38 - Doin' It Well

REGINA STARED IN THE MIRROR. A series of keloid scars made by Jeremy's teeth lined around her areola in a crescent shape. No matter what she used, they were not disappearing, determined to be a continual reminder of her past torment. She'd worked to make sure Simon didn't see them, which was one of the reasons why intimacy was avoided like the plague and strained her marriage. "Not anymore." She pulled the bodice over her breast and exited the bathroom. "It's time to get the rest of my life back."

She couldn't help but smile when she saw the playlist titled "My Gina" on the smart tv's music app screen. She rubbed the remote button with her thumb and pushed. The same music that Simon played in her apartment caressed her ears and permeated through the room. She dropped her lids and swayed her hips as she backed away from the coffee table. Instead of memories of the horrible Instagram episode, her mind drifted to how close they were before the posts ripped between them.

The passion in Simon's eyes were the first thing. They'd burned so fiercely. She rounded the side chair to the center of the room and bent her head back. Thoughts of her love's fingertips emblazoning a trail down her breast came next. She raised her arms and rotated her shoulders to the rhythm. Not feeling him for so long gouged a pit of yearning into her very core. Apparitions of hungry lips expertly traversing her skin created bumps down her arms and every place on her body where the real ones had been. Months dragged like years.

Her husband was very patient with all the rejection. There were times that she sensed his longing. Initially, his advances were triggering, and the torture of that night flooded through her. She'd stiffen and flee. It got to a point where he just stopped sitting or lying too closely to her in bed. Therapy sessions helped Regina purge some of the trauma, so she eventually functioned. Her desire for Simon reemerged from the pain and fear, but her physical scars would then prickle and shut her down, causing a rebuff that made them both wallow in anguish.

Regina broadened her stance and gyrated, led by the sensual tempo. The large expanse of the baby she carried in front of her didn't keep hips from moving the same way they always had, beckoning strong hands to guide them. They demanded Simon——all of her did.

She turned and froze. Her gaze landed on Simon standing with one hand hovering his coat over the entryway rack. Both their mouths agape, she panted while he took in her body covered in a full-length white gown that hugged every curve. His stare lingered on the brown thigh peeking through the long slit.

He dropped his everything to the floor. "Gina."

The dress was on purpose. She was going to entice her husband and have him despite the mixture of desire and terror jumbling inside her. Nothing, not even the scars Jeremy left, would keep them apart any longer. "Come here." She rubbed her tummy and put her hips back to work.

Simon kicked off his shoes and socks and strode to the center of the great room. Regina turned and backed into him then melted against his body. Hot breath rushed over her neck. She reached behind to jibe their hips. His already hard cock pressed into her bottom and drove a surge of passion that flushed out any apprehensions. Weaving her fingers through his hair, Regina moaned, dropped her head against his shoulder and turned it until their lips barely touched. "You feel so good."

"Oh, Babe." His shaky voice matched his quaking chest tightened with raw need. She was so beautiful. His hands floated along her curves—afraid to actually touch. Simon wasn't sure which he feared more—Regina's rejection or an inability to control the hunger tearing through his body. He wanted her so much and for so long. Regina brought his hands to where she undulated. He gently dug his fingertips into her luscious hips. Her heady scent and alluring sighs made him dizzy. "Are you sure?"

She turned in his embrace and hung her arms around his neck. She pressed a finger to his lips. "Shh. No more doubts, okay? I want you, Simon."

He covered her mouth in an unrestrained, torrid kiss. Despite what she said, he still waited for any indication that she was going to be triggered. When she accepted his passionate embrace, he began to caress her curves. They had been terribly missed. He filled his hands with her buttocks, even plumper because of the pregnancy. He nibbled her neck and slid a palm upward until it cupped her enlarged breast.

She sucked in a breath and pushed against his chest. It tightened. *I must be rushing her. She's not ready.* He cast his gaze down to their feet. "I'm sorry, Gina."

"No. It's fine. I liked it." She took him by the hand. "Let's go to bed." He obediently followed two bouncing buttocks.

Regina seated Simon on the black and taupe pinstripe blankets and stood in front of him. He slipped his hands under her dress and dragged her panties down to the floor. He held her gaze and rediscovered her soft folds. She threw her head back and dug her nails in his shoulders. He went further. There was no stopping now. To do so would mean utter despair. He smiled with satisfaction when Regina snatched away from him. She was ready.

He noticed her apprehension when she sat down. "Simon." Anxiety replaced his triumph.

No, no, no. Please don't turn me away. I can't take it. Simon tucked a braid behind his wife's ear. "You're not ready?"

Regina tilted her head. "Oh, hell yes, I am. There's just something I've been keeping from you. It's one of the reasons why I've been hesitant about sex." She picked at a loose thread on the comforter. "Do you remember when I told you I was bitten?"

He nodded and stroked the soft white fabric covering his wife's leg.

"Well, I have scars. I didn't want you seeing them."

Simon cupped the same breast as in the living room. "This one, right?" Jeremy was still a barrier. Regina's inhibition about dressing in front of him all this time made more sense. *All the denial because she's afraid of what I'll think about a few scars?* He had to ease her anxieties. Regina was the thing he wanted most in the world, and he was going to make sure she knew it. "Show me."

She continued to stare out the window as she nodded.

The fabric fell away. After her initial flinch, Simon traced the semi-circle formation with his finger. They were overshadowed by her delectable nipple bidding him to play. He arched his eyebrow. "The girls are bigger." He cast a roguish grin.

She laughed at the air and sniffed. "Yeah, that's one of the perks of pregn—."

Simon drew the nipple between the roof of his voracious mouth and tongue. He crept a hand under the dress and pinched the other nipple between his thumb and finger. Regina sucked in air and leaned away. He wrapped an arm around her back and nudged her closer. He wanted her—all of her—to hell with scars.

"Yes, like that," Regina groaned. She yanked Simon's tie and shirt off and threw his back against the bed. His pants and underwear hit the floor. He lay prone with her kneeling between his legs. She pulled down her bodice and freed both breasts. He teased them until she pushed his hands away, bent down and filled her mouth with him.

She sucked and licked until he begged for mercy. "Gina, stop. I can't. Please."

Her thighs warmed his sides. His hips and torso welcomed the weight of wife and baby. Regina pinned Simon's gaze and reached between them, squeezing and sliding her hand up and down. The pleasure of her insides enveloped him. Her breast jumped to the motion of their lovemaking. The large mound underneath them did as well. She was his, carrying his baby, and driving him out of control. He stilled her hips. "Wait." His chest burned to catch enough air.

"Am I too heavy?"

"No, it feels too good. I'm going to explode."

She brought his hands to her breasts. "Me too, Simon." She resumed. "Me too." The cries of their mutual release almost shook the windows. He felt a warm gush over his groin. Regina crushed his sides between her thighs, continuing to convulse until she finally fell on the bed in a heap.

Simon looked down and gasped. "What the hell?" He rolled on his side. "Gina. I think your water broke."

ঙ঺ঙ঺ঙ঺ঙ঺

"Oh, my God, Toni, it was so embarrassing." The black mid-size car rolled down the tree-lined Queens streets. Regina noticed a steady increase in size of the houses as she got closer to her mother-in-law's. "Simon wouldn't listen to me no matter how many times I told him I was okay. He insisted on going to the emergency room."

"*Aww. He was a worried daddy.*"

"More like nuts. He raced around the apartment like it was on fire. I finally convinced him to take me to Dr. Algiers's office. She took pity on me when I called. Although I think it may have been worse."

"*Why?*"

"She could barely hold in her laughter when she told me that my water hadn't broken, and what I experienced is called a *female ejaculation.*" Regina glimpsed sideways at the rearview mirror. Of course, the driver was listening. She cocked her head. "Are we almost there?"

He lowered his eyebrows and shifted his glance back to the road. "Yes, Ma'am."

Toni's giggling wafted through the phone. "*I can't believe you never had one of those.*"

"Well, I didn't. Have you?"

"*Oh yes. Not like every time but enough to make me want to put up with your brother. He's quite good.*"

"Why did I ask?" The car parked in front of a huge Tudor-style house. Simon's childhood home was slightly bigger than hers. "I'm just coming to Alice's house. I'll talk to you later. Bye." She struggled with her tummy out of the car. The driver put a suitcase carrying enough clothes to outfit her and Simon for the weekend next to her on the porch. "Thank you. How much?"

The driver raised his hand. "It's already paid for, ma'am."

Alice appeared before she could knock. "Gina." Small arms surrounded her. "Come in." She swatted at Regina's hand. "No, he'll bring the luggage inside, won't you?"

Regina sent the driver a sympathetic stare and handed him a large bill. "Thank you."

"Look at you." Alice touched the top of Regina's belly. "You must be ready to have my granddaughter."

"I am." Regina's gaze followed Alice down the tan wainscoted entryway. A formal living room lay at her right and a dining room to her left. In front was a grand staircase. "Dr. Algiers said it will be any day now."

"Then it's a good thing we're going shopping. We should be finished in time to have dinner with Simon. I've prepared his old room. My driver will be here in five minutes."

༺༻༺༻

"No, Alice, no." Regina stared at the tiny floral print sleepwear. "I'm not buying $50 pajamas for a newborn."

Alice shook it. "But it's so sweet. I'll pay."

"You're not buying $50 pajamas for a newborn. I have a job, and I don't have $50 pajamas."

"You've said no to everything. You're going to have this baby any day and you have nothing in the layette." Alice reached in her purse. The girl was being stubborn. *She probably wants to buy some clothes from one of those stores with people in blue vests. I'll not have it.* "Now, your mother may be lecturing in Greece, but she told me to contact her if you became difficult about buying baby clothes." She put the outfit on the table and slid her thumb across her phone screen. Adrian and her immediately hit it off when they met at the wedding. The two were now a unified force of matriarchy to keep the next generation of Youngs and Kents in line. Even Marcus was wary of them. "Do I need to call your mother, Gina?"

Her daughter-in-law folded her arms and pouted her full lips. "Fine. One."

Alice grinned and put her phone away. "Why don't you go over there and select a dress for her to wear home? I'll get the layette together."

Regina glanced at the dresses and smiled. "Okay, but don't go crazy Alice."

"Go." She laid a pair of pajamas over her arm. *I can't get just one. Gina is being unreasonable.* One pair quickly became ten. She walked towards the cashier. It would be too late for her daughter-in-law to protest if the clothes were already purchased. She scanned the store for Regina and narrowed her eyes at the scene before her.

Regina was sliding clothes across a rack. Behind her was a woman with a name tag studying her suspiciously. She hovered around Regina without saying a word. When Regina moved to another rack, the woman trailed a few feet behind. The shifty-eyed clerk provided no help when a dress fell to the floor and Regina struggled to bend down and pick it up.

Alice strode to the register and sat the stack of clothes on the counter, not allowing the cashier to say a word. "Yes, I'm interested in these, but first, I would like to speak to your manager, Collin."

"Right away, ma'am," bubbled the cashier before she called for the manager.

A tall, well-dressed, man emerged from his office and stood next his employee. He bent slightly over the counter garnering a smile that only went as far as his mouth. "Ah, Mrs. Young. It's good to see you again. How can I help you?"

Alice jutted her chin in the air. "Hello, Collin. I come here quite frequently. Every time one of my friends or family members is expecting a baby, grandbaby, and so on."

"Yes, Mrs. Young. It's a pleasure to serve you."

"Usually, I'm satisfied with the service I receive, but I'm not pleased with the way my daughter-in-law is being treated. She's ready to have her baby and needs a full layette. Despite plenty of attendants around her, no one is offering her any assistance."

Collin stood to his full height and peered across the store. "Well that's not acceptable at all. Where is your daughter-in-law?"

Alice pointed. "She's right there."

Collin continued to scan the store. "I don't see her."

Alice placed a hand on her hip. He obviously was looking for an Asian woman. "Really? You don't see that clearly pregnant woman right there?"

He raised his eyebrows and shaped his mouth into an 'O', finally realizing that she meant the Black woman. "Oh, yes."

"Is there any particular reason why your clerks don't think she's worthy of their service?"

"No, of course not, Mrs. Young. There must be some mistake. Gretchen." He waved the woman shadowing Regina to come.

"Alice." Regina called and wobbled to the register at the same time. "I love this one, but It's very expensive." Gretchen stopped behind her.

Alice ran her hand over the dress and smiled at the beaming Regina. "Then she'll have it. You," she snapped and pointed to Gretchen, "take this." The wide-eyed associate looked at her manager's glare and obeyed. "Follow my daughter, and carry whatever she selects until she's finished."

Regina's eyes flashed. The corners of her mouth twitched, indicating that she knew why Alice was being so condescending. "Thank you. I did want to look at some more dresses."

"Then have at it." Alice glanced at the tall manager.

"Yes, Mrs. Young," He reached in a small glass refrigerator behind the counter and took out a few different bottles. He rounded the corner and presented them to Regina. "Would you care for something to drink? We have water and juice."

"No, thank you. Oh." Regina's eyes widened and jaw dropped. She gasped and stared down at the water pooling around her feet from underneath her skirt. "Ma."

"Don't worry." Alice lifted a stack of pajamas and dropped them around Regina's feet. She then stomped the foot of her designer heel on one and wiped around Regina's shoes. Baby didn't like anyone messing with her mama either. "There, that's better. Do you have any plastic bags, Collin?"

"No, Mrs. Young, but we'll get you some towels. Gretchen." The irked clerk raced across the store and brought back a stack of baby bath towels. "Don't worry about paying, Mrs. Young. We'll take care of everything here."

"Thank you." Alice took the towels and wrapped her arm around Regina's waist. "Let's go have this baby. Fun fact. You'll be giving birth in the same hospital where her father was born."

39 - JUSTINE YOUNG

REGINA GRABBED HER GUT, GROANING and gritting her teeth. A ball of pain knotted at the top of her belly and coursed down. She kicked her legs trying to free them from the bedsheets. *Damn hospital corners.* "Where's the anesthesiologist?" She rolled to her side and stared at the empty warmer. Her baby would be there soon.

"They're coming." Alice rubbed her back. "Just breath."

"I can't believe how fast this is happening. The pain won't stop." There were no breaks. Every time one wave of pain ebbed, another quickly followed. Her arms and legs ached from constantly seizing in pain.

"I know." Mercifully, Regina's mother-in-law released her long legs from under the blanket. "I'm looking at the monitor. It should be getting better."

Her tense muscles relaxed as the pain eased. "Where's Simon?" She panted and laid on her back. "Give me my phone."

"No. I'll call him. You hold on because another contraction is coming."

Regina breathed and squeezed the pillow. The contractions were getting stronger. She shrieked through the agony. "Drugs. When am I gonna get some drugs?"

"I told you, they're coming." Alice tucked Regina's braids behind her ear and put the phone near it. "Here's Simon."

"Gina? Gina, I'm coming, babe. There's a lot traffic, but I'm almost there."

She huffed into the phone. "Why didn't you take the train? How much longer? I don't think she's gonna wait." Another pain shot through her stomach and she let out a long moan. "Get your ass to this hospital."

A nurse in scrubs with tiny bunnies on them came in and looked at the monitor. "Well, Ms. Young, you and baby are progressing nicely. I'm going to get the doctor to check you.

Alice took the phone from Regina and walked to the window speaking Korean. she couldn't understand, but the maternal command in her mother-in-law's tone was universal.

Alice set the phone next to the bed. "It's going to be fine. Do you need anything?"

"Ice." Regina sloshed the tiny chunks in her mouth when another contraction and a huge amount of pressure shot through her.

The nurse returned with the doctor trailing. "Okay, Ms. Young. Let's see how we're doing." He snapped on a pair of gloves and sat at the end of the bed. He looked towards the ceiling. "Ten centimeters and fully-effaced. Cancel the epidural." He then began spewing orders at the nurse. "Your baby is ready to come, Ms. Young. You may feel a need to push."

The next contraction deafened her to everyone around. The bottom of the bed disappeared while she struggled to catch her breath. "My husband."

"Unfortunately, baby is not waiting for daddy."

𖤽𖤽𖤽𖤽

Simon stretched to his full length on the bed and lifted his lids. He slowly blinked and curled his lips as he focused on a small fist poking from the blanket. He placed his finger against it. The hand opened and squeezed. His heart melted. Tiny cries sprang out and the pink floral receiving blanket jumped. Justine was awake.

He'd made it to the hospital room just when Regina started pushing to deliver their daughter. The baby was already crowning, and he'd barely had time to hold his wife's hand before the doctor put the little body with a head full of black hair on her chest. It was love at first sight.

"'Morning, princess." Justine paused and stared into the air. She resumed rubbing her fist against her mouth and cheeks. "Are you hungry?" Simon kissed his daughter's forehead. She answered her father with a series of sharp shrieks. The crib across the room remained vacant since Justine established that between her parents was where she would be sleeping. She had a lot of power for such a little person.

Regina's eyes drifted open. She yawned and pulled the bundle closer to her. "She needs to be changed and fed." His wife's drawl attested to another night of waking to care for the precious newborn.

Simon stroked Regina's shoulder. "Stay here. I'll change her."

It was amazing how he could nestle her in his palms. He was scared to even carry her at first, but Regina eased his fears. One week since returning from the hospital, Simon confidently rested Justine's little body on the changing table and went to work.

"Don't forget to rub her belly button with alcohol." Regina rustled under the blankets.

"Got it." He raised the tiny packet in the air. Justine's arms and legs splayed, demanding that her father be quick about getting her back into mommy's warm arms. He obeyed.

Dry and once again swaddled, Simon cooed at the light brown miniature version of his face. "Do you want mommy?" He padded his bare feet across the wood floor and back to the billowing comforter enveloping Regina. "Here's mommy."

Regina propped on one elbow. The scars on her breast disappeared behind Justine's head. Crying was replaced by a soft sucking sound. Regina grimaced and closed her fists into tight balls.

He sat and patted her leg. "Still hurts?" It was amazing how she could bear it.

"A lot." After Justine sucked a few seconds more, the tension in Regina's body relaxed. She smiled down at their daughter, stroking her black hair with her fingertips. "Only at first though. I'll get used to it."

Simon took the buzzing phone from the nightstand and sighed. "It's the caterer. They'll be here in an hour." He kissed his ladies and headed to the bathroom. "I'm going to hop in the shower while

Princess Justine finishes. Then I'll take her so you can get ready." He turned before closing the door and watched his wife beaming over their daughter. So Beautiful and strong. She meant and gave him so much.

❧ ❧ ❧ ❧

Simon looked from his phone and to the bouncer next to him on the counter. He checked to make sure his daughter still slept before hopping off the stool to answer the knock at the door. "Hey, Ma."

"Hello, Simon." His kiss scarcely grazed his mother's cheek. She bypassed his open arms. "Where's she?" Alice shined over the bouncer. "There you are. Look at you." She pulled back the blanket. "You look just like your father when he was a baby. Did you know that? Did you know that, Justine?"

"Tell me about it." Regina strutted across the great room in a long-sleeved emerald maxi dress with her braids in a bun at the base of her neck. She joined Simon's mother in her adoration. "He keeps mentioning it. It's sickening."

"Hey." He put an arm around each woman. "Strong genes."

Alice flicked her son's arm away. "Don't be smug, Simon. It's unbecoming. Gina is the one who had the baby." She opened the bag she'd carried in and handed Regina a box. "I came early because I have something you might like." She washed her hands and proceeded to scooped the baby from the bouncer. "I hope it's the one you wanted."

Regina squealed and tore the box open. "You got it?"

Alice sat on the sofa. "Of course. You need something for Justine's debut to the family." Her hand patted the small back in her arms. Grandma was thoroughly hooked.

Regina lifted the dress in the air. "It *is* the one." She presented it to Simon and glanced over her shoulder. "Oh, Ma. Thanks. Let's put it on her."

It wasn't long before Justine was surrounded by lilac chiffon pleats and nursing comfortably in her mother's arms. Things changed for the better since her arrival. Simon and Regina never felt closer, and even the social media trolls backed off with the attacks.

Elliot's advice to post a picture of them holding Justine with the baby's face turned away from the camera worked. There were still the occasional vicious comments, but those were overrun by supporters quick to "shut that noise down."

Simon gave his mother a proper kiss and answered the door. "Young?" The caterer shot past him holding insulated food carriers. "Excuse me."

Simon peered back into the hallway when someone stopped him from closing the door. "Hey, man. You don't want us to come in?" Marcus grabbed his hand. Caught in a bear hug, Simon coughed for air.

The Kent clan poured into the apartment and made a beeline to the sofa. Adrian took her place next to Alice, and Toni balanced her petite body on the arm. Marcus and Deverell Kent towered over Regina, mooning at Justine—the new woman in their family they'd have to protect.

The caterer rushed past him again. "Enjoy your meal."

"Thank you." Simon slapped a tip into the open hand in the hall and closed the door. He headed towards the din of admiration when there was another knock. "Oh, come on."

"Hello, I've a package for Regina Young." The deliveryman held a large box in front of Simon.

"Okay, thank you." Simon opened the wallet still in his hand and tipped the young man before taking the package. Finally making it to the seating area, he filled the side chair. "You have a package, Gina."

"Who's it from?" Simon read the store's name on the box

Regina shot Alice a suspicious glance. "Ma?"

"I had nothing to do with it." She smirked. "Open it."

He eyed the two women. "What's going on." Something was apparently afoot.

"Nothing." The twinkle in his wife's eyes said otherwise. "Can you open it for me, please?"

He pulled back the tissue paper. "It's pajamas. A bunch of them."

Adrian reached and held one in the air. "Very nice. I wonder who sent them?" Justine startled when all the women on the sofa laughed at what was obviously an inside joke.

"What," asked Simon.

Marcus slapped him on the back of the neck and released a booming laugh. "When will you learn to just leave things alone?"

"Exactly," Deverell agreed with his son. "Trust us, it'll make things easier. Let's eat."

The women continued to chat while the men peeled back the tray lids. Simon focused on his wife and daughter. They truly completed his life.

ACKNOWLEDGEMENTS

Alhamdulillah, I've been blessed by the Creator with a great bunch of people.

A special thanks to my fantastic content editor, Tiffani Burnett Velez for rolling up her sleeves and hitting the ground running to help me polish this work.

A warm thank to Sandra Barkevich for being a patient friend and writing coach. I couldn't have even imagined writing this novel without her gentle guidance, encouragement and support.

Shout out to Rameez Farooqui, a brilliant legal mind and my inspiration for main character Simon Young. Jazakallah for always taking the time to let me bend your ear.

Jazakallah ALKEBULAUN for writing a beautiful and inspirational poem about Simon and Regina's love and as a tribute to interracial couples.

I have to thank my girls–Djamila Abdel-Jaleel, Nadia Anwar, Maritza Flowers as well as my beautiful and talented daughter Hameedah Poulos for listening to me day and night—night and day—and day and night again—as I worked and flustered over finishing this book.

Jazakallah to my wonderful husband, who works incredibly hard so I can do what I love and stays blissfully ignorant about just how much heat I stoke.

THANKS SO MUCH FOR READING!

I hope you enjoyed Simon and Regina's story of love and perseverance. Please leave a review on Amazon and Goodreads so I can continue to bring readers stories!

CONTACT

I would love to hear from you.

Email - laylafied@gmail.com
Website - www.laylawriteslove.com

FOLLOW ME

Facebook - https://www.facebook.com/laylawriteslove/
Instagram - https://www.instagram.com/laylawriteslove/
Twitter - https://twitter.com/laylawriteslove
Amazon   –   https://amazon.com/author/laylawriteslove

SPECIAL BONUS

Start reading the *Brothers in Law* short story and learn how these 6 dynamic men met.

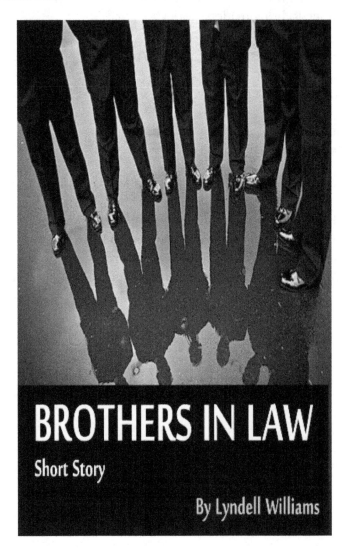

BROTHERS IN LAW
Short Story

By Lyndell Williams

1 - DINNER

SIMON LOOKED AT HIS WATCH AND TAPPED THE DEWY BEER BOTTLE in front of him onto the table. "As usual," he peered across at his law school roommate, "your boy, Adam is late. Where is he? I skipped lunch." He waved the waiter away for the third time. Agreeing to have dinner with the unreliable Adam Kane was a bad idea.

"Relax man." Marcus leaned back in his chair and scratched the black stubble spanning his brown face. "Have some more bread or somethin'. I think he'll be a good fit for this next project. We need a lot of funding, and he's great at getting money out of sponsors."

Simon lifted a crust of dry bread and dropped it back into the wicker basket on the white tablecloth. "That may be, but he's not the most dependable of people. We're always waiting on him." He pulled out his phone and responded to the text. *"Sorry, gorgeous. I'm tied up. I'll be over soon."*

"Yeah, but he comes through in the end." Marcus glanced at Simon's phone and looked at him sideways. "I bet this isn't just about food. What? You got another woman all hot and bothered waiting for you?"

Simon smiled and reclined as he laid his phone face down on the table. "I do have plans for later."

Marcus shook his head and let out a baritone chuckle. "The way you go through women with that smooth Asian game of yours."

"It's the eyes." Simon passed a finger over the thick lid of his hazel eye. "Chicks dig 'em."

"You need to settle down."

Simon raised his hands. "Hey, I'm happy that you found Toni, but I, for one, am not ready to be exclusive." He examined his buzzing phone and raised an eyebrow at the picture his "date" sent. "Oh, yeah. She's ready."

Marcus rolled his eyes and raised his hand. "There's Adam."

Adam dropped his helmet on the table with a thud and tugged at his lambskin biker jacket. "Hey, sorry, I'm late." He tapped the shoulder of the tall man next to him. "I ran into my man, Brandon, and we started talking. He graduated a couple of semesters back and passed the UBE and PA Bar and is already a junior partner at his firm. Brandon Hulse," he lifted his palm to the ceiling, "This is Simon Young and Marcus Kent."

"Hey, man. Congratulations." Marcus shook each of their hands as they sat. "You guys want a beer?"

"No, thank you," Brandon smoothed his tie between the manicured fingers of his umber hands, "I don't drink."

"Brandon is Muslim." Adam pushed up the sleeves of his gray Henley shirt. "That's what we were talking about. I'll take one though."

Simon jutted his chin at the duo. "That's fascinating. Can we order now?" He lifted the menu.

"You'll have to excuse Simon." Marcus signaled the waiter. "He's trying to satisfy his hunger and a bunch of urges tonight."

After a much-deserved glower at his best friend, Simon scanned the menu. "No more banter or distractions. There's a hot woman waiting for me to cool her off."

2 - BRAWL

MARCUS RELEASED A SATISFIED SIGH, tapped his belly and stepped into the evening Boston air with his three companions. It was a very productive meal—things were going just as planned. "Right, how about we meet again at the end of the week and see what progress Adam made with fundraising?"

"Don't worry, Marc. I'll get my mother on it." Adam zipped his jacket and hung his elbow from Simon's shoulder. "There's nothing Vivian Kane likes more than a chance to dress up with her rich friends and throw money at a cause. It helps her feel like she's making a difference."

"Just make sure they're doin' a bunch of throwin'." Simon set his lips in a thin line while tapping at his phone. "This can help a lot of people." He was obviously still wary of Adam's ability to come through—not without cause. Adam Kane was very privileged, which meant he didn't really vest a lot of time or energy in anything—not even his studies. Everything just came too easily.

Marcus opened his mouth but closed it and turned to the faint sounds of grunting and scuffling. "What the—" He peered at the far end of the parking lot. A group of men surrounded another wearing a black leather jacket, jeans and sneakers. Their angry porcelain faces glowed from the light of the street lamp above them. They circled their prey like a pack of buzzards. Clearly, this was no quaint little get-together. They meant to do some damage. Marcus glanced at Simon; the pair stormed towards the scene.

"Why don't you go back where you came from, terrorist?" A White guy shoved the light brown man from behind towards one of his fellow thugs.

Simon scoffed. "You've gotta be kiddin' me. Do they ever get tired of this?"

It was yet another pack of drunken White college students, who had decided to have a little "fun" by jumping a Person of Color unlucky enough to cross their path. It happened more frequently than a lot of people thought. They always chose a victim who didn't appear to be much of a threat and easy to push around. Unfortunately for the crew of 10 knuckleheads that Marcus counted, they chose the wrong guy to mess with that night.

The tall man ducked a punch from the oversized jackass in a red baseball cap. The "victim" then delivered one squarely on the jaw of his attacker. The cap fell off the buffoon's head as he hit the pavement.

Marcus raised his eyebrows. Impressive. He pulled at his zipper. *Definitely not a soft target, but the numbers are still against him.* He dropped his jacket and tugged up the sleeves of his cardigan. "Yo," the collegiate riff-raff simultaneously turned to him, "leave the guy alone."

A lanky blond stalked towards him with a scowl on his whiskerless face. "Who's gonna stop us, coon?" Marcus struggled to keep the corners of his mouth from twitching. Wearing an Abercrombie and Fitch hoodie and designer skinny jeans, the "thug" did not cut an intimidating figure, which was probably why he needed his gang with him.

A rush of air brushed the side of Marcus's face. Adam blasted past him and smashed his helmet against the guy's head. "You like that, huh? You, racist asshole." He tossed the headgear and balled his fists. Marcus shook his head at Simon. Adam was not one to let a good brawl go to waste, especially one where he got to pummel a bunch of bigots. It was his hobby of sorts.

Two more preppie hooligans charged at Adam. A stranger sprang out of nowhere, taking one of them down with a kick to the gut and an elbow strike while Adam decked the other. Fists clenched, he looked over at his new comrade. A street lamp shone on half of the tan man's smug smirk that reached up to his angular eyes. "Yeah," Adam stretched his neck from side to side and puffed his chest, "let's do this." Marcus, Simon and Brandon joined the affray.

It was time to take on hate.

3-PRECINCT

"**Y**OU CAN SIT OVER THERE WITH THE REST OF YOUR GANG." The stubby policeman shoved Faisal in the direction of a row of chairs. He leaned his muscular frame against the wall and poked at his swollen eye. Pain shot from the cut on his lid straight to the back of his head. The stark light blaring down from the police station ceiling only made it worse. *I can't believe they got in a punch. I need to find a ring out here.* He gazed down at the seats filled with three of the five men who came to his aid—despite him being a stranger.

He didn't know anybody at the college. The encounter between him and some of his schoolmates/future clan leaders was the first "welcome" he got since transferring to Boston College less than a week ago to get from under his father's thumb. When they ambushed him on his way to dinner, Faisal was prepared to take them all down, or at least as many as he could. It felt damn good that he didn't have to do it alone. "Thanks," he nodded at the men nursing various scrapes and bruises, "I appreciate you guys havin' my back."

The Black man who first stepped in flexed his hand. "Nah, don't worry about it. They needed to be taught a lesson." Faisal grinned at the familiar Long Island resonance in his deep voice.

The Asian man in the next seat massaged his square jaw. "Yeah." He patted the Black man on the back. "Marc and I know how to handle their kind." Faisal accepted his hand. "I'm Simon."

"I'm Faisal Khan." There was no mistaking the Queens accent either. Not only were they stand-up guys but fellow New Yorkers too.

All their gazes pivoted to the dude in the dress shirt and slacks that exhibited some serious martial arts skills earlier that night. He glanced up from cleaning his blood-encrusted nails and raised his brows over angular eyes. "I'm Quinn Ang."

Simon smiled. "I think we take the same civil procedures course. Thanks for helping out, man."

Quinn crossed his legs and smoothed his hand over his torn trousers. "Of course. I was getting in my car and heard "racist asshole," he scraped at more blood on his pants, "so, I figured there was work to be done." The desk sergeant grimaced at the row of banged up men laughing their heads off.

Brandon and Adam emerged from the office at the back of the precinct followed by the sergeant in a coffee-stained shirt and tie. "Let's go." Brandon waved at them and strode towards the exit.

"What," Faisal pushed of off the wall, "all of us?"

"Yes." Brandon stopped, his gaze followed Adam strutting past him. "Adam called his dad, who contacted his friend—the Mayor, so yeah, everyone."

"You shoulda let me call him earlier." Adam strode into the hallway, raising his voice the further away he got from them. "We would've been home by now."

"You shouldn't have to call your father to pull strings." Brandon followed. "We didn't commit any crime."

"We attacked them."

"No, we were defending," Brandon looked over his shoulder, "what's your name, again?"

Faisal joined them in the hall. This looked like it was about to get ugly. "Faisal."

"We were defending Faisal."

"Okay, Brandon. We were in the right, and when has that ever helped anyone? Look around," Adam spun with his palms up, "where are those goons that started all of this trouble? Gone, 'cause the cops let their White asses out hours ago. Look, I'm the spoiled son of a rich White man. So, I used my privilege like those little punks, but instead of just myself, I got my friends off too," he crossed his arms over his bulky chest, parts of it exposed at the tears of his shirt, "I don't see anything wrong with that."

Marcus stepped between the bickering buddies and pulled Adam by the arm. "I suggest we settle this after we've gotten the hell outta here."

4-DINER

SIMON SQUINTED AND HELD HIS HAND OVER HIS EYES like a visor. He descended the precinct steps, deleting yet another one of multiple incessant messages sent by a very irritated half-naked female. Way too needy. I'm glad I didn't hit that. He scrolled through his contacts for the names of woman who would be just as willing but not so clingy.

"Yo, Simon." Marcus jogged down the stairs with the rest of the fearsome warriors in tow. "Faisal, offered to buy us breakfast."

Faisal fluffed his hair flip. "It's the least I could do. Besides, I didn't get to eat last night because of those jerks."

"I think that's a good idea." Quinn pulled his sleeve cuff and stopped next to Faisal.

Simon shoved his phone in his pocket and rubbed his growling belly. "I can eat." He glanced at Brandon and Adam, slipping scowls to each other. "We can continue The Great Debate." He had similar arguments with Marcus as well as other hard conversations about racism and the law. Learning how to listen to each other made a big difference in preserving their friendship. Adam clearly didn't appreciate Brandon's perspective.

"I know where there's a decent diner not too far from here." Quinn led the group down the busy Boston street.

The tall, fair-haired waitress stopped on her way to the kitchen and suspended the coffee pot in the air, gawking at the diverse crew of gorgeous men swaggering into the diner—none of them the worse for wear after a night in a police precinct. They filled a table and commenced with their morning meal. Lethargy didn't dull any of the deep and witty conversation during breakfast.

"You need to understand where Brandon is coming from, Adam." Marcus poked a mound of eggs. 'Sure, your Kane connections got us out, but there are so many People of Color steamrolled by a racist justice system—Blacks get it especially bad."

"I know." Adam's massive hand dwarfed the coffee cup he put to his lips.

"Then you realize that you were successful in getting just the six of us off, which is not enough." Simon chimed in and dragged his gaze up a white woman at the counter smiling at him and twirling a lock of her long red hair. He smiled back. She descended her stool and sashayed towards them on a pair of long legs in tight jeans. He pulled out a business card, rested his elbow on the table and held it in the air. "Brandon is fighting for people without money or connections and whose race is often a big deficit." She took it and continued towards the exit. He watched her hips sway away. Things were looking up.

Marcus rolled his eyes.

Adam smirked and glanced at Brandon. "I don't know about all of that, Simon. My father is one of Brandon's biggest clients."

"Yeah," Brandon shoved a triangle of toast in his mouth and washed it down with coffee. "He hired me to babysit you, but that's not all I do. I'm working with groups to get people real justice."

"I see nothing wrong in doing both." Quinn motioned for the server and pointed to his plate. "I'm sorry, but this steak is not rare enough." The simultaneous eyebrow raising by everyone staring at the red blood oozing from the hunk of meat that barely had grill marks confirmed that it was.

"I'll get you another, sir." She continued to look back at Quinn as she headed towards the kitchen. What was the deal with him?

"That thing is going to be mooing when she brings it." A chorus of guffaws joined Marcus's and resonated off the chrome and Formica. The men finished their conversations and breakfasts.

They parted, agreeing to a basketball game the next day. By the end of the week, the Brothers in Law solidified their friendships for life.

Thank you for reading the Brothers in Law Short Story. Be on the lookout for Sweet Love, Bitter Fruit - Book 2

Enjoy this excerpt from Sweet Love, Bitter Fruit

SWEET LOVE, BITTER FRUIT

Marcus sipped some cold coffee from a mug. "You said you cleared your schedule. What are you doing with the rest of your afternoon?"

Toni shifted in her seat. "Well, I have an appointment with Dr. Algiers." She jumped at the sound of the ceramic cup hitting the hard wood. "Marc."

"So that's what this little lunch visit is about?" He plopped the rest of the burger on the open wrapper. "What do you need?"

"I was hoping you would come with me. We can talk some more on the way there."

He wiped the coffee off his hand and desk with a napkin. "I've said all I'm going to about this."

Toni raised and leaned across the desk. "Well, I haven't. I'm ready to start treatments."

"You do what you want, but I'm not signing on for another fertility sideshow." It was his turn. Marcus ducked and jumped at the crash of the stapler through the window. Sounds of the city seeped through the hole. "What the hell, Toni?"

Enjoy my published short stories.

Published in *Shades of BWWM* - Love Journey Books

THE RELUCTANT ALPHA - When the life he left summons him back, will Blake Aumont heed its call?

SECOND CHANCE - Lucas made the biggest mistake of his life. Can he make things right, or is he too late?

MY HEART'S TRANQUILITY - Am Muslim Adam Kane has it all – a thriving business, fulfilling faith and loving bride. Is there such a thing as too much happiness?

Published in *Shades of AMBW* - Love Journey Books

I Won't Let Go - Waleed searches for his wife Zina, who ran off for no apparent reason. What will he discover when he finds her?

Turning Around - Justin has to make a decision about the beautiful Monique that may change both their lives.

ABOUT LYNDELL WILLIAMS

Lyndell Williams (Layla Abdullah-Poulos) has a B.A. in Historical
Studies and Literature, M.A. in Liberal
Studies, and an AC in Women and
Gender Studies. She presently teaches
history as an adjunct instructor.

Williams a cultural critic with a
background in literary criticism
specializing in romance. She is the
managing editor of the NbA Muslims
blog on Patheos, a cultural contributor
for Radio Islam USA and a writer for
About Islam.

She received 2017 The Francis Award from The International
Association for the Study of Popular Romance (IASPR). Her peer-
reviewed journal article *The Stable Muslim Love Triangle –
Triangular Desire in African American Muslim Romance Fiction* was
published in the Journal of Popular Romance Studies November
2018.

Lyndell has contributed to multiple anthologies interracial short story
collections, including - *Saffron: A Collection of Personal Narratives by
Muslim Women*, Shades of AMBW and Shades of BWWM.